Tasha Harrison lives in Bright
young daughters. Before becoming a mum she worked as a
freelance sub-editor in London and Sydney on various glossy
magazines and TV guides. Package Deal is her first novel.

To find out more about Tasha Harrison and Package Deal,
please visit www.tashaharrison.com

To Steve + Jo,
Hope you enjoy it,
let me know what
you Think !
Tash x

Package Deal

Tasha Harrison

H+CO

Package Deal

First published in paperback in
Great Britain in May 2007
by Harrison + Co Creative Ltd
Manor Farm Business Centre
Poynings, Brighton BN45 7AG
www.harrisonandco.com

ISBN 978-0-9554997-0-8

Typeset in Adobe Caslon Pro by Harrison + Co Creative Ltd
Printed and bound in Great Britain by Intype Libra Ltd.

I would like to sincerely thank…

Dorothy Koomson for all her invaluable support and for keeping me inspired.

Simon Nye for finding the time in his busy schedule to read Package Deal and for all his advice and encouragement.

Teresa Chris, whose enthusiasm made my day and whose help was much appreciated.

Caroline McCarthy and Sarah Westcott of The Literary Consultancy, for their extra support and belief in this book.

Sophie Coryndon and Dan Street, Jenny Bate and Ric Hatton, John Baron-Kent and Taylor Damien, Julia Faiers, Perry Killington, Dan Biddulph, Debbie Blythe, Phil Jowett, Petra Brannmark, Estelle Hoen and Delphine Neveux for all their interest, positive feedback and encouragement.

My Mum and Dad, for encouraging me to write from an early age and for believing in my abilities.

But most of all, I'd like to thank my brilliant husband Chris Harrison, who wouldn't let me give up writing or trying to get published no matter how hard it got.

For Chris, Ruby and Bonnie

CHAPTER 1

Saturday 1st

Sun, sun, sun. Dazzling, beaming, glorious sun. It engulfed the craggy mountains, tickled the cliff tops and skimmed over the beaches. It swept over tranquil green fields and gently swaying woods. It glinted off the sea and bounced off white-washed garden walls, casting pregnant shadows from the rotund terra cotta vases on every doorstep. Not a cloud in the sky. Not even a wisp of grey or a smudge of white. Just blue, blue, heavenly, everlasting blue.

Vibrant bursts of magenta bougainvillea punctuated the gleaming whiteness of the houses that dotted the hillside. Skinny cats lay asleep beneath olive trees and tables, not so much as twitching an ear as the coach heaved itself past on its way to Skala, squeezing between the houses that flanked the narrow winding road. Locals looked up and squinted. Some nodded. Some waved. An old man riding on a donkey gave a toothless grin and saluted them as they chugged past.

Mia shrunk back in her seat. The Brits were invading. How did these people stand it – and with such good grace? And yet just like everyone else on board the coach, she too yearned for the soothing warmth, uplifting colours and sensual textures of a Greek island. Two weeks of real summer to compensate for the stop-start misnomer of a summer that taunted Great Britain every year. Not that that was the only reason she had come here alone rather than follow her friends to Edinburgh for the festival – but it was reason enough.

"Hang on, did you just say that Tom Hanks lives 'ere? Bloody 'ell, Caz! We come to the right place, ain't we? Hollywood stars an' all that!"

"What's it called, Babs?"

"What?"

"The place where 'e bought his house."

"Dunno. 'ERE! Scuse me, love – whatcha say that place was called where Tom Hanks bought a villa?"

"Fiskardo, in the north of the island," the plump, young rep purred into the microphone in a gentle Irish accent, her frizzy ginger hair bouncing as the coach bumped over potholes in the road.

"That's it, Fistardo."

"Fistarvo?"

"Fistardo. Just remember fist and 'ard. Shouldn't be a problem for you, eh Caz?" The two women snorted with laughter.

Mia rolled her eyes. Could those two possibly talk any louder? She'd suffered them all the way from Gatwick – from the perfume section of the duty-free ("'Ere Caz, smell this Obsession! Bloody gorgeous, innit?"), the ladies loos ("Oh would you Adam-and-Eve it? I got me bleedin' period, Babs! Sod's bleedin' law!"), the departure lounge (*"Why are we waiting? We are suffocating!"*), and then of course they'd sat across the aisle from her on the plane (*"Ere we go, 'ere we go, 'ere we go!"*). She prayed they wouldn't be dropped off at the same apartments.

"OK! Those of you with Hotel Sea Breeze on your envelopes, this is your stop," the rep smiled down the aisle as the coach pulled over and the passengers reached for their hand luggage.

Mia tucked her wavy honey-coloured hair behind her ears and looked at her envelope. She was staying at Eleni Apartments. She prayed the birds-of-a-feather would get off.

"Babs, that ain't us is it?"

"What's the envelope say?"

"I can't pronounce it, but it ain't Sea Breeze."

Mia sighed.

"Follow me everyone." The rep led the passengers off the coach and after collecting their suitcases from the luggage compartment, ushered them along a path to a marshmallow pink building with white balconies surrounded by pine trees.

It looked charming, thought Mia. There was a pool and a café on a terrace next door. She hoped hers would be as picturesque. She was beginning to doubt her decision to opt for an allocation-on-arrival package, but it was all she could afford. Anyway, she had made it to Kefalonia, and that's what mattered – her exact location wasn't important. It was only a small island, a couple of hours' drive from north to south – less from east to west. It wouldn't be hard to get around.

"That looks bloody lovely, don't it Caz?" enthused the voice from behind.

"Yeah, I hope ours is like that."

Two stops later and there were just ten other people left on the bus. Mia cast a quick glance around her. It appeared she was the only person on her own. Not that she cared, but she didn't want anyone pitying her, thinking she had no friends.

"OK everyone. This is Eleni Apartments, our last stop," announced the rep.

A hum of approval echoed around the coach as it pulled off the road and into the drive of what looked like a newly built apartment complex bordering a small rectangular pool, perched on the hillside overlooking the sea.

"Look at the colour of the pool Babs! I ain't seen nuffing like it, 'ave you?"

"I told ya you'd love it, didn't I?" Babs replied smugly.

"Yeah but you wasn't to know the apartments was gonna be nice, you said so yourself. You said it's pot luck with vacation on arrival."

"*Allocation* on arrival, you silly tart."

"Well I dunno do I? I ain't been abroad before."

Mia waited for the other passengers to file past her before she got up from her seat.

"The caretaker's name is Dimitri, but you can call him Jimmy if you find that easier," the rep continued as the driver began to unload their suitcases. "It's a twenty minute walk into Skala, or you can call a cab from the Hotel Flamingo, which is just a five minute walk in the other direction. Hotel Flamingo has a restaurant and a bar, and every Wednesday they have a Greek dancing night which is always a real laugh. My number's on the noticeboard outside the caretaker's room if anyone needs me at any time throughout your stay. Any questions?" She paused and looked around the small group of pale faces.

"No? Well you'll find your keys in your envelopes and I'll be here for another five minutes or so if you need anything." The rep pushed her overgrown fringe out of her eyes and trotted off towards the caretaker's room as the new arrivals eagerly opened their envelopes.

"Number two!" squealed Caz and gripped Babs' arm excitedly. Elbowing their fellow holidaymakers out of the way, they grabbed their luggage which had been deposited next to the coach and hurried down the drive, stilettos clacking, suitcases-on-wheels thundering along behind them.

"Last one in the pool is a ninny!" a middle-aged man called after them in a strong Mancunian accent. He nudged his wife and chuckled. "Those two are as excited as kids."

"Let's hope they don't continue to be as loud as them," the woman muttered under her breath. "What room are we in, Frank?"

Frank fished in their envelope for the key. "Boudoir number one, my sweet."

The woman groaned, resting manicured hands on her wide hips.

"What's up, love?" Frank sighed.

"Well those Essex bimbos are in number two," she hissed.

"Oh get in the holiday spirit, Margaret. Let's try and have some fun while we're here, eh?"

Mia looked at her key as the group started to break up and head towards their rooms. She was in number three.

"Oh dear, unlucky!" Margaret whispered sympathetically as she brushed past, spraying herself with a bottle of Estée Lauder summer spritzer. Mia smiled and turned to get her suitcase.

The room was simple and sparse, yet tasteful. Cream coloured walls, white bed linen and a pine wardrobe in one corner, a kitchenette, table and two chairs in the other – and a pristine white-tiled ensuite bathroom. Mia pulled back the muslin curtains and opened the French doors onto her terrace. Light flooded in and a warm gust of wind sent the curtains into a spiralling dance on either side of her.

Outside, the pool twinkled in the bright sunlight. Fourteen white plastic sunloungers lay neatly around its edges, some in the shade of tall, white parasols. Everything seemed fresh and untouched, like a new bar of soap. Mia leaned against the railings of her terrace and breathed in the sweet aroma of the flowerbed that lay between her apartment and the pool. She glanced around her. There were two apartments to her left, and four apartments to her right, all one storey with verandahs overlooking the pool. The vibrant and well-kept flowerbed lined the front of the verandahs, following the L-shaped layout of the complex around two sides of the pool. It was perfect – in fact, she couldn't have picked a more perfect place had she tried. At the foot of the hillside, the cobalt blue sea gently licked the rocks, while the soft jingle-jangle of goat bells wafted along on the breeze from somewhere above in the hills.

Mia closed her eyes and inhaled the tranquillity. This was heaven. A few more doors opened and people stepped out onto their verandahs, murmuring enthusiastically at the view.

Suddenly a blood-curdling scream followed by a loud splash made Mia jump.

"BITCH! It's b-b-bloody freeeeezing!"

Caz and Babs were in the pool.

"Oops, scuse me French!"

"Keep your voice down Caz! Everyone's looking at you!" laughed Babs, bobbing up and down in the deep end, her short spiky brown hair flattened against her scalp, her large white boobs bursting out of her camouflage-patterned swimsuit like balloons.

"A bit nippy is it?" teased Frank from his terrace, next-door-but-one to Mia's.

"It's alright once you move about a bit," replied Caz, holding onto the side and trying to push a tangle of wet bottle-blonde hair out of her eyes. "Coming in?"

"Yes, in a minute or two. First things first though, ladies," said Frank, taking a cup of tea from Margaret as she joined him on the terrace, her hair coiffed back into place and a fresh coat of fuchsia lipstick on her lips.

She smiled over at Mia. "How's your room, love?"

"Lovely," she replied. "This is much better than I thought it would be. How's yours?"

"Yes, not bad at all. I'm impressed. I did want to go to Venice – it's our fortieth anniversary you see – but Frank's always loved Greece. And I must say, it is a very scenic spot. Did you want a cuppa, love? We brought our own tea bags."

"Oh no thanks. That's very kind of you. I thought I might walk into town in a bit and find a supermarket."

"Right you are, love. Let us know if you find somewhere decent, as we'll be doing the same later, no doubt."

"Sure." Mia turned and went back into her room.

She would have a shower, put a nice summery outfit on and head into town. She walked into the bathroom and turned the shower on. As she kicked off her sandals there was a knock at the door.

"Only me," smiled the rep. "Forgot to tell everybody not to flush anything down the loo. It's a brand new complex – it's only been open a few months – but the Greek sewage system is the same as ever. So even loo roll has to go in the bin provided I'm afraid."

"Thanks for letting me know," smiled Mia.

"You're on your own, aren't you?" the rep hovered in the doorway.

"Yup. Just me."

"Well if you need anything, just give me a shout. But as it happens you're not the only one – there's two other singles staying here at Eleni. We hardly ever get singles – I mean, people coming out here on their own. It's usually always couples – older couples at that. So this is quite a different bunch from usual. The lot that just left barely went in the pool. Couldn't get their zimmer frames down the steps!" she chortled.

Mia feigned a laugh. "Well I'm not entirely on my own. I've come out here to see someone actually."

"Oh yeah? Goodlooking is he?" the rep winked knowingly at her. "You've got to watch these Greek blokes. They're not to be trusted. Take Dimitri for example – *I should know*. They're all the bloody same!" She rolled her eyes. "Oh well, best get on and tell the others about the loo."

"Sorry, I didn't catch your name," Mia smiled apologetically.

"Nikki. Call me if you need anything. Yiasou!"

Mia stood beneath the shower, the hot water pelting onto her head and flowing down her shoulders. She wondered what made people confess details of their private lives to virtual strangers. Or maybe it was a subtle warning: Dimitri's mine, so don't go getting any ideas. *As if.* She'd had enough of men. The girl was right. They weren't to be trusted. Not just Greek men – any men.

"Corfu, Kefalonia, Crete – what's the bloody difference?" a male voice on the other side of the bathroom wall interrupted her thoughts.

"The difference, you ponce, is that one of them is where it's all happening – bars, clubs, pussy – and that one of them, HERE, is where it AIN'T," came the angry reply.

"Craig, we've only just got here. Give the place a chance. We haven't been into town yet."

"According to that ginga bird, there's only one nightclub in Skala, it's the size of a matchbox and it's usually half empty."

"No way! What else did she say?"

"That Kefalonia is a top destination for the silver-haired generation who like to unwind with a bit of sun, ouzo and Greek dancing. In other words, Steve, our Target Ten Shagometer might as well go in the fucking bin right now."

"Don't touch it! I spent hours making that."

"Mate, you have *so* cocked up."

"Oh lighten up – just cos there isn't much nightlife doesn't mean we're not gonna get laid."

"How d'ya work that out?"

"I've noticed some talent already."

"You're not referring to that Irish bint are you? I'm not into ginga pubes."

"She's alright! Anyway, I'm not talking about her. Didn't you see the bird in the room next door to us?" He lowered his voice a fraction. Mia leaned her ear against the wall.

"Nah. What's she like?"

"Not fuckin' bad, mate. Blonde, nice legs. Nice little tits. Her arse is a bit big, but I quite like that."

"Face?"

"Didn't get a proper look, mate."

"Probably a dog."

"There's no pleasing you sometimes, Craig. Anyway, I saw her first."

7

"You can have her, mate."

"Looks like I'm gonna be the first to reach number one on the Shagometer!" Steve bragged. "Anyway piss off, I'm 'aving a dump."

Mia heard the bathroom door slam followed by a loud fart and a double guffaw of laughter. She turned the shower off, wrapped herself in a towel and tip-toed back into the bedroom. *Nice legs, little tits and a big arse.* They might as well have been describing a car: nice tyres, small hooter and a spacious boot. She looked at her breasts in the wardrobe mirror. They weren't that little, were they? In fact, they had definitely got bigger, she observed.

"Caz, stick the kettle on!" Babs boomed outside.

Mia quickly pulled her towel around her. She'd forgotten she'd left the French doors open. She poked her head outside just in time to see Babs heaving herself out of the pool. God knows what crushing description Craig and Steve would assign her: chunky legs, fat bum, two spare tyres and huge melons. A second-hand people carrier with king-sized airbags? She closed the French doors as a dripping Babs sized up the verandah railings and flowerbed, thought better of it and decided to take the longer but more civilised route via the front door.

Mia opened her suitcase and pondered her summer clothes. The denim mini skirt or the short blue flowery dress? The magenta halter-neck top or the white tie-in-a-knot shirt? These precious items remained folded in a drawer for ten months of the year – the weather and the occasion never quite being able to coincide to give them a good airing. The joy of being able to wear them at last almost called for a celebration. In fact it did. The outcome of her visit to Kefalonia didn't matter. She had come purely to gain some knowledge, some understanding of what had happened. Decisions about her future didn't necessarily have anything to do with why she was there. None of it seemed real anyway.

In the meantime, she was there to have a holiday. She pulled on the white shirt and denim skirt and brushed the knots out of her wet hair while forming a mental shopping list: tzatziki, taramasalata, pitta bread, feta cheese, cucumber, lettuce, melon, coffee, milk and a bottle of wine. Perfect. She slipped on her flip flops, threw her key in her bag and stepped outside. As she pulled the door shut behind her she came face to face with one of her desperate-to-get-laid next-door neighbours, leaning against their doorway smoking a cigarette. He wore nothing but a pair of baggy, knee-length swimming trunks, his tattooed arms folded across his skinny, sun-starved torso. Trendy Police sunglasses masking his eyes, he combed his fingers coolly through his David Beckham-style highlights.

"Alright?" he mumbled, fag in mouth.

"Alright," she mumbled back and quickly hurried off up the drive. She could feel his eyes following her as she went, and as she turned onto the main road, she was sure she heard a faint wolf-whistle and a snigger of laughter.

CHAPTER 2

Mia rummaged in her wallet as the woman on the till put her shopping into a plastic bag. Struggling to distinguish Euros from Pounds in the dim interior of the shop, she dropped the change and sent coins rolling in different directions across the floor.

The couple in the queue behind her bent down and helped gather them up.

"Here you go," smiled the girl who was as dark as her boyfriend was fair.

"Thanks," said Mia, taking the coins from her and passing them to the shopkeeper.

"Don't wanna go throwing your money away on your first day," joked the girl.

"How did you know it was my first day?" asked Mia. "Oh, I know – because I'm as white as a sheet!" She examined the skin on her arms.

"No, it's not that," the girl laughed, "we're staying at Eleni Apartments. We were on the same bus as you – same plane too."

"Oh right. The apartments are OK, aren't they? I wasn't expecting them to be anywhere near as nice as that."

"Same with us. I love the way our terrace overlooks the pool and the sea."

The girl's boyfriend tugged at her long black ponytail and nudged her to hurry up and pay for their lone bottle of shampoo.

"I'm Jo and this is my boyfriend Nath – short for Nathan," the girl smiled warmly.

"I'm Mia. Nice to meet you."

"You've done a lot of shopping," Jo nodded to Mia's two bulging carrier bags.

"Yeah. I thought I'd stock the fridge – I fancied some dips and stuff for supper."

"Good idea. We should do that Nath."

"I thought we were going out for a meal," Nath grunted, running a hand over his blond crew cut and twiddling his gold stud earring.

"We are, but we could do with some stuff for breakfast tomorrow."

Nath shrugged and headed out the door.

"See you later," Jo winked and followed him out of the shop.

Back on her terrace, Mia poured herself a small glass of wine and crunched on a mouthful of cucumber and feta. As the sun set behind the hills, the moon hovered above the sea like a distant apparition. It was day and night. Mia flipped open her pocket pad and lazily sketched a couple of sunloungers and a parasol by the corner of the pool. It was a perfect spot. Whoever owned these apartments must be feeling very smug indeed. It was much nicer than any of the hotels she'd noticed in Skala. And although Skala was a pleasant enough little town with a decent sandy beach and a neighbouring wood of pine trees, it was nothing to write home about.

There was a main street that led down to the beach, lined on either side by a string of cheap, vine-roofed tavernas, all offering the standard Greek fare of moussaka, souvlaki, kleftikos and chips. There were a couple of bars – one on the corner with a paunch-bellied waiter with a thick moustache who tried to lure punters in with his jokes, and a trendy, open-fronted bar next-door to the mini-market. The trendy bar looked brand new with its curved chrome counter, mirrored panels, wall-to-wall illuminated optics and TVs tuned in to MTV. However, both were only half full. And instead of the usual swarms of scantily-clad teenagers staggering about arm in arm singing and screeching at the tops of their lungs, the customers were mostly middle-aged, sitting in orderly groups of two or four, sipping merrily on pints and cocktails, baring scorched leather flesh amid a sparse forest of M&S gold spangly twin sets, Next short-sleeved cotton shirts and BHS sandals. They played cards, read papers, marvelled at their knickerbocker-glories and guffawed at each others' jokes.

Yes, it seemed the oiks in the room next-door had indeed cocked up on their destination of choice. This was about as far removed from Ayia Napa as you could possibly get. They might as well have gone to the Outer Hebrides to get laid. Mia smiled to herself and took a sip of wine.

11

"What? All alone?" A young man with floppy brown hair and bright green eyes seemed to appear out of nowhere and leaned across the flowerbed to rest his elbows on her verandah railings.

She sat up straight and tugged at her skirt which had slyly risen to knicker level. "Er…"

"I'm Dimitri – the caretaker." He held his hand towards her. She reached forward and shook it. "And you are?"

"Mia."

"Well Mia, I'm going to the Bora Bora Club tonight. Why don't you come with me?" he asked cheerily, flicking his hair out of his eyes.

"Er…well…" *Talk about forward.*

"Come and dance!"

"Um…I don't really–"

"Come on!" he laughed heartily, "I'm taking some of the others – Caz, Babs, Steve and…I forget his name – oh yes – Craig." He counted on his fingers.

"Where's the Bora Bora Club?"

"On the main street in Skala. And when you arrive you get a free ouzo."

"Oh right."

"Will you come? Say yes – it will be fun!"

"Er…"

"Good decision! I'm gonna take a shower, then I come back to get you."

And with that he strode off, leaped over a sunlounger and disappeared around the corner. Mia got up and went to look at her reflection in the mirror. She wasn't really in a partying mood, and would have been quite content to sit on her terrace admiring the view or reading Wild Swans – a book that had been on her 'to read' list for about three years. Then again, it was nice to be invited out, to be included, not to be alone. And it wasn't every day she got invited out by a tall, dark, handsome stranger. A *very* handsome stranger – probably the local Romeo who had slept his way through summer after summer of young female tourists – and holiday reps. Well he'd be wasting his time with her. Unlike her laddish neighbours, she wasn't there with the intention of getting laid. It was the last thing she wanted. The very thought of meaningless sex made her stomach turn.

She untied the white shirt and swapped it for the magenta halter-neck top. Then she applied some lipstick and mascara. No point making a huge effort. She didn't intend to stay out long.

"*Yiaaaaaaaaaasas pethiaaah!*" yelled Dimitri as they sped past Craig and Steve on the road back into Skala. Mia held onto him for dear life and tried not to move a muscle, even though she felt she was about to slip off the back of the moped. "It was Craig and Steve! Did you see them?" Dimitri yelled over his shoulder.

"Yes," she gasped.

"Are you scared?"

"Just a little!"

"Are you so scared when I go like this?" he slowed the moped down.

"That's fine." She breathed a sigh of relief and relaxed her grip.

"And when I go like this?" he accelerated and Mia clutched onto him again. He laughed. "Just kidding, just kidding! I will go slowly I promise."

He pulled up outside the chrome bar with the big TV sets and Mia slid off the back of the bike and adjusted her skirt. That would be the first and last time she accepted a lift from him.

"Now where are those ladies?" muttered Dimitri as he kicked the moped onto its stand and smoothed back his hair. Mia looked around and spotted them propping up the bar, their large bottoms balanced precariously on tiny bar stools, their fleshy pink elbows leaning on the counter.

"Over there," she pointed.

Dimitri walked over to them.

"Yiasas ladies. You look very lovely tonight," he grinned, putting his arms around them and nodding at a stool for Mia to sit on in a gesture not dissimilar to The Fonze.

"Ooh, ain't he a gentleman, Caz? If I was ten years younger, I'd have you, darling!" cackled Babs, throwing her head back and revealing her large bosoms strapped firmly in place beneath her sparkly turquoise vest-top by a matching high control-factor bra. "It's so nice to be spoken to like that, innit Caz?"

Caz detached a straw from her lips and used it to stir the detergent-blue cocktail she was drinking. "Too right, love. It's a refreshing change to be treated like a lady. English blokes have a lot of catching up to do. You're a lucky girl," she nodded sagely at Mia, discreetly pulling her chiffon leopard-print shirt out of the fold of her belly.

Mia laughed. "Oh, er, we're not together. I just arrived today – I'm in the apartment next to you."

"Course you are! Silly me," Caz rolled her eyes at her mistake. "I thought you looked familiar."

"Got a memory like a goldfish, that one," Babs nudged Mia and winked.

Dimitri roared with laughter. "That is very funny! I didn't ever hear that before. A memory like a goldfish – I like it!"

"Ooh, ain't we entertaining, Babs!" Caz giggled.

"So what's this Bora Dora place like?" asked Babs.

"It is fun. Good music. Good atmosphere. Let's go. I want to dance!" declared Dimitri, slapping the bar and babbling something in Greek to the barman.

"Whatcha say to him?" asked Caz, screwing up her face and straining her ear in an effort to understand.

"I say to him to give me a cigarette you bloody arsehole," explained Dimitri. "He said to me to fuck off you poof."

The barman tossed him a cigarette and grinned, revealing a missing front tooth.

"He is my friend Vasilis," smiled Dimitri, popping the cigarette in his mouth and lighting it.

"What was that – Vaseline?" asked Caz.

"Never mind. Come on ladies, drink up. Let's go!"

Dimitri hopped off his stool and ushered the three women across the road to a newspaper kiosk.

"Just got to buy some more cigarettes, my friends," he said, giving some change to the vendor and saluting him. "OK, let's party!" He hurried ahead of them up some steps between two tavernas and held open a narrow door below a broken neon sign which said 'ora Bora Club.'

Mia followed Caz and Babs towards the bar. The club was small, which was a good thing considering that apart from a few dimly lit faces around the edges, they were the only people in there. And yet the music was pumping, disco lights spinning, and smoke machine hissing out clouds of dried ice in anticipation of the sudden arrival of a large crowd of ravers.

A young Greek barmaid with heavily charcoaled eyes and a tight pink T-shirt handed them each a glass of ouzo. Dimitri greeted her with a kiss on both cheeks and then caught sight of Steve and Craig poking their heads around the door like a pair of hesitant weasels.

"Ela ethó! Over here! Come and meet Marilena and have some ouzo." He waved them over.

"Alright mate," said Craig, pushing his Police sunglasses on top of his head and giving him a friendly pat on the back. "You drive like a nutter, you know that?"

Dimitri laughed. "I think Mia will agree with you."

Mia smiled.

"You know each other? No? Let me introduce you. Steve, Craig, this is Mia. Mia this is Steve and Craig. You are next-door neighbours."

"We met earlier," said Mia, but they had already turned towards the bar.

"And this is Caz and Babs," continued Dimitri, after Steve and Craig had claimed their free drinks.

"Alright lads!" boomed Babs. "Oh it's the Macarena! I love this song. My littluns can do the dance to this. How does it go, Caz?"

"Don't ask me!" said Caz, as Babs started wiggling her fleshy hips.

"Yes, come on, let's dance!" cheered Dimitri, knocking back his ouzo and grabbing Caz around the waist. He propelled her into the centre of the dancefloor and twirled her around.

"Was that just me or did you feel the floor shudder?" Craig smirked at Mia.

"I didn't feel anything," smiled Mia, realising a fraction of a second too late that he was referring to Caz and Babs stomping on the dancefloor. She noticed a tattoo of a naked woman above his skinny bicep and cringed as she remembered the conversation she'd overheard earlier and the ominous wolf-whistle that had followed her up the drive. Oik number two looked more comic than tough with his thick brows, wonky teeth and Kangol woolly hat that was sending beads of perspiration down the side of his face.

"So, you been to Greece before?" asked Steve, adjusting his hat so that

15

the rim skimmed the tops of his eyebrows.

"A couple of times. You?"

"Nah. We usually go to Tenerife or Majorca. But Greece was supposed to be where it's all happening this year," said Steve.

"Really? What, Kefalonia?"

"Unfortunately not," snarled Craig through gritted teeth.

"Young Steve here got his islands mixed up when he went to book the holiday. I told him Faliraki or Ayia Napa. I don't know how he ended up booking Kefalonia, but there you go – that's Steve for ya."

"He's a right whinger, this one," sighed Steve. "Fancy another drink, Maria?"

"It's Mia. I'll just have a Coke please."

"You've barely touched that ouzo. Don't ya like it?"

"Not really. Here you have it." She handed him the glass.

"Cheers." Steve knocked it back in one go and turned back to the bar as Dimitri returned from the dancefloor.

"At last, some party people!" he grinned. "You know the last guests at Eleni were all in their fifties. Every single one."

"How do you know? Did you ask them?" asked Craig, lighting a fag with a shiny silver Zippo lighter.

"Yes. I try to get them to come here, but they prefer the Greek dancing night at Hotel Flamingo – which is also fun, you must come to that too. But they don't want to go to nightclubs."

"You asked every single one of them how old they were?" repeated Craig in disbelief.

"Some I ask, some tell me. I talk with people all the time. I am always at Eleni and people like to talk to me and play cards with me. They tell me all about themselves. One woman told me she had slept with more than one hundred men. One man told me he couldn't get it up no more. Another woman told me she lost twelve stones in two years."

"Here Babs, did you hear that? A woman told Dimitri she lost twelve stone," panted Caz, rejoining them and patting her fuzzy blonde perm into place.

"I lost weight an' all," announced Babs proudly. "Guess how much!"

"Two grams," mumbled Craig into his ouzo.

16

"Eh?" Babs cupped a hand to her ear. "Whatcha say?"

"Ten stones!" guessed Dimitri.

"Six," offered Mia.

"Nearly," replied Babs. "Five stone, I lost. I weighed seventeen, now I'm twelve. That's partly why I'm 'ere with Caz. My husband didn't like the fact I'd got slim."

Steve and Craig choked on their drinks.

"Why not?" asked Mia.

"Cos I got more confident, didn't I Caz? When I was big, you see, I didn't think much of myself. But now, I can wear all nice clothes, go out dancing...I get more attention off blokes, and he hated that. Pissed 'im right off. So one day I says, 'Stuff ya', and packed his bags for him."

"We both did," agreed Caz.

"You both what?" asked Steve.

"Chucked our 'usbands. That's why we come here together – to celebrate." Caz and Babs clinked glasses.

"And did you say you have kids?" Mia asked Babs.

"We both do. They go to school together. Just like we used to. Me oldest Mark is fifteen. And her eldest Davey is fourteen. And our younguns are both twelve. My youngun's a girl, Debbie. Hers is another boy, Ricky."

"I don't believe you have children so old," gasped Dimitri.

"It's true innit, Caz?" laughed Babs. "Here you're pulling my leg, Dimtree. How old d'you think I am?"

"You are both thirty-three I think," grinned Dimitri.

Caz and Babs squawked with laughter.

"Oh you aaaare lovely!" wailed Babs, giving him a hug. "I'm forty-one and she's forty."

"No!" exclaimed Dimitri, feigning outrage. "And you?" he turned to Mia.

"Guess," smiled Mia.

Dimitri tilted her chin upwards to make an assessment. "Hmm...let me think..." He turned her face gently to the left and right. "You are twenty-five!" he concluded.

"Twenty-nine, I reckon," piped Craig.

"Thirty-one actually," announced Mia.

"No way – I'm losing my touch," said Dimitri. "Usually I always guess right. OK, I guess Craig and Steve now."

Craig and Steve stood side by side pulling silly faces while Dimitri sized them up.

"Eighteen!" he teased.

"Fuck off!" spat Craig.

"Relax – I'm just joking, malaka! You are…hmmm…you are both twenty-four."

"Bang on, mate," said Steve. "Craig, it's your round. Buy the man a drink!"

"A beer please my friend," said Dimitri. Craig pulled out his wallet and turned to the bar. No more offers were forthcoming.

"Oh well, what will you 'ave, Babs?" asked Caz.

"Bloody Mary, darling. I'm gonna have another dance."

Babs strutted back onto the dancefloor to join the three other lone souls gyrating to The Bee Gees' Stayin' Alive. Mia sipped her Coke and watched as Babs proudly wiggled her slimmed-down – and yet still rather ample – behind, clad in shiny black leather trousers that reflected the flashing lights like a beachball. Babs sang along merrily to the music, running her chubby fingers through her spiky brown hair.

"Who does she think she is?" sighed Caz, shuffling past Mia onto the dancefloor with two Bloody Marys.

Mia turned around to find herself face to face with a closer than expected Steve and Craig. She looked over their shoulders to see Dimitri leaning over the bar talking into Marilena's heavily pierced ear.

"So how comes you're on your own?" asked Craig.

"Mind your own business Craig, you nosy bugger," snapped Steve, finally giving in to the heat and whipping his woolly hat off.

"I'm sure she can speak for herself. So how come you're on your Jack Jones – if you don't mind me asking?"

"Just fancied a break on my own for a change. Most of my friends went to Edinburgh for a summer holiday – for the festival a few weeks ago – but I wanted guaranteed sunshine."

"So couldn't you get no one to come with you?" asked Craig.

"Shuddup Craig! Stop asking personal questions! Sorry about that,"

Steve rolled his eyes.

"That's quite alright. The truth is I didn't really want anyone to come with me. I'm quite at ease in my own company. Unfortunately other people seem to have a problem with it."

"Yeah but you've got to admit, it's not really normal going on holiday on your own, is it?" continued Craig. "Most people go in couples or with mates."

"Loads of people go off backpacking on their own – that's acceptable – so why shouldn't people go on a package holiday on their own? Why does everyone have to be coupled up? Since when did having a partner become a prerequisite of enjoying rest and relaxation?"

"Eh?" grunted Craig.

"What she's basically saying, mate, is that she's quite happy on her own," explained Steve.

"Yeah, but don't you feel a bit of a Nobby No-mates when you're eating in a restaurant and you're sitting all by yourself?"

"No. Why should I? I've got friends. They're just not here, that's all. And that's my choice. I could have gone to Edinburgh with friends, but I wanted sun, sea and sand instead."

"So how come none of your mates didn't wanna come to Greece?"

Mia took a deep breath. "Some of them are serious theatre buffs and have friends who are performing in plays at the festival – so they were set on going to Edinburgh. Some of them couldn't afford to go abroad, and the few who would have been willing, I didn't really want to share an apartment with for a fortnight. OK?"

"Fair enough." Craig turned to Steve and jerked a thumb towards the bar. "Your round, mate."

"Mia, another Coke?" asked Steve.

"No thanks. I think I might make a move actually."

Craig glanced at his watch. "It's only twelve!"

"Yeah, I'm quite tired after the journey today. See you later. Enjoy yourselves." Mia walked over to Dimitri. "I'm off now, Dimitri. Thanks for inviting me out."

"What? So soon? But the night has not even begun!"

"I know, but I'm tired."

"Let me get you another drink!"

"No thanks." Mia edged away. Dimitri grabbed her wrist and pulled her back.

"Come on! What will you have? Maybe you should try Sex On The Beach. That'll get you in the mood!" He winked at her.

She noticed Marilena eyeing her suspiciously from behind the bar and released herself from his grip. "I'm leaving now, Dimitri. Good night," she said sternly.

"Then let me give you a lift back to the apartment – please." He begged, stubbing out his cigarette.

"No thanks, I'll get a cab."

"I will drive slowly I promise – come on!"

"Good night, Dimitri." Mia turned and headed for the door.

Dimitri shrugged in defeat.

As Mia reached the exit, she noticed a tall, lanky, fair-haired man with small round glasses hovering hesitantly in the doorway.

"Excuse me," she said politely.

"It doesn't look very busy in there, does it?" said the man, moving not quite enough for her to squeeze past.

"It might pick up later," shrugged Mia.

"D'you think so?" The man still didn't move.

"One can but hope." Mia tried to get past but two girls squeezed in the door behind him, accidentally elbowing him out of the way. The man regained his balance and was about to ask Mia a further question when he realised she had gone.

CHAPTER 3

Sunday 2nd

"Morning my sweet!" Frank beamed as he strode onto the terrace, holding in his belly as he struggled to button up a short-sleeved shirt. Mission accomplished, he stretched his arms up in the air before attempting to wrap them around his wife.

"The kettle's boiled. Help yourself." Margaret barely glanced at him, but continued painting her long nails a deep merlot red to match the floaty Nicole Fahri dress she was wearing.

"Don't I get a kiss? What's the matter – didn't you sleep well?"

"Not particularly."

"Why not? Bed not comfy enough? I slept like a log." Frank extracted a piece of fluff from his grey moustache, inspected it and blew it into the breeze.

"Yes, so you did."

"What's up love?"

"You know what's up." She tried to pat her new sandy-blonde hairstyle into place without jeopardising her wet fingernails.

"Oh love, please. Yesterday was a long day. We were up at six."

"You slept on the plane – and on the bus," Margaret snapped. "You slept most of the bloody day."

"Forgive me pet, I'll make it up to you tonight."

"Promises, promises…"

"Keep your voice down, Margaret. Or do you want the whole world to know our business?" Frank retreated into the kitchen, robbed of the smile he'd woken up with that morning. He'd been so full of joy – a great night's kip complete with complimentary Carol-Vorderman-in-a-bikini dream, followed by waking up to a room full of sunlight and breezy warmth and realising it was the first day of his annual holiday and more importantly,

21

his retired life. Superb. No commute, no office, no grey drizzle, no washing up in the sink, no moodiness from the wife… You just couldn't have it all, could you?

"Fancy another cup, pet?" he called out to Margaret.

"Please," she replied tersely over her shoulder, screwing the lid back onto the pot of nail varnish.

Frank carried two small cups of tea out onto the terrace. "Bit small these cups, aren't they?"

Margaret ignored him.

"Brave, that girl coming out here on her own," he remarked, nodding towards their next-door neighbour-but-one's closed shutters.

"Yes. Just goes to show you don't need a partner to get on with life and enjoy yourself," said Margaret, taking a sip of tea.

Frank stared at the sea. What was that supposed to mean? Was it a hint, a threat? He decided to ignore it. "Isn't it beautiful here? Simply stunning," he breathed.

"Don't start."

"Don't start what?"

"Your retirement fantasy. It is lovely here, yes I'll grant you that, but it'd be deader than a morgue in winter."

"Like I keep saying, pet, it'd be our summer home. We'd spend the winter in Tunbridge Wells – or if you really want to up the budget of our summer home, we could sell up and buy somewhere back in Manchester near your parents to spend the winter…"

"I'm not moving back to Manchester, even if it is just for six months of the year," said Margaret defiantly. "Anyway, I'm sure we can find something affordable in Spain or Italy – somewhere a little more sophisticated."

"Somewhere where there's more shops and everything costs an arm and a leg, you mean."

"How about Capri? Our friends would be so envious." Margaret wrinkled up her nose in delight at the thought.

"Capri? Don't be daft woman! What do you think I am – a millionaire? If we bought a place in a location like that, we'd have to rent it out to friends, friends-of-friends and Joe Bloody Public for eleven months of the year to pay off the mortgage."

"You'd ask our friends to pay?" Margaret's heavily mascaraed eyes stood out on stalks. "Over my dead body!"

"We'd have to – anyway, that's what people do. It's what they'd expect."

"My friends wouldn't expect to pay – they'd be mortified. They wouldn't make us pay to stay in their holiday home."

"If you're referring to the Mansfields, I don't recall ever being invited to stay in their holiday home."

"They invited us to come out this summer!"

"That's because they knew it was our fortieth anniversary and that we were more than likely to say no! Anyroad, I wouldn't want to be renting it out all the bloody time – I'd want to be in it me bloody self!"

Margaret rolled her eyes and blew on her wet nails. Frank sighed and noticed the piece of fluff that had previously been caught in his moustache was now entrenched in his fingernail. The scraping of chairs and the clatter of cutlery being spilt onto a table echoed around the pool. They looked around. A few verandahs away, a couple were sitting down to breakfast.

"Union Jack swimming trunks," observed Margaret dryly. "And you want to buy a house here…"

"Bush – top bloke. That's what *I* think," said Nath, scratching his stubble and turning the page of his Daily Star.

"Eh?" Jo took a mouthful of muesli and opened her magazine.

"George Bush." Nath passed Jo a page of his newspaper. "He's been voted number three in the World's Greatest Wankers poll after Saddam Insane and Osama Bin La-la."

"I'm surprised he's not number one – how can you possibly think he's a top bloke?" asked Jo, glancing at the page disinterestedly before handing it back.

"He was right to nuke Iraq and get rid of that nutter – who was butchering his own people anyway."

"I don't think Bush's reasons were anything to do with liberating the Iraqi people." Jo pushed her wispy black fringe out of her eyes.

"Course not, he got his mitts on some more oil for us lot while he was at it – good lad!" Nath joked, a dimple forming in his left cheek as he grinned at her.

"*Good lad?* He's pure evil, Nath. That man is almost single-handedly responsible for global warming by turning his back on the Kyoto agreement. All he cares about is the American economy – he doesn't give a shit if half the world is under water in a century's time."

"Well according to what it says in here," Nath pointed at his paper, "we'll all be living on Mars by then, so it won't matter."

Jo groaned. "Why don't you read a real newspaper anyway, instead of The Titty Times?"

"I should think The Titty Times has got more news in it than New Woman."

"New Woman is a magazine. It's not supposed to have news in it. It's supposed to have fashion, beauty, gossip and women's issues."

"Women's issues! What does that mean – what kind of tampons should I use? Are my baps too big? How do I achieve orgasm?" Nath laughed, then lowered his voice. "Oy, you don't fake your orgasms do you?"

"Ha, ha! Wouldn't you like to know!" Jo stretched her arms above her head and yawned, pushing her 34C bikini-clad chest provocatively towards Nath.

"Honestly, Jo. You don't, do you?" he asked worriedly, looking at her breasts.

"Nath, I know we've only been together for six months, but believe me, I wouldn't waste my time with a bloke who couldn't satisfy me. Faking is for martyrs."

Nath sat back and grinned. "Shall I grab us a couple of sunbeds?"

Jo smiled. "If you think you've fulfilled your duties in the bedroom…"

Nath reached forward and slid his hand up her sarong. "This is just a trick to get me out of my Union Jack trunks, isn't it?"

Jo giggled. "Oh look, there's what's-her-name…Mia!" She batted Nath's hand away and waved. Mia waved back from her terrace and disappeared back inside her room.

"Quite a fit bird, that," Nath teased.

"Shut up you. Get in the bedroom and get your trunks off!"

"Yes mistress. Be gentle with me."

Mia put the kettle on and looked in the cupboard for a mug, but all she could find was two small cups. What was the point in making cups that small? Three mouthfuls and it was empty. She tipped a teaspoon of decaf coffee into each one. She would drink them back to back, thus sparing herself the inconvenience of having to get up and get a refill. Strange the things you did when you were on your own. Strange, but liberating with no one to tell you you're strange.

She thought back to the night before in the Bora Bora and Craig's barrage of questions. She felt quite irritated by his small-mindedness. Obviously Craig was the type of person who never did anything on his own. He probably spent twenty-four hours a day in the company of other people. How sad – especially for the poor sods who had to put up with him. And what about Dimitri? She hoped she hadn't offended him by refusing to stay. But if she had…well, that was too bad.

Stepping back onto her terrace, she exchanged greetings with Frank and Margaret and sat down at her table. She took a sip from one of her coffees. It probably looked like she was expecting someone to join her. Oh well. Not today.

She opened up the 'Welcome' leaflet she'd found on the bedside table and scanned it for information on car hire. Good, there was a place in Skala – she'd set off after breakfast. She looked at her watch and was surprised to see it was eleven o'clock already. There was, of course, a two hour time difference – but even so, she hadn't expected the morning to be nearly over already. It was time to get a move on. All of a sudden Mia felt her stomach churn. Could she do this? Should she be doing this? She didn't have to – just because she was here didn't mean she had to go through with it. She rushed to the bathroom and bent over the toilet bowl, but nothing happened. Gradually the feeling of nausea subsided and she returned to the terrace.

OK, here was the plan. She would hire a car, buy a map, find out where the town of Sami was and then make it part of a day trip. Once in Sami she'd look up the address, and if she couldn't find it or it turned out to be the wrong one, then so be it – she would go and find a nice beach somewhere – perhaps the pretty one in the leaflet. After all, she was on holiday. A holiday that just happened to be in Kefalonia. But deep down she knew she wouldn't be able to relax until she'd done what she'd come to do.

25

CHAPTER 4

Mia locked the car door and took her bearings. So this was Sami. Small, tranquil and picturesque. It made Egham seem like the pits of the Earth in comparison. According to her guide book, this was where they had filmed most of Captain Corelli's Mandolin. She strolled along the waterfront, past a string of tavernas with their checked tablecloths fluttering in the breeze, and stopped to admire the pretty view of fishing boats bobbing up and down in the harbour.

There were lots of tidy little shops selling lace tablecloths, souvenirs, postcards and snorkels. Feeling peckish, she went into a bakery and bought a slice of cheese and spinach pie.

"Efharistó," she thanked the man behind the counter.

"Parakaló," he smiled.

"Um, could you tell me where this road is please?" she showed him the scrap of paper with the address on it.

The man eyed the address with a frown on his face. "Hmmm…" He stroked his moustache in thought. Mia waited patiently. How big was this town? It had seemed pretty small to her. Surely he would know the road. Weren't people in small Greek towns all related to each other anyway?

"OK," he announced. "You must go out of this shop and turn left. Then you cross the road. Then you must walk up the hill and take the second turning on your left. Walk for a few minutes and take the next street on your right. This is the street you are looking for."

Mia repeated his directions slowly, locking each turn to memory in time with the man's nods. Thank God most people here spoke English. She wouldn't have understood a word of that had he spoken to her in Greek.

"Thanks." She left the shop and followed his directions.

It didn't take long to reach Napoleontos Street. At least the sign looked like it said that. It was hard to tell with the Greek alphabet – some letters were the same, but some made no sense whatsoever. She counted the houses. There it was, number six. Mia's heart started thumping. She felt butterflies in her stomach. Perhaps she should have phoned first? But she'd been over it a dozen times. If she phoned first she might get knocked back immediately. No, definitely best to just go for it – or else what was the point in coming all this way?

Mia walked up to the house, smoothed her hair into place, took a deep breath and knocked on the front door.

CHAPTER 5

"God, that's a bit rough," said Jo, squeezing some more factor fifteen onto her palm and smoothing it onto her legs. "Did you have any idea that she might be feeling…you know, having second thoughts?"

"Well looking back on it now, yes I suppose there were clues, but I was so in love and so excited about the wedding, I would never have picked up on them." Simon took a deep breath and scratched a mosquito bite on his ankle.

Jo had never seen such long, skinny, painfully white legs. They were like silver birch saplings. What was more puzzling than why Simon's fiancée had done a runner at the altar, was what she'd seen in him in the first place. He seemed like a nice enough guy, but he was definitely no oil painting. Jo wondered what miracles she could work on him if she got him into her salon. A hair cut for a start. It was all over the place. And an eyelash tint – just a subtle one, but he was so fair, he looked like he didn't have any. She would encourage him to grow a goatee. Always a good option for a man with no chin. Hmm…what else? Oh yes, sort out those glasses, mate. John Lennon specs may have looked cool on John Lennon, but then he was a millionaire pop star with hordes of screaming groupies chasing him around. The guy could have worn a turnip on his head and got away with it. You, on the other hand, cannot. Contact lenses for you, darling – or else some sleek Armanis, but then again, that might look like he was trying too hard. Bless.

Anyway, it couldn't have been his looks that had attracted her to him.

"What do you do for a living?" asked Jo.

Simon took a swig of water from his bottle. "I work for an IT helpline."

"Right." So much for the uniform/money/power theory, then. Unless – "Do you have to wear a uniform for that?"

"No, I'm in a call centre. I can wear what I want so long as I look smart."

"What does your fiancée – sorry, ex-fiancée – do?"

"Shelley works in a creche."

"And at what point during the wedding did she er…change her mind?"

"Just before saying 'I do'. She went pale, just stared at me, and then turned and ran out of the church."

"Blimey. Just like in a soap opera."

"She didn't even say sorry. I've heard nothing from her since. *Selfish bitch.*"

"Well, you're very brave coming away on your honeymoon alone. Don't know if I could have done it."

"It wasn't like I had any choice. The tickets were non-refundable and non-transferable. And stupidly, I was hoping she might change her mind at the last minute and come with me, so we could work things out."

"Oy, Jo!"

They both turned round. Nath was in the pool, leaning over the edge behind them. "I'm going inside for a kip. Alright?"

"OK, I'll join you in a bit," Jo replied.

Simon turned back to face the sea and reached for his bottle of Soltan as Nath climbed out of the pool. Jo blew him a kiss. Nath grinned and held his finger and thumb up to his forehead in an 'L' shape, mouthed 'Loser' at Simon's back and padded back to their apartment, leaving a trail of wet footprints behind him. Jo admired Nath's broad shoulders which had turned slightly pink from the sun. Now there was a man with a fine physique. He disappeared behind the building and re-emerged ten seconds later on their verandah, beckoning to her while performing some pelvic thrusts on an unsuspecting chair. Jo tried not to giggle and turned back towards Simon. She was about to excuse herself but missed the opportunity.

"We'd been together for three years, you know," Simon sighed deeply. "You'd think you'd know someone inside out in that time, but it just goes to show, you never can tell."

"I'm sure there are plenty of other people who have been in this situation," Jo tried to sound reassuring. "I'm sure the vicar must have seen it a thousand times before."

"Do you think she's been seeing someone else?" He sat up straight on his sunlounger.

How was she supposed to know? "It's possible, but there's no point jumping to conclusions. You need to talk to her. You deserve an explanation. And if you don't get a satisfactory one, you should…"

"What? I should what?"

"Well if it was me, if my fiancé jilted me at the altar and then let me go off on our honeymoon alone without so much as an apology, I'd say 'good riddance to bad rubbish.' I don't think I'd want to see him again, quite frankly."

Simon stared miserably at the sea. "But I still love her."

Now what was she supposed to say? 'You'll get over it, mate'? Or, 'she'll probably turn up on the next plane, begging forgiveness'? Out of the corner of her eye she noticed Nath was still on the verandah, waggling his tongue at her in a suggestive manner. She stood up.

"Listen, I'm baking out here, I'm going to pop inside to cool down for a bit. I know this is a boring old cliché, but what is meant to be will be. If you don't work things out with your fiancée, then there's a reason for it – there'll be something better in store for you."

"You're very optimistic," Simon squinted up at her.

"It's the only way to be. That's life, isn't it? Anyway, if I were you I'd cover up – you're starting to burn." Jo gave him a friendly pat on the shoulder. "See you later."

Caz and Babs smoothed their towels out on the sunloungers and placed their bottles of Piz Buin next to their flip flops.

"Bloody hell it ain't 'alf hot," gasped Caz, putting her sunglasses on and fiddling with the back of the sunbed to get it at the right angle.

"Pass us the paracetamol," mumbled Babs. "Me head still hurts."

"You only had one half an hour ago." Caz rummaged in her bag for the painkillers.

"Yeah, well I was stupid. I should've taken two, shouldn't I? One's no good. Makes no bleedin' difference. How's your head anyway?"

"Not too bad. I switched onto Cokes at about one, didn't I?"

"Did you? I don't remember that."

"I don't suppose you remember trying to grab Dimitri's little man, either."

30

"*What?*" Babs sat bolt upright.

Caz cackled. "Had you going there, didn't I?"

"Cheeky cow. Mind you, I wouldn't blame meself if I did. That man is bloody lovely. Shame he ain't a bit older."

"Shame we ain't a bit younger," sighed Caz.

"Well girl, I'll tell you this much. I felt younger than I 'ave done in ages last night. I enjoyed every minute we spent at that Bora Bora place."

"I'm surprised you remember much of it. You was well gone."

"So was you."

"Not as much as you. You never had the same drink twice. It's no wonder you're still hungover."

"Caz, it was the first night of our holiday. You gotta go a bit mad on the first night ain'tcha?"

As Babs reached for her paperback, the high-pitched notes of the Dallas theme tune echoed around the pool. "Caz, you have got to sort out your mobile ring tone. That is well embarrassing!" hissed Babs, looking over her shoulder at the various raised heads and disapproving frowns around the pool.

Caz took her phone out of her bag and pressed it to her ear. "Whatcha want? I told you, Wayne, they need new trainers – both of 'em…That's how much trainers cost these days, innit? You can't expect them to wear those ones. It's Nike or Adidas – they won't touch nothing else…Have it your own way, Wayne, but don't call me later when you've got World War Three on your hands. Anyway, must dash, I'm going for a swim. Ta-da!"

Babs rolled her eyes. "Don't tell me – he wants to get them Dunlop or something."

"Worse – Asda's own. They're refusing to go in the shop with him."

They roared with laughter.

"Right, I'm going in the pool," announced Babs, getting up. "Coming?"

"In a minute. I need to get really hot first."

Babs walked over to the ladder and lowered herself carefully into the water. Gripping the hand-rail she grimaced as her buttocks skimmed the surface. "Christ," she muttered through clenched teeth.

"Come on you big wuss!" Caz teased from her sunbed.

"You'd never believe I was once captain of Southend women's swimming team, would you?" Babs announced to the svelte red-haired woman in a white bikini who was sitting with her feet over the edge of the shallow end. The woman smiled.

Babs let go of the ladder and plunged in. "SheeeeeezzUSS!" she spluttered. "How comes this water's so bleedin' cold?" She swam to the shallow end, teeth chattering. "'Ere, I'm alright now. It's just getting in that's the hard part. Know what I mean?" she said to the red-haired woman.

"Oh, it's wonderful once you've warmed up a bit. Really refreshing," she replied.

"That's a nice tattoo – what's it say?" asked Babs, nodding towards a small pattern on the woman's toned arm.

"It's Thai for Shantee. That's my name. I lived in Thailand for a couple of years – so I thought I'd get a tattoo in Thai as a souvenir."

"Oh…very nice," said Babs, slightly baffled. "I like your bikini 'an all. Better than this thing I'm wearing. I'm not convinced about the camouflage pattern – Caz says I look like a lezzer."

The smile on Shantee's face stiffened. "Actually camouflage is very fashionable at the moment – regardless of one's sexuality."

"Yeah, well, as long as I don't go shaving me head I s'pose I can get away with it," said Babs. "Right, I'm gonna do ten lengths without stopping. Nice talking to you."

Shantee got up and walked back to her apartment, carrying her towel over her shoulder. Let go, she told herself. Let go. The silly woman didn't mean to be offensive. Obviously Southend was a bit behind when it came to political correctness. Still, it wasn't looking like a lesbian that 'Babs' needed to worry about. Looking like a big, fat dumpling, though…now surely that was cause for concern. Shantee caught herself again. Let go! Release the irritation! *So* not important. Funny though, how even though Babs had not introduced herself, you'd have to be deaf not to know her name. Or the other one, Caz. Perhaps they were a bit deaf – that would explain not only why they were so loud, but also why they hadn't heard of gay rights.

Shantee paused to clear her mind of negativity. Tossing back her long, straight hair and proceeding, she tripped over a hose lying across the path and just managed to steady herself before stumbling into the caretaker who was watering the flowerbeds.

"Opaaa!" chuckled Dimitri. "You are OK?"

"Yes, fine," Shantee laughed nervously. "Away with the fairies. Didn't see you there."

"Oh," sighed Dimitri, "it's not like beautiful women not to notice me."

Shantee narrowed her eyes beneath her bold, henna-red fringe. Here we go, she thought.

Dimitri laughed. "Relax. I am joking – not that you are not beautiful, of course!" He grinned at her warmly.

"Sorry, I should have been looking where I was going."

"I don't mean to be rude," said Dimitri, assuming a serious expression, "please don't take this the wrong way, but you have a very incredible body. I have never seen such a toned woman – or man, either. I am thinking you are an athlete, but you do not have too big muscles."

Shantee smiled. There was nothing like praise for her figure to win her over. "I teach yoga and meditation," she explained. "I do about six hours of yoga a day. That's how I keep in shape."

"You don't run or swim, things like that?"

"I swim occasionally, but it's mainly down to yoga."

"Well I think I will have to learn some yoga myself. I'm not so toned as I used to be." Dimitri pinched a roll of flesh on his hips.

"You don't look too bad to me. Still, I can't recommend yoga enough."

"Really? You will teach me some, then? Show me some positions?" he grinned, a twinkle in his eye.

So that's where he was coming from. Smug little smart-arse! She smiled wryly. Men – they really were all the same.

"Oh, no, no, no!" laughed Dimitri. "No, I don't mean I want to learn yoga in your bed. I am serious. You can teach me here, now – over there on the grass. Wait, I will turn the hose off. I want to know yoga, I promise. I am serious! I am turning into a fat bastard." He hurried over to the tap, turned it off and rolled up the hose.

Shantee sighed and followed him to the strip of grass next to the drive. She placed her towel next to her feet and stood facing him.

"The rep told us your name, but I'm afraid I've forgotten it," she said.

"Dimitri."

33

"Dimitri?"

"Yes, your pronunciation is perfect. You speak Greek?"

"No."

"Don't worry. I will teach you in return for yoga. What is your name?"

"Shantee."

"OK, teach me, Shantee. I stand straight like this…?" Dimitri stood to attention.

"Feet hip-width apart, knees loose, tailbone tucked in. Relax a little."

"OK say it again, slowly please…hip-feet…"

A white rental car turned into the drive.

"Yiasou Mia!" Dimitri called. Mia waved out the window and pulled up in the small car park behind the apartments. "Look – Shantee is teaching me yoga," he beamed as she locked the car and walked towards them.

"So I see," she replied.

"You want to join in with us?" he asked.

"Maybe another time. Did you enjoy yourself at the Bora Bora last night?"

"Yes, you should have seen Caz and Babs. They are crazy! When I left at two o'clock, they were still there dancing and singing. They were very drunk. Especially Babs – she fell over. It was very funny."

"What about Craig and Steve?"

"They met these two girls and bought them lots of drinks, but later their boyfriends arrive. So they were disappointed. And Simon arrived just as you were leaving."

"Sounds like you had fun."

"Sure, next time you must stay longer. Shantee, you must come too."

Shantee smiled. "We'll see."

"I'll see you later," said Mia.

"Hello? Do you want to learn some yoga, or can I go for my shower now?" asked Shantee impatiently, as Dimitri watched Mia walk towards her apartment.

"Sorry. Yes, ready. Teach me."

"Right, well if you look into my eyes, rather than over my shoulder, I might believe you're paying attention."

"Sorry. I'm looking at you and only you, beautiful yoga teacher."

34

"And give the flirting a rest – I'm gay. Just pay attention if you want me to teach you something."

Dimitri's eyes widened. "You're a lesbian? It's not possible!"

"Don't you believe me?"

"No – I mean yes – I don't know. I'm just surprised."

"Do you have a problem with it?"

"No, of course not. Just a shame, that's all. Such a waste! Such a body!" He sighed.

Shantee smiled. A right smooth talker, this one. A real ladies' man – Kefalonia's very own Casanova. She wondered if he had a sister.

CHAPTER 6

Monday 3rd

Mia woke with a start, her heart racing. It was just a bad dream – a very weird, bad dream. She'd been running down a crowded road clutching a jam jar full of water. There was something else in the jar – a gherkin or a pickled onion perhaps. She reached the zebra crossing. The traffic lights were on red, the green man signalling her to cross, but the cars refused to stop. She started shouting at the drivers, swearing at them, trying to memorise their number plates, but every time she tried to cross the road, they sped up, nearly running her over. Mia hurled abuse at them and ran to a phone box to call the police and report them. But the police had changed their number. It was no longer 999, but consisted of eleven digits, which Mia repeatedly dialled incorrectly, hanging up and starting again, over and over. Panicking that time was running out, she realised she had left the jam jar on the kerb. Luckily it was still there. She picked it up and ran back to the phone box, only someone was now in it having a good, long chat. Mia held the jam jar up to the light. The object in it wasn't a gherkin but a seahorse. It looked at her with big, scared eyes. *Don't leave me*, it was saying. *Don't desert me.* The person in the phone box hung up and left. Mia grabbed the phone. It was dead – the cord had been cut in two. The receiver was no longer attached to the phone, and there was blood on the ground.

That was the point at which she had woken up, anxious and disorientated, frustrated at not being able to remember the eleven-digit phone number. It was just a dream. A stupid dream. She shuddered. Best to get up straight away, have a shower and forget about it. Wash the demons away.

Margaret placed two bowls of cornflakes on the table and went back inside to bring out the tea.

"Hurry up, Frank. The coach will be here in ten minutes."

"Have you seen me travellers cheques, love?" came the agitated reply.

"They're in the inside pocket of your suitcase."

"Ah yes. Thanks, pet."

"What d'you need those for anyway? We should have enough cash to last us till mid week before we need to get those out." Margaret took a spoonful of cornflakes and sprinkled on some more sweetener. "Frank? Did you hear me?"

"Yes, pet…er, well you see, I paid for the excursion in cash, and last night's meal in town…" Frank appeared on the verandah, holding a pair of socks in one hand and his sandals in the other.

"Yes, but we should still have a fair bit left over," Margaret frowned at him. "You didn't pay too much money in the restaurant last night, did you?"

Frank hesitated. "Well I couldn't resist buying you a little present yesterday. But don't ask me what it is, cos it's a surprise. So you'll just have to wait till our anniversary." Frank smiled lovingly at his wife. A brilliant and cunning lie. However, now he really would have to slip off and buy something nice for her. Only it wasn't going to cost him fifty quid like last night had. Oh no. Twenty, tops – unless he could win the money back from Dimitri in another round of Poker or that other game they'd played that he'd never heard of before.

Margaret smiled and reached for her cigarettes as he sat down and pulled on his socks.

"You're not wearing socks with those!" she gasped as he reached for one of his sandals.

"Why not?"

"Because I refuse to be seen with you if you go out like that. It is the epitome of bad taste. I mean, if you want to look like a German tourist, then fine, and if you want to be laughed at by everyone on the coach, then on your own head be it – but I shall be sitting as far away from you as possible." Margaret popped a cigarette in her mouth and lit it, inhaling deeply.

"Oh bloody hell woman! Alright, no socks!" Frank pulled them off and chucked them back inside the room. "Satisfied? If I get blisters though, it'll be you who has to find a chemist to get me plasters."

"But really, Frank, how do you expect a woman to find you attractive wearing socks and sandals?" asked Margaret, exhaling a funnel of smoke.

"I'm not concerned about looking attractive, I'm concerned about being comfortable while walking around. Anyway, how do you expect a man to find *you* attractive when all that comes out of your trap is bullshit and clouds of toxic chemicals? Not to mention your ashtray breath. I shall be sitting as far away from *you* as possible!"

Margaret was about to launch an attack on his paunch belly when another voice butted in first.

"I have to say, darling, I agree with your wife. Socks and sandals just don't look right together." Caz stepped out of her French doors and leaned over the railings between their terraces. "But don't you worry about blisters – I come armed with plasters of all kinds. Hang on – I'll go get you some!" she disappeared back inside again.

Margaret pursed her lips. Just how long had that Essex airhead been eavesdropping on their conversation?

"Cheer up, pet, she's on your side," whispered Frank, tucking into his cornflakes.

"'Ere you go darling," Caz passed him a handful of plasters over the railings.

"Very kind of you indeed," smiled Frank. "Much obliged."

"No worries, love. So where are you two off to today? Somewhere nice?"

"We're doing an excursion up to Fiskardo in the north of the island," Margaret replied through tight lips.

"Oh, so are we!" beamed Caz. "The coach'll be 'ere any minute and I ain't had any breakfast yet. I'd better hurry up. Toodaloo!"

"Ta-ra love," said Frank, as Caz vanished again. "Nice lass, isn't she?"

Yes, thought Margaret silently – if you liked lasses of the bovine variety.

Mia sat down on her verandah with her two cups of decaf and a plate of fruit and watched as a coach approached Eleni Apartments on the winding coastal road. It slowed to a halt just out of sight behind the complex. A couple of doors slammed and she could hear muffled voices as people boarded the coach.

Once the coach had parted, the only noise that could be heard was the jingling of goat bells on the hillside. No one else was outside yet. Mia closed her eyes and relished the peace. Yesterday had been a big disappointment. All that build-up, the adrenalin, the hovering around on the street wondering if she was doing the right thing. Only to find out it was the wrong address. Still, she had known that it probably wouldn't be straightforward.

Mia clutched the new address she'd been given in her hand. It was in Argostoli, the island's main town – a good hour or so in the car from Skala. The woman at number six Napoleontos Street had seemed fairly confident that this was where Mia would find her 'friend'. Mia wasn't so sure. What if it wasn't the right place? What if there was no answer? What if she was unwelcome? All those questions had got the better of her the day before and she had returned to Skala, relieved at having a reason to postpone the big moment. She would have to get a grip on herself today.

"Morning." Shantee was standing by the pool in front of her verandah. Mia jumped. "Wow, you were miles away!"

"Sorry," smiled Mia. "I didn't see you there."

Shantee leaned over the flowerbed and rested her elbows on the railings. "Not going on the excursion to Fiskardo?"

"No, I'm going to have a look at Argostoli today. The coach has already been and gone for Fiskardo."

"Yes I could hear your nextdoor neighbours getting all excited about going to find Tom Hanks' house. It was as if they expected it to have a round, blue plaque above the door."

Mia smiled. "You must mean Caz and Babs."

"Who else?" Shantee rolled her eyes. "Nice people by all means, but yesterday I felt tempted to steal their mobile phones and throw them over the cliff."

"They've brought their mobiles? God, I'd never bring mine on holiday. You'd never get any peace and quiet."

"Exactly. They were going off every half an hour yesterday. First it was something to do with kids and trainers, then the other one got a call from her mum asking how to set the video recorder. So much for being 'free at last'!" Shantee made little quotation marks with her fingers.

"What do you mean?" asked Mia.

"I take it you haven't seen the T-shirts, then?"

39

Mia shook her head.

"Well I won't spoil it for you," Shantee grinned. "Right, I'm off for a swim. Have a nice time in Argostoli."

CHAPTER 7

Fiskardo's waterfront bustled with tourists in the late afternoon sun. They sat themselves down excitedly in the cafés lining the harbour, snapped endless photos of the pink and yellow bougainvillea-covered houses, and scanned the postcard racks for the best pictures of the pretty views that lay before them.

"You're better off without her, pal. God knows I could do with a holiday without the wife!" Frank laughed while noticing an impressively large fish in the water just yards from their table. Margaret raised her eyebrows in a bemused manner and stubbed out a lipstick-stained cigarette in the ashtray. "Only joking, pet. You know how much I love you." He drained his pint of beer and shifted his chair into the shade of the umbrella.

"I don't think that's what Simon really needs to hear, is it Frank?" said Margaret, hoisting up her dress to tan her portly pink legs.

Simon stirred his coffee, staring into the small, foamy brown vortex he had created. "I tried to phone her last night but I just got the answering machine. I left a message. Said I could forgive her if she'd just tell me why…"

Margaret looked at Frank and shrugged. He shrugged back. "How about I get some more drinks in? Or an ice cream even? We've got time before the coach goes," he offered, glancing at his watch.

"No thanks," mumbled Simon.

"Frank, there's not enough time, love," Margaret frowned at him. "We have to meet back at the coach in ten minutes, the rep said."

"Stop worrying about the time, Margaret – I'll get a Cornetto or something that I can take with me. Alright?" Frank patted the change in his pocket and headed towards the café. Margaret watched as he looked in the outside fridge at the ice cream selection and then darted into the gift shop next door. Perhaps he'd spotted a souvenir in the window to get for the kids, she thought, although there was something shifty about the way he'd

41

looked over his shoulder before going in. She turned back to Simon as two large shadows fell across the table.

"My my, we are looking serious," joked Babs, squashing into the chair next to Simon's. "Don'tcha like Fistardo, then?" she nudged him and cackled.

"There's nothing wrong with Fiskardo, it's quite lovely," said Margaret, begrudgingly moving up her chair so that Caz could fit in at the end of the table. "Unfortunately Simon has had a bit of a bad luck lately, and we were just discussing that."

"Oh dear, what's happened to you, then?" asked Caz, giving Simon a concerned look.

Simon attempted a smile. "It's nothing really..." he said as Frank rejoined them.

"Oh well, I won't stick me nose in," said Caz, taking a large bite of Cornetto. "Oy, you'll never guess what – I reckon we saw Tom 'anks earlier."

"It weren't 'im, Caz!" Babs rolled her eyes and sniggered.

"Might've been – it was hard to tell cos he 'ad sunglasses on," said Caz excitedly.

"My fiancée left me at the altar," interrupted Simon. "I haven't seen her since. This was supposed to be our honeymoon." He took his glasses off, gave them a rub and put them back on again.

"Shit-a-brick!" spurted Babs. "She dumped you at the altar? What a silly bitch!"

Margaret sighed. The last thing this poor man needed was these two getting him all worked up into a tiz.

"How comes she got cold feet then?" asked Caz, a mouth full of ice cream.

Simon shrugged. "That's what I keep asking myself, but it doesn't look like I'm ever going to find out."

"Well, if you ain't heard from her since," said Babs, "I'd say it's more than just a case of cold feet. Sounds to me like – without meaning to be rude or nothing – but it sounds to me like she don't love you no more."

Margaret's jaw fell open. The audacity! Some people's tactlessness defied belief. "I hardly think it's fair to make that judgment when you've never even met the woman." She turned to Simon. "Listen love, who knows why she did what she did. But I'm sure she's feeling dead rotten about it – she's probably trying to find the courage to face you and explain. By the time you get home, she'll be desperate to talk to you and sort it all out. If she didn't love you, she wouldn't have got as far as half way down the aisle – she'd have cancelled it months ago. I'm positive."

Simon looked at Margaret, a faint glimmer of hope in his eyes. "D'you think so?"

"Yes, love, I really do."

Babs wolfed down the last inch of her Cornetto and dusted the crumbs off her lap. "She might be right," she began, her mouth still full.

"*She* has a name," interrupted Margaret.

"Oh, I DO beg your pardon," said Babs, suppressing a belch, "It's Marge, innit?"

"Margaret, NOT Marge."

"As – I – was – saying," said Babs, giving Margaret a frosty side-glance, "Margaret might be right, but she don't know any more than I do what your fiancée's state of mind is. On the one hand, as Margaret said, she must love you not to have called the whole thing off ages ago. BUT, on the other hand, she might not have had the guts to call it off any sooner cos she didn't wanna hurt you. But to let you go off on your honeymoon without trying to explain to you why she couldn't marry you, well – I wouldn't get me 'opes up that she's gonna be on her knees, grovelling for you to take her back the minute you walk through customs at Gatwick airport."

Simon's hand trembled as he placed his cup back on the saucer.

Margaret glared at Babs, her eyes bulging like a cartoon bull about to stampede.

"Look, I'm just being straight with you," Babs continued nonchalantly. "Most people will just try to make you feel better, tell you what you wanna hear. But you won't be doin' yourself no favours unless you prepare yourself for the worst. Know what I mean?"

Simon's eyes turned red and watery.

"She didn't mean to upset you, pet," Margaret patted his hand.

"*She* has a name," Babs announced.

Margaret arched an over-plucked eyebrow. "Barbara, I believe?"

43

"Wrong! Babs. Like Babs Windsor."

"Which is short for Barbara."

"It is for her, but it ain't for me. I was born Babs – it's on me birth certificate."

"Well now we all know," Margaret smiled acidly.

The pool glinted and swayed as Shantee completed her second round of thirty laps that day. Resting against the edge and dipping her head back into the water, she caught her breath back and stared up at the glorious blue sky. It was divine. Pure tranquillity – well apart from Beavis and Butthead giggling over a pair of breasts in FHM every so often, but at least they knew how to have a conversation without shouting. In fact, in the absence of Caz and Babs, the complex was so quiet you could practically hear people's stomachs rumbling.

The black girl with the high ponytail was sitting on the pool steps, half in and half out of the water. She was leaning back, eyes closed, head tilted towards the sun, as if modelling her sparkly silver bikini for a fashion shoot. She was slender and curvaceous, with skin that looked as smooth as a pebble. She was stunning. Shantee looked away. She had come to relax, meditate and be alone. She had to stay focused.

Beavis and Butthead started giggling. Shantee looked over at them. Beavis was holding up a pin-up of a topless woman, pointing to her crotch and muttering something about 'having missed one'. Butthead scrutinised the picture before passing it back and replying in a low voice, "If that was my ho, I'd tell her to sort it out or else I'll pluck it out with me teeth." They both grunted with laughter.

Shantee rolled her eyes in disgust.

"Dickheads," muttered her companion in the pool, shaking her head.

Shantee smiled.

"Oy – Jo!" The girl looked up. Her boyfriend was waving at her. "I'm just gonna nip over to that hotel down the road and pick up some beer and a paper. D'you want anything?"

"No thanks. See you in a bit." She winked at him and slunk down a few steps so that only her head remained above water. "Typical lads!" she whispered to Shantee, nodding towards Craig and Steve. It's ridiculous that it's seen as unsightly. It's only natural after all. I mean, they're allowed to have it, so why shouldn't women?"

"And yet we willingly conform," sighed Shantee. "It's our own fault really. No one's forcing us to have bikini waxes."

"Yeah, but if you don't, you get idiots like them giggling at you and making you feel embarrassed."

"At least when you've got a partner you don't have to worry quite so much."

"Not so sure about that. Nath's with them on that one. He likes a nice, neat landing strip. Luckily I run a beauty salon with my best mate, so we always do each other the honours. Bloody painful though. Men have no idea."

Shantee laughed. "I'd love to watch those two having their pubes waxed."

"Oy – I heard that!" Craig lowered the back of his sunlounger and turned onto his front to face the pool.

Shantee groaned under her breath.

"We were just saying that even cosmetically-enhanced supermodels don't seem to meet mens' standards these days," said Jo.

"Ah, now that's where you're wrong," said Craig, getting up to sit on the edge of the pool. "Personally, I prefer a woman who's all real. I mean, nothing against the bird in the magazine – she's a very sexy woman – but, the old silicone implants and rubber lips don't do it for me. I prefer natural boobs, a bit more swing than bounce. Know what I mean? What do you think, Steve?"

Steve joined him, swinging his legs over the edge of the pool. "Well mate, I know what you're saying, but I don't think you'd kick Pamela Anderson out of bed for farting, would you?"

Craig and Steve chuckled while Jo and Shantee exchanged unimpressed looks.

Not wishing to head down this road any further, Shantee decided to change the subject.

"I was looking at the tattoo on your back earlier," she said to Craig. "Is it Urdu?"

Craig nodded, pleased that he was attracting female attention.

"Let me see it," said Jo.

Craig turned around to reveal an arch of blue letters between his shoulders.

"What does it say?" asked Shantee.

"Beckham," Craig announced proudly.

"As in David Beckham?" asked Jo, trying not to laugh.

"That's the one," winked Craig.

"Why Beckham?" asked Shantee, also struggling to keep a straight face.

"*Why Beckham?*" Craig turned to Steve with a mock-mystified expression on his face.

"Allow me," offered Steve, squinting at them – his eyes all but disappearing beneath his thick brows. "Obviously you ladies don't watch football."

"We know who David Beckham is, thank you very much," said Shantee.

"Then you would be aware ladies, that he is both the best football player the world has ever known – apart from Pelé maybe – and was England's best chance of winning the World Cup and bringing our country the biggest victory since the end of the Second World War – not forgetting 1966 of course," said Steve.

"In other words, the man is a national hero," explained Craig, practically salivating.

"So why in Urdu?" asked Jo. "Do you speak it or something?"

"No," Craig replied defensively. "Becks has got a tattoo on his arm in Urdu which says 'Victoria'."

"Oh, I seeeeee," grinned Jo. "It all makes sense now."

"Very original," nodded Shantee approvingly, winking at Jo.

"Oy!" said Craig. "I might have to dunk you if you carry on being cheeky. Steve, d'you think these ladies are asking for a dunking?"

"Mate, I seriously do."

"Don't even think about it!" snapped Jo. "If my hair gets wet I'll kill the pair of you!"

But Craig and Steve were already in the pool and swimming towards them, excited grins on their faces.

"Oh shit," muttered Shantee. "I think they've got the wrong message."

"It might be time to flash them our overgrown bikini lines," laughed Jo, wading as fast as she could towards the steps.

"Girls! Where ya going?" called Steve, as Jo and Shantee swiftly exited the pool.

"See you!" teased Jo. "I'm going to make some coffee. Would you like one?" she asked Shantee.

"Mmm, you read my mind," Shantee glowed.

Mia waved to Shantee and Jo as she locked the car door and walked towards her apartment. People were forming friendships already. She felt a twinge of insecurity. Then again, she hadn't come to Kefalonia to make friends.

She had found the address by herself this time. It had been surprisingly easy. Argostoli was certainly a lot bigger and busier than Sami or Skala, but the directions she'd been given with the address had been easy enough to follow.

She had parked outside the house and sat waiting in the car, trying to calm her nerves and summon the courage to go and knock on the door. Finally, she had shaken herself into action and opened the car door. As she did so, the door of the house burst open and two young teenagers – a boy and a girl – scampered out, followed by a middle-aged woman wearing a flowery headscarf, who locked the door behind her. The woman said something to them in Greek which sounded like an order to hurry up. Within seconds all three had disappeared down an alleyway out of view.

Mia fell back into the driver's seat, her legs trembling. This couldn't be right, surely. A Greek woman with two teenagers? It couldn't be the right address…could it? Mia cursed. She'd missed her bloody chance now. She should have just got on with it rather than sitting there trying to predict every possible outcome. God knows how long it would be before they came back.

She had switched on the ignition and set off slowly, driving aimlessly around town hoping to spot them again. She wanted to get a closer look. They were Greek. There were kids. It couldn't be the right house. She went back and checked the number on the front door. No mistake there. Perhaps they were friends visiting? No, they'd had a key. Family, relatives? It was pointless guessing. But new thoughts were seeping into Mia's mind.

47

Thoughts she hadn't allowed herself to have before. Thoughts she wasn't prepared for.

After scoffing a quick snack in a café in the main square, she had returned to her stake-out for another two hours, until she had become aware of a neighbour sitting on their front doorstep looking at her suspiciously. It was time to give up for the day.

Back in her apartment again, she tried to put uncomfortable thoughts out of her mind and forget about it – have a swim, read her book, soak up the sun. She kicked off her sandals and changed into her bikini. She stood sideways in front of the mirror and held her stomach in for all she was worth. It wasn't as flat as it used to be that was for sure – but she could still get away with it. She peeped outside from behind the curtains. Craig and Steve were the only people out there, and they were adjusting their sunbeds into lying position, backs to the pool.

Mia parked her towel and bag at the other end of the pool from Craig and Steve – who hadn't stirred as she'd walked past, her flip flops clapping on the paving stones. She took out her book, quietly dragged the sunlounger under the shade of the parasol, sat down and spread herself out. It was so peaceful here. There was virtually no noise – just the occasional car on the coast road, and the goats on the hillside, jingling their bells as they grazed.

The horizon stretched before her – just sea and sky as far as the eye could see. Blue sea, blue sky. Not grey sky, not white sky, not patchy blue and white sky. Blue sky. Pure, unadulterated blue. Mia gazed up at it and drank it into her consciousness, into her very being. Greece was blessed. All those weeks of grey and drizzle back home, gridlock traffic, the damp patch on the kitchen ceiling, splitting up with Max, quarrelling with mum and dad. Thank God she had come here. It hadn't been an easy decision to make, but now that she was feeling calmer and having had time to absorb the day's events, being here was worth it – if only for the sun's gentle caress, the soothing blue sky, the time to think.

"You are the slowest reader I have ever seen."

Mia looked round, shielding her eyes from the sun. Dimitri sat down on the sunlounger next to hers and lit a cigarette.

"You haven't turned the page since opening the book ten minutes ago," he commented, exhaling smoke and trying to wave it away from her.

Mia smiled. "I was deep in thought."

"What were you thinking?"

"I was thinking I'm glad I came here. I really needed some sun, sea and…" she trailed off.

"And…?" Dimitri cocked his head to one side and studied her, an expectant grin on his face.

"Well not sex, that's for sure. Space – sun, sea and space."

"Space? You mean like not so crowded?"

"Yeah, I suppose. But also space from people I know. It's good to be on your own sometimes, isn't it?"

Dimitri nodded.

"So how are your yoga lessons going?" she asked him.

"Shantee taught me some positions – I mean postures yesterday. She does six hours of yoga a day, you know. That's why she has such a perfect body."

OK, mate. No need to rub it in. She looked down at her own body. It might not be perfect but it wasn't too bad. Shagathon Steve had given her the thumbs up at any rate.

"So Shantee's your type, I take it?" Mia teased.

Dimitri smiled and shook his hair out of his eyes. "Type? I don't have a type," he said sounding serious all of a sudden.

"Do you have a girlfriend?" Mia asked. "I don't mean to be nosy or anything, but I thought that pretty barmaid in the Bora Bora was your girlfriend?"

"Marilena? One time she was, but not now. No, I don't have a girlfriend – I don't want one. I am thirty-three and I am probably the only man on this island over the age of twenty-eight who isn't married. People don't understand, but this is how I like it – it's my choice. My mother is always asking me when I will meet a beautiful girl, get married and have children. I tell her maybe when I'm fifty. It makes her very sad. She lives alone since my father died, and my two younger sisters both moved to Athens – one to study at university and one to get married. She hopes I will meet a woman, get married, have kids and buy the house next-door to hers. I tell her to stop dreaming."

"Why? Why would that be so terrible?"

"Are you kidding?" Dimitri looked at her as if she was mad. "You British love Kefalonia. But you only see it for a week or two in the summer. There are lots of tourists here and it seems alive and beautiful – paradise. I live here all my life and I've had enough of this fucking place. There is nothing for me here. I am bored. I am trapped. I want to get out and see the world."

"So what's stopping you?"

"What's stopping me, my friend, is money. Greece is a poor country compared to England. I am a caretaker – a gardener, a cleaner. You think I earn much money?"

Mia was starting to feel uncomfortable.

"I earn next to nothing. And what I earn has to last through the winter, in case I can't find work."

"What work do you do in the winter?"

"Anything I can find. I've worked in a supermarket, a petrol station. One winter I worked as a fisherman. It's all shit."

"So what would you really like to do?"

Dimitri gave a defeated shrug and took a deep drag on his cigarette. "Sometimes I think I would love to be a teacher. Or maybe I would like to run my own travel company."

Mia was surprised. She was sure he was going to say Formula One racing driver or Hollywood actor – something glamorous, something so out of reach it wasn't worth pursuing. "Neither of those sounds too impossible to me."

"Maybe. But I wasn't very good at school. I didn't pass my exams."

"Well, in England they're crying out for teachers. They'd take you with open arms – although obviously you'd have to train first."

Dimitri looked thoughtful. "You think I could be a teacher?"

"Why not? My Mum used to be a teacher. She said the two most important things you need to have are enthusiasm and total confidence in yourself so that you're in control of the class. You rounded up a bunch of strangers to go out dancing without any problems."

"But I'm not so clever." His green eyes looked forlornly into hers.

"You're clever enough to speak fluent English. I can't speak any other languages."

"I can speak a bit of German too," he said brightening up. "There is a hotel in Skala where they get mainly German tourists. I worked in the bar there one summer."

"Dimitri, you're intelligent – all you'd have to do is train. Loads of people do badly in school. We're often too young and immature to realise the importance of education, either that or we get teachers who are crap and can't teach."

"You think I'd be a good teacher?"

"Sure. You've got charisma and confidence. Kids love that."

Dimitri beamed. "You really think so?"

"Yes. Now stop fishing for compliments." She picked up her book again.

"What about you – what do you do?" he asked.

"I'm a dentist."

"Really?" Dimitri looked impressed. But then his expression turned to one of fascination combined with disgust. "Doesn't it bother you putting your fingers in the mouths of strangers?"

"Have you ever slept with a stranger?" Mia asked him bluntly.

Dimitri shrugged. "Yes."

"Presumably more than once?"

He shrugged again and looked away. "So what?"

"So why should putting my fingers in someone's mouth bother me any more than you sticking your tongue in someone's mouth – or anywhere else in their anatomy for that matter?" she snapped.

Dimitri looked at the ground. "OK…good point," he mumbled.

"Obviously it doesn't bother me at all or I wouldn't be a dentist," she said more calmly. After all, he was only the umpteen-millionth person to ask her that question.

"But what about when you get an old man with really bad teeth and smelly breath?"

Mia sighed. "There's a lot of old people who live on their own and don't know how to look after themselves properly – it's very sad. I'm glad I can do something to help, even if it is only something small like alleviating their toothache. In fact, it's amazing how many young people don't know how to look after their teeth properly in this day and age." She looked at him for signs of boredom. Most people switched off at this point, changed the subject, or suddenly remembered they had something to do, someone to see…

"How do you mean?" he asked, running his tongue over his top teeth. "You brush your teeth in the morning and in the evening. Everyone knows that."

"Not everyone. Do you ever use toothpicks?"

"If I eat in a taverna."

"You should use a toothpick every day too. People think flossing is better, but it isn't as effective as using toothpicks." She looked at him again. Miracle – he was still awake.

"I didn't know that," he replied. "You use a toothpick every day?"

Mia smiled. "Not *every* day."

"Do you think I have bad teeth?" Dimitri opened his mouth wide and then clamped his jaws together, grinning like a Cheshire cat.

"They look pretty good from here – although – open wide again…"

Dimitri lowered his jaw while Mia sat up straight and craned her neck to see the backs of his bottom front teeth.

"You've got a lot of tar building up down there. When was the last time you went to a dentist and had them cleaned?"

Dimitri frowned. "Hmm…" He counted on his fingers. "Don't know. Ten years ago?"

Mia laughed. "And how many cigarettes do you think you've smoked in that time?"

He smiled. "Don't scare me please. Oh shit – look!" Dimitri pointed behind her.

Mia turned around and followed his gaze. "What?"

"Look at Craig and Steve – they are red like lobsters."

Mia rested her eyes on the two lads who were fast asleep on their sunbeds. She gasped. "Ouch! They are going to be in serious pain tomorrow!"

Dimitri flicked his fag butt over the cliff and got up.

"Gently," advised Mia. "Don't wake them up too quickly – they'll have a heart attack!"

She watched Craig and Steve's chests rise and fall in oblivious harmony as Dimitri walked up to them and hesitated.

"Craig, Steve," he called softly. There was no response from the slumbering bodies. "Pssst!" He looked over at Mia and shrugged. "CRAIG! STEVE! WAKE UP YOU BLOODY BASTARDS!"

Craig and Steve jolted awake, a mixture of panic and fear on their faces.

"What the fuck...?" squeaked a startled Craig, blinking up at the silhouette towering above them.

"You're on fire, my friends. You are pink like taramasalata," Dimitri grinned at them.

They looked down at their legs.

"Sssssssshit," mumbled Steve, struggling to sit up.

"Steve, you knob – I thought I told you to put the umbrella between us!" snapped Craig.

"I put it so its shadow was right on us, but the sun's moved."

"That's what the sun fucking does you idiot! Why didn't you move it?"

"Why didn't *you* move it, you twat?"

Craig stood up and winced. "Fuck – I can hardly move!"

"I think you have had enough sun today," said Dimitri, trying to sound serious.

"I think you're right, mate," said Steve, slinging his towel around his shoulders like a cape.

"How bad is it?" Craig asked Dimitri, turning his back to him.

Dimitri looked at his back and whistled. "Bad."

"I'm going in," said Craig and walked off.

"What about me?" Steve turned his back to Dimitri. Dimitri cringed. Steve looked over his shoulder and saw his expression. "Don't say anything, mate. I get the picture."

He scuttled off after Craig. Dimitri looked down at the empty sunbed and picked up a plastic bottle. He held it up. "Coconut oil," he announced to Mia.

Mia shook her head and laughed. "I thought that stuff was illegal."

Dimitri looked at his watch. "I must go now," he said. "See you later." He dropped the bottle of coconut oil back onto the sunbed, nodded at her and left.

Mia waved at his retreating figure. At last she had the entire terrace all to herself. She walked over to the pool and climbed down the ladder, before lunging backwards into the cool water. The sky reigned blue above her head, the water transparent beneath her chin. The day's frustrations drifted away and a tide of calm washed over her as she swam lazily along on her back.

Dimitri dealt the cards like a professional. It occurred to him that he had forgotten to mention to Mia that he had also once worked as a croupier at a casino in Corfu. Not that it was any more impressive than any of his other jobs. Still, she thought he'd make a good teacher. Was she just being polite, perhaps? No, she had seemed to mean it. She was not a false person – feisty perhaps, but not false. No one had ever said that to him before. Then again, he'd never confided to anyone before about his real ambitions. He felt an unfamiliar glow of competence within him as he pictured himself standing in front of a class of small children and pointing to the blackboard as they watched his every gesture, hungry for knowledge.

"Come on, ladies!" he called over his shoulder. "Why are you taking so long? You don't need any more make-up, you are beautiful enough already! Let the evening begin!"

Caz whipped the curtains aside and giggled, fluffing up her dyed blonde curls. "And what would Sir like to drink?" she asked in an unsuccessful attempt to assume a posh voice.

"What have you got?" Dimitri lit a cigarette.

"Babs – what we got?"

"Well," came the reply, "in the Bar del Babs, we've got one bottle of JD, one bottle of Tia Maria, a bottle of Malibu, four cans of lager, Coke and lemonade. Take your pick!"

Dimitri raised his eyebrows. These ladies had come prepared. "Lager please."

Clad in purple leggings and a baggy white T-shirt, Babs padded barefoot onto the verandah carrying a glass and a can of lager, and plonked them on the table in front of him. "That will be a million trillion Euros, please Sir," she announced, pulling out a chair and sitting down.

Dimitri chuckled. "Ladies, don't you know it is the custom when gambling that drinks are on the house?"

"Who said we was gambling?" asked Caz, placing two glasses of Tia Maria and Coke on the table and looking down at her chest to make sure nothing was escaping out of her low-cut top.

"I did," said Babs. "I told Dimitri that he'd better watch out or else I'd thrash him at Arsehole, and he rose to the challenge. Ain't that right, Dimitri?"

Dimitri grinned. "I told her that no one ever beats me – I am the king of cards," he explained to Caz.

Babs turned to Caz. "See? So I said, 'We'll see about that mate – twenty Euros says I'll whip your smutty butty'."

"So are we playing for money?" asked Caz, sitting down next to Dimitri and picking up her cards.

"That, ladies, is up to you." He exhaled slowly towards the sky, making his floppy fringe levitate on a gust of smoke and stubbed out his cigarette in the ashtray.

"How much is ten quid in Euros?" asked Babs.

Dimitri did a quick calculation. "Sixteen Euros."

"Hang on – I ain't gambling ten quid, I hardly ever play cards," Caz protested.

"A fiver then – you gotta add a little excitement to the game, aintcha?"

Caz nodded her consent.

They each plucked their cards into a fan.

"Oy, what game are we playing?" asked Caz.

"Arsehole," said Dimitri. "The game, Arsehole. Babs chose it."

"Oh that makes sense," smiled Caz.

"Gentlemen first," said Babs, nodding to Dimitri.

Silence fell over them and the atmosphere became serious with the concentration of play. Caz slapped a card on the table and smacked a mosquito on her leg. Frowning, Babs drained her drink and poured herself a refill before chucking a card on the pile. Dimitri scrutinised his hand and lit another cigarette, inhaling deeply. He tossed a card onto the table and winked at Babs as she eyed him suspiciously, running her fingers through her spiky hair. Starting to look confused, Caz picked a card up from the table and groaned.

"Ladies and gentlemen, we have a winner," stated Babs, spreading her hand out on the table for all to see.

"Shit," muttered Dimitri, throwing his cards into the centre of the table.

"Eh? What?" Caz looked confused. "Oh bugger, I'm getting confused with that other game, Blackjack or something. I was trying to get me cards to add up to twenty-one!" She burst out laughing.

"You silly trollop!" Babs let out a loud cackle.

Dimitri smiled. "Maybe I have met my match at last, Babs. Finally someone who can make this simple game interesting. I am impressed."

"Let's play again," said Caz. "I was playing the wrong bleedin' game last time!"

"You deal them this time," Dimitri instructed Caz.

Babs stood up and wiggled cheerfully into the apartment, returning five seconds later with another can of lager and another litre bottle of cola. She replenished hers and Caz's glasses with a generous measure of Tia Maria and added a meagre dash of Coke.

"Ladies, it is only fair to warn you that I am just warming up," Dimitri winked at them.

"Yeah, yeah, yeah!" sung Babs, sitting back down again. "You've met your match me ol' China. I'll have you by the Niagaras within the next half hour!"

"What?" Dimitri looked at her, baffled.

"Rhyming slang," explained Caz, shuffling the cards slowly. "Her folks come from the East End of London originally."

"Ah yes," Dimitri nodded. "I know some rhyming slang. Trouble and strife, wife. Loaf of bread, head. Right?"

"Right!" chimed Caz and Babs.

"So what is 'china'?"

"China plate, mate," said Babs.

"Niagara Falls, balls," grinned Caz, dropping the cards all over the floor. Dimitri laughed and bent down to help her pick them up.

Several drinks and games of Arsehole later, Dimitri decided that perhaps it was time to let Babs win again. He'd let her win the first game, as was his usual custom, but he had won the seven games since, and she obviously wasn't going to give up.

"Babs you silly slapper, cut your losses now or you'll be well out of pocket!" urged Caz, who had decided to gamble chewing gums in lieu of cash after the second round.

"No bleedin' way!" slurred Babs indignantly.

"Here, take it back," said Dimitri, pushing his winnings back towards Babs.

She pushed it straight back at him. "I will WIN that back fank you verr much."

"Ssssh!" Caz raised her finger to her lips. "Keep your voice down, woman."

"SORRY! Am I making too much NOISE?" Babs called over Caz and Dimitri's shoulders. They turned around to see who she was addressing.

A pair of feet was resting on a chair just outside the French doors of the neighbouring apartment. They swung onto the ground and Mia leaned forwards, holding a book in one hand and a cup in the other.

"Don't worry," she smiled. "I barely heard you I was so engrossed in my book."

"Why don't you come and join us?" asked Dimitri, smiling at her.

"Oh no thanks, I can't put this down."

"Whatcha reading?" asked Caz.

"Wild Swans," replied Mia.

"Oooh – I know the one – by Naomi Campbell. I read it ages ago. Brilliant, innit?"

"Er, no, this one's about three generations of a Chinese family."

"Oh," said Caz.

"It's fantastic," enthused Mia. "I really recommend it."

"Right…Sure you won't join us?" asked Caz cheerily.

"Come on!" urged Dimitri. "Caz and Babs need help – they are losing."

Mia shook her head. "Another time. Thanks anyway." She leaned back in her seat and put her feet up again.

"Deal the cards!" demanded Babs.

"Say please," Caz scolded her.

"Please," Babs frowned and let out a long, deep belch.

Caz fell about laughing. "See what I have to put up with?"

Dimitri stared at Babs, speechless. Babs noticed his expression and built herself up to belch again.

"No – please don't!" Dimitri pleaded.

Babs growled a second time and then cackled wildly while Caz clutched her sides in hysterics.

"Excuse me, do you mind?" Margaret barked as she pushed open her terrace door and stepped onto her verandah in a crimson nightie, arms folded across her chest.

Dimitri stood up. "I am so sorry to disturb you," he said sincerely. "Don't worry, we will be quiet now and I am leaving anyway."

Margaret glared at Caz and Babs before going back inside muttering "no respect for others" just loud enough for them to hear.

Dimitri glanced at his watch. "Almost midnight – time for me to go. Babs, I insist you take back this money. We can play again another day."

"I ain't takin' it back," said Babs defiantly. "I got me pride you know. Like I said, I'll win it back fair and square. Just name the time and place and I'll be there."

"As you wish," Dimitri pocketed the heap of notes that lay on the table and shook both their hands. "I look forward to a re-match."

"Night," said Caz.

"See ya," said Babs, tipping a night cap of Tia Maria into her empty glass.

He nodded to them and saw himself out. He was about to walk straight up the drive when he found himself pausing outside Mia's front door. It was late, but she had still been reading by her terrace doors when he had left. He knocked lightly. A few seconds later, the door opened a fraction.

"Mia, it's me, Dimitri," he whispered.

"Yes?"

"I just wanted to say thank you."

"What for?" She opened the door a fraction wider.

"For what you said to me earlier…About me making a good teacher."

"No problem," she smiled.

He hesitated. What did he say now? "You are a nice person."

"Thank you…er… so are you."

Was this an invitation? No, she was just being polite again. What was he doing? This wasn't how he usually played the game. He never, *never*, knocked on a girl's door – he always let them come to him. And yet he couldn't drag himself away, as if a magnet lay hidden beneath the ground where he was standing.

"Good night," he said finally.

"Kali nikta," she replied and closed the door. God she sounded sweet speaking Greek. He slapped himself on the cheek. Get a grip. She was just another tourist, like all the others before her and all those yet to come. She may not have flirted with him yet, but she would. As sure as eggs were eggs, she'd be giving him the green light before she got on that plane back home. He strutted off up the drive and became aware of the scratching of scrunched-up notes in his jeans pocket. He smiled to himself. Another successful night's winnings…and it was *so* easy.

CHAPTER 8

Tuesday 4th

It was now or never, Mia told herself as she crossed the road and rang on the doorbell of the caramel-coloured house.

The door opened. It was the woman she'd seen yesterday – without the headscarf. "Yes?" she asked in an English accent, her strawberry-blonde bob swinging above her shoulders.

Mia looked into her eyes. They were grey-blue, like her own. "I'm looking for Gwen Griffiths," her voice came out as little more than a whisper.

"You've found her." The woman stiffened and looked at her expectantly.

"I'm Mia…your daughter."

Silence. Gwen stared at her, her lips slightly apart. She didn't blink, twitch, or reel backwards from the shock as Mia had always imagined she would.

"Now's not a good time," she said at last, a hint of unease in her voice.

Not a good time. *Not a good time?* Mia looked at her blankly. Words deserted her.

"My parents-in-law will be here any minute."

Mia felt her heart beginning to thump against her rib cage. *Not a good time?*

"I just wanted to talk – I don't want anything from you," she tried to explain. "I don't want money or anything." Mia could feel a lifetime's worth of resentment simmering away in the pit of her stomach.

"Can we talk tomorrow? Sorry, but you should have called me first," said Gwen, with a slight flicker of irritation.

"You might not have wanted to talk to me." Mia felt a tingle in her nose and a lump in her throat.

"Come back tomorrow. One o'clock?" She looked anxiously over Mia's shoulder.

Mia nodded and turned to go. Before she'd even taken a step, the door had shut behind her. Her eyes filled with tears. *Now's not a good time.* Her parents had been right. This woman wasn't fit to be a mother. You'll only get hurt if you find her, they'd warned. She unlocked the car, got in and slammed the door shut. She had to find a secluded spot fast. She didn't want anyone to see her cry.

"Free at last."

"Eh?"

"Free at last – that fat bird's T-shirt." Nath cracked open a beer and put his feet up on the railings of their verandah.

Jo looked up from her book to see Babs adjusting the parasol by her sunlounger. On her large bouncing chest were the words, 'CAZ & BABS – FREE AT LAST' in the same bold black style as the classic 80s 'FRANKIE SAYS RELAX' T-shirts.

"Free from what?" asked Nath.

Jo shrugged. "How should I know?"

"Free from work? Free from kids? Free from Wormwood Scrubs? Free from what?"

"Why don't you go and ask them?" she suggested, glancing again at Babs, who was trying to discreetly pluck her bikini bottoms from between her white, dimpled buttocks.

"So what's your new friend up to today?" Nath asked.

"Shantee? Dunno. She said something about going for a walk up in the hills near Skala, I think." Jo put her book down on the table, tightened her ponytail and reached for her suntan lotion.

"She's a bit odd, isn't she?" said Nath. "Fit, but odd."

"Why is she odd?"

"All that stuff about reincarnation and reaching enlightenment."

"What about it?" Jo squirted the sun cream down her legs and massaged it in.

"Sounds like a load of old bollocks to me."

"Well personally, I thought it made a lot of sense."

"Well *personally*, I thought she was talking out of her arse."

Jo sighed. She picked up her book again and then dropped it back down on the table. He could be so narrow-minded sometimes. "You haven't exactly given the matter a lot of thought, have you?" she said impatiently.

Nath blinked at her.

"I mean it's not like you've read books about it, researched the subject on the internet or given a nanosecond of your time to weigh up the various arguments before reaching the conclusion that it's a load of old bollocks."

"I don't need to weigh it up. The idea that you die and then come back to life as someone else is bloody fruit-loopy. What's the point?"

"She explained the point yesterday. You keep coming back until you learn how to live a spiritually enlightened life. So each lifetime, you are a wiser, more spiritually developed person than in your previous life."

"I still don't see the point."

"Well maybe you should read some books on the matter before you dismiss it as being rubbish."

"Can't be arsed. If I come back, I just hope I come back as David Beckham."

"You can't come back as someone who's already here, *thicko*."

"Alright then, I hope I come back as a goodlooking – sorry, an *even better looking* – world-famous, stinking rich footballer with a popstar wife with nice tits." Nath tried to tickle her under the ribs.

"Because, let's face it, those are the important things in life," Jo rolled her eyes. Sometimes she wondered what she was doing with a guy like Nath. And then she looked at his perfectly toned pecs, his soft blue eyes, mischievous grin and well-endowed package, and tingled all over. What he lacked upstairs, he more than made up for downstairs. And he made her laugh, too.

"Being happy and comfortable is important," he argued.

"And being rich and famous is the only ticket to happiness and comfort?"

"No, I'm not saying that," groaned Nath, taking a swig of beer and spilling some on his vest top. "What I'm saying is, being loaded doesn't half help.'

"Being a millionaire can also make you extremely miserable. Think of all the famous actors and popstars and minted socialites that end up topping themselves or spending their lives in and out of rehab centres. Look at

George Best. He threw away everything that David Beckham's got cos he couldn't stay off the booze." Jo lifted her sunglasses on top of her head and looked at him smugly.

"Yeah well that's just a small minority of minters who don't know how to spend their mint."

"So what would you do if you came into a million tomorrow?" she asked, reaching across the table for her sparkly lip gloss and applying it to her pout.

"Aha, the golden question!" Nath stretched his muscly arms and grinned. "£500,000 on a new gaff. Surrey or Berkshire, somewhere like that, plus £150,000 on a pad in Spain – both with a pool, naturally. £50,000 on a nice set of wheels, £100,000 to start up my own business, £185,000 in the bank to earn interest and occasionally buy some smart threads or whatever, £5,000 to split between my family and £10,000 to take the lads on the holiday of a lifetime."

Jo looked at him. "At last, a topic that you have given your full consideration."

"Well, you've gotta be prepared – you never know when your luck might come in." He produced a lotto ticket from his pocket. "Two lucky dips, babe. One for me, and one for me." He winked at her.

"And where do I fit into that masterplan of wealth and luxury?"

"Play your cards right, darlin', and you could be living in my five-bedroom Surrey pad, and if you're very, very good, I might even let you drive my motor."

Jo reached over as if to kiss him and flicked him on the nose.

"Ow!"

"Nice to see you've apportioned a generous percentage to your parents," she pursed her glistening lips.

"I think that's more than fair – you're forgetting that they'd get free holidays in my Spanish villa, staying for as long as they like. Anyway, they're not materialistic people, my parents. If you gave them a million, they wouldn't know what to do with it."

"Unlike you."

"Well they'd just put it in the bank and forget it's there. Then, when they needed to buy a new washing machine or something, they'd still look for the cheapest one – and then they'd say, 'Oh we can't possibly go on holiday this year, we've just had to fork out for a new washing machine'. A million in the bank wouldn't change their lives one bit."

Jo laughed. "Good for them. Are you sure you're not adopted?"

"Enough of your cheek, girl, or I'll have to show you who's boss."

"Are you going to tell me off?" Jo's eyes sparkled.

"I think you're asking for it," Nath smiled slyly, tossing his empty beer can into the bin behind him.

"What will you do to me?" she licked her lips coquettishly.

"I think you deserve nothing short of a good spanking."

"Is that an immediate penalty or a deferred punishment?"

Nath glanced down at his trunks and nodded towards the bedroom. "You. Naked. By the time I count to three."

Jo sprung up and skipped inside, doing a suggestive little wiggle in front of the bed. She undid her bikini top and dropped it on the floor. Nath closed the French doors behind him and drew the curtains.

"Why don't we leave the curtains open?" breathed Jo. "Let them all have a good look."

Nath gave her a baffled look. "Er…I'd rather this was a private party," he said coming towards her and tugging the bows at the sides of her bikini bottoms.

Jo shrugged. "Whatever…" She pulled Nath towards her and they tumbled backwards onto the bed, a heap of entwined limbs.

"Am I burning?" Sitting upright on her sunlounger by the pool, Caz strained to look over her shoulder at her back. "Should I put me T-shirt back on?"

"Nah. Stick some more factor thirty on. You'll be alright," said Babs, turning back to her magazine.

"'Ere – I saw those two lads earlier," whispered Caz. "They was like beetroots. Burnt to a cinder!"

"They're not the only ones looking red-faced," muttered Babs, looking up and spotting Margaret striding away from Frank with tight lips and knotted eyebrows. Frank altered the back of his sunlounger to horizontal, lay back and pulled his hat over his face with a heavy sigh.

"Peace at last," whispered Caz, interpreting Frank's body language.

"God knows how he stands that old witch nagging him all the time," said Babs.

"It's their fortieth anniversary, you know."

"Yeah, so she said," yawned Babs. "How old d'you reckon she is?"

Caz screwed up her face. "Hmm…dunno. If she's been married forty years, she's gotta be somewhere near sixty, ain't she? Too old to be wearing gold high-heeled slingbacks with them fat ankles at any rate."

"We should ask Dimitri. I bet he knows how old she is."

"'Ere, talking of Dimitri, I reckon he likes that girl, Mia, the one next-door to us. He went all quiet after you asked her if we was making too much noise last night."

"You reckon?"

"Yeah, he kept lookin' over at her."

"Young love, eh?" Babs yawned again.

"Just think, we used to feel that way about Wayne and Trev once upon a time," sighed Caz.

"We was also in love with George Michael and the lead singer of Frankie Goes To Hollywood. We didn't half pick 'em."

"Come on, Babs. Your Trev weren't that bad. He weren't the most romantic bloke in the world but at least he came home every night."

"Yeah, expecting his dinner on the table and his shirts ironed," Babs muttered sarcastically.

Caz sighed. They'd had this conversation many times but she could never get Babs to see that Trev wasn't nearly as bad as she made him out to be. It seemed to Caz that Trev's greatest crime was worrying that Babs would leave him – an insecurity that Babs seemed happy to take advantage of. OK, so Trev was a bit of a drip – he could have encouraged Babs while she was dieting, rather than getting all uptight about it. He could have bought her a nice sexy negligée to celebrate her reaching her target weight, but no, the stupid plonker had brought home a lamb korma with extra onion bhajis, a king-sized tub of Chunky Monkey ice-cream and a 12-pack of Tennant's Extra – all Babs' favourites. Babs' evil, banned, naughty favourites. She'd gone ballistic and hurled it all over the kitchen (except for the beer which naturally she'd drunk to help her calm down). It was a desperate act of self-defence, she'd claimed – lose the food or abuse the food. Trev hadn't supported her in something that was very, very important to her. And yet he did love her. And he tried to treat her right…sort of.

"Trev always washed up though," said Caz, wiping the sweat from her forehead. "Wayne never bloody washed up. Wayne was never bloody there."

"Well he was driving lorries all over the shop, so of course he was gonna be away a lot."

"It don't take three days to get from Manchester to Southend."

"That only happened once," said Babs, loosening her watch strap to measure how her tan was coming along.

"Cos I threatened to throw him out if he done it again," blurted Caz.

There was no comparing them in Caz's opinion. Wayne was a good-for-nothing through and through. He was a cheat and a liar. She'd caught him out too many times. When he came home with a bottle of wine and a bunch of flowers it meant one thing and one thing only – there was a new pair of knickers hanging from the mirror in his driver's cab. Babs was wrong: Wayne and Trevor were completely different. Trevor was an idiot, but Wayne was a bastard.

"At least Wayne was romantic," said Babs, watching a paraglider sail across the horizon.

"Are you mad? He just tried to keep me sweet so he could get up to all sorts behind my back. Trev, on the other hand, really loved you. He loves your kids an' all. He'd have done anything for you, Babs."

"Yeah – when I was fat." Babs sneered as she watched the paraglider plop into the sea and the boat rally round to pick him up, leaving a frothy white line behind it.

"He just worried that now you was all confident about how you looked, you might run off with someone else," Caz continued. "It's not like you did much to reassure him."

"He didn't deserve to be reassured," snapped Babs. "He didn't trust me. Kept buying me Terry's chocolate oranges when he knew I was paying good money to get weighed each week. He never bought me bleedin' nothing before then."

"I know he was a bit of a prat sometimes, but he never cheated on you.

He never gambled your savings down the pan neither."

"OK, so he weren't as bad as your Wayne. But he couldn't give me what I wanted either. The only thing I want from Trevor these days is that he's there for his kids. And you're right, he is. So I'm happy." Babs turned the page angrily, almost ripping it from the magazine.

Caz put her sunglasses on and picked up her Danielle Steele. Well it was pretty clear – Babs no longer felt anything for Trev. Poor old sod. She felt sorry for him. Only a week ago he'd turned up on her doorstep, drunk and crying that he wanted Babs back. Listening to him, she'd realised he wasn't such a bad bloke after all, and that there were two sides to every story. She could imagine Babs wasn't the easiest person to live with – she could drink too much sometimes, get all wound up and angry, and yet he'd loved her with all his heart. In fact, they seemed ideal for each other in many ways. It was a shame, a real shame. Caz couldn't help feeling that her friend was throwing something decent away that she would later regret.

She'd promised Trev she would try to talk some sense into Babs, but it looked like he was going to have to face facts and move on with his life. If only the silly bugger had told her she looked gorgeous after losing five stone they might still be together. Men – they really were a useless bunch. Who knew what went on inside their pea-sized brains?

Women, thought Frank from beneath his sun hat. What were they all about? Can't live with 'em, can't live without 'em. Certainly could live without Margaret for a while, though. Must be the menopause. No, that happened ten years ago, didn't it? How long is it supposed to last? Wasn't it just a matter of their periods stopping? In that case, one month they had periods, the next, they didn't. Simple. So that lasted…one month? Right, obviously couldn't be that then.

What was her problem? He just couldn't work her out at the moment. One minute she was all over him, five minutes later, she was frostier than a frozen haddock. He'd given her what she wanted last night and she had seemed to enjoy it. God knows she'd been bending his ear about it for weeks. He was sixty-five for pity's sake. And he'd worked hard all his life. Now he was retired, all he wanted to do was relax. He'd earned it. He'd grafted day in, day out, since the age of fifteen, knowing that one day he would leave his career behind and have time on his hands – time that he had spent many a happy hour dreaming about. Time to play golf. Time to go fishing. Time to read all those books he'd never got round to buying. Time to travel, explore, go for long strolls in the countryside, along the coast.

And then there was the Big Idea – to buy a holiday home somewhere abroad, preferably Greece, where he and Margaret could spend their summers. Of course Margaret had made it quite clear that Greece wasn't her cup of tea for a holiday home. She wanted it to be Tuscany, Marbella, or the Cote d'Azur. Somewhere more 'upmarket', as she liked to say.

Now he was a fair man and a good husband. He'd looked after his wife and she'd never wanted for anything. So he didn't quite have the same libido he'd had twenty or thirty years ago, but he kissed her and cuddled her and told her he loved her often enough. He took her out for meals to all her favourite restaurants. He took her on holidays. He bought her jewellery and shoes and handbags. When she wanted something, he gave it to her. When they disagreed on something, either they compromised, or more often than not, he'd let her have her way. What more could a woman ask for? So it was only fair that for once in her life, Margaret should give in to his wishes for a change.

She knew how much he loved Greece. She also knew how much they could afford for a second home, and France, Italy and Spain were simply not within their budget. At sixty-five, potential financial troubles were not what he needed. Why couldn't Margaret see that? The woman thought money grew on trees. She hadn't done a day's work since Maple and Maple's went bust ten years ago. Even then her job had been a paltry nine till four with an equally paltry salary that she had insisted was hers and hers alone. She had never once contributed to the mortgage, or the bills – he even paid for the weekly shopping.

Fair enough, so she had finally seen the error of her ways, but it was too late by then. She'd been redundant for three years before she took a good look at herself and suddenly offered to contribute to their joint living expenses. With what? he'd asked her. She hadn't exactly gone to a great effort to find herself another job. Instead she'd kept her hand in doing repairs and alterations for Judith at the drycleaners, which she'd put towards the weekly shopping. She'd also sacked the cleaner and deigned to do the housework herself – although no one was supposed to know about that. No one was supposed to know that she did a bit of stitching for Judith either. She told people she occasionally did embroidery for an old friend who worked as a wedding dress designer. Pure fiction!

That was what he didn't understand about Margaret – her obsession with class and social status. It was as if life was one big competition and she was hell-bent on winning. He often wondered if she'd married him just because all those years ago, at the grand old age of twenty-five, he'd been the only man she knew who was making something of himself. And of course he'd been a goodlooking lad in those days. Plenty of ladies would have accepted a proposal of marriage from him. Back then, he was quite a catch. Mind you, so was Margaret – there was no denying it. She had been a fine looking woman in her day. And she still looked good from time to time, depending on her weight – not that she was fat as such, just a tad broader around the hips, a bit saggier in the bust department and a bit chubbier around the ankles. But that was only normal for a woman of her age. It wasn't as if she'd let herself go – on the contrary, nothing was more important to Margaret than her appearance. In fact recently she'd been spending even more time than usual at the local salon. She'd done something with her hair – he wasn't quite sure what, and her eyebrows looked…different somehow. Better. Yes, he had an attractive enough wife, it was true. So why did he no longer feel attracted to her? Was it age? Familiarity? Fatigue? Lethargy?

On the outside they seemed like the perfect couple. They had everything: a nice four bedroom house with a spacious garden, two cars, two lovely grown-up children and two grandchildren. But on the inside, things weren't quite so idyllic. They practically led separate lives. Margaret was always out – meeting Gillian for a cappuccino, getting her highlights or her nails done, going swimming, lunching with Hilda, playing bridge with that arrogant prat Marcus and his long-suffering wife Rosemary. He didn't mind. He quite liked the peace and quiet, not to mention the freedom to go fishing for the weekend with George. But when they were together, they didn't have a great deal to talk about. In forty years of marriage they'd had their fair share of ups and downs, but now they had entered a stage which was neither up nor down. They just coasted along. They were friends, companions. Hell, what else were you supposed to be in your mid-sixties? The fact that they were still together without too many an argument was a success, surely?

And yet something was missing. The fact was, he just wasn't interested in her life, and she wasn't interested in his. They both tried to seem interested but he knew that was just it – they had to *try*. And nothing he ever did was good enough. She didn't like his new suit. She complained about his grey hair. He never remembered to water the plants. He said something insensitive to Gillian. He forgot to mow the lawn. That's what their conversations really boiled down to – the running of the house. They never seemed to spend any real time together. Once or twice he'd tried to tell her this, but she had ignored him. Then on other occasions she had a go at him for being "barely aware of her existence". It was as if she couldn't make up her mind whether she wanted to be left to her own devices or pestered into doing things together. They never did anything alone together – apart from the occasional meal at the outrageously over-priced Da Vinci's, where they usually bumped into one of her friends and ended up joining them.

That was the point of this holiday, he had told her when they booked it. To spend some time together. It was their fortieth anniversary, after all. They needed to be alone together, focus their attention on one another, have some fun. Quality time, as their daughter called it. Were they having fun? He wasn't sure. *He* was enjoying himself. He was in his favourite country, in a beautiful spot. The weather was fine and the food as tasty as ever. He was reading a great book – could hardly put it down – and he'd satisfied his wife the night before. Well sort of. But something was niggling him. Margaret wasn't happy. Perhaps he should have taken her to Venice after all. But it was so expensive. Why spend one week in Venice when you can spend two or even three in Greece for the same money? Then again, it was their fortieth. And she'd always wanted to go there.

Frank took off his hat and sat up on his sunlounger. He would promise to take her to Venice for her birthday in March. That would cheer her up, get him back in her good books. He got up and slipped on his sandals.

"Had enough of the sun?" chirped Caz, as he picked up his book and newspaper.

"Enough of the sun? Never!" he winked. "Er, you haven't seen the wife have you, love?"

"She went that way," said Caz, pointing to the far end of the complex.

"Ta love. See you later." He put his sun hat back on and headed off to his apartment.

"Right, time for a swim!" Babs announced in a loud voice. Standing at the edge of the pool, her 'Free at last' T-shirt just covering the bottom of her swimsuit, she pinched her nose and jumped in.

Water splashed on to Shantee as she sat down on a sunlounger and opened up 'The Art Of Breathing'. She took a deep breath and exhaled slowly. This, at least, was good practise.

"*No I can't get you out of my 'ead, boy your love is all I think about!*" sang Babs as she clung on to the edge of the pool, pulling pouty faces at Caz.

Caz giggled. "Come on then Kylie, let's see you do twenty lengths," she barked.

"Sod off!" said Babs. "I ain't seen you do one yet!"

"All in good time. I'm reading your Hello at the moment. According to this, Ulrika Jonsson's only thirty-nine. I thought she was more like forty-six."

"Too much sunbathing," said Babs, floating on her back.

Shantee tried to concentrate on her book, but she kept thinking about Jo. They'd had a real laugh yesterday. They were totally on the same wavelength. It was nice to meet someone who you got on with instantly, effortlessly. She hadn't mentioned her sexuality, because somehow the moment hadn't seemed right, but she knew it wouldn't be a problem. Jo seemed like an intelligent, open-minded person. She wasn't too sure about Nath, though. They made an odd couple, in fact. Physically, they looked like a perfect match. They were both tall and toned and attractive. But mentally, they didn't quite add up.

She could imagine them jogging on treadmills side by side at the gym, munching popcorn while watching the latest blockbuster, and drinking and dancing at a party. And she could picture them traipsing around the high street shops together or having sex. But that was where her imagination ran out. What did these two talk about when they weren't discussing the latest blockbuster, party or things they'd bought? There was obviously more to Jo than that, whereas she doubted there was more to Nath than met the eye.

Jo had flawless skin, with immaculately plucked eyebrows. She had pouty heart-shaped lips and a long, smooth nose. She had carefully manicured fingernails and, blood-red toenails. Shantee imagined herself kissing Jo and then gave her head a good hard shake. *Stop this at once*, she told herself. *The girl is unavailable and straight. You know better than that. And you came here specifically to be at ease with solitude. You are taking a break from relationships. You are getting to know you.*

Shantee focused on the page in front of her. She read the first paragraph again. And then again. It was no good. It was going in one ear and out the other. She might as well go and do that walk she'd planned. She'd been hoping to catch Jo by the pool and invite her and Nath along, but their curtains were still drawn. Perhaps they'd gone out already.

She was about to get up and get her things together when the tall blonde guy from the end apartment threw his towel over the sunlounger adjacent to hers. To get up and leave at the exact same second he sat down might look rude. Still, she noticed there were several pairs of empty sunloungers around the pool – each with their own parasol. Why didn't he choose one he could have to himself?

"It's so hot out here," he gasped, making himself comfortable.

"Take a dip in the pool – that'll soon cool you down," she said. "It's lovely."

"I can't," he replied.

"Why not?"

"I can't swim."

"Oh. Can't you just hang out in the shallow end?"

"I would if Shelley was with me, but I won't on my own. I know it sounds daft, but I'm scared of drowning – even in the shallow end."

"Oh dear. Where's Shelley then?" asked Shantee nonchalantly.

"Shelley's my fiancée…or rather, my ex-fiancée."

"Oh." She wasn't too sure whether to probe any further or not. It sounded delicate. She picked up her book again. '*As you wake up, gradually become aware of your breathing. Breathe in slowly and deeply, taking the air as deep into your lungs as it can go. Hold it and release, breathing out slowly and steadily.*' She glanced at her new companion. He smiled at her pitifully. He seemed in need of company.

"Er…so I take it you won't be going in the sea then," she said, spotting

Dimitri in the distance walking along with a shovel and a hosepipe coiled over one shoulder.

He laughed emptily. "No, the sea petrifies me more than the pool."

"So why did you book a sun, sea and pool holiday?" asked Shantee. Were his eyes looking slightly watery?

"Shelley's idea. She wanted to come here for our honeymoon. She'd never been to Greece before. She saw a picture in our local travel agent of Myrtos Beach – you know, the scenic one on the front of the Welcome brochure – and decided we had to come to Kefalonia."

Oh dear. Ex-fiancée, honeymoon booked, man on his own. That didn't sound too good.

"So, er...how come Shelley's not here with you?"

"We didn't get married," he said flatly, tilting his head back and closing his eyes.

Right. Sorry for asking, thought Shantee. Obviously the subject was now closed, although he'd been the one to open it. What a strange guy. He could have sat anywhere around the pool but he chose to sit right bang next to her. Then he starts talking about his ex-fiancée, and then he makes her feel as if she's being nosy.

Shantee itched to get up and go. She looked over at Jo's apartment. The curtains were still drawn.

"Right then," she breathed, sitting up.

"She called the wedding off about fifteen seconds before she was supposed to say 'I do'," he murmured.

Shantee sighed and leaned back again. It looked like she was going nowhere fast. "I'm so sorry," she said dutifully. This Shelley, whoever she was, had obviously seen sense in the nick of time. There was something about this guy...he was too...something...

"I'm Simon, by the way," he turned to her and held out his hand.

"Shantee," she replied, shaking it.

"As in shanty towns?" he smiled at his own joke.

"Exactly," she said dryly.

"It just goes to show, you never know what's around the corner in life," said Simon.

"Very true." She needed an excuse to get away. This man was oozing negativity and it was literally making her come out in goose bumps. "I'm afraid you'll have to excuse me, I…er, I'm absolutely dying for the loo." She stood up and gathered up her things.

"Don't worry, I can keep an eye on your towel for you," offered Simon.

"Ah, well actually, I was going to go for a walk."

"Oh right, where to? I might come with you," he squinted up at her.

"Um, well, I'm meeting someone actually. Perhaps another time?"

"Oh OK. Never mind." His face fell. "Have a nice time."

"Thanks. See you later." She made her escape round to the front of the building. She was about to let herself into her apartment when Dimitri called her name. She turned around. He was leaning on his shovel, shirt tied around his waist, the middle-aged woman with the naff gold slingbacks was standing next to him.

"When's my next yoga lesson?" he called cheerfully, waving her over to him.

"Well I was about to go for a walk," she replied. "Maybe later?"

"Great. She teaches yoga, you know," he informed his companion.

"Oh how wonderful. I used to do yoga," she smiled.

"How's your shower?" asked Dimitri, winking at her.

Shantee looked at him blankly.

"Remember you said yesterday your shower wasn't working properly?" He winked at her again a little more obviously this time. "I can fix it now if you like?"

"Oh," said Shantee, grasping that he needed her to go along with it – whatever *it* was. "Yeah, sure. I forgot all about that. Thank you."

Dimitri beamed at the woman. "Please excuse me, Margaret. Nice talking to you. I'm sure tonight will be your lucky night. I can feel it!"

"I hope you're right, Dimitri," she giggled girlishly.

Dimitri quickly ushered Shantee back towards her apartment door.

"What was all that about?" asked Shantee.

"I think she wanted to go to bed with me," he whispered.

"Are you sure?" Shantee laughed. "She's here with her husband, you know."

"So what?" Dimitri shrugged. "She said he is spending most of his time asleep or reading a book, and she is starting to feel lonely."

"That doesn't mean she wants to jump your bones." Shantee opened the door and waved him in. "She's old enough to be your mother!"

"This is true, but it isn't the first time."

"What? She's chatted you up before?" Shantee closed the door behind him.

"Not her. Last year, a German woman. She was fifty-five. She was on holiday with her husband who was a bird watcher."

"What, as in the feathered variety or do you mean he had a roving eye?"

"Birds that fly and go chip chip." Dimitri flapped his arms and sat down at the table.

"Right," Shantee chuckled, sweeping her hair up and tying it into a ponytail. "Coffee?"

He nodded as she put the kettle on and took the standard two small cups out of the cupboard beneath the sink. "He was always going to the woods to watch the birds," he continued. "Late at night, early in the morning, most of the time. He was even writing a book about birds. She was lonely and she asked me if I wanted to keep her company."

Shantee raised an eyebrow. She wasn't sure if she wanted to hear this, but it sounded like a good story to tell at dinner parties – the Greek gigolo she'd met in Kefalonia who bedded married older women. "Go on…"

"She was beautiful. Like a movie star. She didn't look her age. I took her all over the island on my moped – to Assos, Fiskardo, Myrtos."

"And?" Shantee smirked, picturing the scene while filling the cups from the kettle.

"And what? You have a dirty mind," he grinned, pulling his cigarettes out of his shirt pocket. "Can I smoke?"

"If you absolutely have to," she sighed.

"I absolutely have to." He stood up to open the French doors, grabbed himself an ashtray from under the sink and sat back down again.

"So you didn't sleep with her?" she asked as he lit up.

"Of course I did! Are you mad? She was begging for it! In fact, she was an exception to my rule."

"What rule?"

"I never sleep with the same girl twice," he said matter-of-factly and

75

blew a smoke ring into the air.

Shantee frowned and handed him a cup of coffee. "Come again?"

He laughed as she folded her arms and leaned back against the sink. "No! *No* come again. I only sleep with them once – apart from Heidi, because it was a bit different – but if you sleep with them twice, they think you're going to ask them to stay forever, marry them, have babies and all that shit…" He pulled a nauseous expression.

"A real heart-breaker," Shantee gave a shallow smile, wondering what it was that could have hardened him in this way, and whether he was truly immune to feeling more than just sexual attraction for a woman.

"I don't hurt anyone," he said defensively. "I make them understand it's just for fun. Sometimes, if they really don't get the message, I pretend that Marilena at the Bora Bora is my girlfriend."

"Have you ever had a girlfriend?"

"Sure. I did go out with Marilena for a little while, but I didn't love her so I said we are better as friends."

"So have you ever been in love?"

Dimitri smiled wistfully and looked down at his feet, his floppy brown hair falling in front of his eyes. "Do you have any sugar? I like my coffee *gleeko*."

Shantee handed him a couple of sachets of sugar she'd bought at the mini-market in Skala.

"One time I was in love. A long time ago," he said, tearing the sachets and pouring the sugar into his coffee.

"How old were you?" Shantee asked, hoisting herself up to sit on the draining board.

"Eighteen. I took tourists out for boat rides from Skala's main beach. She was nineteen."

"A tourist?" she took a sip of coffee.

"Yes, English. We fell in love. I cried when she left to go home," he grinned, as if amused that he could ever have behaved so childishly. "We wrote to each other. I tried to save up the money to visit her in England but the airfare was too expensive. The next year she came back in May for two weeks. I was so happy – I had been counting the days. I asked her to marry me and she said yes. She wanted to live here in Kefalonia. I wanted to live in England but I loved her so much I was happy to stay. I introduced her to my mother. My mother loved her. Then she went home again and she was supposed to come back in October for two weeks."

"Did you plan to get married when she came back?"

"No, the following year. Anyway, she didn't come back." He stubbed out his cigarette, squashing the butt in half with his index finger.

"Why not?"

"She met someone else," he shrugged. "Actually she had started seeing him before she came out in May, but she didn't tell me that until we split up in September. She had been lying to me."

"And were you faithful to her while she was in England?"

"I know you won't believe me, but yes. My friends thought I was crazy. They think you don't have to be faithful until you are married. I disagree. When you tell someone you love them you should be faithful from that moment on."

"So this girl who broke your heart," Shantee paused and looked at him. "Is she the reason you won't sleep with the same girl twice?"

Dimitri thought for a moment. "Maybe. Who knows?"

"Don't you want to fall in love again?"

"One day perhaps. When I meet the right person. I don't see her yet."

"How would you know? You don't give anyone a chance by the sound of it."

"I will know when I meet her," he said confidently.

"Love at first sight?" Shantee shook her head and tutted, her red ponytail swinging above her shoulders.

"You don't believe in it?" he asked.

"Nope." She drained her coffee. "*Lust* at first sight, sure. Love – that's different. How can you love someone without knowing them?"

"*You just know.* It's a feeling, a connection." He looked at her incredulously.

"That's how you felt when you met this girl when you were eighteen?"

"Yes. The first time I looked at her I knew."

"Forgive me for saying this, but you knew what exactly? You spent a grand total of four weeks in her company over the course of a year. And then you found out she was seeing someone else. Sounds to me like you didn't know her very well at all."

77

Dimitri finished his coffee and shrugged. "What about you – have you ever been in love?"

"Yes, a few times. It's different each time. I've had my heart broken, and I've broken a few hearts too."

"Men or women?" he asked with a fascinated grin.

"Both."

"Have you ever slept with a man?"

"Gosh, we are being nosy, aren't we?" she teased, secretly pleased at his interest and the flirtatious spark in his eye. Five, ten years ago, she might have flirted back – she might even have gone to bed with him, but not any more. Cute though he was, men were a thing of the past – and so were casual flings.

"Well, have you?" he persisted.

"Yes. I had a boyfriend for five years in my late teens, early twenties."

"When did you realise you preferred women?"

"When we had a threesome with another girl at a party."

Dimitri grinned, evidently impressed. Shantee instantly regretted being so honest.

"Tell me more," he demanded.

"There's nothing to tell. The girl gave me her number. I met up with her a week later and I realised I fancied her."

"And your boyfriend? Did you break his heart?"

"I'm afraid so. Still, he's married with three kids now and hasn't looked back since, while I've been single for nearly two years."

"Two years? You haven't had sex for two years?"

"I said I was single – not celibate. Although, I haven't had sex for the last eight months and I'm trying to keep it that way for another four."

Dimitri looked perplexed. "Why?"

"My therapist recommended it. I need to be at ease as an individual. I need to feel thoroughly independent and self-sufficient before I embark on another relationship."

"But why can't you have sex in the meantime – it's not the same as having a relationship."

"True, but it gives you a fix. It fills in the void. I need to deal with the void alone. I need to feel the void, accept it, be at peace with it. Once I've achieved that, I'll be ready to have a relationship."

Dimitri frowned. "Are you allowed to masturbate?"

Shantee laughed awkwardly, trying to hide her embarrassment.

"Sorry – that was a personal question," said Dimitri, lowering his eyes. "I'm fascinated, that's all. I never met anybody before who choose not to have sex for one year. You know, Shantee. You are a very unusual person. I like you very much. I respect you." He stood up and passed her his empty cup.

"Er...thanks." She'd never known how to respond confidently to a compliment.

"I must go and plant that tree. Thanks for the coffee."

"You're welcome. See you later."

Dimitri patted her on the back and opened the front door, peering cautiously from side to side. The coast was clear.

As she watched him retrieve his shovel, Shantee wondered how long it would take him to make a move on Mia. She had already noticed the way he looked at her.

CHAPTER 9

Steve heaved himself off his bed and limped slowly to the door, avoiding a couple of empty beer cans and gasping with each step. He opened the door ajar to find an attractive, petite brunette dressed in shorts and a T-shirt.

"Hello," the woman beamed, flicking her long brown hair over her shoulder. "You are Craig or Steve?" she asked in a strong Greek accent.

"Er…Steve," he said, confused. "Who are you?"

"I am Maria. Nikki told me I *have* to see you."

"Eh?" Steve scratched his head. "Oh, I get it. So she thinks it's funny does she? Is she selling tickets to come and see the freaks at Eleni Apartments or something?"

Maria gave him a puzzled look. "She said you were really bad, she beg me to come and see you. Normally, I don't do this on my days off."

"She *begged* you did she?" Steve shook his head in disbelief. "That cheeky cow!"

"Steve, you nonce!" Craig shoved him out of the way and yanked the door open. "Come in," he ordered Maria, ushering her into their apartment. "While you were in the shower," he whispered into Steve's ear, "Nikki came back to tell us about hiring mopeds, and when she saw the state of me she insisted on getting the local nurse to come and take a look at us. I told her we were fine, but obviously she didn't listen."

"Look, if you want me to go, I go, but now I am here, you might as well let me look at you," Maria shrugged. "I mean, I don't care – it's up to you."

Craig took in her long shiny mane, smooth olive skin, big brown eyes and shapely brown legs. Typical. A tasty-looking bird turns up on your doorstep the one day of the year you resemble a pork scratching. *Think Beckham*, he told himself, assuming a bow-legged footballer's pose and discreetly clenching his fists in an effort to flex his biceps.

"You might as well look at us now you're here," he said coolly, turning his back to her so that she could glimpse his tattoo.

"No problem," she replied, glancing around her.

As Maria took in their sizeable stash of duty-free Jack Daniels, portable stereo and CD collection, Steve spotted two bumper packs of condoms sitting brazenly on the table and quickly threw a tea-towel over them. Then he gasped as he noticed their Shagometer – a phallic-shaped chart with ten notches on either side, each one accompanied by a cut-out pair of pneumatic breasts – lying on top of a newspaper. Quick as a flash, Steve flipped it upside down and sat back down on his bed.

Craig offered her a cigarette as she grimaced at his red-raw chest. She shook her head and tutted disapprovingly before breaking into a grin.

"Did you fall asleep in the sun?" she asked.

"You could say that," Craig lit his cigarette and shot a scathing look at Steve.

"Do you have some calamine lotion?" She looked from one to the other.

"Nope." Spotting a pair of dirty boxer shorts on the floor, Craig discreetly kicked them under the bed.

"OK, you are lucky because I have some cream with me, but it is only a small tube, so you will have to go to the pharmacy and buy another." She reached into her leather shoulder bag and took out a pink tube with Greek writing on it. "Rub it on where you are red – it is probably easier to do it for each other – twice a day, and keep out of the sun. When you go out, cover your skin and try always to stay in the shade. And no alcohol today or you will be ill." Maria handed Craig the cream and got up to leave.

"Can you just rub some on my back before you leave?" asked Craig. "Knowing Steve, he'll scratch me."

Maria smiled. "OK, quickly. Turn around." She took the cream from him and squeezed some onto her fingertips.

Craig turned his back towards her and grinned at Steve as she massaged the cream across his shoulders.

"Wow, you have *big* tattoo," she remarked. Craig and Steve sniggered.

"All the girls say that," Craig replied.

"Does it say 'Lobster Man'?" Maria giggled.

"Very funny," Craig said wryly.

"OK, finish. You?" she gestured to Steve.

81

"No, I'll sort myself out thanks," Steve swung his legs back onto the bed.

"Fine. We say goodbye then," she smiled a warm, pearly-white smile, threw the tube of calamine lotion to Steve and headed for the door. "Remember, no sunbathing!"

As the door closed behind her, Craig eased himself gently onto a chair.

"Nice bit of totty," said Steve, arranging the pillows behind him. "She had a lovely pair of norks on her – you should've asked her out, mate."

"What, looking like a fucking tomato? She'd have pissed herself laughing."

"She looked at you with a sparkle in her eye, mate." Steve yawned and unscrewed the cap on the little pink tube. "Anyway, red today, bronze tomorrow, my son. The totty will be queuing up at the door when they check out our tans."

A smile slowly spread across Craig's crimson face. He hadn't thought of that.

Frank walked along the coast road at a leisurely pace. The sun was still going strong at five o'clock and he'd left his sunglasses back at the apartment. He also should have worn his hat – nothing looked more ridiculous than a sun-burnt bald patch. Perhaps he should have waited till it cooled down a bit before going for a stroll. But then he'd only intended to walk as far as the Hotel Flamingo, having imagined that's where Margaret had disappeared to. Unable to find her there, he'd decided to walk on and have a wander. She was probably sulking somewhere, which suited him fine as he fancied a half hour or so of freedom.

The view was medicine for the soul. On one side of the road the craggy hillside stretched up towards the sky, and on the other, it fell down towards the sea. There was even a tiny secluded beach down there – barely visible from the road, you had to stand closer to the edge of the cliff to see it properly. There wasn't much in the way of civilisation after the Hotel Flamingo – just scrubland full of bushes, rocks and grazing goats and a couple of small crumbly-looking houses up ahead. As he paused under an olive tree to wipe the sweat from the back of his neck with his handkerchief, a bony white cat crept out from behind a bush and miaowed at him. He bent down to stroke it which met with instant purring approval. Margaret hated cats. She would usually shoo them away before he had a chance to get anywhere near them.

Frank walked on. It was a fabulous spot. He couldn't believe it wasn't covered in hotels and apartments. No doubt it soon would be – if Eleni was the latest addition to the resort of Skala, then it was only a matter of time before it had a next-door neighbour, and another, and another. He stopped as he reached one of the two small ramshackle houses. This place looked like it had seen better days. Such a shame – what with its million-dollar view. Surely it deserved better upkeep than this?

As he squinted up at the roof, the front door opened and an old woman dressed in black appeared on the doorstep. Frank nodded politely and moved on when the woman called after him. He turned around and looked at her, wondering what she wanted. She was beckoning to him and smiling. She started to walk towards him and laughed. Confused, Frank smiled back. What was so funny? The woman pointed to his feet. He looked down to see the bony cat staring up at him expectantly.

"He followed me!" he chuckled as the woman bent down to pick up the cat. "Looks like I've made a new friend."

The woman laughed, the cat miaowing happily in her arms. "My cat... he is bad!" she said in a husky voice.

"Friendly little fellow, aren't you?" cooed Frank, tickling the cat's ears. "What name does he go by?"

The woman frowned. She didn't understand.

"Name? What's his name?" repeated Frank slowly.

"Ah, Thomas," she stated.

"Like Tom and Jerry?"

A friendly look of confusion. Perhaps she hadn't heard of Tom and Jerry.

"You live here?" asked Frank, pointing to the house.

"Nai, enai to spiti mou," nodded the woman. Sounded like a yes.

"You...Hotel Flamingo?" she asked.

Frank shook his head. "Eleni Apartments."

"Ah," the woman beamed. "My son, caretaker Eleni Apartments."

"Indeed?" asked Frank. "That would be Dimitri, then?"

"Nai, Dimitri. My son." The woman released the cat which slunk off towards the house.

"Nice lad, Dimitri," nodded Frank. The woman frowned again. "Dimitri-is-a-nice-lad – a good boy."

"Ah nai," she laughed girlishly. "My son…is good boy."

Frank was about to give her a polite nod and make his way back to the apartments when she touched his arm. "Café?" she asked.

He hesitated and looked at his watch. Conversation would be an effort – but no more of an effort than it was with Margaret. Oh why the hell not? If Margaret complained she only had herself to blame for going off without telling him. And besides, it was always nice to meet a few of the locals.

Inside, the house didn't look quite so dilapidated. It was clean and tidy – and cosy, if equipped with only a sparse sprinkling of basic furniture. There was also a very nice smell coming from the oven. Frank felt his stomach rumble.

The woman made him a cup of instant coffee. He'd been hoping for a Greek coffee, but as most tourists turned their noses up at it, he wasn't surprised she'd gone straight for the ubiquitous Nescafé. She sat down opposite him with a glass of water and smiled at him. She wasn't as old as she'd appeared at a distance, he observed. It was the black clothes she was wearing – they were the standard garb of old widows. Her face was actually quite handsome, if a little weathered. She was probably the same age as him, or younger even. Was she a widow? Probably not an appropriate question to ask.

"What-is-your-name?" he asked slowly and deliberately.

"Mi-lene-Vasiliki," she replied in the same tone, her eyes smiling mischievously.

"Va-?"

"VAS-EEL-EEK-EE," she repeated.

Frank nodded. "Vasiliki."

She smiled. "Nai! Good! Esí?" She pointed to him.

"Me? I'm Frank."

"MI-LENE-FRANK," she annunciated slowly, indicating him to repeat.

"Mi lene Frank," Frank scratched his moustache.

She laughed and clapped her hands. "Nai, kala! Padrevestai, Frank?"

Frank smiled nervously. Nope, didn't get a word of that. Vasiliki threw back her head and laughed at the blank look on his face.

"You…er…wife?" she asked taking a sip of her water and pointing at his wedding ring.

"Yes, I have a wife – Margaret – two children, and two grandchildren." Frank made a knee-high gesture with his hand to signify the more recent additions to his family.

She pointed to herself and held up three fingers. She then lowered her hand to knee-level with a sad pout and shook her head.

"You have three children and no grandchildren?" interpreted Frank. She nodded.

After they had exchanged all their families' names and ages, Vasiliki got up to attend to whatever was cooking in the oven. As the oven door opened, a heavenly aroma wafted swiftly towards Frank. It surrounded and intoxicated him. His stomach growled loudly. Vasiliki grinned and patted her stomach. "Pinas eisai!" Indeed, he was ravenous.

Frank glanced at his watch. He ought to be getting back before he gave Margaret more ammunition to shoot him with. He took a swig of coffee and stood up as Vasiliki placed a plate of steaming hot moussaka in front of him. "Ela," she smiled, patting him on the shoulder and urging him to sit back down. "Try." Well, what was a man supposed to do? It would be the height of rudeness to refuse such warm hospitality.

The sun was setting, casting long, tangled shadows from the trees. Dimitri sat on the stone wall, smoking a cigarette in the amber light and watching old Spiros the fisherman set out on his boat from the beach below. Another day, another sunset, another catch of fish…another van load of laundry, another blocked drain, another de-weeded flowerbed. He inhaled deeply, sucking the cigarette down to its butt before flicking it in an arch to the ground. There were probably a few thousand of his cigarette butts scattered around the length of this wall. He looked down at the beach again. Old Spiros had gone but a woman was sitting by the water's edge, staring out to sea.

She hugged her knees to her chest. It looked like Mia. Dimitri sat up straight and strained his eyes. Yes it was her – the wavy hair, the stripy halterneck top, the denim shorts. He hopped off the wall, his spirits lifted, and started towards the steps that led down to the beach. And then he stopped. She would have to come back this way shortly. He turned round and hoisted himself back up onto the wall. He lit another cigarette and smoothed back his hair. He would wait.

Mia was sitting very still. Curled up in the distance, her body made a sort of egg shape, gradually blurring into the shadows as the sun dipped below the hills. He got the impression she was sad. Or maybe she had seen him and was coyly waiting for him to notice her and go down and join her. Many women had tried that tactic before, but he always stayed put and waited for them to come to him – which they inevitably did.

Finally she got up. Dimitri smoothed back his hair again. He was about to light another cigarette when he stopped himself. She didn't seem keen on the habit. But then what to do with his hands? Leaning back, he tried to assume a relaxed pose. He looked stupid. He leaned forward and lifted one foot up onto the wall. Too contrived. He reached for his packet of Camels and lit one. That was better. More natural. As Mia came into view at the top of the steps, he quickly turned his face away. He would pretend, as usual, not to have seen her, and any second now she would come over and say hello. Any second now. Any…second…

Dimitri looked round. She had walked straight past him! Had she not seen him sitting right there? How could she have missed him? Or was she avoiding him? Damn it – he shouldn't have knocked on her door last night. He had appeared too keen. She was playing hard to get, of course. He liked her style – but it wasn't going to work. He flicked his cigarette on the ground, sprung off the wall and trod on it. Up ahead Mia turned into the drive of Eleni Apartments. Dimitri hung back until she was out of sight and then followed her. It was only half-past seven – she was bound to go and sit on her verandah. He could walk past as if he was busy doing something in the complex.

He turned into the drive and walked round to the pool area. He looked over at her verandah. Her light was on, but the French doors were closed and the curtains drawn. He couldn't just sit there and wait, and knocking on her door was out of the question. As he stood there, the black girl and her boyfriend came out on to their terrace. They nodded at him. He waved back and walked off – without a broom or a hosepipe in his hand he looked like he was loitering. Dimitri felt agitated. He decided to go into Skala and have a drink with Vasilis or Marilena. He paused as he walked back past Mia's door – maybe he should invite her along for a drink…? *No way, malaka!* He gave his head a brisk shake. By the end of the week she would be following him around like a lost dog. Patience, Dimitri, patience. Besides, there was always Karen, that flirtatious new travel rep over in nearby Poros to kill the time.

CHAPTER 10

Wednesday 5th

It was one o'clock. Mia put her watch back in her bag. She pretty much had the pool to herself. It seemed most people had gone off on the excursion to the neighbouring island of Ithaca – home of Odysseus as it had said in the Welcome leaflet. The only other people around were Frank and Margaret – who were lying on sunbeds at the other end of the pool, reading – a quieter than usual Craig and Steve sitting behind two large newspapers on their verandah, and that tall guy, Simon, who was sitting on his terrace fiddling with his mobile phone.

Mia put on her iPod headphones. She wasn't really listening to it – it just served as a good deterrent so that people wouldn't come over and start talking to her. How anyone actually read and listened to music at the same time, she didn't know. Out of the corner of her eye she could see Simon shaking his mobile and cursing under his breath. He kept huffing loudly and looking despairingly around him. As if by gut instinct, she had manoeuvred her sunlounger so that it faced away from him. He seemed like a nice enough guy, but there was something about him. Behind the smiles and the friendly nods she sensed an air of discontentment – loneliness, perhaps, but with a prickly edge. Whatever it was, it was enough to make her look away whenever he came into her line of vision.

She picked up Wild Swans. She had almost finished it. Fortunately it was gripping enough to keep her from fuming over Gwen – although when she'd finally put it down last night, she hadn't been able to sleep for replaying the scene in her head over and over again. *Now is not a good time*. Well of course it wasn't, she thought acerbically. There obviously never was a good time for Gwen Griffiths or Mihalopoulou or whatever her name now was. After all, this was a woman who had decided not long after giving birth, that now wasn't a good time to have children. She had left a six-month-old

Mia with her father and simply left. She had started to realise what bringing up a child really meant and decided she just couldn't do it. So what if she was only eighteen? Eighteen wasn't so shockingly young. Fourteen, maybe – but not eighteen. She knew what she was doing – she came from a family where sex was discussed openly, so there were no excuses on that front. She had told Dad she was on the pill – that the pregnancy was a fluke accident. But neither Dad nor Gran and Granddad had ever seen any evidence of the pill among her things at home. Had she told them the truth? Did she carry it around with her all the time in case she forgot to take one at home? Or had she never been on it in the first place? In which case she would have been fully aware of the risks she was taking.

Gran's theory was that Gwen had got pregnant in order to get Dad to commit to her. Despite being a faithful and generally reliable boyfriend, he had been aloof and non-committal about the future, which had made Gwen anxious to know where she stood. However, Gwen had apparently denied Gran's suggestion, sticking to her fluke accident story like glue.

Dad had asked her what she'd wanted to do, whether she wanted to keep it or not. He had said he'd stick by her whatever decision she made. So why had she chosen to go ahead with the pregnancy? It would have been straightforward enough to have had an abortion if she had wanted – both Dad and her parents were completely behind her. No one was pressuring her to do anything. It was her choice entirely. A pregnant teenager couldn't have asked for a more understanding family.

Another thought occurred to Mia – Gwen's new family didn't know about her. From the way Gwen had behaved, it seemed they probably didn't even know she existed. She hadn't expected Gwen to have children. The thought had occurred to her many years ago that she might have a gaggle of half-siblings somewhere that she didn't know about, but after careful consideration she had decided this was highly unlikely. It was only logical that Gwen wouldn't have other children because she'd had one and realised it was a big mistake – one she wouldn't want to repeat. She'd sacrificed a lot to re-gain her freedom, so she was hardly likely to give it all up again. And besides, she simply wasn't the maternal type.

The gradual realisation that the teenagers she'd seen two days ago must be Gwen's children – *her half-brother and sister* – was like a slow-motion punch to the stomach that hadn't made contact with her yet. It was too unreal.

When Mia had set off for Kefalonia, she had been prepared to hear what Gwen had to say. She couldn't imagine that anything this woman said would excuse what she'd done or make her feel any better, but she had been prepared to listen – purely to get the answers she needed to resolve her current situation. After all, it was the whole reason why she had come here. Not that Gwen needed to know about that. It was none of Gwen's business – as if she'd care anyway! In fact if it wasn't for her current situation, who knows…she might never have felt inclined to track down this sad woman. Right up until a few months ago, it was just a lazy thought, a daydream she indulged in less and less frequently as she grew older. One that she had intended to follow up some day when she had nothing better to do. And yet, here she was. The time had come, brought about by an unexpected twist of fate. *Now* she needed to see her. *Now* she needed an explanation. It mattered *now*.

The fact that Gwen had gone on to have more kids, however, was a startling blow. It changed everything. It meant that Gwen *was* maternal. It meant she didn't abhor the idea of bringing up children and being responsible for them. It meant she didn't prize her freedom and responsibility-free existence above everyone and everything else. It meant she was capable of love – didn't it? For a moment Mia entertained the appealing idea that Gwen had been a treacherous mother to her two other children – that she hadn't cuddled them when they were babies, that she smacked them and locked them in a cupboard for not doing their homework, that she frequently left them home alone while going off on holiday by herself. But it wasn't the story she'd glimpsed the other day. It may have been just a thirty-second insight into their lives, but the picture looked like a happy one.

Did Dad know she had kids? He couldn't have done or he would have told her. He had warned her not to have any expectations, but like Mia, he hadn't thought it likely Gwen would choose to be a mother again. Anyway, the two of them had had no contact for over twenty-five years. Even Gran and Granddad hadn't spoken to their daughter for almost as long. All communication had died – hence the out-of-date address. That was all Mia

90

had known about her mother after Gwen had turned twenty – that she had gone to live in Kefalonia. Not a single one of Gwen's relatives knew that she was married, that she'd had children. Not long after Gwen had abandoned Mia as a baby, Gwen's family had abandoned her. As the years went by, the rift grew deeper and deeper until Gwen's name was no longer mentioned. Gran and Granddad had more or less adopted Dad into their family and helped him bring up his daughter. They even called him 'Son'. Gwen's older sister Jan had tried to keep a line of communication open with her for a few years, but that too had eventually weakened and snapped. And now Jan felt pretty much the same as the rest of them – Gwen had chosen to abandon her baby, to leave the country and turn her back on her family. Contact was non-existent. Gwen didn't know that Gran had been hospitalised for a fortnight and nearly died after being mugged three years ago. She might not even know that Dad had married Linda when Mia was seven. For all each party knew, the other could be dead.

So Gwen could stuff it. She'd probably be looking at her watch right now, wondering where her estranged offspring was and panicking about the interrogation she had hoped would never catch up with her. Well she'd just have to panic a little longer. After all, if you could make your child wait another day after not giving them a minute of your time for thirty-one years, then you could sample your own medicine. And Mia hoped it tasted very bitter indeed.

There she was. At the side of the building just a few yards behind Mia's sunlounger, Dimitri took off his shirt and slung it over a post. He wasn't supposed to strip off at work, no matter how hot it was, but the boss was in Athens on business so he could do as he pleased. He planted his shovel in the flowerbed and started to dig, scooping out football-sized holes and heaping the earth into small mounds behind each one. In went the new bushes, back went the soil, éla! The job was done and a fine shiny sweat christened his tanned olive skin. He checked his reflection in the window above the flowerbed. He may have gained a fraction of extra flesh around his hips, but he still had a damn good body if he did say so himself. At least that was one good thing about his job – it kept him fit.

Leaning the shovel over his shoulder, he strutted into the pool area and waved casually at Mia. She waved casually back and turned back to her book. Right. Just what was it with this girl? Was she blind? Was she gay? No, there couldn't possibly be two gorgeous gay single women in these apartments – God wasn't that cruel. He walked over to her.

"Yiasou, ti kanis?"

Mia took off her headphones. "Kalá, efharistó."

Dimitri grinned. "Your accent is excellent. What else can you say?"

"That's about it really…" she shrugged.

"I saw you last night, near the beach. But I didn't see you until you walked past me – did you see me?" He hoped he sounded casual.

"Er, yes…I saw you, but you looked like you wanted to be alone. I didn't want to disturb you, and anyway, I was rushing."

"*Rushing?*" he gave her a baffled look. "No one rushes in Kefalonia."

"I needed the loo," she lowered her voice.

"Ah," he smiled, although he didn't believe her. This was a strange way of playing hard to get – it was almost as if she wasn't interested in him. No woman he'd set his eye on had ever really resisted him before, and although some of them tried to feign indifference, they always crumbled in the end. A casual nod in their direction, a spot of labour with his shirt off, a lift into town on the back of his moped, and within twenty-four hours they'd be ripping his jeans off in their apartment, straddling him on the beach, or pinning him up against the wall in his caretaker's cupboard. It was an easy life. Too easy, really.

"Tonight there is Greek dancing at the Hotel Flamingo," he said. "Will you come?"

"Um…"

"No um. Come, please. You will have a good time. Everyone is coming from Eleni Apartments, they tell me already this morning. If you come, maybe you will see me dancing." He winked at her jokingly.

"Oh, *that* I must see," she smiled. "What time does it start?"

"Nine o'clock. But come early and I will buy you a drink."

"OK, I'll see you there."

"Endaxi. Good. See you later, alligator."

"In a while, crocodile."

Dimitri did a sharp about-turn before she could see the grin on his face.

By the end of the night, he'd be fighting her off. He hoped he wouldn't have to shell out on too many drinks though. Usually it was the women who bought him drinks. Still, he needed a challenge. Screwing tourists had been getting boring lately. And travel reps were definitely off-limits after last night's regrettable experience with Karen, the man-eating rep from Poros. They'd only been doing it for two minutes when she'd drunkenly slurred that she was going to ask to swap locations with Nikki so that she could be with him all the time. It was the worst sex he'd had in months. It was bad enough coping with Nikki's schizophrenic behaviour – meaningful looks one minute, catty remarks the next ever since he'd made the foolish mistake of letting her win a game of Poker at which the stakes were sexual favours rather than cash. The last thing he needed was two women scorned on his doorstep.

As he collected his tools from the freshly planted flowerbed, he made a mental note to buy some more condoms before the day was out.

Craig stood in front of the mirror and tilted his baseball cap down a bit further so that his face was barely visible. This was not good. This was *seriously not good*. He squirted some aftershave on his jaw and gritted his teeth at the sting. There had been no improvement after twenty-four hours and three tubes of cream. He felt like punching something. Luckily Steve was behind a locked door on the toilet.

Craig had woken up at midday and eased himself stiffly out of bed to check out his glowing new tan, but the reflection that smiled back at him was just as crimson as the day before – if not more so. The smile fell off his face like a fridge magnet that had lost its stick. When Steve had woken up ten minutes later and laughed at him, it wasn't long before the smile had faded from his face, too. The pair had spent the entire day indoors or on the terrace – their top halves hidden from view by The Sun and The Daily Express, their bottom halves shielded by two large St George's cross beach towels hanging over the railings.

By evening their sun burn would be tan-tastic, so all they had to do was sit it out, keep rubbing in the love potion given to them by Nurse Nice-Norks, and wait for the sun to set. But it wasn't to be.

"No way, Steve. I ain't going out like this!" hissed Craig as a raspberry-pink Steve emerged from the bathroom. "*Fuck me!*" Craig quickly covered his nose and mouth and grimaced. "Open the fucking window in there, will you – I can smell that from here." He grabbed a newspaper to fan the air around the room. "Christ, you dirty bastard! What have you done in there?"

"Three logs," announced Steve proudly, "two golf balls and a couple of Maltesers."

"Shut up you twat!" Craig grinned despite himself. "I hope you haven't blocked up the bog."

"Nah mate. It was a large parcel but delivery was successful." Steve reached for the calamine cream to give himself one last coating before getting dressed.

"We can't go out like this Steve, we're gonna be a laughing stock."

"It's not that bad," said Steve, examining his arms. "Maybe we should wear long-sleeved shirts?"

"I didn't bring any."

"You can wear one of mine." Steve opened the wardrobe and threw him a psychedelic-patterned shirt.

"Where d'you buy this? Help The Aged?" smirked Craig.

"Alright, don't wear it," Steve snatched it back.

"Only joking, you moody tart," Craig grabbed the shirt back again and put it on.

They stood side by side in front of the full-length mirror, zipping up their jeans and buttoning their shirts. As Craig looked around for his wallet, Steve put his baseball cap on.

"What are you doing?" asked Craig, frowning at him.

"Eh?" Steve tilted the cap down over his forehead.

"You can't wear that."

"Why not?"

"We can't *both* wear baseball caps, dick-weed," Craig looked at him incredulously.

"I need the visor to hide my face, so I'm wearing it," Steve stated matter-of-factly.

Craig lit a cigarette and rubbed his forehead wearily. He took a deep drag and put his arm around Steve in front of the mirror.

"Steve," Craig tried to keep his voice calm. "Look at us," he nodded towards their pink baseball-capped reflections.

Steve looked in the mirror and shrugged. "So?"

"If we were to walk down the street in Bromley looking like this," explained Craig, "we would be pointed at, laughed at, spat at, mugged and beaten to a pulp. We look like a cross between Bros and a couple of glacier cherries for fuck's sake. ONE OF US HAS TO LOSE THE HAT." Craig glared at Steve.

Steve took off his baseball cap and flung it on the bed. "The beers are on you, mate," he huffed. "You can fuckin' line 'em up, too."

CHAPTER 11

Frank made his way through the lively Hotel Flamingo bar as Elton John's Crocodile Rock competed with the noise of enthusiastic chatter from the growing number of hotel guests, tourists and locals who had come to see the Greek dancing performance. He carefully placed a glass of sparkling mineral water on the table in front of Margaret and sat down next to her, giving her hand a perfunctory squeeze and taking a thirsty gulp of his pint. They had barely exchanged a word all day. He couldn't tell if she was in a mood with him, or just subdued in her own thoughts. She got like that a lot these days – went a bit quiet, pensive. He didn't pry, the peace was invaluable.

"Oh look, there's our friends Caz and Babs," Frank waved.

As they approached, Margaret balked at the realisation that they had two vacant chairs at their table. There was no escape.

"Come and join us," urged Frank, feeling the red-hot glow of Margaret's annoyance burning through her skin like a Ready-brek halo. "We'll have a good view of the dancing from here."

"That's very kind of you Frank," smiled Caz. "Shall we, Babs?"

"Well if you're sure we ain't interrupting a private conversation…" said Babs.

"Not at all," Margaret smiled thinly. "We've talked so much these last few days, we've run out of things to say."

Frank chuckled uneasily. The first half of that sentence was a blatant lie, the second half the blatant truth. Still, whenever he did try to make conversation with Margaret she either ignored him or bit his head off. Better to keep your gob shut and speak when spoken to.

"Nice tan coming along there, Margaret," offered Caz politely.

"Thank you, yes I'm trying to build it up gradually. I bought this wonderful sun milk range by Estée Lauder – my skin has never felt so good."

"Unlike those two poor buggers," cackled Babs, nodding towards Craig and Steve as they attempted to slide towards the bar unnoticed, sticking cautiously to the shadowy edges of the room.

"Good God, they look like they've been dunked in a barrel of ketchup," quipped Frank. Caz and Babs guffawed with laughter. Even Margaret couldn't resist sniggering as Craig surreptitiously pulled his baseball cap visor so low he had to tilt his head back in order to see the barman.

Babs stood up. "Can I buy anyone a drink?"

"I'm alright thanks, love," said Frank, patting his pint of Carlsberg.

"Bacardi and Coke, darlin'," grinned Caz.

"Nothing for me, thanks," said Margaret.

"You sure, love? What's that you're drinking? Looks like fizzy water to me – we can't 'ave that! Come on, what will it be? Wine, ouzo, Bacardi, gin, vodka–"

"I'm not drinking at the moment," Margaret interrupted her sharply and then tried to soften her voice, "I'm on a course of anti-biotics, so if you insist on buying me a drink, I'll have another mineral water – sparkling, no ice and a slice of lemon – thank you."

"As you wish," Babs raised her eyebrows and winked mischievously at Frank before heading to the bar.

"Quick – hide that stool!" Jo whispered to Shantee. Shantee shoved the stool under the table and shifted her chair to obscure it from view as Simon entered the bar and scanned the bustling, smoky room for familiar faces.

"Huddle!" ordered Nath. The three of them stuck their heads together and laughed loudly, feigning lots of excitable body language that gave the impression of a lively, funny, and impenetrable discussion.

"I don't mean to be nasty, but I don't think I can hack another conversation about his fiancée," Jo whispered apologetically, gloss shimmering on her pouting lips.

"You're not being nasty," said Nath. "You're doing the bloke a favour – look, he's found a new victim. Someone he hasn't bored the shit out of yet."

They looked round to see Simon edging his way nervously along the bar to where Mia was perched on a stool, sipping a glass of wine.

"Poor girl. Perhaps we should rescue her," said Shantee, straightening her back and rolling up the sleeves of her floaty beaded chemise. "She looks like she's got enough problems of her own to deal with."

"Who, Mia? Are you sure? She always seems so cheerful whenever I've seen her," frowned Jo.

"Believe me, I can tell," Shantee lowered her voice. "When she thinks no one's looking at her, that smile vanishes and a knot appears between her eyebrows."

"Perfect," smiled Nath. "Two misery-guts together. They can keep each other company and we don't have to feel bad about not inviting them to join us. What were you doing ogling at her, anyway?" he teased Shantee with a nudge and a wink.

"I wasn't ogling – merely observing," smiled Shantee. "Although, she's an attractive girl, wouldn't you agree?" she asked casually.

"Mmm, not bad at all," nodded Nath. "But, personally speaking, she doesn't do it for me like this one does," he grinned, putting a proud well-sculpted arm around Jo, who sighed cheerfully and leaned her head against his shoulder.

Shantee smiled politely. At least they agreed on something.

As Simon turned to the barman to order another bottle of Sol, Mia sneaked a look at her watch. Bloody Dimitri. She'd arrived at eight-thirty, expecting him to be there already, but the place had been practically empty. She'd made polite conversation with the barman and picked up a few more words in Greek, and then as luck would have it, Simon had shown up and joined her at the bar. Now she knew why her gut instincts had been prodding her to avoid him. In the nicest possible way, the guy was a loser. No sooner had she thought it than she felt guilty. He was a nice enough person – friendly, polite, he'd offered to buy her a drink – but for the last twenty minutes he'd done nothing but talk about himself.

She had so far learned that he had worked as an IT helpline operator for the last three years since leaving his job at Dixons or somewhere; he lived in Basingstoke with his cat called Pudding and his goldfish called Spock; his fiancée – sorry, ex-fiancée – Shelley looked like Sarah Michelle Gellar from Buffy The Vampire Slayer (he then took a photo of her out of his wallet and she looked more like Janice the machinist from Coronation Street); and he was on his honeymoon, heart-broken, bewildered, "his future torn from his hands".

OK, so he'd had a rough time. She felt for him. It must have felt awful being jilted at the altar – being dumped, having your wedding cancelled and being publicly humiliated all in one go. She couldn't imagine how dreadful that must have been. She wouldn't wish it on her own worst enemy. But what did it take to spend two minutes asking her what *she* did for a living, where *she* lived, how come *she* was also here on her own?

Simon pushed his glasses back up his nose and passed her a Coke. "So I've turned off my mobile phone," he continued. "If she tries to call me now, it'll be too late. It's over."

"Good for you," Mia smiled politely as she spotted Dimitri walking through the door. He waved at her and stopped to greet a couple of male friends. She couldn't help noticing how handsome he looked in a simple black T-shirt and dark jeans. All of a sudden she felt slightly fluttery. She'd been looking forward to making her escape from Simon, but now she felt more comfortable where she was. How bizarre – she'd been fine, if a little bored, but in the last ten seconds since he'd walked in the door, her self-confidence had done a runner. Well, as Dimitri was late, he'd just have to join her and Simon at the bar, she thought to herself. It wasn't like they could just walk off and leave Simon there alone.

"Shelley was never any good at making decisions," continued Simon. "My mum pointed it out to me many times, but I could never see it. She used to change her mind back and forth, back and forth…"

"Yiasas, my friends," boomed Dimitri, grabbing them both around the shoulders and giving them a friendly hug. "Who can I buy a drink?" he asked eagerly, noticing their full glasses.

"I'm fine thanks," said Simon warily, taking a glug of beer.

Mia pointed to her glass of Coke and shook her head. Her mouth had gone dry.

"Mia, I'm sorry for being late – my mother kept trying on different clothes and asking me what I thought. She took ages to make up her mind – can you forgive me?"

Mia looked into his smiling green eyes. She bet there weren't many women who could hold a grudge against this guy for long. He was gorgeous, full of life, and had an infectious warmth about him.

"I think I can forgive you," she smiled. "As long as I get to see you dancing later."

"Don't worry, you will see me dancing."

"Will you wear your traditional costume with the bobbles on the end of the shoes?" asked Simon. See – Dimitri could even get Simon to come out of himself for five seconds, so irresistible was his charm.

"You must be joking, malaka!" laughed Dimitri. "I don't wear that if you pay me to. Well, depends how much you pay me…Please, come with me, I can see a table over there where you will be more comfortable and have a better view of the dancing." He guided them by the elbows away from their bar stools to a table at the other side of the room. "Look – that is my mother!" He waved at a lady wearing a black shirt and trousers and a headscarf sitting next to an old man in the corner. Mia and Simon waved at her and she smiled timidly back.

"You look like her," said Mia. "What's her name?"

"Vasiliki," he replied. "OK, excuse me please, I must move a few tables out of the way so we can dance in the centre of the room."

As Dimitri set about shifting tables and relocating people with the barman, Mia and Simon found themselves sitting in silence.

"So what do you do?" Simon asked finally.

Hallelujah! thought Mia. *A question for me at last!* "I'm a dentist," she answered.

"Oh, what a coincidence, Shelley's dad is a dentist. Although he's retired now. He retired early because of health problems. He's got a dicky heart – has to take it easy…He gave me an old dentist's chair for my birthday last year. It's a vintage one. Pudding loves it. It's his favourite place to sleep…"

Mia was about to start humming softly to herself when the Seventies compilation CD that had been playing since she arrived was replaced with a Greek music CD, and the twang of bouzoukis filled the room. People started clapping their hands in time to the music as three young women in traditional dress skipped into the centre of the room. Holding hands they skipped from side to side, crossing one leg in front of the other and back again, their long skirts swinging with each step. The audience whistled and 'opa'd' as they twirled each other around, each one smiling from ear to ear and gazing confidently at their audience.

Mia looked around the room. Frank, Margaret, Caz and Babs were all clapping in time. So were Jo, Nath and Shantee. Dimitri's mother was clicking her fingers and swaying from side to side with the old man in the corner. On the other side of the room, lurking in the shadows, Craig and Steve looked bored and restless. She watched as Craig nudged Steve and pointed to an overweight woman whose clearly visible white G-string was threatening to snap in half several inches above her waistband.

The three women curtsied as they ended their dance while the audience clapped and whooped. Then the music began again and they re-joined hands and skipped around the edge of the make-shift dancefloor, their skirts sweeping the laps of the cheering crowd.

"They're good aren't they?" Simon shouted into Mia's ear. "Shelley doesn't know what she's missing. I wish I had a camera phone – I'd love to send her a picture of us having a great time with the dancers in the background."

Caz and Babs clapped enthusiastically as the girls bowed at the end of their third dance and skipped off to thunderous applause.

"It's my round," announced Caz, getting up. "Tell me what you want quick – I think the boys are on next, and I don't wanna miss our lovely jubbly Dimitri."

"I'll have a half this time, please, Caz," said Frank.

"I'll have an orange juice, thank you," said Margaret.

"Are you sure you don't want a cheeky vodka in that Mags? Go on – one won't hurt you!" urged Caz.

"No thank you, I'm afraid I don't get on very well when I mix medication and alcohol."

"I always mix medication and alcohol!" blurted Babs. "And I'm alright, aren't I?"

That was debatable, Margaret thought to herself.

"Oh look, there's Vasiliki, Dimitri's mum," said Frank, pointing across the room. Margaret followed his gaze to where a slender, middle-aged woman was sitting between an old man and a pregnant lady, laughing heartily with her companions. Despite the head-to-toe gloomy black attire, she could see instantly where Dimitri got his good looks from.

"I'll just pop over and say hello," said Frank.

"Tell her to join us," suggested Babs. "She can dish the dirt on Dimitri then!"

"She doesn't speak much English, unfortunately," said Frank as he excused himself.

"I must just pop to the Ladies," said Margaret, also getting up. "Do excuse me."

Glancing over her shoulder, she saw Caz and Babs mimicking her and laughing. Margaret lifted her chin and smiled to herself. Imitations always looked cheap – class wasn't something you could fake.

"Dimitri's on next," said Jo, as Shantee returned from the bar with another pitcher of beer.

"Alright, alright – try not to look too excited." Nath folded his arms, an unimpressed look on his face.

"Well he is *extremely* goodlooking," teased Shantee. "God knows why he's working his arse off digging up flowerbeds when he could easily be strutting his stuff down a catwalk."

"You're right," agreed Jo. "If he lived in London, he'd have been pounced on ages ago by some talent scout and would probably have a part on Holby City by now."

"Holby City? More like a Hollywood blockbuster, I'd say!" said Shantee, knocking back a large mouthful of beer.

Nath frowned. "I don't get it. What's so bloody great about him?"

"Come on, Nath, don't take it personally – even you can see the man is gorgeous," said Jo. "It doesn't mean anything. We're just checking out the talent, that's all – we're just observing, scanning, processing other people–"

"You shouldn't need to 'process' other fellas when you're with me," he protested.

"Poor old Nath," laughed Shantee. "Tell you what, let's process some girls too – to make you feel less insecure."

"I'm not insecure," snapped Nath. "Her over there, she's not bad."

Jo and Shantee turned round to see who he was pointing at. A girl with long blonde hair, a slinky figure clad in pistachio green flairs with a matching strapless top, was sitting arm-in-arm with her boyfriend, looking very pretty and 'spoken for'.

"Yes, she's cute," said Shantee. "Not my type, but definitely a babe."

"Are you a muff-muncher or something?" Nath shot her a dubious look.

"Honestly, Nath, just because a woman finds another woman attractive doesn't make her a lesbian," Jo flared her nostrils at him. She turned to look at the blonde girl again. "I think she's attractive, too."

"What about her fella, then?" asked Nath.

"Hmm…no," mused Shantee. "Not *my* type at any rate."

"What *is* your type?" Nath asked irritably.

"Easy," replied Shantee, winking sideways at Jo. "Tall, slim, dark and beautiful."

"I'll drink to that," grinned Jo, reaching forward to clink glasses.

The music started up again as Dimitri and two other men skipped into the centre of the room, clapping their hands above their heads and encouraging the crowd to do the same. The three men formed a line with Dimitri in the centre. With arms around each other's shoulders they lurched forward, dropping down on one knee, before springing up and dropping onto the other. The audience cheered.

"SEXY!" shouted Babs and let out a piercing wolf-whistle.

Dimitri grinned and glanced over at Mia who was watching him, smiling. Good, he thought. His dancing hadn't failed him yet. His mother had joked ever since he was a boy that it was their family forté. "Dimitri, my handsome little man," she had often said, "no Marinakis man has ever failed to win the heart of a woman after dancing for her. After all, that is how your grandfather won the hand of your grandmother, and that is how your father seduced me!"

The crowd was clapping, and most of the girls in the audience were staring wide-eyed at him. He sprung down onto one knee to clap as one of his fellow dancers, Yannis, a tall man with a bushy beard, did a solo in the middle of the floor. Then it was his turn. "NICE BUNS!" shouted Babs as Caz banged the table and cheered. Jo and Shantee whistled. With his hands on his hips he twisted and twirled, sprung forward, leaped back, hopped to one side, swayed to the other, before finally sliding down on to one knee again to let his other fellow dancer – the young, long-haired Manos – take centre stage. Aware that most female eyes remained firmly fixed on him, Dimitri looked over at Mia again. She glanced away quickly.

Dimitri and his companions bowed to another round of applause. But they weren't finished yet. As the familiar notes of Zorba The Greek echoed around the room, the three men performed the dance they'd done a thousand times, and the crowd sang along, playing air-bouzouki and clapping their hands in time to the music. "OPA!" yelled Frank. "GO ON MY SON!" shouted Babs. "YEEHAR!" screeched Jo. Dimitri clocked Mia. She was clapping and smiling. It was the most relaxed she had looked since arriving in Kefalonia. Simon, on the other hand, clapped with an expressionless, dazed look on his face. He didn't look like he was enjoying himself at all. Maybe that was because he liked Mia and she wasn't interested. A smile spread across Dimitri's face. Tonight she would be his.

The three women skipped back into the centre to join the men. The music and the clapping started up again as the dancers joined hands and formed a circle, moving two steps forward, one step back and rotating round, slowly gathering speed. Tall, bearded Yannis darted into the crowd, grabbed a giggling Caz and Babs, and ushered them towards the dancefloor, signalling them to join hands with him and Dimitri. Then one of the women broke free and grabbed a protesting couple from their table, and dragged them into the circle. Shantee slunk back in her seat. Craig and Steve turned hastily towards the bar.

"Come and join in everybody!" shouted Dimitri, waving to Jo and Nath, who stood up hesitantly before being yanked into the growing circle by Manos as he flew past. One of the women invited Mia and Simon to join in. Simon eagerly stood up but Mia politely declined, remaining rooted to her seat. He sat back down again.

"You go ahead," she insisted.

"No it's alright," he mumbled.

Dimitri swept towards them, released his neighbours' hands and grabbed Mia.

"Éla Mia! You saw me dance, now I see you dance. OPA!" He pulled her towards the circle, yelling over his shoulder to a startled-looking Simon to join them.

Dimitri and Mia pushed into the rotating circle. Mia smiled as she found herself gripping Frank's hand, who was in turn holding Vasiliki's. She looked round for Margaret, but couldn't see her. The ring of people danced merrily round and round. Out of the corner of her eye Mia noticed Simon trying to break in, but they were all moving too fast. As she flew past, he tried to grab her arm but missed and stepped back hesitantly. She shrugged apologetically from the other side of the room and signalled to him to slip in between Jo and Nath. But despite almost tripping them up, they seemed oblivious to him. Eventually, Vasiliki spotted him and welcomed him in. At this point the circle had grown so large that it broke and transformed into a conga, which made its way off the dancefloor and around the edge of the room like a gyrating snake, swallowing up all those in its path.

"Let's get out of here," Craig nudged Steve, making him spill beer down his chin.

"Good idea," agreed Steve. "We'll need to call a cab to take us to the Bora Bora, though."

"Fuck that – I'm not going there looking like this!" balked Craig, lighting a fag.

"No one's gonna notice how red we are in the nightclub," argued Steve, draining his beer and following Craig out of the bar into the reception area next-door.

Craig pulled a face. He wasn't convinced.

"No one'll see in there – it's too dark and smoky," insisted Steve, signalling to the receptionist to call for a cab.

"No one'll see cos there's never anyone bloody in there!" snapped Craig. He sighed. "Steve you really are a plonker, you know that? First you book the wrong bloody resort, and then you burn us both to a cinder. You'll be the bleedin' death of me, mate."

Steve ignored him. He stepped outside into the fresh night air. Craig followed him and dragged on his cigarette.

"Well it's either the Bora Bora, back to the apartment or stay here. What would his highness prefer?" asked Steve sarcastically.

"Oooh, temper temper!" whined Craig, turning his back on him and staring up at the starry night sky. "To be honest, mate, it don't make much difference cos we ain't gonna pull tonight looking like the bleedin' Tomato Twins."

"Let's stay here then," snapped Steve and walked swiftly back inside.

"Alright, keep your hair on, Vera," said Craig, trying to work out where the Great Bear was. "You're such a whinger, Steve, you know that?" he continued, flicking his fag butt towards a tree.

"Do you mind?" a woman's voice barked out of the shadows.

Screwing up his eyes, Craig could just make out a plumpish figure with a mobile phone pressed to one ear. "Sorry darling!" he sneered. "You shouldn't be lurking in the bushes – someone might think you're a prossie." Craig stuck his fingers up at her, but the woman had already turned her back on him.

"Listen Derek, I can't answer that yet, I already told you…" she spoke in hushed tones into her phone. "I can't just throw forty years away without giving it one last chance. Yes, it is the last chance…*Yes, I promise.*"

Craig sniggered. "Forty years on the game – 'kin'ell, how many blokes d'you reckon she's had in that time, Steve? …Steve?" Craig turned around to find himself alone, cursed under his breath, and looked around to check no one had seen him before lighting a fag and swaggering back inside.

"Watch out for the pot holes," warned Dimitri, lightly touching her elbow to guide her around a dip in the road. Even in the dark, he knew where every hole and bump was between here and Skala, hence he hadn't had a moped accident for twelve years. The last one had been somewhere in the middle of the island, and he had been drunk at the time. He'd broken his left leg and left arm. He was lucky, it could have been much worse. But he'd learned his lesson.

He felt the soft skin of her arm and closed his fingers around it, squeezing her reassuringly as he tugged her slightly to the left of another small hole and released her again. He smiled as he pictured Simon looking at them like a startled rabbit, trapped within the chain of the conga as he swept Mia out of the bar, waving at him as they left. Poor Simon, there was no mistaking the disappointment on his face. But surely he couldn't have thought he stood a chance with a girl like Mia? Dimitri frowned. He felt slightly mean – after all, the poor guy deserved a break after his fiancée troubles. Still, he couldn't afford to let sympathy get in the way of his chances with a beautiful woman.

"Whoops," Mia tripped over another pot hole. Again he took her arm, lightly, casually. He didn't usually have to pick his moves so carefully. He breathed in her perfume. It was sweet like magnolia. A sweet fragrance for a sweet girl. Five minutes and they'd be at her door. Another five minutes and they'd be in bed…at least, he was pretty sure they would be. The signals had been green all night long. Plenty of eye contact; meaningful hand squeezing while dancing; and she was happy for him to take her arm just now. But for some reason he didn't dare slide his hand down to meet hers. Too risky. He didn't want to ruin his chances before getting to her door. They turned into the drive of Eleni Apartments.

"Thanks Dimitri, I'll be fine from here," she stopped and smiled, her blue eyes shining up at him.

"Please, I am a gentleman. Let me walk you to your door," he insisted, his eyes tracing the contours of her hips, exposed above her baggy combat trousers.

"Honestly, there's no need," she insisted back with a little laugh. "I'll be quite safe."

The opportunity was fading fast. Dimitri lunged forward and kissed her on the lips.

"GET OFF!" she shouted, pushing him away.

Startled, he stumbled back a step.

"I'm not interested, OK?" she shouted at him. "Just because I'm on my own doesn't mean I came here to get laid."

"I…I thought you liked me…" he mumbled, confused.

"As a friend, but that's all. Get it?" she snapped and turned swiftly on her heel.

"Mia!" he called after her. He started to follow her but then thought better of it. He kicked the wooden fence angrily and lit up a cigarette. Never in all his days had he been even politely turned down – let alone physically pushed away. And never in all his days would he have given a shit if a girl had told him to get lost. None of them ever meant anything to him anyway.

Dimitri inhaled a ball of smoke into the depths of his lungs and expelled it with a sigh and a curse. So what? he told himself. It was just another day and another girl. So why did he feel like he'd just made a huge mistake? He didn't want Mia to think badly of him. Her opinion of him mattered. She seemed different. He was confused. Obviously he'd drunk too much beer and done too many 360-degree twirls on the dancefloor. He gave his head a brisk shake and turned to go home.

CHAPTER 12

Nath grinned and ducked down beneath the surface of the water. "Christina Aguilera," he said popping up again and shaking the water from his face.

"I said name a woman you *respect*, not a woman you'd like to shag," groaned Jo, leaning back against the steps in the shallow end of the pool.

"*Excuse me*, I do respect Christina Aguilera. She's got a great voice," said Nath, splashing water in her face.

"OK, not including singers and actresses," said Jo, splashing him back.

Nath thought for a minute. "Melinda Messenger."

Jo pinched him tightly on the arm.

"OW! She's not a singer or an actress – she's a TV presenter."

"I was thinking more along the lines of Mother Teresa, Aung San Suu Kyi, Mo Mowlam, Kate Adie…"

"Aung Samsung who?"

"Never mind," said Jo impatiently. "You've heard of Kate Adie, surely?"

"Um, excuse me, you asked me who I respected and I gave you my answer – Melinda Messenger."

Jo laughed. "Go on then, why do you respect her? Because she's pretty with big tits?"

"Actually, I respect her cos she stood up for herself in the Big Brother house when the other celebrities were giving her a hard time."

"Gosh, that's SO admirable. She really is an amazing woman. Do you think she'll win an award for that?"

"And that's not all!" declared Nath. "She got rid of her silicone implants. She had them taken out – said it was a mistake and she was old enough to know better now. That, in my opinion, is a brave thing to admit – and it sets a good example to young women. Although personally I think she should've kept them in."

Nath manoeuvred himself on top of Jo and pressed his thighs into hers.

"Don't Nath – not here!" she turned her face away as he went to kiss her.

"No one's looking," he protested. "Besides, you were well up for having an audience the other day."

"Yeah, behind a window, but not in the middle of the pool," she looked at him as if he was stupid and wriggled free from his grasp.

Only women could contradict themselves in the same sentence and think you were mad for not knowing what they were talking about, thought Nath as Jo swam to the other end of the pool in a steady front-crawl.

He turned around to see Shantee perching on a sunbed, smoothing sun tan lotion onto her arms. He narrowed his eyes. He couldn't put his finger on it, but there was something about her he didn't like. Shantee looked up and waved at him. He nodded.

Jo swam back towards the shallow end, stopping level with Shantee's sunlounger. She leaned over the edge of the pool. "How's your head this morning?" she asked.

Shantee laughed. "Could be better. How's yours?"

"I'm fine, surprisingly," said Jo.

"Jo, can you see if I've covered all of my back properly?" Shantee asked, screwing the top back on the sun cream bottle and twisting her back towards her.

"You've missed a bit in the middle," observed Jo. "Hang on, I'll do it for you – you don't want to dislocate your shoulder." She heaved herself out of the pool in one majestic movement and took the bottle from Shantee. "Oh, I've read that book," said Jo, pointing to Shantee's copy of The Art Of Breathing. "It helped me conquer my panic attacks a few years ago. It's brilliant."

Nath leaned back against the steps in the water and watched as Jo massaged the cream between Shantee's shoulder blades. A mild feeling of irritation began to surface within him like a bubble rising to the top of a pint of lager. Shantee always seemed to be hanging around. Admittedly he hadn't minded at first – after all, it made him look good having an attractive woman hanging off each arm. But enough was enough. Two is a company, three is a crowd. Why couldn't Shantee piss off and leave them alone for five minutes? He nosedived beneath the water and swam along, re-emerging in the middle of the pool. An idea occurred to him. Take Jo out for a romantic meal. And in the meantime, he'd have to think of a subject to discuss over dinner so that he could show off his knowledge. He racked his brains.

Mia drove aggressively. She'd been honked at twice by slimy local men who were no doubt married with five kids. That Dimitri was unbelievable. Who did he think he was, lunging at her like that? What a narcissistic, big-headed, arrogant arsehole! First he turned up late, then he managed not to buy her a drink all evening, and then he had the nerve to assume she was gagging for it. She had thought Max was a prize dickhead, but Dimitri could give him a run for his money any day.

Then again, Dimitri was just a dumb Romeo. He was only trying his luck with her like he would with any woman. He was so busy thinking what hot stuff he was he'd misread the signals. Still, she'd suffered much worse than an unwanted, clumsy kiss in her time. At least he hadn't been going out with her for two years before dropping the bombshell that he'd been seeing someone else and was going to emigrate to America with her. And as if the bombshell wasn't bad enough, the timing of it couldn't have been more hurtful. How could Max have detached from her like that with such ease, without any emotion – well, apart from unjustified anger and false accusations. And what was she supposed to have done wrong? He was as much to blame. How he could turn his back on her like that, so coldly, after two years? She just didn't understand. And yet there was an uncomfortable feeling of familiarity about it all. She hoped she never laid eyes on Max again lest she punched his lights out. Mia swerved the car as a cat shot out across the road. The car behind beeped, making her jump.

"Alright, alright!" she yelled and pulled a sharp right at the turning for Argostoli. She was going to see Gwen. No more pussyfooting around. It was time to talk, and she didn't care who was 'about to turn up'. If her family didn't know she existed it was Gwen's problem, not hers. She'd had two days' grace to break the news, and now it was confrontation time. And boy was she ready for it.

She slammed the car door shut, marched across the road to Gwen's house and knocked loudly on the door. If they were out, God knows what she would do. She was so angry she'd probably do something stupid like punch the door. Luckily, the door opened before Mia could entertain any more self-destructive ideas.

"Come in," said Gwen, standing aside to let her through. Without a word, Mia entered the house and stood in the hallway. "This way," Gwen pointed towards the kitchen.

"Where are your kids?" Mia asked, unable to disguise the anger in her voice.

"Out," replied Gwen.

"Your husband?"

"Working. Please, sit down. Would you like something to drink?"

"Water, please." Mia hesitated before sitting down at the large wooden table and took in her surroundings. It was a snug, cosy kitchen with a stone floor and a rustic old cooker beside a giant mantelpiece. The walls were plain brick up to chest-height, and white above. And everywhere you looked there were photographs of Gwen's children. Some were of them as babies in frames on the mantelpiece. In others, stuck to the fridge with magnets or pinned to the cupboard door, they were toothy toddlers, chubby ten-year-olds or spotty adolescents. And then there were certificates – all in Greek of course – for various achievements, and pictures they had drawn as children. It was enough to make Mia want to projectile vomit across the room.

Gwen placed two large glasses of water on the table and sat down opposite her.

"So, what happened to you yesterday?" she asked calmly, tucking her short strawberry-blonde hair behind her ear.

"What happened to you my whole life?" Mia retorted levelly, the blood pumping through her veins and round her head. She took a sip of water and looked out the window at the back garden. She could see a swing and a hammock. It was all very cute and perfect. And now she was here to cause dangerous ripples in an otherwise harmonious little family pond.

Gwen took a deep breath. "Of course. Let's get straight to the point, seeing as that's basically what you came here to find out." She took a sip of water. "I'm not sure I know where to start."

"Well, how about we start at the beginning with the conception," Mia said scornfully.

"You're very angry – understandably, I suppose," said Gwen, meeting Mia's eyes.

"What did you expect?" snapped Mia. "Do you think it's no big deal giving birth and then abandoning your child?"

Gwen looked down at the table. She fiddled with a gold hoop in her earlobe, sighed and rubbed her eyes wearily. "I suppose I knew this day would eventually come," she said at last. "I was expecting you to turn up years ago, but-"

"You didn't answer my question," interrupted Mia loudly.

"No…no, I think it's a very big deal. It's huge. I was there, you know."

"*You were there?*" Mia laughed. "What – by astral projection? Sorry to refresh your memory, but you *weren't there*. You left, remember? And you never came back."

"What I meant is that it was a huge deal for me, too."

"Oh, poor you."

"I'm not looking for sympathy, Mia. I know I don't deserve any. I came to terms with that a long time ago. In Greece, a mother who deserts her child is worse than a murderer."

"But in England you can get away with it?"

"Of course not!" Gwen's voice rose. "Why do you think I left the country?"

"I don't know. Why did you leave the country? You could have moved to another part of England."

"I moved in with Jan for a few months and visited you at weekends. But – understandably – her patience and sympathy ran out after a while and she told me to go back to Mum and Dad's and sort my life out."

"But you didn't."

"No."

"So why couldn't you bear to be my mother?" Mia's eyes welled up but she fought back the tears. "What was it about me that was so horrific you couldn't stand to be anywhere near me?"

"Oh Mia, it wasn't like that. I've thought a million times how I would explain it to you one day and in all these years I've never found the right words." A single tear fell from Gwen's eye. Quickly, she wiped it away.

"You've *got* to explain it to me," Mia banged her fist on the table. For a second she could see herself from the outside. It was bizarre. There she was, shouting accusations at a complete stranger in an unfamiliar kitchen. It was like an intense dream – a dream she'd had many times. Only this time it was real. "You've got to have an explanation for why you turned your back on your six-month-old baby, your boyfriend and your family – each of whom loved and supported you. They didn't even pressure you to have the baby in the first place. It was your choice!"

Gwen buried her head in her hands. Mia couldn't tell if she was crying or not. She didn't feel good about making her cry, but at the same time, Gwen had brought it all upon herself. She'd obviously thought she was off the hook, having expected her daughter to turn up a long time ago, probably at the age of sixteen or seventeen when she no longer had to get permission from her father. An age where Mia would have still been a child, unable to confront Gwen on an equal footing. But Mia had never shown. She had been tempted to find her mother many times, but resentment always kept her away – why should she have to track her down? Gwen should come to *her*. But circumstances had changed. Decisions had to be made and answers were needed.

"Look at me," she ordered Gwen. Gwen half-lifted her face from her hands. Her eyes looked tired and red, but there were no more tears. "I'm waiting for an explanation," Mia said calmly.

Gwen took a sip of water and looked out of the window. She fiddled with her earring nervously, cleared her throat and took another sip of water.

"I'M WAITING!" shouted Mia in exasperation. "Why did you leave me? Where did you go? Where were you all the times I needed you – when I took my first steps? When I spoke my first word? When I started school? When I went to hospital to have my tonsils out? When I got the leading role in the school play? When I started my periods, when I had my first boyfriend, when I first had sex? WHERE THE FUCK WERE YOU?"

Gwen burst into tears. Suddenly a burly man with thick dark hair and a thick dark moustache appeared in the kitchen, making both women jump.

"OK, that's enough!" he ordered, standing at the head of the table and putting a protective hand on Gwen's shoulder.

114

"No it's OK, Andonis. Please, I'm fine, really. Go," Gwen patted his hand and tried to push him towards the door.

Mia stared at him, shaken by his sudden entrance.

"What do you want from us?" he asked Mia gruffly, glaring at her.

"All I want is an explanation," she said, trying to keep her voice steady.

He took out his wallet and pulled out a thick wedge of crisp new notes. "How much?" he asked, chucking the wad of money on the table. "How much *explanation* do you want?"

"Andonis, she hasn't come here for money. Please go back to work, everything's under control. I can handle it," urged Gwen, looking anxiously up at her husband.

"I don't like anyone shouting at my wife," Andonis growled, pointing at Mia. "So, I'm going in the next room, and if I hear raised voices again, I will remove you from this house with my bare hands." He turned and left the room.

Mia could feel herself trembling. This was all so, so wrong – she wasn't the guilty party. She stood up.

"He won't bother us again," said Gwen. "Please sit back down. Please understand, this is all new for him – he didn't know anything about this until two days ago when you turned up. I only told him later that day. It's all a bit of a shock for him."

"Sounds like you're pretty good at shocking people," said Mia, walking past the money on the table and standing by the kitchen door. "I suppose I know how he feels, having never really recovered from the shock that my mother didn't want me." She turned and headed down the hallway towards the front door.

"Mia, wait!" Gwen called. But the door had already slammed behind her.

Frank released Margaret's hand and pointed at the dilapidated cottage. "Ta-daaah!" he beamed.

Margaret raised her Chanel sunglasses and blinked at the broken windows, the holes in the roof and the clumps of weeds sprouting out of the crumbling walls.

"Can you picture it?" grinned Frank, his eyes dancing with excitement.

115

Margaret opened her mouth, but no words came forth.

"Margaret, *please* tell me you can see the potential," he implored, turning towards her and grasping her hands. "*This is it*, love. This is the one – I can feel it in here." He patted his chest. "If Dimitri hadn't told me it was for sale, I'd never have known – it must be fate!"

Margaret's upper lip twitched. He *had* to be joking. When they had walked past the house nextdoor a hundred yards back – where Dimitri and his mother lived as Frank had been only too keen to point out – she'd started to suspect what was coming and braced herself to keep calm and cheerful to avoid getting into an argument. She tried to smile.

"Ha haaaa!" laughed Frank, punching the air. "I knew you'd be able to visualise it. Happy anniversary, sweetheart!"

Margaret's jaw dropped. "Frank, you haven't…have you?" she croaked.

"Nearly, but not quite. I didn't want to sign on the dotted line until you'd seen it, but that's all it requires – my signature – plus a wee deposit of course."

Margaret stared at the derelict house. She could actually see straight through a broken window, through the missing door at the back to the sea beyond. Had he lost his mind?

"Frank, love," she sighed, "I can see why you thought this might be a good idea, but personally, I was under the impression that we were still at the choosing a country stage. And if you can just cast your mind back a few days, we were not in agreement about Greece – let alone Kefalonia, Skala and that heap of bricks over there."

"Let me stop you right there, love," interrupted Frank, still grinning. "That heap of bricks has a million-dollar view – as you can clearly see. Now, Vasiliki's nephew Gregoris is a builder, plumber, you-name-it-he-does-it, and he's already given me a very reasonable quote to transform it from rubble to dream house. The price of the land plus the price of the restoration is so cheap, Margaret, we'd be fools to turn our backs on this opportunity."

"But Frank, what about Italy, France, Spain? You know Greece isn't my favourite country. The food's not that nice, the language has another bloody alphabet for God's sake, and there's not a right lot to do around here, is there? Come on, love, we need to consider all the options first."

"The food's fantastic – you should have tasted the moussaka Vasiliki gave me the other day, it was divine – we just haven't found the right restaurant yet, that's all. And we'll have all the time in the world to get to grips with the language once we're out here – and in the meantime, everyone's more than happy to speak English anyway. And as for things to do – we've got a whole island on our doorstep just waiting to be explored! Hey – I've even found out there are some designer shops in Argostoli." Frank beamed. "What more could you ask for?"

She wasn't getting through to him. She'd have to speak the only language he understood – money.

"OK, fine. Now supposing we do it up, and spend our summers in it, and then something happens and we need to sell. How much more profit could we make on a property in the south of France than a property on cheap-as-chips Kefalonia?"

"Oh come on, Margaret. You know as well as I do that it's all relative. A property in the south of France will cost us God knows how much more than a house here. And besides, Kefalonia's going up in the world. If it's good enough for Tom Hanks, it's good enough for me!" Frank gazed lovingly at his retirement dream.

Margaret shivered, goose pimples spreading across her arms. She looked at Frank as he picked his way through the overgrown bushes to the front door and caressed the walls of his beloved pile of rubble. She was no longer the love of his life. And he was no longer hers. She knew it in her heart, but she had made a decision to give their marriage one last go. Frank was taking her out that evening to 'an exclusive restaurant' to celebrate their fortieth wedding anniversary – although nothing in the slightest bit upmarket had caught her eye in Skala. She didn't want to ruin the occasion, but if they were going to make it to their forty-first anniversary, it was time to lay her cards on the table. Cards that Frank, bless him, wouldn't appreciate at all.

Mia turned into the drive of Eleni Apartments, almost running over Frank and Margaret in the process. She flashed up a hand in apology, allowing them to walk down the drive in front of her, and drove slowly into the parking area, a tear trickling down one cheek.

Leaning her head on the steering wheel, Mia allowed the tears to stream down her face. She'd just completed a circuit of the bottom half of the island, having driven from Skala to Argostoli to the airport and back to Skala again. She had known she wouldn't be able to change her flight, but the way she was feeling she had nearly tried to bribe the woman behind the ticket desk. It was only when she had noticed Nikki the rep standing a few feet away that she'd given up and driven back to the apartment. Well, one thing was for sure – she wouldn't be making any more visits to Argostoli before flying home. Perhaps it was a good thing. At least now she could just relax and have a holiday. No doubt Dad would say "I told you so" and Gran and Granddad would be all hugs and sympathy, but it hadn't been a complete waste of time coming here. It was good for her to find out for herself what her mother was really like. All her life she'd only had other people's accounts and opinions to rely on. At least now she knew that they were absolutely right. There would be no more doubts, no more confrontation fantasies, no more reconciliation daydreams. She had faced reality and it was time to move on.

Gwen's inability to offer her an explanation had been insulting enough, but being threatened by her husband was the icing on the cake. She had been made to feel like the proverbial skeleton in the closet – a threatening, unwanted reminder of the past. The husband had treated her like a criminal, offering her money to leave them alone. The tears fell even harder. Anyone would think she was the spawn of the devil the way they had behaved. She took a tissue out of her pocket, dried her eyes, blew her nose and tried to pull herself together. It was time to accept reality and be practical and business-like again. Her mission was accomplished. The result of her research was that her mother had not wanted to know her, either as a child or as an adult. No explanation had been gained, but it almost seemed irrelevant now. How this affected her current situation, she wasn't sure, but she needed to make a decision soon and it was crucial that it was the right one.

She got out of the car, locked it and walked quickly to her apartment, not noticing Dimitri watching her through the small window in his caretaker's cupboard.

"Who is it?" asked Mia, without opening the door.
"It's me, Dimitri," came the reply.
"What do you want?"

"I want to apologise for what I did last night."

"Apology accepted."

"I would like very much to apologise to your face."

Mia hesitated before opening the door ajar. "I'm listening."

Dimitri looked her in the eye. "I was an arsehole yesterday – *a total malaka*. I want you to know that I am truly sorry and I will *never* behave like that again. Please can you forgive me?"

"Fine, let's forget about it." She closed the door again.

Dimitri knocked again. Mia yanked the door open. Now what?

"Please, Mia, I saw you crying in your car just now and I feel horrible. I am a stupid, immature bastard and I don't deserve your forgiveness."

"That was nothing to do with *you*," she said indignantly. "*You* weren't the reason I was crying. God, don't flatter yourself. I don't know you well enough for you to have that kind of effect on me. You pissed me off, that's all."

Dimitri pondered her words. "Of course." He screwed up his face and sighed. "Now I feel even more stupid. I'm sorry." He looked down at his feet and back up into her eyes. "But no matter how much of an arsehole you think I am, I don't think I can leave this doorstep until I know you are OK."

He seemed genuinely concerned, thought Mia. But then again, this was still the same man who had tried to ram his tongue down her throat less than twenty-four hours ago. "I'm fine," she said tersely.

"Please can we start again?" he asked. "You inspired me the other day – you gave me hope that I could be a teacher one day. You are a nice person and I would very much like to be your friend. Please can we forget how I behaved last night? *Please*? I am not such a bad guy, I promise you. If you are upset, perhaps I can cheer you up? I am a good listener – that is, if you want to talk to somebody."

She bit her lip. Perhaps it would do her good to open up to someone – it had been a while. And it was better than sitting on her own stewing for the rest of the day. Just so long as he didn't try to pull any funny business again. But she got the feeling he wouldn't – not after that heartfelt plea at any rate. "Come in," she sighed and held the door open for him. Dimitri stepped inside. "Coffee? Orange juice?"

"No thank you." He stood uneasily, looking around the room at her things.

"Take a seat."

He sat at the table in front of the sink and took out his cigarettes. "May I smoke?"

She opened the French doors part-way and passed him an ashtray.

"Can I ask why you were crying?" he held her gaze as she pulled out a chair and sat down with a glass of orange juice.

"It's a long story," she replied.

He lit a cigarette and blew the smoke away from her towards the verandah. "This is Kefalonia – I'm not in a rush," he offered softly.

"My head bloody hurts, Caz," moaned Babs, lying on her sunlounger in the shade of the umbrella.

"Don't you moan to me," said Caz unsympathetically. "I warned you you'd pay for it if you had those tequila shots after drinking all that Bacardi and ouzo. You're your own worst enemy, Babs Blatchford. Honestly, you just don't know when to stop."

"Don't have a go at me," whined Babs. "I feel bad enough as it is."

"Good!" snapped Caz, turning the page of her Danielle Steele. "You know Babs, if you cut down on the booze you'd probably lose another stone."

"If I lose any more weight, I'll disappear!" protested Babs.

Caz bit her tongue to stop herself smiling. "Yes, no wonder Kate Moss hasn't had much work lately what with Babs the super-waif from Southend lording her skinny bones all over the shop."

"Enough of your cheek, girl," grumbled Babs, clutching her forehead and rolling onto her side. "I ain't in the mood today."

"Oh look, here come the likely lads," said Caz, looking up from her book as Craig and Steve climbed off two mopeds on the main road outside the complex. "Look, they've got themselves some wheels – maybe we should do that too, Babs?"

Babs didn't reply. Caz looked down at her. She was fast asleep.

Craig stood in front of the bathroom mirror and admired his crisp golden tan.

"Steve, my son, pack the johnnies," he called over his shoulder. "The boys are back in business!"

Steve turned up the portable stereo and leaped into the bathroom behind him waving two boxes of Durex.

"Nice tan, son," Steve nodded at Craig's bare-chested reflection. "Almost as nice as mine!"

"Steve, mate, *let's get ready – I said, let's get ready ready – let's get ready-to-bang-some-booty!*" Craig rapped into his comb, assuming a gangsta pose.

"*Booty!*" echoed Steve into an imaginary microphone.

"*Cutie booty with nice big boobies.*"

"*Boobies!*"

"*I said yo I wanna ho with her titties on show.*"

"*Show!*"

"Steve, get lost – I need a wazz," Craig pushed him out of the bathroom and closed the door.

"Oy!" shouted Steve through the door. "Where to first, mate? I've got a map here."

"Dimitri said Lassi probably had the best clubs on the island," Craig shouted back.

"Lassi…" Steve scanned the map. "Found it! We should take our jackets in case we end up sleeping on the beach."

"Dunno about you mate, but I ain't gonna be sleeping on the beach – I'm gonna be sleeping in some bird's bed."

Steve laughed. "I christen this map Steve and Craig's Totty Tour of Kefalonia. Three days of dancing, drinking and humping ho's!"

Dimitri drained the last mouthful of coffee and reached over to put the cup in the sink. "That is a long story," he said quietly. "You are a brave girl."

"Brave? Stupid more like," smiled Mia. "Curiosity got the better of me. I wanted to meet her. I had to know what she was like."

"Does she look like you?"

Mia thought for a moment. "We have the same eyes and the same complexion. But other than that, I couldn't see any other likenesses. Anyway, that's not so much what I was curious about."

"Of course," said Dimitri. "You wanted to know why she left you. My mother would be shocked at what your mother did."

"But I also wanted to find out if I was like her – not if I looked like her, but if there were any other similarities…"

"Like what?"

Mia shrugged. It was doing her good talking to Dimitri, but she didn't want to tell him too much. He was an extremely good listener, and in her vulnerable state she felt in danger of spilling out her life story – from the day her mother left her to the day just six weeks ago when Max accused her of playing dangerous games and warned her not to contact him again.

"I don't think you are like her," Dimitri shook his head and stubbed out his third cigarette in succession.

"How do you know?" asked Mia. "You've never met her and you barely know me."

"I know you just well enough to know you would never hurt anyone the way she hurt you." He looked into her eyes and smiled. Mia returned his gaze and looked away. Those green eyes were dangerously appealing.

"You can't be sure of that. I mean, I can't guarantee that I'd never hurt anyone badly – I'd hate to think I could treat someone the way she treated me, but what if I did? I must have inherited some of her genes."

"Have you ever hurt anyone before?"

"I suppose so, yes."

"Who?"

"I've broken up with a boyfriend or two, fallen out with the odd friend over the years. Gave my parents a hard time a bit when I was a teenager. I haven't always been proud of my behaviour, but I don't think I've ever done anything deliberately malicious – although, when I was at school I never stood up for the kid who was being bullied. I didn't bully her too but I stood there and laughed – which is just as bad – just so that I could avoid being bullied myself."

"At school?"

"Yeah."

"At school I punched another boy's front teeth out."

"*Ouch.*"

"Yes, Vasilis can tell you all about it – he still has a tooth missing. He forgave me though. We're best friends now. School is different Mia. We all act like arseholes at school because we are young and stupid. It's not the same as being an adult and leaving your baby."

"Yes, but what if…" she trailed off. "What if *I*…"

Dimitri leaped to his feet.

"Whatif was a man who lived all alone.
He never went out for fear of the unknown.
Each of his actions was preceded by debate:
What if it went wrong and he got caught out by fate?
Whatif grew old never knowing real life.
He never made friends, never looked for a wife.
He never went to work, he never had fun.
He never laughed out loud, never spoke to anyone.
He never got hurt, never made a mistake,
Never took risks, never suffered heartache.
Whatif died at ninety, an impressive old age.
But not a soul knew he'd turned his final page.
His soul passed to heaven, where God awaited his arrival.
God said, "So what if you're a genius at survival?
At living life fully, you score nought out of ten.
Back to Earth you go, to take the test again."

Mia laughed. "Did you make that up?"

Dimitri sighed. "No, it was an English friend of mine – a teacher, in fact."

"There's a lot of truth in it."

"Yes. And you worry too much. You're a nice person. Besides, who knows what your mother's reasons were for leaving – maybe it has nothing to do with you."

"But that's exactly what I'm trying to find out."

"And she didn't tell you anything – no clues, *nothing?*"

Mia frowned, annoyed at herself. "I got a bit impatient. I suppose I should have given her more time."

"So go and see her again."

"Maybe…" The thought of another encounter with Gwen's husband Andonis made Mia's heart start hammering away again. "…Maybe not."

"How much do you want answers to your questions…?" he challenged her, his green eyes sparkling.

Mia smiled. Dimitri would definitely make a good teacher. He seemed to have a knack of bringing out the best in people – brightening them up, making them take life less seriously for five minutes. The perfect antidote to a class full of hormonal teenagers. "We'll see. But thanks, I feel better now."

"So you no longer think I'm a malaka?"

"No."

"Phew. And again, I'm sorry for last night."

"It's forgotten."

Dimitri looked at his watch. "I should go now," he announced.

"Doing anything exciting tonight?" she asked.

"Well, first I promised to do a favour for your neighbour Frank, and after that I'm playing cards with Nath."

"Oh good luck then, I hope you win."

"I *always* win," Dimitri winked at her and turned towards the door.

I'm sure you do, Mia smiled to herself, admiring his broad shoulders as he saw himself out. With looks like those – along with that happy-go-lucky confidence – he probably got away with all sorts.

CHAPTER 13

Frank took Margaret's hand and kissed it as a transparent wave lapped at their feet.

"Happy anniversary, mon amour," he smiled, pulling out a chair for her to sit down on.

Frank surveyed the presentation of his surprise and smiled to himself. He'd done well – the wife was impressed. The candle was flickering, the white linen table cloth was shimmying softly in the breeze, and the orange sunset was glinting off the rims of their champagne glasses. He sat down opposite her and popped the cork out of a bottle of alcohol-free sparkling grape juice. After pouring her a glass, he then opened a demi-bottle of champagne for himself.

"I'm amazed we've got the beach to ourselves," smiled Margaret, looking round at the small secluded cove. "How did you manage that?"

Frank winked at her. "I pulled a few strings." He raised his glass. "To us."

"To us," Margaret clinked her glass against his.

As if on cue, Dimitri arrived at their table, looking smarter than usual in a black shirt and trousers, carrying a tray of hors d'oeuvres.

Margaret beamed up at him. "My, my, we *are* looking handsome!" she giggled.

He smiled. "I had my orders." He placed the dishes on the table. "Bon appétit, and happy anniversary." He bowed and quickly disappeared, taking the tray with him.

"I must say Frank, when you said 'exclusive restaurant' I couldn't imagine where you had in mind. None of Skala's restaurants really match that description, do they?"

"No, my pet. I checked out each and every one, but none of them were good enough for my lovely wife."

Margaret marvelled at the dishes on the table. There were delightful little filo pastries coated in a creamy yellow sauce, soft courgette parcels sprinkled with thyme, crisp, succulent-looking deep fried calamari, dolmades, fresh bread and olive oil.

"Well dear, I must say I am impressed. This is quite charming. And who made this lovely food?" she asked.

"Vasiliki."

"Oh," Margaret's smile was laced with a bemused raised eyebrow.

"It was her idea, actually," said Frank. "I was asking her where I could find a special restaurant, and to be honest, I didn't think she'd understood a word I'd said, but then she got Dimitri to translate and it turned out she was suggesting preparing a meal for us to eat on the beach."

"What a lovely idea. I must thank her."

"Get stuck in, love," Frank nodded eagerly towards the meze. "Mmm, delicious," he enthused, biting into a filo pastry. "You see, Margaret, it's like I was saying – those restaurants are just providing what they think the tourists want – pizzas, kebabs, chips…but once you taste some real Greek cooking. By 'eck, there's nothing like it."

Margaret chewed daintily on a dolmade. "Yes, this is certainly an improvement on that stodge we had the other night."

Frank took another sip of champagne. "So my love. Here we are – just the two of us. Isn't this a fabulous spot to have dinner?"

Margaret smiled at him. "Go on, say it," she rolled her eyes.

"Well, just think love, we could dine on this beach every night for the rest of our lives if we bought that house up there. Wouldn't you like that? There's no one else here apart from us – how many places can offer that, eh? France, Spain and Italy – they're too over-crowded. You can never get away from people in those places."

Margaret dipped a hunk of fresh bread into the small dish of olive oil.

"Frank, it is a stunning little spot and I can see why you love it – I really can, love. It's very, very…well, *you*–" Margaret paused. "But it's just not…*me*."

Frank sighed. "OK, love, I know. I know it's not you. I love it – I'd move in to that little cottage tomorrow – even in the state it's in – if only you felt the same way, but you don't, and that's fine, love. We'll find somewhere else." He scratched his moustache and slid his glasses back up his nose.

126

"I'm sorry, Frank," Margaret sighed.

"No, love, don't be sorry. It's got to be right for both of us – we'll find somewhere eventually. You liked Fiskardo though, didn't you? That's a bit more sophisticated than this particular spot. Perhaps we should have another look up there – we might as well give the island a proper going-over while we're here."

Margaret frowned. "*Greece* isn't me, love..." She reached for her cigarettes and popped one in her mouth.

Frank looked out at the sea. It was fair enough. Greece just wasn't her cup of tea. She couldn't help that anymore than she could help not liking prawns. No point forcing the issue.

Dimitri returned to collect their plates and replaced them with two steaming plates of plump stuffed tomatoes, brimming with chopped onions, rice, chopped parsley and dill, accompanied by slithers of grilled aubergine and a glistening cucumber, tomato and feta salad.

"Oh, I say!" beamed Margaret, fluttering her eyelashes at him. "Thank you Dimitri. Do pass my compliments to the chef!"

"Well, the chef herself will come to help you clear the table and collect the plates in an hour or so," said Dimitri. "But I'm afraid you must excuse me as I have another engagement to attend." He winked at Frank.

"Taking out that pretty young Mia?" Frank jibed. "I noticed you couldn't take your eyes off her last night."

Dimitri smiled shyly. "No. Not tonight," he said, looking slightly downcast.

"Well have a nice evening," said Margaret. "And thank you for helping Frank put together this wonderful surprise."

"*Ohi problema*," Dimitri saluted them and made his way back up the hillside.

Frank scratched his forehead. "Where were we? Oh yes. Listen my love, we've got all the time in the world to work out where to buy a second home. There's no hurry. This is a big thing for both of us and you've got to be happy, too."

He raised his glass again. "To our holiday home, wherever it may be," he said cheerfully. But inside, his spirits had wilted like a candle in a greenhouse.

Margaret raised her glass with a contented smile.

127

"Now let's change the subject," announced Frank, reaching into his pocket and pulling out the small present he'd sneaked off and bought in the gift shop in Fiskardo. He pushed it across the table towards her, drained his glass and pulled out a bottle of lager from a cooler-box beneath the table.

"Oh, Frank, you shouldn't have," she smiled reluctantly, picking up the small prettily wrapped parcel. Did he detect a note of disappointment in her voice? She hadn't even opened it yet.

She pulled at the ribbon and undid the paper. The necklace and earrings slipped out onto the table. "Jewellery," Margaret said, the smile just visible on her lips.

"Sorry love, I wish I could have got you something more glamorous, but well, I was trying to keep an eye on the budget, and well I thought these would look beautiful on you, love."

Margaret fingered the cheap necklace and earrings. "It's the thought that counts," she said as kindly as she could. "Thank you."

Frank scratched his ear. He felt uneasy all of a sudden. She hated the jewellery, that much was obvious, but for some reason she wasn't having a go at him about it. And that was unnerving him.

"I've got something for you, too." Margaret leaned down towards her handbag and sat back up again holding a small blue parcel tied with a silver ribbon. "On the one hand, it's nothing exciting, but on the other hand, it is," she said in a strange tone and handed the gift to Frank.

Margaret sat back and watched as Frank unwrapped his present, a baffled look on his face. He cast the wrapping paper and ribbon to one side and held up the little screw-cap bottle, squinting at the label in the fading light.

"Viagra?" he frowned. Margaret smiled smugly. Frank chuckled. "Very funny, love. You had me going there for a minute!" He looked at her.

She stroked the stem of her glass with a polished fingernail and looked him in the eye. "I'm not joking Frank."

Shantee admired Jo's tall, slender figure, clad in pastel pink hipsters and a tight white vest top as she squeezed herself into the booth, slid up towards her and handed her a bottle of Becks.

"Shantee, I don't know how it happened but I'm as pissed as a fart," she laughed. "I can't have drunk that much, can I?"

"What have you got this time?" grinned Shantee.

"Don't know, don't care!" laughed Jo. "Something with rum and kahlua in it." She took a long sip through a curly straw. "No offence to my boyfriend, but it's nice having a night out without him. He'd have been a right pain if he'd come along. He'd be ripping the piss out of this Bora Bora place for a start. Here's to Dimitri for taking him off my hands for one night!" She raised her glass up in the air.

"It seems to me you're actually very different," said Shantee, taking a sip of beer.

"That's true," laughed Jo. "But you know what they say – opposites attract."

"So, is he *The One?*" asked Shantee.

"Hmm…" pondered Jo. "Not sure yet. But I'm not in any hurry to get hitched and settle down or anything. However, although we might have different opinions about a lot of things, we do have great sex – and I mean *fantastic* sex. So I'm happy to stick with him for the time being." She batted Shantee on the arm and let out a howl of raucous laughter.

Shantee smiled. "What kind of things don't you agree on?"

"God, you name it…He thinks the government should build more roads to improve traffic, whereas I think cars should be banned altogether. He thinks no more immigrants should be allowed in the country, no matter how desperate their situation is. He reckons 'England is full'," Jo made quotation marks and pulled a silly face.

Shantee rolled her eyes.

"Exactly!" huffed Jo.

"What else?"

Jo took several large gulps of her cocktail while she thought. "He thinks Liam Gallagher is cool – I can't stand him. He says homophobic things-"

"Who? Liam Gallagher?"

"No, Nath."

"Really?" Shantee sat up straight, her raised eyebrows hidden behind her red fringe.

"I'd never usually tell anyone that, I'm too embarrassed. But I don't think he really means it, he just hasn't thought it through properly."

"Sounds like a lot of differences of opinion to me," said Shantee.

"I've tried to educate him, believe me," said Jo. "But he's stubborn. He's like an old bulldog."

Shantee laughed.

"What about you?" asked Jo. "Anyone special in your life at the moment?"

"Not at the moment," she replied. "I'm giving myself some time out from relationships. I need to be by myself for a while. I'm quite happy being single though – I thought I'd be lonely but I'm not."

"So did you break up with someone?"

"Yeah, it wasn't working. She wanted children, I didn't. That's a serious difference of opinion." Shantee watched to see Jo's reaction.

"Yeah, you're right," said Jo. "Luckily Nath and I haven't had to deal with any big stuff like that yet." Jo polished off her cocktail. "God, Shantee, I hope Nath hasn't said anything to offend you – I don't think either of us realised you were gay."

"Don't worry," Shantee smiled. "I only take offence when someone's being nasty or malicious – not when they're being thoughtless. It's not worth it."

"Hey – it's Abba! I love this song. Come on, let's dance!" Jo grabbed Shantee's arm and pulled her out of the booth and onto the dancefloor.

"You are the dancing queeeeen, young and freeeee, oooonly seventeeeeen!" wailed Jo drunkenly, gyrating her hips provocatively in the centre of the dancefloor. She grabbed Shantee by the hand and spun her round.

"Steady there, girls!" a bald middle-aged man leered at them with a glazed glint in his eye as his rotund, grey-haired friend leaned towards Shantee and breathed into her ear.

"Looks like you two could do with another drink. What d'you fancy, love?" he squeezed her bottom.

Shantee balked at the simultaneous stench of his breath and fondle of her buttock. Before she had time to react, Jo butted in. "Sorry gentlemen but my partner and I prefer to buy our own drinks. See ya!" Jo swept Shantee away from them towards the bar and ordered two more beers.

Shantee laughed. "They're still staring at us, the sad old fools. I wonder what their poor wives would say…"

"Perhaps they haven't got the message," grinned Jo and pulled Shantee towards her in a suggestive embrace.

"Wehey!" jeered the men. "Usually this kind of show costs extra!"

Shantee released herself from Jo's grip. "I don't think we should encourage them," she said, taking a swig of beer.

"You're right," said Jo, steadying herself against the bar. "Sorry, I was being silly."

Shantee smiled. "Let's go and sit down."

Jo followed her back to the booth in the corner of the club and slid in beside her.

"Have you ever kissed a woman before?" asked Shantee, feigning casual interest.

"Not properly..." admitted Jo.

"Would you like to?" she asked, smiling softly.

Jo giggled and shrugged. Shantee placed a hand on her knee and leaned towards her. She brushed her lips against Jo's, lightly at first, then harder. She began to slide her hand up towards Jo's hips when suddenly Jo lurched back. "I think we should go back now. Nath'll be wondering where we are." She stood up and clambered out of the booth.

Shantee screwed up her eyes and wished the ground would open up and swallow her. She tried to think of something to say but her mind was blank with embarrassment. Slowly she squeezed out of the booth and stood up. "OK, let's go," she murmured.

"I was just leaving," smiled Dimitri as Jo walked in through the door.

"Where's Yogi Bear?" asked Nath, taking a swig of beer.

"Gone to bed," said Jo, kicking off her heels and lying down on the bed. "Urrrrgh...I feel sick."

"Uh-oh," groaned Nath.

"OK, I leave you to be alone," said Dimitri, standing up and pocketing his winnings.

"We're having a re-match, mate," Nath prodded him in the chest. "Just as soon as I've been to the bank, yeah?"

"I don't think it's a good idea," Dimitri frowned and stroked his stubble. "I keep telling you I'm on a winning streak. I was given a blessing by the priest at Agios Yerasimos last Sunday, and this week I have won every game I've played – it's amazing. I don't want you to lose any more money, my friend."

Jo raised her head off the pillow. "Have you been gambling, Nath?"

"Only a few quid, babes. Go back to sleep." Nath leaned closer to Dimitri. "I like that Boo game you taught me. Let's have one more round."

"You've been saying that all evening," said Dimitri, walking towards the door. "I'll feel very bad if I win again."

"Not as bad as me," muttered Nath. "I was gonna hire a car with that wad. We'll have to go to the bank again now."

Dimitri paused and pulled out the money from his jeans pocket. "Here, take half of it back, endaxi?"

"No mate, you won it fair enough. I'll thrash you next time, so spend it while you've got it."

Dimitri shook his hand. "See you tomorrow. Kali nikta."

"Kali nikta, mate," said Nath, seeing him out. "Oy!" he called as Dimitri walked up the drive, "Where does this priest live? I could do with a dose of good luck myself!"

Nath closed the door and cursed under his breath. He was already in debt up to his eyeballs. How had he managed to lose so many games in succession? Obviously he needed to practise his Poker – or rather his Boo skills. Either that or get a blessing from an old Greek priest. He glanced over at Jo. She was fast asleep. If she knew how much cash he'd just lined Dimitri's pocket with she'd go ballistic. She was always going on about how careless he was with money and this time he'd literally given it away. *Idiot*, Nath sighed, kicking himself. There was only one thing for it – he'd have to win it back.

CHAPTER 14

Friday 7th

Margaret put her hairbrush into her handbag and looked at Frank. He was snoring loudly and muttering in his sleep. It was half-past nine already and it would probably be half-past ten before he'd slept off all the beer he'd drunk the night before.

She wasn't really sure where they had left things last night, but one thing was for sure, when the time had come to hit the hay, Frank was well and truly past it. Despite the trouble he had gone to organise their romantic anniversary dinner on the beach, when push came to shove, there was only so much pushing and shoving one could do without one's husband's participation.

She had dropped enough hints before they'd left for Greece, some of them subtle, some of them not so subtle. Short of spelling out the fact that their sex life needed urgent attention, she had given him all the clues a man could hope for. A strategically placed magazine article on the subject of stale sex-lives; a documentary on the female orgasm that she'd recorded accidentally-on-purpose instead of Match Of The Day; the diamond earrings she stopped to look at every time they walked past the jewellers; the surprise birthday party that Gillian's husband had organised for Gillian, where he had presented her with a pearl necklace and a couple of airline tickets to the Seychelles in front of everyone; the Italian property brochures; the Venice holiday brochures; the Men's Health supplement on getting and maintaining an erection she'd gently suggested he should read.

And the result of all those nudges and hints? A holiday in the most downmarket resort on Kefalonia; a hideous pair of earrings and matching necklace that couldn't have cost him more than a tenner, and one twelve-minute screw that resulted in zero orgasms for either party. Oh, and not forgetting the near-purchase of a pile of bricks on a scrubby piece of land down the road. Margaret pressed her hand to her heart – she would have died had he said he'd already gone and bought it. She'd been very polite explaining how she felt about Greece, *very polite*. In truth it was cheap, tacky, cheesy, and full of commoners – both Greek and British.

Outside a horn sounded. Margaret checked her lipstick in the mirror and propped the note she'd left for Frank against his bedside lamp. She was going on a day trip to Lixouri on the other side of the island. She needed a day to herself to think. It was clear Frank was not happy about her refusal to consider the cottage he'd fallen in love with, and he was even more put out by her 'gift' last night. She hadn't even dared mention the sex and relationships counselling she had booked for them. There was no doubt that was going to really get his back up. But if he refused to go, then what was she supposed to do…? She glanced at her mobile phone as she closed the door behind her. There were no new messages. She sighed and walked up the drive to where the coach to Lixouri was already waiting.

"Good morning," Mia smiled nervously as she walked towards Dimitri who was standing at the top of the drive with a giant sack of bed sheets at his feet.

"Kali mera," he smiled back. "Going to the beach?"

She nodded, patting her beach bag. "Would you like to join me?"

"I wish I could but I must work. It's laundry day, and I must water all the flower beds, sweep the drive and the pool area, and many other boring things."

"Of course," said Mia, sensing he didn't sound too disappointed. Perhaps she had depressed him yesterday with her lengthy account of her visit to her long-lost mother. Oh well – at least he wouldn't attempt making another pass at her now that he knew she came with a suitcase full of angst and bitterness. "That's a shame. Perhaps I'll see you later," she smiled.

Dimitri nodded. "Have a nice time."

She walked on. Was she imagining it or was he definitely a fraction cooler towards her than he had been the day before? Could she really have bored him witless going on about Gwen and her horrible husband? But then he'd said such nice things. He'd said she wasn't the type of person to hurt people the way she'd been hurt herself – and he hardly even knew her.

For a fraction of a second Mia considered turning back and telling him she was grateful for their talk yesterday, but when she looked over her shoulder, he was heaving the giant sack of laundry into the back of a van.

She carried on along the road a short way until she came to the steps that led down to the beach. She looked over her shoulder again but she could no longer see Dimitri. As she descended the uneven steps, she felt loneliness tickling at her – ever so slightly, like a single strand of hair resting on the skin. She would have appreciated his company for a while.

As Mia hopped off the bottom step onto the shingle, she spotted Shantee sitting on a rock, perfectly poised in the lotus position, eyes closed, looking like a slimline Buddha. Mia wondered whether to go before she saw her. She may have been feeling lonely but she wasn't in the mood for polite chit-chat.

Too late – Shantee's eyes were open and they were resting on her. She smiled as Mia made her way towards her.

"I won't disturb you," said Mia, "I'm going to have a swim and read my book."

"Actually I've just finished doing my morning meditation," Shantee smiled. "How are you? Haven't seen you around much." She swung her legs so that they were dangling over the edge of the rock.

"Oh I've been all over the island." Mia perched on a neighbouring rock, still clutching her bag.

"Sightseeing?"

"Sort of. Well, visiting relatives actually." She didn't have the mental energy to invent stories about where she'd been when she hadn't really been anywhere worth mentioning.

"Oh, how fantastic," exclaimed Shantee. "How wonderful having family in a place like this!"

"Well I don't know them very well. It's the first time I've come here and I thought I might as well look them up. What about you – have you been having fun?"

Shantee seemed to glass over for a second. "Er, yes," she answered as if she was trying to remember what she'd been up to since arriving. "Yes, I've been doing lots of yoga and meditating, been on some walks in the hills – oh, and you were at Greek dancing night, weren't you? That was a laugh wasn't it?"

Mia nodded.

"Dimitri's a very talented dancer isn't he?" said Shantee.

"Yeah," Mia mumbled.

"And something tells me he's got a crush on you," Shantee smiled slyly.

Mia felt her cheeks burning. Had Shantee seen him trying to kiss her the other night?

"I think he has a crush on most women," said Mia dismissively.

Shantee shook her head and grinned. "Well I've definitely noticed him looking at you by the pool – and at the Greek Dancing night, he couldn't take his eyes off you!"

Mia shrugged and fidgeted with the strap on her bag. "He's a nice guy but I'm not looking for a holiday romance."

Shantee straightened her shoulders. "You know what? Neither am I!" she announced proudly.

Mia gave her a quizzical look. Shantee laughed. "Ignore me," she said brushing a fly off her arm. "It's great being single, isn't it? Being independent, being your own boss. Not having someone else to compromise with the whole time – and more importantly, not feeling lonely. Not feeling like you're one half of a whole and the other half's missing." Shantee pretended to stick two fingers down her throat. "Don't you think?"

"Er, yeah, sure," said Mia.

"You are single, aren't you?" asked Shantee.

Mia wished she'd legged it back up the steps before Shantee had opened her eyes. She wasn't in the mood for celebrating singledom.

"Yes I am," she sighed.

"Sorry – I don't mean to be nosy," said Shantee. "That was insensitive of me."

"No, not at all. I split up with my boyfriend a few months ago. It hadn't really been working for some time."

"Oh, I'm sorry. Probably a bit premature to be asking you if you're enjoying being single. I mean, it takes some time getting used to once you've just come out of a relationship."

"To be honest I felt more alone in the relationship than I do now."

"Are you still friends?"

Mia imagined Max hand-in-hand with his new girlfriend at the top of the Empire State Building, gazing romantically at the Manhattan cityscape. She thought back to the day he'd icily told her it was over, that he'd been seeing someone else. And then she recalled the telephone conversation they'd had later, when he had refused to acknowledge what she was telling him and accused her of trying to blackmail him.

"Friends?" she half-laughed. "I don't know what I ever saw in him – as a human being, let alone as someone I thought I wanted to spend the rest of my life with."

"Wow," breathed Shantee beneath raised eyebrows. "He really hurt you, then?"

"I wouldn't say he's damaged me irreparably," said Mia. "In fact, he's done me a favour, as it'll take one seriously special man to get into this heart again. Not that I'll never trust anyone again – but you know...I suppose it just boils down to a case of once bitten, twice shy."

A small fish jumped out of the sea nearby and plopped back in again. Mia looked down and marvelled at the transparency of the water.

Shantee stared peacefully ahead. "So our poor Dimitri doesn't stand a chance then?" she teased, looking up and squinting in the sun.

Mia laughed. "I'm sure he's utterly devastated!"

A waiter placed two bottles of beer on the table in front of Jo and Nath and flipped off the lids with his bottle opener. With one arm draped around Jo's shoulders, Nath picked up his beer and took a long, satisfying, thirst-quenching swig.

"WHAT A GOAL!" he boomed, half-standing up, fists clenched triumphantly.

The customers all cheered and one leaped forward to turn up the TV that was stationed on a shelf on the taverna terrace.

"Did you see that?" Nath removed his arm from around Jo.

Jo rolled her eyes. "He scored a goal – so what?"

"Bloody hell woman, you've no idea have you? The odds of him getting that in were practically a million to one. I'm no batty boy or anything but I'd happily make sweet love to Wayne Rooney right now. The boy's a genius!" Nath shook his head in wonder as he watched the goal replayed in slow motion on the screen. "Bloody genius!" he repeated and took another mouthful of beer.

Jo tried to concentrate on her book but it wasn't going in. All she could think about was last night. Poor Shantee must be feeling awful. She'd knocked on her door earlier but there had been no answer. She wanted to apologise for rushing off like that. And not just that – she had flirted with Shantee, she had led her on. She had encouraged her to make a pass at her, and why? Because she'd wanted it. And then to back away like that – it wasn't fair to her.

"Don't you reckon?" Nath nudged her.

"Reckon what?" she asked.

"I said, they're bound to equalise in the second half, don't you reckon?"

Jo shrugged. "If you say so."

"What's up with you today? You've been in a right mood since you got up this morning," Nath grumbled.

"Sorry, I've just got something on my mind. In fact, last night–"

"Bloody HELL!" shrieked Nath, punching the air. "He's done it again!"

The customers cheered and banged the tables as a close-up of Wayne Rooney's sweat-drenched face beamed across the taverna, before his team-mates pounced on him in a group-hug. This was followed by another slow-mo replay of the ball skimming the out-stretched fingertips of the goalie.

"That's it – I'm shagging that man!" Nath slapped his hand on the table, his eyes fixed on Wayne Rooney's triumphant face. "Like I said, I'm no fudgepacker, but that man is a–"

"*Stop making homophobic remarks!*" hissed Jo angrily under her breath.

Nath turned sharply towards her. "Calm down, I'm only joking," he retorted.

"Well, it's not funny. For all you know the people at the next table could be gay and could get up and come and thump you one in a minute. So grow up!"

"What the hell's got into you today? Is your period due?" he griped.

"No it bloody isn't! Can we go now please? We need to talk."

Nath stared at her as if she was mad. "England is playing Spain and you want to leave – *now* – before we've even reached half-time?"

"Exactly," snapped Jo.

"NO CHANCE," Nath exaggerated his lip movements for extra emphasis and turned back to face the TV.

Jo stood up and threw her book in her bag. She hovered for a few seconds to see if Nath would follow but he ignored her. Pushing her chair noisily under the table, she marched off. Nath turned his head a fraction to watch her go but was soon distracted by a free kick for Sheringham.

Jo plonked her bag down and spread out her towel on Skala's sandy main beach. Perhaps it was a good thing Nath was glued to the football. Telling him about last night could be a big mistake. He wasn't keen on Shantee anyway, so to tell him that she was a lesbian and that she had made a pass at his girlfriend probably wasn't a good idea. But it wasn't just last night that she needed to get off her chest. It was more than that.

Firstly, admitting to Shantee about how different she and Nath were had started to niggle her. She had always known she and Nath were complete opposites and it had never really bothered her until now. But his stubbornness, ignorance and general immaturity were beginning to get on her nerves. Nath believed the divorce rate would plummet if women stayed at home to bring up the kids. He thought homosexuality was wrong because it was "disgusting and didn't involve pro-creating". He thought fox-hunting was "only natural" because man had hunted animals since the dawn of time. And most incredibly of all, until she had put him right, he had thought the Dalai Lama was a special, superior type of llama – like a Queen bee.

Jo drew in a long breath and exhaled slowly. Admittedly, it was only in the last three months they'd actually started talking to one another – the first three months their liaisons had been purely sexual – which was probably why the sex had been so good. They had met up at parties and ended up in someone's bedroom or bathroom, and afterwards, they had parted without arranging to see each other again. Eventually their spontaneous meetings had developed into dates to the cinema or to a Formula One race – a rare mutual passion – both of which weren't really the kinds of places you could hold much of a conversation, and then it was back to her place or his for more orgasmic sex. And of course his job had been a turn-on. He'd worn his fireman's uniform for her in bed umpteen times and it still sent shivers down her spine. Plus he was up for trying almost anything – a definite bonus.

But the more they got to know each other, the less they had in common. Jo leaned back and stretched herself out on the sand. It didn't matter of course, she was young – only twenty-six – she was in no hurry to settle down and get married. She was having far too good a time. That was just it – she was enjoying herself. She and Nath were having fun. It didn't matter if it wasn't going anywhere. As long as they weren't at each other's throats arguing all the time…and they weren't. They just had different opinions about stuff, that was all.

She relaxed a little. At least she had got that straight in her head. But then there was the other little thing – the little thing she'd been ignoring since she was eighteen. The little thing which, after last night, was becoming increasingly difficult not to acknowledge.

"Frank, I don't want to get you into trouble so soon after your special anniversary," said Dimitri stubbing out his cigarette and shuffling the cards.

"How's she going to find out?" Frank nudged him and threw a wink over Dimitri's shoulder at Shantee who was sitting on her terrace reading.

Shantee winked back. "Your secret's safe with me," she said not too loudly in case Caz and Babs heard at the other end of the pool.

"Why don't we move to your verandah?" Dimitri suggested. "We will be more comfortable there."

"Better not, in case the missus comes back," said Frank, scratching his moustache. "We're alright here – besides, we're only playing two more games."

"You said one more just now."

"Well if I lose, we'll play again."

"OK Frank, but don't say I didn't warn you, Father Yorgos–"

"I know, I know," interrupted Frank impatiently. "Father Yorgos from Agios Yosa-yosa-yos has given you a lucky blessing. Well let me tell you something sonny Jim – your mother has given me a lucky blessing." Frank rolled up his sleeve to reveal a beaded bracelet.

"Komboloi," Dimitri smiled. "Hmm, you will need those worry beads if you lose again."

"According to your mother, these will bring me much luck."

Dimitri lit another cigarette. "My mother likes you. She said you are a nice man. So I hope they do bring you luck or I will feel bad about beating you for the seventh time."

"Your luck has to run out some time, my friend," grinned Frank as he shifted the parasol to reclaim the shade. "Poker is all about patience. Deal the cards!"

Shantee smiled and turned the page of her book. She was feeling better about last night now. She had thought it through several times and decided she most certainly hadn't misread the signals. There had been an undeniable attraction between them – she hadn't just imagined it. However, it was just as well nothing more had happened. It wasn't good karma to come between two people. If Jo wanted to go out with that brainless oaf, that was her business. Anyone could see they weren't compatible.

Anyway, it was all for the best if Jo had thought better of her behaviour – she wasn't the only one who was supposed to be resisting temptation. She only had a few months to go until she'd completed her one year of celibacy, so it would be a real shame to blow it now. Perhaps she should avoid drinking too much from now on. Strict goals had a habit of losing their importance after a few beers. Then again, she was on holiday. Maybe it was Jo she should avoid, instead.

"Alright, Mia – that's a nice tan you've got coming along!" Frank waved to Mia as she hung her towel over the fold-away laundry rack on her verandah.

"Thanks, yours is looking pretty good too," she replied. Dimitri watched her as she bent over to pick up a clothes peg.

Frank threw his card down. "Come on Dimitri, we haven't got all day, the wife'll be back soon."

"Sorry." He drew a card from the draw pile.

"God knows how you keep winning with all these pretty girls around distracting your attention," chuckled Frank, laying down another card. "Have you asked her out yet?" he whispered, nodding in Mia's direction.

"I'm not her type," said Dimitri quietly, studying his hand carefully while fiddling with his shirt sleeve.

"Don't be daft, lad, you made a right handsome pair at the Hotel Flamingo the other night. Your mother said so 'n'all."

"Maybe," Dimitri placed his card. "But in a week's time she will be gone."

"I suppose you're right," said Frank. "Shame though…Oh shittin' nora – scuse my French. How do you do that?"

Shantee looked up from her book. Frank was staring in bewilderment at the heap of cards on the little plastic table. "So…you win again."

Dimitri shrugged. "I told you, Father Yorgos-"

"I want to meet this Father Yorgos. I'm not going back to England until he's given me a blessing. You'll be a millionaire if this lucky streak of yours continues!"

Dimitri laughed dryly. "I wish. If I was a millionaire I wouldn't be stuck on this bloody island, would I?"

Sighing heavily, Frank pushed a wad of notes towards Dimitri and rolled his eyes at Shantee who shrugged sympathetically.

"So, you still want to play again?" asked Dimitri.

"Perhaps not," frowned Frank. "Margaret will go berserk if she finds out. Let's call it a day."

"As you wish." Dimitri stood up and shook his hand. As he did so, Shantee noticed a small flash of white on the inside of his shirt sleeve. She strained her eyes. There it was again. Frank got up, slipped on his sandals and shuffled back to his apartment as Dimitri tucked his winnings into his shirt pocket. As he turned around he nodded to Shantee.

"Buona sera, bella donna!"

"Oh, he speaks Italian too, does he?" Shantee raised her eyebrow.

"Si, naturalmente! Won't you invite me in for a coffee?" He made his hand into a cup.

Shantee folded her arms and pursed her lips. "I suppose so…" she mused.

"I will come round the front," he announced and walked swiftly towards the far end of the pool, nodding to Caz and Babs who lowered their magazines and nudged each other with a giggle as he walked past them.

"How is my favourite yoga teacher?" Dimitri beamed as she opened the door.

"The eternal charmer," Shantee eyed him suspiciously and closed the door behind him.

"Why so serious?" asked Dimitri, pulling a silly face.

She fixed him with a knowing look. "How many card games have you won this week?"

Dimitri laughed. "More than usual! I'm on a lucky streak. I was blessed by Father Yorgos at Agios Yerasimos."

"Indeed…" Shantee turned away from him to put the kettle on.

"What? Don't you believe me?" Dimitri's smile vanished as he leaned against the wardrobe. "I took Father Yorgos' younger sister to the beach last month. She is disabled and can't go out very often because she needs someone to take her. Her mother is old and ill and Father Yorgos is always so busy. So he blessed me, and now I'm having lots of good luck."

Shantee handed him a cup of coffee and a couple of sachets of sugar. "Good for you. So how come I saw a card poking out of your sleeve when you finished your game with Frank just now?"

Dimitri stared at her, his cup poised half-way to his lips. "I think you are mistaken, Shantee. I am not a cheat," he said solemnly.

Shantee sat down on her bed, crossed her legs and looked him squarely in the eye. "Dimitri, I know what I saw," she said gently.

He didn't reply but sipped his coffee and stared aimlessly out the window.

"Frank's a nice guy. You can't go conning money out of nice people."

Dimitri rested his cup on the edge of the sink and lit a cigarette. He inhaled deeply, allowing the smoke to seep out of his nostrils.

"It's not fair," continued Shantee. "They've worked hard to afford this holiday."

"I never encourage them to play," said Dimitri. "It's their own greed that gets the better of them every time."

"Greed? You're hardly in a position to talk about their greed. What about *yours*?"

"What about mine?" snapped Dimitri. "I don't put a gun to their head and say, 'Play cards with me or die!' I never encourage them. They have a choice. I warn them that I am on a lucky streak and that they are bound to lose – but after three, four games they are still willing to risk their money. And, it is always them who choose the stakes – never me. That way, I know they are only losing what they can afford to lose."

"But you're not playing fair," said Shantee.

"Fair? You think my life is fair? Digging up flower beds, unblocking toilets, collecting the laundry – for what? How many countries have you been to in the world, Shantee?"

"What's that got to do with anything?" she shrugged.

"Just answer my question."

Shantee pondered. "Twelve or thirteen?"

"Name me some of them."

"Look, don't try and change the–"

"Name me some!" demanded Dimitri. "Greece…France?"

"France, Italy, Spain, Thailand, India…"

"Guess how many countries I've been to? One – that's how many. I've never been out of this fucking country. I've been to Athens twice, Corfu twice and Zakynthos once, and I'm thirty-three! You think I can afford to go anywhere with what I earn? Most of it goes to my mother since my father died and my sisters left home. No life's not fair, Shantee, and what I'm doing is no big crime. I'm not hurting anybody."

"How do you know you're not hurting anyone? You don't know what their bank balances are."

"I know their bank balances aren't as bad as mine or they wouldn't be here."

"Even if you're not hurting them," said Shantee, "You're hurting yourself."

Dimitri frowned. "How am I hurting myself?"

"You've got your pride haven't you? You can't feel too good inside knowing that you're cheating innocent people, lying to their faces, being friendly and nice while all the time you're stealing from them."

Dimitri stubbed out his cigarette and promptly lit another one.

Shantee reached forward and touched his hand. He snatched it away. "I know you're not a bad person, Dimitri," she said softly. "I know you've got a good heart – I can tell you feel bad about what you're doing by just looking at you. It's in your body language – the way you sit, the way you stand, the smoke you're poisoning yourself with, the downcast look in your eyes."

Dimitri looked away. "So what would you do in my situation?"

"I wouldn't steal from people. I won't take what doesn't belong to me," she said resolutely.

"That's easy for you to say. You have money, you can travel, you can escape. You can choose a different job, move to a different house, take a holiday, eat at nice restaurants, buy nice clothes. You are free."

"Dimitri, if it's one thing I know, it's that what goes around comes around. If you carry on conning people like this, you'll get bad karma. Do good things and you'll get good karma. And good karma equals freedom. If you helped Father Wotsit's disabled sister, you probably didn't need to cheat. You should have trusted his blessing."

Dimitri pulled out a chair, sat down and slumped forward, resting his forehead on the table.

"You'll never get off this island and do something with your life if you carry on the way you are," said Shantee. "Fucking and chucking women, stealing from people, chain-smoking your life away. No wonder you're stuck here – you're stuck in a never-ending circle of bad karma."

He slowly propped himself up on one elbow and folded the empty sugar sachet in half, then quarters and then eighths. "What you said…it makes sense. You are right," he glanced up at her with a sad smile. "I hate myself. I am the biggest arsehole malaka in Kefalonia – *in the world*. Nothing ever changes and it's my fault." He tossed the crumpled sugar sachet into the sink. "What shall I do, Shantee? How can I change my life?"

Shantee leaned her elbows on her knees and rested her head in her hands. "You could start by giving that money back to Frank – and to anyone else you've ripped off this week."

Dimitri balked. "*No way, José* – they will hate me. I'll lose my job. I'll lose the money I've saved, and worst of all," Dimitri paused to light another cigarette, his hands trembling slightly, "my mother will disown me – and probably the rest of my family, too."

Shantee considered this for a minute. She got up and sat down at the table opposite him. Dimitri jogged his leg up and down nervously under the table.

"Do you need the loo or something?" she asked.

Dimitri looked at her, baffled.

She gripped his leg firmly under the table until it went still.

"Sorry," he mumbled. "I'm nervous. *Please* don't tell anyone, Shantee. *Please*." His deep green eyes searched hers for sympathy – a tactic that no doubt worked wonders when trying to let down some poor smitten woman he'd bedded. She didn't blame Mia for resisting his charms. Although, ironically, a well-balanced woman like her was probably just what he needed. Men – they were fairly pathetic on the whole. They always needed a good kick up the arse before they did anything worthwhile. Women, on the other hand, were always light years ahead.

"How are things going with Mia?" she asked.

"What do you mean?" he frowned.

"You like her, don't you?"

He shrugged. "I like everyone."

"Come on Dimitri, you can't fool me – or haven't you learnt that by now?" Shantee shifted her chair next to his and slid an arm around his shoulder.

"Yes, I like her very much – she is beautiful and a nice person – so what?" he said irritably.

"Is that all?" she held his gaze. "I saw you with her at the Hotel Flamingo the other night. You didn't take your eyes off her from the moment you arrived."

"Shantee, I look at women all the time. I told you – I don't like to get involved."

"Why? Because you might get hurt again?"

"Look, it's always the same. She will be gone in a week and I'll never see her again."

"You'll definitely never see her again with that attitude."

Dimitri sighed. "She knows I'm bad news."

"But you're not bad news. You're good news – well from now on, you are. You're turning over a new leaf."

Dimitri looked at her. "Turning over a new leaf? What does it mean?"

"You're starting again – shedding your skin." She stood up enthusiastically and paced the room. "If you want to get out of the vicious circle you're trapped in, you've got to be proactive. It's time to get honest – with yourself – not just with other people."

"No more cheating people," he smiled nervously.

"And at the same time, no more cheating yourself of the abundance of blessings the universe has to offer – if you're prepared to take the risks." She turned and looked at him, eyes ablaze with karmic wisdom.

Dimitri's forehead wrinkled with curiosity.

"It's payback time, Dimitri. You've got to pay back anyone you've cheated in the last week – and then it's time to put your heart on the line and risk getting it broken. Then and only then will you be able to break the pattern you're in." She folded her arms triumphantly.

"Shantee – I already told you, if people find out I was cheating them, my life won't be worth living."

Shantee sighed. There she was, helping him and pointing the way forward and all he could do was make excuses. He was beginning to annoy her. She didn't want to be party to his petty theft – which wasn't exactly petty by the bulge in his shirt pocket. It wasn't right that he should swindle a nice old man like Frank. She liked Dimitri, but if he didn't want to take responsibility for his actions and sort his life out – well, why should she care what karma came his way?

"You'll find a solution," she said ominously. "Otherwise, who knows when one will find itself for you?" She arched an intimidating eyebrow at him.

Dimitri swallowed and lit another cigarette before spotting one still smouldering away on the edge of the ashtray.

Nath tiptoed up behind Jo as she sat on the bed filing her nails and put his hands over her eyes.

"Fuckwit," she muttered as he slid his hands down towards her breasts.

"Two all!" He presented her with a bottle of wine.

"Like I care," she huffed, unimpressed.

"Still in a strop then?" he opened the bottle of wine and poured them both a glass. "Blurggh – that's disgusting!" he grimaced, picking up the bottle to read the label.

"It's retsina – it's made with pine resin or something," explained Jo.

Nath opened the fridge and took out a can of lager. "That's more like it," he sighed, pulling back the ring. "So then, are you going to tell me what I've done wrong or shall we play twenty questions?" In his experience of women, they wouldn't tell you what was bugging them because you were supposed to know already. Of course he never knew, so it usually took twenty questions to get to the answer, which was usually something like, 'You didn't tell me I looked nice today' or 'Why haven't you proposed to me yet?' But first you had to go all round the houses…

He pulled out a chair and swung his feet up onto the table. Jo put down her nailfile and bit her lip.

"OK, then. Let me see, did I forget to tell you what a hot bitch you look in that tight T-shirt?" he asked, taking another glug of lager from the can.

Jo ignored him.

"Not that then. Is it because I ignored you during the football?"

She rolled her eyes.

"Two down, eighteen to go. Hmm…I'm not getting any clues either. Oh hang on – is it cos I said 'fudgepacker' earlier?"

"You're so narrow-minded," seethed Jo. "Anyone would think you just arrived in a time machine from 1873 or something. Nobody uses words like fudgepacker and poof anymore unless they're thick, ignorant and uneducated."

"Ooooh! Miaow!" laughed Nath. "Anyone would think you're bloody gay the way you carry on!"

"How d'you know I'm not?" she shot at him.

Nath coughed and put down his beer. "Well you wouldn't be with me if you were," he frowned. "What are you on about anyway? Are you trying to tell me something? Did you cop off with that basket-case Shantee last night or something?" he laughed and belched.

Jo looked at him in disgust. "Yes, actually, I did," she said smugly.

"Yeah, yeah, whatever," Nath rolled his eyes and drained the last mouthful of lager from his can, before chucking it across the room into a waste paper bin. He tilted precariously backwards in his chair. "Look, whatever I've done, I'm sorry. I've drunk too much to play twenty questions, so how about we shag and forget about it?" He winked at her and touched his crotch suggestively.

"You're a real prat, you know?" Jo hissed at him and stormed out of the room, slamming the door behind her.

Nath swung back into an upright position and took his feet off the table. He was truly mystified as to what was wrong with her. He should have paid her more attention while the football was on and he shouldn't have said the fudgepacker thing. She was so uptight about some things. It was only a joke for God's sake. He didn't care about poofs – as long as they kept their distance from him, and as for dykes, well if they were fit porno stars then that was more than alright with him. But if they were shaven-headed, flat-chested mingers then that was…well, scary more than anything. That was just plain fucked up. Why would a woman want to go out with another woman who looks like a bloke? Might as well just go out with a bloke, surely? It just wasn't logical.

And as for that 'stepping out of 1873' comment, well, excuse him for having an opinion. He was a normal bloke. A bloke's bloke – not some airy-fairy new-aged hippy with their head in a self-help book.

As Nath paused in front of the French doors he caught sight of Shantee hanging up her bikini on the back of a chair on her verandah. He ducked back behind the curtains. Now there was a stupid airy-fairy hippy with a head full of shit. Nice arse though, he thought as he watched her bend over in her lycra shorts. Funny – everything had been fine between him and Jo until *she* started hanging around like a bad smell. She said the weirdest things, too – all that reincarnation bollocks, how learning to breathe properly could prevent cancer, and all that 'processing women' stuff at the Greek dancing night. Definitely something not right about that one. Was she a dyke? Nath eyed her beadily through the curtains. She better not have tried to get her lezzie lips on Jo or there'd be trouble…

He folded his arms and turned away from the French doors. He would have to try and keep that Shantee at arm's length from now on. She was obviously having some kind of unhealthy influence on Jo and it was affecting their relationship. He should never have agreed to play cards with Dimitri the other night – he'd given Shantee the perfect opportunity to have Jo to herself. And he had intended to take Jo out for a romantic meal. Good job he'd never said it out loud or he'd really be in the dog house. He'd do it tonight instead – have a shower, sober up, put on his best threads and take his lady out. Just the two of them. All it took was a bit of wining and dining to get Jo eating out of his hand. Women were simple creatures really. That's why they were called birds.

Mia put down her book and went to open the door. The face that greeted her made her start.

"What do you want?" she asked, her voice shaking.

Andonis removed his sunglasses. "I want to talk."

"How did you find me?"

"I followed you the other day after you left," he shrugged. "May I come in?"

"Why? So that you can intimidate me again? I don't think so."

"I come only to talk in a civilised manner. I don't come to hurt you."

"And *I* never came to hurt you or Gwen."

"Please, may we go inside? I will leave as soon as you wish."

Mia stepped aside.

"Come to up your offer?" she asked sarcastically as she closed the door.

"No." Andonis sighed heavily and paused at the foot of her bed. "All I care about is my wife and her happiness. I think you come to make trouble for her – to punish her."

Thought had crossed my mind a few times, mused Mia. "All I've ever wanted from Gwen was some acknowledgement that I exist. She brought me into this world – *by choice* – and she turned her back on me, *by choice*. I've never known why, apart from what other people have told me over the years. But now I need to hear it from her. She owes me that much."

"She owes you *nothing*," Andonis replied bluntly. "The world is not a fair place. Babies are abandoned every day – sometimes by parents on drugs, sometimes because the parents are killed in war, many reasons. She left you in the care of a good family. She suffered guilt and loneliness. She was cut off by her own parents. She has paid her dues."

Mia couldn't believe his coldness. She could feel her blood boiling and struggled not to let it show. There was only one way to behave with this man, and that was professionally – not emotionally. She took a deep breath and looked him in the eye.

"Does Gwen know you're here?" she asked.

"No. And she's not going to find out," he said authoritatively.

"All I want is an explanation. It doesn't matter whether I like it or loathe it. Whatever it is, I'll accept it and be on my way. I'm not here to cause trouble or to try to become a part of her life, so there's no need for you to feel so threatened. It's Gwen's turn to have her say. For the last thirty years other people have spoken for her – just like you're doing now. Why don't you let her speak for herself, give her the chance to offer *her* version of events? She might well appreciate the opportunity to wipe the slate clean after all this time."

Andonis bowed his head and stared through the French doors at the pool beyond. "My children do not know about this. Neither do my parents. If you make trouble…" he looked at her, the lines on his forehead drawn into a deep frown.

"I promise not to interfere with your family," she said calmly. "But please don't interfere in Gwen's and my business either. Let her make her own decisions. Women have the freedom to do that in Greece don't they?"

Andonis scowled at her. "Of course they do."

"Then let *her* decide if she wants to talk to me. She'll only resent you if you try to bully her into doing what you want."

"Know this – nothing can come between Gwen and me," Andonis growled.

"Then what are you so worried about?" snapped Mia. "I told you, all I want is an explanation. I have no intention of causing trouble for your family – I don't enjoy confrontation you know."

"Why now?" Andonis asked suddenly.

"Why not now?" Mia shrugged.

"You could have done this years ago – why are you coming here now? What is it you really want?"

"For the last time, all I want is an explanation," Mia was starting to lose her patience. "I didn't come before because I was hoping she would come to me. Then I realised she probably never would, so I finally decided to get it over and done with."

Andonis studied her face. "There is something else," he said. "You have another reason."

"I don't want anything else – especially not money, if that's what you're thinking," she protested. "I do alright for myself thank you very much. Besides, you don't strike me as having that much anyway."

Andonis took a step towards her. "I don't trust you."

Mia's heart started to beat faster.

"I'm warning you – if you cause any trouble, if you upset my wife, you will be sorry," he breathed.

Before she knew what she was doing, she reached out and touched Andonis's arm. "Please don't see me as a threat," she urged, trying to drown her anger and fear with all the warmth and sincerity she could muster.

Andonis looked down at her hand on his shirt sleeve and back into her eyes before turning and striding towards the door. As it banged shut behind him, Mia flopped onto the bed, her heart pumping like a runaway steam train.

CHAPTER 15

Saturday 8th

The sun beamed down as Dimitri plunged the broom into the bucket of hot soapy water and attacked the grubby concrete around the giant rubbish bin at the foot of the drive.

"Looks like hard work," commented Simon as he walked past with a paper tucked under one arm.

"It is," replied Dimitri, without looking up.

Simon leaned over the white wooden fence that lined the drive. "I hear you're a card player," he said.

Dimitri leaned on his broom and looked up at him.

"I wondered if you fancied a game later?" Simon asked.

Dimitri smiled and shook his head. "I think my card playing days are over," he said. "Sorry."

"Oh." Simon took off his glasses, rubbed them on his T-shirt and put them back on again. "Why's that then?"

"I need to take up more healthy sports," Dimitri continued sweeping. "Like swimming maybe. I wish I could use the pool here but I'm not allowed. It's empty right now – good time to go for a swim…you can have the place to yourself?"

"I can't swim," Simon replied bluntly. A vein in his temple twitched. "Actually, have you seen Mia?" he asked.

Dimitri looked up again. "No."

"Right. Well if you see her, would you tell her I'm looking for her?"

"Ohi problema," Dimitri nodded and dunked the broom back into the bucket.

As Simon walked back down the drive, hovered at Mia's door and then disappeared round the corner towards the pool, Dimitri felt uncomfortable. He leaned the broom against the large dustbin and lit a cigarette.

He'd knocked on Mia's door himself earlier but there had been no answer. He'd looked by the pool but she wasn't there either. He'd been all geared up, ready to ask her out – ask her if she wanted to go for a drink or a ride or something. In nervous anticipation he had smoked ten cigarettes – and it wasn't even midday yet. He would give up smoking at the end of the season once and for all – it would be part of his turning over a new leaf.

He'd given a lot of thought to what Shantee had said the day before. He'd sat on his wall that night, staring at the reflection of the moon in the sea, smoking and considering his life. He wanted more than this. He knew he could do so much more than just push a broom around. He had much more to offer than that. He was desperate to get out of Kefalonia. He was suffocating here, dying slowly, smoking himself to death. He pulled the cigarette out of his mouth, dropped it onto his booted foot and kicked it hard like a football. He'd been acting like a loser. He could see that now. And all this time he'd thought he was so cool, so in control. All the women he'd allowed to seduce him and then told there would be no second 'rendezvous'. He had been so proud of himself. His friends called him the Conqueror – they slapped him on the back, bought him drinks, tried to calculate the number of women he'd slept with over the years. They'd praised his promiscuity, said he was a legend, marvelled at the beautiful women they saw on the back of his moped. And yet they all had wives or girlfriends. For all their admiration, he knew that not one of them would trade what they had for what he had. For they had love in their lives, and he had nothing.

Over the years he had never acknowledged his loneliness. In the summer he was busy working, chatting with the tourists or having fun with some girl or other. In the winter he spent more time with his friends, or in the company of Yota, a forty-year-old mother and divorcee who lived in Argostoli, and who was quite content with his sporadic visits. He had immersed himself in other people so that the only time he spent alone was when he escaped to his secret spot up in the mountains, or sat on the wall near Eleni Apartments, looking out over the sea. All these people, they all had someone significant in their lives. He had no one – except for Mama, and all she wanted was for him to find a wife and settle down. She would be mortified if she knew how he used women – and even more devastated if she found out about his cards scam.

He knew Shantee was right – he needed to wipe the slate clean or nothing would ever change. But apologising and paying people back? It was suicide – the whole island would know about it within days. And if he didn't, would she tell on him? He recalled her icy expression as she'd told him to find a solution. She didn't strike him as a bluffer – and he would know. Perhaps he could give Shantee all the money he owed the day they all left – then she could pay them back for him when they were all sitting comfortably on the plane home. But somehow, he couldn't see her agreeing to that.

As he was sweeping, he spotted Mia walking up the road from Skala towards him. He waved to her. She waved back. What was it about this woman that was different from all the others, he wondered? She was here all on her own, she was sweet, warm and friendly. She had told him things no one had ever said to him before – that he could be a teacher, a good teacher. She hadn't seen him as some poor useless caretaker, she had seen him as a person, as an equal. And her interest in him hadn't been sexual. He knew many of the women he'd slept with over the years were using him as much as he was using them. But Mia hadn't even seemed to notice him in that way. Dimitri felt his heart start beating as she turned into the drive.

"Got time for a coffee?" she asked merrily, leaning over the fence in the same spot Simon had done just a few minutes before.

"Of course," smiled Dimitri, his eyes sparkling with anticipation. Even just a simple exchange like that brought an entirely different person out in him. Until now he never would have agreed to a coffee with a woman he wanted to bed as he had always been feigning disinterest. And after he'd slept with them, he'd be trying to make it clear it wasn't going to happen again. For the first time he was saying yes to a coffee with a woman whom he was deeply attracted to. It was unknown territory.

"You seem much happier today," he observed, pouring the bucket of water down the drain and following her to her apartment.

"I just called my Dad from a phone box in Skala," she replied, unlocking her door. "I got a visit from Gwen's husband Andonis last night. He thinks I want to cause trouble. I tried to pacify him but I'm not sure I succeeded. Anyway, I told my Dad everything and he made me feel better. He said he supposed he could understand where Andonis was coming from – although that gave him no excuse to make threats – and that I handled it the best way I possibly could. I wasn't sure whether to tell him about their kids or not, but I did, and he said that it was none of our business."

Dimitri followed her inside and put the kettle on while she put her groceries in the fridge. "What else did he say?" he asked.

"That Gwen probably felt so bad about what she'd done that she just didn't know how to justify herself, and having two teenage kids to explain made her feel even more ashamed."

"Does he hate her?" Dimitri spooned some coffee into the two small cups.

"Not anymore. He did for a while though. But when he met Linda he fell in love again. She helped him a lot. She never once encouraged him to hate Gwen – she couldn't, he was living with my Gran and Granddad, Gwen's parents, when she met him. Now she's almost as close to them as he is. She's always said that hatred can kill a person, eat them up inside. She's right. I felt awful when I was shouting at Gwen the other day. But I couldn't stop myself, I needed to let it out."

Mia pushed open the French doors and stepped outside. Dimitri followed her and handed her a cup of coffee.

"This Andonis – did he try to hurt you last night?" he asked.

"No, he was just trying to unnerve me," Mia sat down and pulled out a chair for him. "He thinks I want revenge or something ridiculous. Like Dad said, you can't blame him for being apprehensive – especially as he never even knew I existed until a few days ago."

"If he tries to scare you again, he will have *me* to answer to," said Dimitri, fists clenched, anger bubbling in his eyes.

Mia smiled. "That's what Dad said. But hey, I'm not worried – he won't do anything – he's just trying to protect Gwen, that's all. At the end of the day, he knows it's up to Gwen, not him, to decide whether or not to have contact with me. Anyway, enough of that. Let's change the subject."

Dimitri slurped his coffee and imagined himself rushing to Mia's rescue and throttling Andonis. Perhaps he should be more vigilant – keep an eye on her at all times. He yawned. "If my boss saw me sitting chatting on a guest's balcony when I should be working, he'd sack me," he said, looking around nervously.

156

"Where is your boss?" asked Mia.

"Athens I hope." He shifted his seat into the shade and immediately noticed Simon, lying on a sunbed with his back to him. Dimitri wondered whether or not to mention that Simon had been looking for her. He supposed he ought to – after all he could turn round at any minute and see them.

"Simon was looking for you earlier." He went to pull his Camels out of his pocket but stopped himself. He would see how long he could go without smoking.

"Oh," said Mia, looking over at the gangly white body draped over the sunlounger, one hand clutching a mobile phone, the other grazing the floor in slumber.

"I think perhaps he likes you," grinned Dimitri, testing the water.

Mia frowned. "I think he's just lonely. You know what happened to him, don't you?"

"Who doesn't? Everyone knows the story by now." Again Dimitri's fingers crept towards his cigarettes and nearly took hold of the box before he realised what he was doing. He sat on his left hand and clutched his cup tightly with his right.

"I feel sorry for him," said Mia. "Although he's not making it easy for people to be around him right now with all that negativity."

Dimitri breathed an inner sigh of relief. At least she wasn't interested in him then. Perhaps now was a good time to ask her out.

"Maybe he just needs a shoulder to cry on and then he might start to get over it," she said, looking sympathetically at Simon.

Dimitri tensed up again. Did that mean she intended to offer Simon her shoulder? He grabbed his cigarettes, flipped open the box, popped one in his mouth and lit it hungrily. But why was he worrying about that skinny white flagpole? The very idea that any woman could find this man attractive would have seemed ludicrous a few days ago, but then again, the idea that this very woman could resist his own charms had also seemed ridiculous. Perhaps Mia preferred the sensitive, weedy type? He felt his confidence ebb away.

"So, will you go see your mother again?" he asked, trying to distract her attention from Simon. "I will come with you if you are worried about Andonis."

Mia threw back her head and sighed up at the sky. Dimitri looked at her upside-down face, her hair dangling wavily down her back. He fought the urge to reach out and stroke it.

"What would it achieve?" she asked, still looking up at the sky. "She could hardly look at me, let alone look me in the eye. I think if I went to see her again I would only end up causing myself more grief. I was talking to Shantee yesterday and she made an interesting analogy."

Dimitri raised an eyebrow. "Analogy? What is this?"

"I'll explain," said Mia, sitting upright again. "She said that expecting to get something from someone who had nothing to give you, was like going to an empty well to get water."

Dimitri thought for a moment. "OK, so your mother has nothing to give you. She is an empty well."

"Exactly," said Mia. "And people tend to keep going to the empty well because they keep on expecting it to have water in it. It takes time to learn that the well is unlikely to ever have water in it."

"So you don't give your mother another chance?"

"Dimitri, all my life she's known where to find me. I was kind of hoping she might want to give *me* another chance." Mia turned and looked him in the eye.

"Perhaps you are right," he smiled. "You don't deserve to be hurt again."

She smiled back at him and patted him on the shoulder. "We'll see. I haven't made my mind up yet. Another cup?" She stood up and strode towards the kettle.

"I should get back to my work," said Dimitri, as he watched Simon sit up, scratch his head and blink in the sunlight. Their eyes met. Simon frowned at him. Dimitri nodded politely, but Simon looked straight past him to where Mia was shuffling about by the sink.

Dimitri narrowed his eyes as the bumbling Simon gathered his things and stood up, again looking hesitantly beyond him into Mia's apartment. Dimitri stubbed out his cigarette and stood up to leave, all the time keeping Simon in his line of vision. It appeared he had a potential rival.

"I fancy a nice big strawberry ice cream," said Babs, grinding to a halt where the sand of Skala beach seeped into a shady area of pine trees near the main road.

Caz followed her gaze across the road to an ice cream parlour where a few people were sitting at tables outside contentedly licking brightly coloured glistening dollops out of cones.

"Now you're talking," agreed Caz enthusiastically. She was starting to become conscious of always opposing Babs' ideas, usually because they involved alcohol, so it was a relief to agree to something harmless at last.

They crossed the road together and went into the shop. The man took their order and told them to sit outside and he would bring the ice creams to them.

"And two coffees as well please!" called Babs over her shoulder.

For a second Caz thought she was going to say 'two beers'. She breathed a sigh of relief. Babs's drinking had escalated considerably these last few days. First she had started drinking at six in the evening – nothing wrong with that, they were on holiday after all. But it had gradually got earlier and earlier. Yesterday, Babs – still suffering from a hangover – had ordered a beer as they'd sat down to lunch at the terrace restaurant in the Hotel Flamingo. Caz hadn't even opened her mouth to protest when Babs had snapped, "Oh shut up – hair of the dog is the next best thing to paracetamol!"

Caz wondered whether it was worth broaching the subject again. It was likely to put Babs in a mood, but something had to be said. She couldn't go on like this, she'd give herself liver failure. The waiter delivered their ice creams and coffees.

"Mmm, this is lovely," said Caz, tucking into her soft scoop of chocolate.

"I could stay on holiday for ever," sighed Babs, running her tongue around the edge of her strawberry ice cream to prevent it from dripping.

"Don't you miss the kids?" asked Caz.

"Not yet."

Caz looked at her. She wasn't joking.

"I feel free, Caz. Don't you? Every day I drive those kids around, feed 'em, clean up after 'em, make sure they do their homework, listen to their whining, and I do a full-time job, and I've got Trevor ringing me up every

159

other day bending my ear about getting back together. I'm in no hurry to get back, believe me!"

Caz licked a chocolate dribble from the side of her cone. "You'll be dying to go back by next Saturday."

"I bloody won't," humphed Babs.

"You bloody will."

"I bloody won't."

They sat in silence for a while, finishing their ice creams and soaking up the sun.

"How about we have a quiet night in tonight?" suggested Caz. "I could do with detoxing for a day. My skin feels all dried out and I've got bags under me eyes."

Babs popped the last inch of cone into her mouth and crunched. "I'm alright meself," she said with her mouth full. "I've been drinking plenty of water every morning to keep myself hydrated. We can stay in if you want, though. We should drop in at the little supermarket and pick up some nosh for dinner, and a bottle of wine – you never know, you might change your mind later."

Caz rolled her eyes.

"Babs have you any idea how many units you've drunk since you've been here?"

"What do you mean *you*? *We've* drunk more like. Quite a few I'm sure. But that's what holidays are for, innit? Letting your hair down, having a good time."

Caz stared at the back of the woman sitting in front of them who was quietly writing postcards. She was wearing a shirt covered in pink dots. The longer Caz looked at it, the more it made her eyes go funny. It was a lost cause telling Babs she was drinking too much. Perhaps she'd improve when she got back home. But then, even Trevor had voiced his concerns that time he'd come round. He'd said he found a bottle of rum hidden behind the bleach in the cupboard under the sink one time. Caz had found it odd, but hadn't thought it that big a crime. She was always hiding the contents of her liquor cabinet from the kids. But she had noticed that Babs' capacity for alcohol seemed to have increased in recent months. If they went down the Black Horse in Southend, they'd get through three rounds of beers, and then Caz would switch to orange juice while Babs had another beer. Again, that in itself wasn't that big a deal, until it got to last orders and Caz would drink up her orange juice ready to go home, and Babs would say, "'Ang on, they're not booting us out yet," and head to the bar for one last pint. How Babs had managed to lose five stone while increasing her alcohol intake was beyond Caz.

"'Ere, ain't that Margaret?" Babs whispered, nodding towards the woman in the pink dotted shirt.

"Oh yeah," said Caz, recognising the gold handbag on the empty seat beside her.

"Didn't realise it was her with that daft straw hat on," grinned Babs. "Wonder where Frank is?"

"Probably got himself a one-way ticket on a fishing boat to Italy," whispered Caz as Margaret's handbag started to buzz and vibrate. The pink dotted sleeve reached into the bag and pulled out a mobile phone. She pressed a button and held it to her ear.

Caz and Babs listened.

"*Where have you been?*" she demanded anxiously into the phone.

Babs rolled her eyes. "Poor Frank, she don't half keep him on a tight leash."

"Not yet..." continued Margaret. "It's not that simple...Yes I know... No I haven't forgotten. You're on my mind all the time...Don't ask me that, darling. I can't promise anything...Yes...Of course I'll let you know..." Margaret then mumbled something into her phone and hung up, staring wistfully towards the sea.

"Ey up lasses! Have you seen my trouble and strife?" a voice boomed, making Caz and Babs jump. Frank was standing on the pavement outside the ice cream parlour terrace.

"Ah, there she is!" He lifted his leg over the short wall, nodded to Caz and Babs and crept up behind his wife to tickle her.

Margaret squirmed. "Don't Frank, you know I hate that!" she grumbled.

"I can't believe you've let me sleep in two days on the trot and then buggered off without me," Frank said cheerily, winking over at Caz and Babs. Margaret followed his gaze and jolted at the sight of her two neighbours sitting behind her.

"Well you looked so peaceful," she replied sweetly. "I didn't want to wake you – you obviously needed your sleep."

"I was looking for you all over the shop." Frank smiled stiffly. "Ah, postcards! S'pose I ought to send one to the office. No doubt they'll have forgotten me already. Fancy another cuppa, love?" Frank went inside to order them both a coffee, his cheery face transforming to a disgruntled frown.

"Morning!" Margaret called cheerily to Caz and Babs. "Didn't see you there. How are you?"

"Fine thanks," they replied in unison. "Yourself?" asked Caz.

"Yes, good thanks. Isn't this weather wonderful?" Margaret breathed in the sea air and smiled lovingly as Frank sat back down beside her and unfolded a newspaper.

Caz and Babs exchanged furtive looks.

"Shall we go?" said Babs, getting out her purse to pay.

"Mmm," nodded Caz, standing up.

They paid inside and waved to Frank and Margaret as they left.

"There's something going on there," whispered Babs as they walked past.

"You're not wrong," Caz whispered back.

The road twisted and turned, following the contours of the hills. The sun glinted off the sea and the breeze ripped through their hair as Craig and Steve raced each other on their mopeds, heading north towards Myrtos Beach.

Steve swerved to avoid a pothole.

"Watch it!" yelled Craig, swerving to avoid him.

They whizzed along the road side by side, grinning as they pushed their mopeds as fast as they could go.

Steve felt strangely invigorated by last night's events. Things hadn't exactly gone according to plan, but at least their luck looked like it was beginning to change finally. They had gone to a club in Lassi and got chatting to a couple of not bad looking German girls who were island-hopping with backpacks. They'd bought the girls some drinks, had a bit of a dance, bought them some more drinks, had another dance, bought them some more drinks – cocktails this time – ploughed in there for a bit of a snog, had another dance and then somehow managed to lose the girls on the crowded dancefloor. At first Steve had felt annoyed at losing them – just when things were looking very promising, too. As the girls had sipped their cocktails, they'd apologised for not getting a round of drinks in (one had left her wallet behind in their room, the other only had five Euros on her). But they had promised to make it up to the boys back in their apartment where they had a bottle of tequila, and a separate bed and lounge area...

The girls had said they were just off to the toilets for a pee and they'd meet them back on the dancefloor and go back to their apartment together. Seizing the opportunity to empty their bladders, check their reflections and share out the condoms, Craig and Steve also headed off to the gents. But five minutes later, back on the dancefloor, the girls were nowhere to be seen.

"They must have thought we'd gone and left them!" groaned Steve, smacking his forehead in disbelief.

Craig had scanned the room three times over like a secret agent on the hunt for a wanted terrorist. "They've gone," he confirmed.

"Oh *fucking hell*," Steve kicked an empty Coke can across the floor.

"It was *your* bloody idea to go to the bog at the same time as them," snapped Craig. "We should have waited until we got back to their place."

"Yeah, yeah, blame me as usual. You didn't have to come with me – you could've stayed here and waited for them."

Craig lit a cigarette. "Those cocktails cost me a fucking fortune," he spat.

"Oy – you don't think they buggered off on purpose, do you?" asked Steve.

Craig took a drag of his fag. "Looks like we'll never know," he said dryly.

The pair of them had stayed in the club until it closed at around five a.m. and then spent the rest of the night on the beach. Steve silently cursed himself for listening to Craig and not bringing a jacket with him.

As soon as the first café opened at eight o'clock opposite the beach, they had gone to get breakfast – the full monty: eggs, bacon, sausage, beans, tomatoes and fried bread. They had cleaned themselves up in the café toilets and then jumped on their mopeds, deciding to head to Myrtos Beach with its white sand, famous turquoise water and with any luck, an array of topless totty.

The German girls had become a taboo topic, neither of them daring to admit to the other that the two sly bints had more than likely been leading them a merry dance all evening. Steve had kept his eyes peeled for them all morning before leaving Lassi, lest they emerged out of a nearby apartment block or hotel. But then, what would he say to them? Still, on the positive side, at least they'd both got themselves a snog and a bit of a grope, and strictly speaking, there was no actual evidence proving the girls had done a runner. Perhaps this was just a mere sexy taster of things to come.

Steve pointed to a sign for Myrtos Beach and overtook Craig. Craig grinned and sped up, levelled with Steve and then overtook him, giving him the finger as he went. A beep made them both jump and Craig pulled in to the side of the road as a flashy Kawasaki GPZ600 tore past them – a muscly bloke with a bandana up front and a petite brunette clinging on behind, long hair streaming in the wind.

"Cunt!" spat Craig, staring daggers at the back of the bike. He sped up. Steve tried to keep up with him.

The Kawasaki slowed down a fraction, allowing Craig to catch up. The brunette swept her hair out of her face and waved. It was Nurse Nice-Norks – *Maria*.

Craig nodded at her coolly and tried to keep up with his opponent.

"Slow down, mate!" Steve called out. "You can't compete with that motor. Don't even try!"

Craig shot him a dirty look, took a cigarette from behind his ear, put it between his lips, threw another smooth glance at Maria, and drove straight over a pothole.

Steve froze as he watched Craig wobble from side to side, veer to the edge of the road and collide with a small boulder. Both Craig and his moped catapulted over a bush and landed side by side in an earthy field.

Steve and the Kawasaki skidded to a halt. Maria hopped off the back and clambered through the bush to where Craig was lying spread-eagled and staring vacantly up at the sky. She knelt down next to him as Steve and her muscly friend hurried over and squatted down on his other side.

"Are you alright?" gasped Steve, panic and adrenalin pumping through his body.

Craig blinked. Maria leaned over him and touched his face. "Can you tell me your name?" she asked loudly.

"Craig," groaned Craig.

Maria glanced worriedly at Steve and turned round to say something in Greek to her companion. "He is going to call the ambulance," she announced.

"I don't need one," said Craig, the strength returning to his voice. "I'm alright – no thanks to him," he hissed, glancing at the young Greek on his mobile phone. "Your boyfriend cut me right up."

Maria frowned. "He is not my boyfriend, he is my brother. And he didn't cut you up – you were in the middle of the road going all everywhere like a crazy man. So, can you sit up? Is anything broken?" She examined his grazed knees and elbows.

Craig dragged himself into a sitting position. "I don't need an ambulance," he repeated and stood up.

Maria tried to stop him. "You may be concussed – you should go to the hospital."

"I'm fine," snapped Craig. He picked up his battered moped and flipped it onto its stand. "The bike, on the other hand, is twatted."

"I agree with Maria, mate," said Steve. "You should get yourself checked out. If you cark it I don't want to be humping your dead body back home, do I?"

"Thanks for that, Steve," Craig rolled his eyes and looked at the dents on the side of his moped.

"Come on, it won't take long," said Maria. "If they say you are OK, you can leave quickly – and while they examine you, Steve can get you another bike in Argostoli."

Maria turned to her brother, and again the two babbled away in Greek.

Steve nudged Craig. "I don't know why you're arguing with her, mate – I thought you fancied her?" he said in a low voice. "There she is, this gorgeous nurse with nice norks and sexy legs all concerned about you and wanting to get you to hospital – and there you are, all dazed and confused and needing medical attention after an accident. You really must be concussed or you'd have had her giving you the kiss of life by now!"

In the blink of an eye, Craig flopped to the ground. Maria spun around. "What's the matter?" she asked, rushing over to him. "Are you OK?"

Craig grimaced and rubbed his forehead. "My vision's gone all blurry," he whined. "And I'm feeling short of breath."

At that moment the ambulance came into sight and pulled up beside them. Two men jumped out and crouched down beside Craig as Maria explained to them what had happened. They put their arms round his shoulders, lifted him up and helped him towards the ambulance.

"I'll follow on behind you," said Steve, heading towards his bike. "Oh – what about your moped?"

"Don't worry," said Maria, "my brother already call the garage to come and find it. You can get a new one from Argostoli or Skala – there is same garage in both towns." She smiled at him.

Steve thanked her and nodded his appreciation to her brother.

"OY!" Craig lifted his head from the bed inside the ambulance. "Aren't you coming with me?" he looked anxiously at Maria.

"Who *me?*" she pointed to herself with a big grin. "No, my duty is done. Don't worry, you are in good hands. They will look after you."

Craig flopped back on the pillow, cursing.

Steve sniggered. "Don't worry, mate. I'll be there for you."

"Fucking grrrrreat," groaned Craig, as the paramedics bolted the ambulance doors behind him.

The water felt cold and cleansing against Mia's skin as she darted along the bottom of the pool, determined to make it from one end to the other without surfacing for air. At just two metres short of the deep end she flew up to the surface, rubbing the water from her eyes and gasping for breath.

She looked back at the distance she had swum underwater and noticed Simon had returned to the pool and was sitting on the steps in the shallow end, watching her.

"Well I was close," she smiled at him.

"Yes," he agreed. "You nearly did it."

"Can you do it?" she asked, pushing herself into the centre of the pool and treading water.

Simon shook his head. "Can't swim," he mumbled.

"Oh."

"I used to get all panicky on school swimming trips – even in the shallow end. I refused to take my arm-bands off and move from where my feet could touch the bottom. So I got as far as wading, really. Never made it to actually swimming. I got too scared, made a big fuss, and eventually they let me just sit at the side and watch."

"That's a shame," said Mia, coming to rest beside him on the steps.

"Oh, it's never bothered me too much. I'm not really the sporty type." The sun bounced off Simon's spectacles as he tilted his head back. "Shelley was the sporty one. She went jogging every day. She thought she was fat. I told her she wasn't, but she wouldn't listen."

Mia sighed. If this was going to turn into another long, self-pitying rant...

"Why do women think they're fat when they're not?" asked Simon.

"Good question," she replied, wondering whether to escape now or give the poor guy a chance.

"Do you think you're fat?" he asked, running his eyes down her body.

"I suppose I have my fat days," she replied, lowering herself in the water.

"But you're not fat at all. You've got a great figure."

Mia smiled awkwardly. "Oh...er, thanks."

Simon blushed.

"I suppose women are faced with images of the ideal body so much that they can't help but aspire to look like that," she said.

"It's stupid," Simon said angrily. "All those pictures of supermodels have been air-brushed and messed about with. And they have hairdressers and make-up artists do them up for hours before the photo's taken. Anyone could be a model with a bit of grooming and air-brushing – even me!" He grinned despite himself.

Mia laughed.

Simon smiled. It was the first time she'd seen him smile, Mia noted. And he did seem to have a sense of humour buried beneath all that woe.

"That one's a bit of a ladies' man, isn't he?" said Simon in a low voice, as Dimitri walked past them with the hosepipe coiled over his shoulder and nodded at them.

"I dunno, is he?" shrugged Mia, waving to him.

"You ought to watch out," whispered Simon. "A girl on her own like you in a Latin country like this…"

Mia suppressed a smile. "Oh, he's harmless. Probably cos there's no Latin in him, what with him being Greek."

Simon blushed again. "It's just that I noticed him…"

"What?"

"Looking at you. From what I've heard, it sounds like he's got a bit of a reputation…"

"Well thanks for your concern, Simon, but he's just being friendly, that's all." She wondered if Simon had witnessed Dimitri's clumsy pass at her. No, he would have said so. He'd have probably tried to intervene.

"I don't mean to be nasty or anything – he's a nice guy," said Simon, trying to backtrack a little.

"He *is* a nice guy," agreed Mia, looking around to see if he was still there.

"Anyway I expect you know how to handle yourself if anyone tried any funny business," said Simon. "But if you need my help at all, I'm only over there." He pointed to his apartment.

Mia mumbled a thank you and tried to keep her lips from twitching into a smile.

"Of course Shelley practised karate, so she had no problem looking after herself if anyone tried anything on her."

"Have you heard from Shelley?" she asked, curiosity suddenly getting the better of her.

Simon looked dolefully down at the water. "No."

"Have you tried to call her?"

"Several times. If she could just tell me why she did what she did. I just haven't got a clue – did I do something wrong? Was she seeing someone else? Has she got terminal cancer? I haven't a clue!" Simon threw his arms up in the air and brought them splashing down into the water.

"Sometimes I think perhaps we're not supposed to know," said Mia gently. "You can't force the other person to tell you why they did what they did. Sometimes you just have to accept it and move on."

"That's easy for you to say," he mumbled. "Your fiancé didn't just leave you at the altar."

Mia bit her lip. She couldn't be bothered to enlighten him to the fact that he wasn't the only one with problems. "Well, that's enough swimming for me today," she smiled, standing up. "My skin's gone like a prune."

"Maybe we can have a drink or something later…or whenever?" Simon blurted rather too eagerly.

"Er, yeah," Mia waded up the steps out of the pool. "OK…see you."

As she wrapped her towel around her and padded back to her apartment, she could see him smiling out of the corner of her eye. A drink with Simon. How on earth was she going to get out of that?

CHAPTER 16

Jo handed the two menus back to the waiter and examined her fingernails. They needed filing and re-painting – she had chipped one last night while climbing over the rocks on the small hidden beach near their apartment complex. She had been hoping to find Shantee down there, but there was no sign of her anywhere. Was Shantee avoiding her? She didn't blame her if she was. Anyway, apart from apologising what else would she say to her? That she did find her attractive? That she had wanted to return that kiss? It wasn't right – it was Nath she should talk to first. She needed to tell him what she was feeling before she went and acted on the emotion and would then have to confess to being unfaithful. She didn't want to lie to him – he deserved to know why she was acting the way she was. He wasn't going to like it, and it was probably going to mean the end of their relationship, but perhaps that was for the best. The last thing she wanted was to go behind his back and hurt him.

Nath cleared his throat. "When you didn't come back last night, I was so worried," he said. "It really made me realise how much–"

"I was back by nine," Jo interrupted. "And I was only ten minutes' walk away on that little beach. You couldn't have looked for me very hard."

"I didn't even know that beach existed," protested Nath.

"But if you'd asked someone if they'd seen me – which you didn't – they'd have asked you if you'd tried the beach."

Nath rolled his eyes. "Look, I'm trying to apologise so will you just give me a chance? I've been trying really hard all day to find out what it is I'm doing wrong. I was gonna take you out last night for a nice meal – I got all dressed up for you – but by the time you came back…and then we argued…Bloody hell, just tell me what's going on in your head, will you? I've apologised for slagging off gays, I've apologised for ignoring you during the football, I've apologised for everything else I can think of that I may have done wrong, and short of apologising for being born, I don't know what else I can say!"

Jo sighed as the waiter returned with a bottle of red wine and poured them each a glass.

"I'm sorry," Jo murmured.

"Eh?" Nath wondered if he'd heard correctly.

"I said I'm sorry." Jo looked up at him. "You did piss me off yesterday but you did apologise and I shouldn't have gone off like that. I just needed time to think, that's all. I wasn't pissed off with you anymore, I just needed to be by myself for a while."

"If you weren't pissed off with me anymore, then why did you need to be by yourself?"

"Because there's something I need to tell you, but I don't know how to say it and I'm scared of how you're going to react. I'm scared you're going to judge me and make me feel bad. But then if you do, I'd know you were a cock and not someone I want in my life anymore."

Nath looked at her, bewildered. "Well bloody tell me what it is then," he said, exasperated. "Are you up the duff?"

Jo shook her head and the colour returned to Nath's cheeks slightly.

"Just tell me, Jo," he begged.

"You promise not to be horrible?" She looked at him, her eyes full of apprehension.

Nath reached forward and took her hand. "You're my girl," he said reassuringly.

"I think…" Jo swallowed to lubricate her throat. "I think I'm bisexual."

Nath stared at her in disbelief and slowly pulled his hand away. Silence hung over them as her confession sank in. Jo looked around her. Other people were heartily twirling spaghetti around their forks, laughing and whispering sweet nothings to one another.

Nath picked up his glass of wine and took several big gulps. Jo took a small sip from hers. The waiter arrived swiftly to top up their glasses and deliver a basket of garlic bread. Life seemed to stop for a moment – the pair of them sat suspended in action while the rest of the world continued to bustle about its business all around them. For a brief moment, Jo felt serene. She'd finally said it, after all these years of pushing it away, burying it beneath all the other goings-on in her busy life. It was out, and as yet, she was still sitting there, in one piece, the aromas of red wine and garlic suddenly gaining her attention over the blurred face sitting opposite her.

"It's that fucking Shantee weirdo, isn't it?" piped Nath suddenly, just as Jo's mind had begun to wonder. She quickly snapped back to reality. "What's she been saying to you?" Nath growled.

"*Calm down, Nath.* We're in a restaurant. I don't want any scenes," Jo lowered her voice.

"Just tell me what she's been saying," he demanded.

"Look, this goes way back to when I was eighteen," said Jo. "I had a crush on my tutor at university. She was-"

"*She!*" Nath hooted and shook his head in amazement.

"She was in her early thirties, beautiful, full of energy and enthusiasm – not one student missed her tutorials."

Nath twitched and chipped a piece of dripping wax off the candle in the centre of their table. "How very jolly hockeysticks," he muttered.

"I used to think about her all the time," continued Jo. "I was attracted to her. I wouldn't admit it to myself at the time, but I was always 'accidentally' bumping into her in the canteen or the bar on campus, asking her if she fancied joining me for a coffee..."

"And?" Nath scowled at her. "Was she a dyke?"

"No," snapped Jo. "No she wasn't."

"So, what happened?" asked Nath, feigning boredom and stuffing a slice of garlic bread into his mouth.

"Nothing happened," shrugged Jo. "She was straight."

"So you never..." Nath gesticulated the words he couldn't bring himself to say.

"I never told her, she never knew, nothing happened, and soon after I started going out with Jamie and forgot all about it." Jo took another large sip of wine. "That's just it, Nath. I've never done anything with a woman..."

Nath grimaced and looked away.

"I've only ever been with men. I've had crushes on women-"

"Well crushes don't mean anything. It doesn't mean you're bisexual. If you actually did...do something with a woman, you'd probably feel sick."

Jo shook her head. "I don't think so. But the truth is I don't really know, because I've never allowed myself to explore that side of me."

"So what are you saying?" asked Nath, his mouth full of garlic bread. "You want to go off and shag a bird? Aren't I good enough for you anymore? Are you getting bored of me? I don't get it – I made you come four times the other night. Or maybe you have been faking after all?"

Jo tried not to lose her patience. Nath's reaction was understandable, she told herself.

"Nath, sexually speaking, you're the best I've ever had," she tried to take his hand, but he pulled it away like a sulking child.

"Well, obviously I'm not enough for you or we wouldn't be having this conversation," he said miserably. "Why now, though? What's brought all this on? If you've known about this for years, why have you suddenly decided to bring it up now?"

Jo looked down at a scattering of crumbs on the tablecloth.

"It *is* Shantee isn't it?" he gave her a piercing look. "You'd better bloody tell me what's been going on, Jo."

CHAPTER 17

Sunday 9th

Frank walked briskly along the road to Skala. He was no longer enjoying this holiday. It had been a big mistake coming here. He should have booked somewhere in Italy to keep that grumpy old witch happy. But he was trying to be sensible, thinking of the future – of *their* future. The less they frittered away on expensive holidays and luxury items, the more they'd have to spend on their holiday home. And after the way she'd been harping on about finding some kind of Italian Sloane Street-on-Sea location to buy a property, they shouldn't have indulged in a holiday at all, but stayed at home, sold the cars, rented out the garage and lived on gruel and water all year.

Money. She really did think the stuff grew on trees. It was his own fault. He should have been tighter with it. He should have made her take more responsibility. She'd never even opened a bill for God's sake! He'd always taken care of everything. No wonder she thought there was an endless supply of funds. No, Margaret, there wasn't. And now that he'd retired, she'd soon find out that the money tree in the back garden was no longer producing fruit.

But that wasn't the only thing that had got his goat. As if giving up on that golden opportunity of a cottage down the road hadn't been painful enough, he'd agreed to go on a property-searching holiday in Lake Como next May. Como! He laughed to himself as a car sped past him on the coast road. He'd only gone along with her silly ideas because it would be worth the look on her face when she got to see the price tags attached to the villas in the province where Italy's top fashion designers and footballers lived. Then he planned to give Margaret a little maths lesson: sell house for smaller house back home, leftover capital plus savings equals smarmy Como estate agent pissing himself with laughter. But then you couldn't tell

Margaret this. She had to find it out for herself – the hard way.

And there was more. Viagra. *"Viagra!"* He spat the word out loud, looking round to make sure no one was behind him. He wondered how she would have responded had he handed her a brochure for a cosmetic surgeon specialising in breast implants and liposuction. It wasn't him who needed medication – it was her who needed a transformation. She might look alright when she was dolled up to the nines with her tummy-hugger tights and push-up bras disguising the flaws beneath her clothes. But remove all that regalia and what was she? A flabby sixty-year-old with sagging breasts and a pot-belly – just like him. He couldn't see how Viagra was going to make that any more exciting or sexy.

And it got worse – *worse!* She wanted them to go to sex and relationship counselling! A stitch pierced Frank's side. He stopped for a minute to catch his breath. He breathed in the fresh sea air and tried to identify a large boat on the horizon. Probably a tanker on its way to Italy. He carried on walking. Sex counselling – had she lost her mind? He had agreed to the property search in Como, he had said he was willing to give the Viagra a go, but sit and discuss what you did with your bits and bobs in front of some know-it-all with a clipboard – not on your nelly, mate. Of course Margaret had gone berserk at him when he'd said as much. For a minute, he'd thought she was going to scream at him and that the whole complex would be able to hear, but she just about managed to keep her voice under control. Twenty-five good years she reckoned she still had in her. Her father had lived to eighty, her mother to eighty-five and her aunt to ninety. And, according to Margaret, twenty-five years was too long to spend being ignored in bed.

But he didn't ignore her, he'd argued. Why did it have to be up to him all the time? She never lifted a finger to try and seduce him. She was out of her frocks and into her nightie so fast, he was beginning to think she wore it underneath her clothes.

Frank muttered under his breath. She was bullying him, just like she used to. And he was giving in to her demands, just like he used to. But what could he do about it? It wasn't worth the arguments, the silent treatment, the vanishing acts, or worst of all, the return to her favourite old vice. God, no. He was too old for all that. He laughed a hollow, bitter laugh as his late father's words came back to him: "Son, it happens to us all. One day you'll be making love, the next you'll be making vows, then you'll be making babies, and then you'll be making a run for it."

He thought of the crumbly little cottage and its charming, friendly neighbour Vasiliki. He imagined himself sitting on a rock on the beach, dangling a fishing rod above the water, or enjoying a Greek lesson over a coffee in Vasiliki's kitchen. Heaven, pure heaven. Just a signature away.

Frank followed the road as it turned the corner into Skala and breathed in the fresh sea and pine-scented air. He stopped at the supermarket to buy himself a newspaper and then headed into the open-fronted bar with the illuminated optics and large TV sets. As he ordered himself a pint at the bar, he felt a tap on the shoulder.

"Alright, Frank?" It was Caz, holding a couple of cocktails.

"Oh, hello, love. How are you?" he asked, trying to appear bright and breezy.

"Not bad. Yourself?"

"I'm fine – just came down here for a sneaky pint and a paper," he winked. "Bit early for cocktails isn't it?"

Caz nodded towards where Babs was slouching over a table, eyes fixed on the wall-mounted TV. "Madam over there had a sudden craving for a Tequila Sunrise. Mine's non-alcoholic. Fancy joining us?"

"Why not, indeed?" Frank followed Caz to their table and sat down.

"What's that then, Babs?" asked Frank, gesturing to the TV screen.

"A Britney Spears video," replied Babs, yawning.

"Oh dear, oh dear, been having too many late nights have we?" he teased.

Babs smiled sleepily. "I'm not used to all this freedom, Frank. Gotta make the best of it."

"I understand entirely," he said sincerely and took a sip of his pint.

"I can't keep up with her," joked Caz. "She can drink me under the table any day. I can only take so much booze these days. I used to get blind drunk when I was seventeen, eighteen, but now – well a couple of glasses of wine and I'm 'alf asleep. I think I've done pretty well this holiday, haven't I, Babs?"

Babs rolled her eyes. "So you keep saying. Anyone would think I'm an alcoholic the way she goes on," she grumbled. "I mean, I'm hardly waking up and pouring neat whisky down my throat first thing in the morning on a park bench covered in newspaper, am I?

"Of course not, love," Frank reassured her. "But alcoholics come in all shapes and sizes, you know. Once upon a time I went to an AA meeting with a friend who wanted to stop drinking, and I expected to see exactly the type of character you just described. Well, you know what – there wasn't a single tramp in the room. Instead there were smartly dressed men in suits and ties, fashionable young women with their designer shoes and handbags, there were people from all walks of life – young, old, male, female, black, white, rich, poor, upper class, working class. It was an eye-opener, I can tell you. Because had I passed any of those folk on the street, I never would've taken any of them for an alcoholic."

Babs propped herself up on her elbows, opened her lips and caught the straw of her cocktail between them, like a frog catching a fly. "Are you trying to tell me something, Frank?" she asked, releasing the straw from her mouth.

"Not at all, love," Frank chuckled. "I'm sure you've nowt to worry about, Babs. I'm just saying, you don't have to be a down'n'out to be an alcoholic. It's a common misconception."

Babs took another sip of her cocktail and then excused herself to go to the ladies'. As soon as she was out of earshot, Frank leaned towards Caz.

"I hope I haven't offended her," he whispered.

"To be honest, Frank, I think she needed to hear that. I'm worried about her, you know. She has been drinking a lot more than she used to, although that's strictly between you and me."

Frank winked. "My lips are sealed."

"So, this alcoholic mate of yours, is he alright now?" asked Caz.

"Well, he doesn't drink anymore, put it that way," Frank replied. "But just recently he's been back to his bossy old self."

Caz looked at him, intrigued.

"Alcoholics are skilled manipulators, you know," Frank mused, as his eyes drifted towards the TV screen.

Mia was glad she was properly dressed when she opened the door. Had she still been wrapped in a towel as she had been five minutes previously, she probably would have dropped it in shock.

"I called your father," said Gwen, standing nervously on the doorstep. "He told me where you were staying, and the caretaker told me which room you were in."

Mia looked over Gwen's shoulder at an anxious Dimitri who was standing a few feet away holding a pair of shears. She glanced at him and stood aside to let her mother in.

"I am just here if you need me," whispered Dimitri, retreating to a nearby flowerbed.

"Don't worry, I'll be fine," she whispered back and went inside.

"Nice apartment," said Gwen, looking around the room.

"Would you like a drink?" asked Mia.

"Just water, thanks," said Gwen, her mouth already sounding dry.

Mia poured her a glass of water and gestured to her to sit down.

"So, why are you here?" she asked, remaining standing.

"I wanted to apologise for what happened the other day. I felt terrible about it. Andonis was aggressive because he was scared that you wanted to cause trouble. He's also furious with me for not telling him about you." Gwen pushed her short hair back behind her ears, but it flopped forward again.

Mia resisted the urge to say something sarcastic. Oddly, she felt more in control of her emotions being on her own territory, as it were. It tipped the balance slightly. Her mother was coming *to her* to apologise – it made her feel stronger.

"Why didn't you tell him before?" Mia asked.

"He comes from a strict background, religious, morally upright. His parents would never have accepted me if they knew…and I wasn't sure if he would. Getting married and starting a family meant a lot to him right from the start. I fell in love and I needed the stability – it had been a long time since I'd had any in my life. I didn't tell him because I didn't want to risk losing him."

Mia nodded. It seemed like an honest answer – albeit for a dishonest action.

"Mia, your turning up out of the blue like that was an enormous shock to my system. Although I had always imagined you'd look me up one day, when year after year went by and you never did, I gradually came to the conclusion that you had decided you didn't want to."

Mia noticed a thin film of perspiration on Gwen's forehead. She didn't answer but waited for her to continue.

"After your sixteenth birthday, I was positive I'd get a call or a letter," said Gwen. "I suppose I was better prepared for you then."

"Why didn't *you* call *me*?" asked Mia, the anger that had been dormant for the last few days gradually reawakening.

Gwen looked at the ground and sighed. "I did try to call you a couple of times – once was on your twelfth birthday. Your father wouldn't let me speak to you. He said you were going through a difficult time at school and he didn't want you getting all upset…"

Mia thought back to her twelfth birthday. She couldn't remember the actual day, but she would never forget that year. She had been bullied at school by a girl in the year above, a girl whom she'd accidentally bumped into in the playground while playing with her friends. The bullying had lasted throughout the entire year until the older girl had discovered a new victim whom she had pushed down the school stairs. This resulted in a broken leg for the victim and – not a moment too soon – expulsion for the bully.

Had she been allowed to speak to Gwen on the phone, would it have brought her comfort and happiness? Or would it have made her feel more miserable than she already was? She didn't know. And although she could understand her father's reasons for not letting Gwen speak to her, she wondered why he'd never mentioned it. She'd always believed Gwen had never once tried to make contact.

"So you tried to call me on my twelfth birthday. When else?" asked Mia, determined not to be put off by this new information.

"I tried calling again the summer you took your O-levels. I left a message on your answering machine with my home number in Greece – I wasn't living with Andonis then. But no one called me back."

"You could have kept trying."

"Out of respect for your father, I didn't want to cause problems. And I wanted to speak to you with his blessing. When he never called me back, I realised I would probably never have his blessing, and that I should probably wait until you were older and more independent before I tried to get in touch with you."

"So I got older and you still didn't get in touch. Why?" asked Mia, folding her arms.

"One reason was because I got married to Andonis and he didn't know about you. The other was because after the age of sixteen, you were free to get in touch with me if you wanted to, and you didn't. So I let go."

"You could have written to me. I never received a single letter."

"I wrote so many," Gwen smiled sadly.

"So where are they? Lost in the post?"

"I never sent them." Gwen looked up at her, eyes glassy with restrained tears.

"Why not?"

"I wanted to. I got as far as putting stamps on them, but none of them ever made it into the postbox. I always stopped myself at the last minute. You were very young when I first started writing – four or five. You wouldn't have understood who they were from – that's if your father had given them to you, which I knew he wouldn't. I carried on writing to you until I married Andonis."

"You could have sent the letters to Gran and Granddad to pass on to me."

"My parents were ashamed of me, Mia – deeply ashamed. After I left, they were dumbfounded that I was of their flesh and blood. They could not believe the daughter they had brought up, loved and cared for, could abandon her own daughter and her entire family. They were horrified by my behaviour. When you were still little, they begged me to come back and be the mother I had chosen to be. They lectured me, sent me on guilt trips, made me feel like…like scum. They praised David for coping so well. They worshipped your dad. Still do, I'm sure. He was a hero in their eyes. Me? I was a spoilt, selfish bitch with no conscience. After I'd been gone a few years, they finally gave up trying to make me come back and said they wanted nothing more to do with me. I was no longer their daughter. I sent them a Christmas card every few years, just to let them know I was still alive. They never replied." Gwen finished her glass of water and looked at the pile of books on Mia's bedside table. "Wild Swans…don't know that one. Oh, Wuthering Heights – had to read that one at school. Cathy and Heathcliff – great stuff. Do you remember the Kate Bush song? You were probably too young."

"I remember it very well," said Mia, sitting down opposite her at the small table. "It was one of my favourites. Dad used to take the micky out of her strange dancing and make me laugh. He bought me her album for my birthday one year."

Gwen smiled. "I can just picture him," she said. "I bet he's been a brilliant father."

"He didn't have a choice," said Mia. "What are your kids' names, by the way?" she added scathingly.

Gwen stiffened and took a deep breath. "Mind if I have another glass of water?"

Mia gestured to help herself. "Katerina and Yorgos…or Katty and George as I sometimes call them," she mumbled as she filled the glass from the tap.

"How old are they?"

"George has just turned fifteen, Katty is thirteen."

"Do they know they have an older sister?"

"Not yet. Andonis and I plan to tell them soon. Andonis just needs a bit of time to get used to the idea himself first. He seems to be coming round though. This is a big thing for him to accept. For a few days I was worried I'd lost him."

Mia could feel jealousy and bitterness bubbling away inside her. She thought back to Mum's warning that negativity and anger could lead to cancer. Then another thought distracted her – did Gwen know about Mum?

"Did you know that Dad got married when I was seven?"

"Yes, Mum and Dad told me." Gwen seemed relieved to shift the focus from her children. "It was one of the last conversations I had with them. That was another reason I didn't make more attempts to contact you. You had a new mother – a wonderful one according to my parents. Your life was complete and you were stable, happy. I didn't want to stick my nose back in and start causing trouble-"

"That's bullshit!" Mia snapped more aggressively than she'd intended.

"I'm sorry, but how can you say 'my life was complete'? My life has never been complete because I have never known my real mother. Yes, Linda has been a brilliant mother and I wouldn't trade her for you in a million years, but don't tell me my life was 'complete'. That's just a convenient excuse for you to feel better about leaving me and forgetting me."

"Mia I have *never* forgotten you," Gwen looked at her beseechingly.

"Two phonecalls in thirty-one years and a heap of letters that you never sent – that you probably never even wrote, more like!"

"Mia I lost count of the number of letters I wrote–"

"Where are they then? Let's see them. Did you bring them with you?" Mia leaned her elbows on the table and looked at her expectantly.

Gwen sighed as if she knew she was fighting a losing battle. "I wanted to, but I couldn't find them."

"Of course you couldn't!" Mia laughed dryly.

"Mia on my life, I swear to you I kept all the letters I wrote to you in a box which I kept hidden in our attic. I went up there last night to look for them but I couldn't find them amongst all the junk. They must be up there somewhere, so I'll keep looking until I find them."

"Right," Mia nodded sarcastically. "Why don't you look for all the birthday and Christmas presents you never sent as well while you're at it. Perhaps they're hiding in a trunk somewhere, too?"

"Mia, nothing can excuse what I did–"

"That's true, but as you haven't even tried to give an excuse–"

"Exactly!" Gwen barked, leaping up from her seat. "I can't give you one because I haven't got one," she lowered her voice again. "You can sit here and call me all the names under the sun, Mia, because I deserve them. I cannot excuse what I did. But I've lived with the guilt and the self-hatred all my life and at times it's nearly killed me. I was wrong – what I did to you was unforgivable. But I've had to forgive myself or else I'd be six feet under by now." She turned her back to Mia and pushed her hair back behind her ears again. "I wasn't in love with David. He was a good man and I cared for him dearly. At first I thought it could work, I thought I felt all the right feelings, but the closer it got to giving birth, the more I realised I couldn't spend the rest of my life with him."

"You didn't have to."

"I also realised, too late in the day that I wasn't ready to be a mother. It was far too late to have an abortion. I suggested giving you up for adoption and David flipped his lid. So did my parents, just as I knew they would."

Mia froze, the hairs on her arms standing on end – a feeling of nausea welling in her stomach.

"I didn't want to give you up for adoption," Gwen said quickly. "Of course I didn't, but I was just trying to think of the right solution. Then after you were born, when I told David I didn't love him and that I couldn't be a mother, the only solution was for me to leave. At least I knew you were in the most loving hands there could ever be. I was an empty person then, Mia. When I was pregnant I would see small kids in the supermarket screaming their heads off and I just wanted to scream right back at them. I concluded that there wasn't a maternal bone in my body and that I was incapable of loving a child. I didn't even fall in love until I met Andonis when I was in my thirties. It was only then I discovered that I wasn't devoid of normal emotions and that I could be selfless enough to bring up a child after all. God blessed me with a second chance. And now that you're here, perhaps I'm being blessed with a second chance with you…?" Gwen looked at her, her eyes full of sorrow and hope.

The words 'abortion' and 'adoption' rang in Mia's ears. She stared numbly ahead of her, her eyes boring a hole through the cupboard under the sink.

"Mia?" Gwen sat back down at the table and put her hand on her arm. Mia stared at it. This was the first time her mother had made physical contact with her since she was a baby. A tear fell from her eye. "Do you think we could be friends?" asked Gwen softly.

Mia burst into tears and quickly hid her face in her hands. Thirty-one years of pain and anger gushed out in heavy, breathless sobs. Wiping tears from her own eyes, Gwen put her arm around her and held her as she cried.

When the tears stopped, Gwen stood up and went to the bathroom, returning with a hand full of tissues for them both. Mia took a wadge and blew her nose as Gwen sat back down again, this time hesitantly keeping her hands together on her lap.

"I don't know," Mia said finally. "I don't know if I want to be your friend."

"I don't blame you," said Gwen.

"I don't know how I feel. Part of me has always wanted to be your friend – ever since I was little. But part of me hates you with a passion, and I don't know if I can ever overcome that feeling."

Gwen weighed up her words in silence.

"It's probably best if I go now," she said eventually. "Give you some time to think and decide how you feel. But perhaps we could meet again in a few days…just to see whether you want to get to know me or not?"

Mia considered this.

"Katty and George are at school all week and on Wednesday morning Andonis is going away on business for a week, so you could come over for lunch any day from Wednesday onwards and we could spend the afternoon together."

"Maybe," said Mia. "I'll think about it."

"No pressure," said Gwen. "I'll understand completely if you choose not to come. So I'll leave it up to you to call me and let me know." She stood up, pulled her handbag over her shoulder and walked towards the door. "I'd like to get to know you Mia. Of course I know I can't expect you to feel the same way about me." She opened the door and then paused. "By the way, your father wanted you to call him after I'd gone. Probably wants to make sure you're alright." She smiled briefly and closed the door behind her.

Mia remained in her chair, her head throbbing with confused emotions. A wave of nausea overcame her and she scrambled quickly to the bathroom. As she retched over the toilet bowl, Gwen's words flooded back to her: *It was far too late to have an abortion. I suggested giving you up for adoption…*

How could you? thought Mia as she wiped her mouth only for the tears to start all over again. *How could you have wanted to get rid of me so desperately? I was just a baby – I wasn't even born yet.* As the nausea subsided, Mia leaned back against the wall. She recalled what Gwen had said about Gran and Grandad finding it hard to believe that Gwen was of their own flesh and blood. Suddenly her mind seemed a lot clearer. At least Gwen had helped her make up her mind about one thing.

As for 'doing lunch' and 'being friends'…the way she felt right now, if Gwen was the last human on Earth, nothing could be less appealing.

CHAPTER 18

The shadows from the folded parasols stretched like long, thin torpedoes across the paving beside the pool. In the distance a herd of goats jingled their way along the road on their way to a new pasture. Dimitri glanced at his watch as the sun began to descend above the hills. His heart fluttered at the thought of what he was about to do and automatically he reached for his cigarettes. He popped one in his mouth and folded down the last parasol before lighting it.

He stood and scanned the pool for any litter, forgotten cups or belongings. Margaret smiled at him from her verandah where she was sitting reading and smoking a cigarette. Shantee, wrapped in a towel, waved at him as she shut her French doors and drew the curtains. And there was Simon, sitting on his balcony, feet up on the railings, a bottle of beer in one hand, his mobile in the other. Dimitri nodded at him, but Simon either hadn't seen him or was pretending not to have noticed him – his eyes were fixed anxiously on Mia's closed French doors. He seemed, observed Dimitri, to be waiting for her to make an appearance on her verandah.

Just then, Simon's mobile rang, making him jump and leap to his feet. For a brief moment he froze, just looking at the phone and letting it ring. Finally he held it tentatively to one ear.

"Shelley," he announced shakily, before disappearing inside his room and closing the doors behind him.

Dimitri took a drag of his cigarette and shook his head pitifully. Had it been him, he would have let that phone keep on ringing, throw it over the cliff and head off to a nightclub with his mates. Anyway, at least that would keep Simon busy for the next five minutes while he went to ask Mia if she wanted to join him for the evening.

He flicked his cigarette over the cliff and made his way to the front of Mia's apartment.

"Hi," he said cheerfully as she opened the door.

"Hi." She looked slim and sexy in baggy black draw-string trousers and a white vest top. Dimitri drew a deep breath. "I thought maybe you need some cheering up, so I wondered if you wanted to come and see one of my special secret places in Kefalonia – somewhere really beautiful?"

Mia smiled.

"Is that a yes?" he asked.

"Yes it's a yes," she nodded. "Yes I do need cheering up and yes I would like to see one of your special secret places."

"OK, good. Take a jacket or something because it is cold at night sometimes."

He waited on the doorstep as she fetched more clothing.

"Does this mean we have to go on your moped again?" she asked, closing the door behind her and following him up the drive.

"Come on – you loved it!" he laughed, hopping on his bike and kicking it off its stand. "Admit it!" He patted the saddle. Mia laughed and climbed on behind him. He revved up the engine and turned his head towards her. "Mia, you don't need to worry, I would never do anything to hurt you," he said sincerely, hoping she understood what he was really trying to say.

Mia raised her eyebrows. "Glad to hear it. Now drive slowly or else!"

Dusk faded into night as they followed the coast road north. As they came towards Poros, Dimitri took a detour down some back roads to make sure they didn't cross paths with Karen the mad rep. On the other side of town they rejoined the coast road and continued north around several hills until eventually Dimitri pulled over and parked the bike. Mia hopped off and looked around her. There were no houses or signs of life. Just the sea on one side, a steep hill on the other.

"We are going up," he announced, nodding to the hill. "Come, I will take your hand. It is tricky to see where you are going in the dark."

Mia took his hand and tried to follow exactly in his footsteps. "Is it far?" she asked.

"No," he replied. "Pende lepta – five minutes. Can you count to ten in Greek?"

"No."

"OK, by the time we reach ten, we will be at the top. Ena – repeat, please."

"Ena," she repeated.

"Thio."

"Thio."

"Not hard 'th', soft 'th'. Like 'the', not like 'theatre' – like 'then' and 'this'. OK?

Mia tried again. "Thio."

"Nai! Polí kalá! OK, ena, thio, tria. Repeat please!"

"Ena, thio, tria."

"Tessera – mind your step, there is a rock just there."

"Tessera."

"Pende."

"Pende."

"Exi, eftá, octó, enyá, theka!" Dimitri laughed and hauled her up a steep gap in the rocks.

"Exi, eftá, octó, enyá, theka!" she repeated.

Dimitri stopped. "You already know it," he grinned suspiciously.

"Honest – I don't," she protested.

"Then you are a good learner."

"You're a good teacher. A natural, obviously. I can really see you in front of a class full of kids. You'd be great at it."

"You think so?"

"I know so."

He released her hand and scrambled over some more rocks, beckoning her to follow. As she joined him he took her hand again and led her along the hillside, through a forest.

"This is scary in here," said Mia, looking above her at the tops of the tall trees.

"We are lucky there's a full moon tonight," said Dimitri. "Otherwise, we would see nothing – not even our hands in front of our faces."

Mia shivered.

"You are cold?"

"No."

"Scared?"

"No."

He resisted the temptation to pull her to him there and then. That really would scare the shit out of her and then he would have blown it yet again.

"Nearly there," he assured her, and two seconds later they were out of the woods and on the crest of the hill.

"Turn around," he said, releasing her hand again.

"Wow," Mia beamed. All she could see was the sea, for miles and miles, stretched out before them into the distance, a rumpled indigo blanket with a moon-kissed silvery pathway to the edge of the earth. "It's stunning," she gasped, breathing in the fresh night air.

"Am I cheering you up?" he asked, feeling pleased with himself.

"Yes, thank you," she turned to him, giving him a friendly pat on the shoulder.

Now, maybe? he thought. No, too soon. "You are cheering me up too," he said instead.

"How's that?" she asked.

"I never believed I could be a teacher until I met you." He fumbled in his pocket for his packet of Camels, but fought off the urge to take one out. "Here, you can sit down." He sat down and spread his jacket on the grass next to him for her to sit on.

"So, what are you going to do about it?" she asked, sitting down next to him.

He shrugged. "Look to find training and get qualified."

"Really?"

"Yes, really. I am thirty-three Mia. For seventeen years I have pushed brooms, pulled pints, dug flowerbeds, pumped petrol, caught fish, played cards and smoked cigarettes. If I carry on living like this I will either die of boredom or lung cancer. It is time for my life to change – I'm serious."

"Do you think there's a training course here in Kefalonia?" she asked.

Dimitri pouted and gave in to the temptation to plant a cigarette between his lips. He tried to light it but couldn't get his lighter to spark. "The best one is in Athens. But even better would be to train in London," he smiled at her. "You said before they need teachers there?"

Mia nodded. "My Mum – that is my stepmum, Linda – used to teach in a primary school. Now she just gives private lessons to dyslexic kids. But she's always going on about how British schools are going to end up with no teachers left."

"Why?" asked Dimitri, shaking his lighter and still failing to get a spark out of it.

"They're fed up with low pay, too much bureaucracy being introduced to their daily workload, having to teach classes of over thirty kids. It's not an easy job, that much I know."

"Their wages can't be as low as mine," said Dimitri. "And a large class of kids doesn't worry me. As for easy jobs, I think I've done enough of those."

"Well I think you should go for it," said Mia.

"So, what happened with your mother?" he asked.

"She tried to befriend me, but…I don't know if she's someone I want to get to know."

"But if she's trying to make up for what she did…?"

"I don't know, Dimitri, it's just a gut feeling. I can't trust her. She tells lies. She said she'd written me loads of letters over the years but never sent them. So I asked her where they were and she said she couldn't find them. It's bullshit. There are no letters. And she kept trying to turn the tables on me – saying she'd expected me to turn up years ago, and as I hadn't, she'd believed I wasn't interested."

"Maybe this is fair enough to assume," Dimitri said softly.

"Maybe, but she could've got up off her arse to come and find *me*. That's what I can't understand – wasn't she at least curious to know about me, to see what I looked like?"

"I'm not disagreeing, but just because someone doesn't come to see you, doesn't mean they don't think about you – perhaps all the time."

"That may be so, but it's not good enough. Nowhere near. I've been thinking, you know – I've already got a mum who loves me, so why am I pursuing one who doesn't?"

They sat in silence as Dimitri considered what she'd said.

"I think she looks like you – a little bit," he said timidly.

"Do you think so?" Mia wasn't sure if that was good or bad.

"She's not as beautiful as you though." Dimitri could feel his heart beating. Damn his lighter – he desperately needed a cigarette. He was about to put his heart on the line, tell her how he felt. It was the scariest thing he'd ever done. Mia smiled shyly at the compliment.

"Sorry," said Dimitri. "I didn't mean to–"

Mia leaned towards him, plucked the unlit cigarette out of his mouth and kissed him. Dimitri enveloped her quickly in his arms and kissed her passionately back. At last he could touch her hair, her skin, the nape of her neck. For a few moments he lost himself completely in their embrace. Gently tracing her skin from her chin down to her collarbone, he lifted his lips away from hers to look into her eyes and make sure he wasn't imagining what was happening between them.

"How many girls have you brought up here then?" teased Mia, her arms wrapped around him.

"None," he replied solemnly. "You are the first."

Mia raised an eyebrow and grinned. "I don't care," she insisted. "Go on, you can tell me."

"I swear you are the first," he said. "I only take special people to my special places, and I haven't met anyone special for a long, long time."

Mia smiled. "That's very sweet."

Dimitri put his finger on her lips. "I want to tell you something. And I want you to believe me because it's the truth."

"OK," she whispered obediently against his finger.

This was it. He was taking a risk – just like Shantee said – and so far his chances were looking good.

"I'm falling in love with you."

She looked up at him, his finger still resting on her silent lips.

"I tried not to but I can't help it," he shrugged. "I don't fall in love since I was a teenager. Now here you are, and my heart won't listen to my head."

"Ssh," Mia insisted. She removed his finger from her lips and kissed him gently.

Nath tossed and turned in bed. He knew that Jo was wide awake as well, but there was no way he was going anywhere near her – not after what she'd told him. He turned angrily away from her onto his side, pulling the cover tightly with him. She pulled it back. He yanked it for all he was worth.

"Oh for fuck's sake Nath!" she snapped, sitting up in bed. She pulled the cover gently but firmly so that it rested evenly over both of them and slid back down beneath it again, turning onto her side so that they faced away from each other.

Nath scowled in the darkness. He couldn't believe she'd cheated on him

– with a woman! Snogging someone else was bad enough as it was, but snogging a woman? What would his friends say if they found out? He'd be a laughing stock – he'd never hear the end of it.

That Shantee – that sneaky conniving dykey slag. Boy was he going to give her an earful tomorrow. If she wanted to act like a bloke and steal his woman, perhaps he should treat her like a bloke and give her what for. He clenched his fist tightly beneath the sheets and wondered if they'd been laughing at him behind his back. What if they'd done more than just snog? What if they'd– ugh! He screwed up his face. He didn't want to think about it. No, she'd have told him if they had. He knew Jo well enough to know she couldn't keep something to herself when it was bugging her.

And what about all that business about "needing to explore that side of her"? What the fuck was that supposed to mean? Was she saying she was dumping him? Or was she saying she just needed to go and try it out, find out if it was all in her head, realise it was a big mistake and come back to him? She couldn't dump him. No way. They were the perfect couple. All his mates were dead jealous of him. She was gorgeous – a total babe. She looked like Naomi Campbell – in fact she was better looking than Naomi Campbell *and* she had bigger tits. She looked smart and she was smart. She had a degree, but she didn't brag about it. She owned her own beauty salon. *She owned it!* She was successful, she was going somewhere and he was damned if she wasn't going to take him with her. He'd never meet another woman like her. And the sex was mindblowing. She was up for anything. Most girls got uptight about trying some things, but not Jo. She couldn't dump him – not only would his mates take the mick out of him, they'd all be trying to get her into bed.

Nath felt all hot and sweaty. His heart was beating faster than if he'd just taken speed. He was crazy about her. She was *his*. She couldn't be bisexual – she was mad about him too, wasn't she? They'd been all over each other for the past six months, there was no way she could have gone off him just like that. How could she prefer Shantee to him? It didn't make sense. She'd always claimed to like broad-shouldered men. Men with meat on them. Men who knew what to do in bed. Shantee didn't quite fit that bill, somehow. OK, so Shantee wasn't a bad looking woman, but she was weird. She sat cross-legged for hours on end chanting like a fucking spaced-out hippy. She read weird books about how to fucking breathe for God's sake! Breathe in, breathe out. There! How fucking hard was it? Although hadn't Jo said she'd read that book? He rolled his eyes.

Nath let out a long sigh and tried not to let the image of them kissing sneak into his head. If she wanted to end it, then fine – but not because she fancied another bird. Oh no, he wasn't having that. As if that wasn't gutting enough to deal with, he wasn't going to allow himself to be put in a situation where his mates would give him grief for the rest of his life. He didn't want to become known as the bloke whose bird left him for a lezzer. He could imagine the jokes now. They would get porn films out and pretend they'd just watched his ex going down on another woman. He thought back to a film he'd watched on the adult channel at his mate's house with all the lads. Two birds – one Japanese, one white – one was a copper, the other a con. They'd given each other a good going over in a prison cell with handcuffs while a male officer watched through the peephole in the door. His mates had been cheering and jeering at the male officer to get in there and give them both a good seeing to.

Nath's eyes sprung open. He stared up at the ceiling as the idea gradually came into digital-sharp technicolour focus, and a grin slowly spread across his face. Sweet Mary mother of Jesus, he'd seen the light.

CHAPTER 19

Monday 10th

Craig rolled up his newspaper to swat a fly that had taken a liking to his left knee cap. He aimed and swatted, missing the fly and whacking his leg, leaving newspaper print smudged across his skin and suntan lotion smeared across the paper. He cursed under his breath as the fly returned to his knee and rubbed its forelegs together as if it was having a laugh.

This was without doubt the worst holiday he'd ever been on – and it was all Steve's fault. He watched Steve in the pool, chatting to one of those two fat mingers, Caz, in the shallow end. He was clueless that boy. He had no idea about street cred, no idea about what was cool and what wasn't, and couldn't tell his sex, drugs'n'clubbing resort from his pensioners' paradise if his life depended on it – which it would next time. Not that there would be a next time. This was definitely the last time they went on holiday together.

He gritted his teeth as Steve and Caz laughed at some no doubt pathetic joke in the pool. Where was the other one – Babs? He spotted her chubby legs lying on the bed beyond the French doors of their apartment. Bit of a boozer that one, looked like she was sleeping off a hangover. At the other end of the pool, he could see another loser – Simon the pie-man. He was always on his own – a right Nobby No-mates. Not surprising really, seeing as all he could talk about was his ex blowing him out at the altar. Craig smirked. Why would any bloke in his right mind go around telling everyone that he'd been dumped – on his wedding day to boot. Had he no shame? This place was full of losers. Yeah, well done, Steve. Kefalonia rocks.

He and Steve had been mates for years, and they'd probably be mates forever, but sharing a room with Steve was another matter. He left his half-finished bowl of cereal next to the bog, attracting the local ant colony into the bathroom. When he shaved he didn't wash out the sink. He walked around the apartment brushing his teeth – swallowed the toothpaste – and then left his smeggy toothbrush on his bedside table, or even the kitchen table. And worst of all, the dirty bastard farted in his sleep – loudly enough to wake Craig up, several times a night.

He hated to admit it, but he couldn't wait to go home. There was no totty on this bloody island – apart from Nurse Nice-Norks who had packed him off in an ambulance not in the slightest bit bothered that he might be about to cark it. It was a disaster. Neither he nor Steve had got their leg over once, they'd been burnt to a cinder, they'd been led up the garden path by two hairy-armpitted Krauts, he'd crashed his moped and nearly killed himself – in front of Nurse Nice-Norks and her macho meat-head brother – and now he had to pay two hundred quid for the damage done to the bike. A complete fucking disaster from start to finish – and they still had the best part of a week to go.

Steve did a handstand in the water and toppled over as Caz shrieked with laughter. Craig unrolled his newspaper and opened it at page three to study the mouthwatering assets of nineteen-year-old busty Beth from Humberside. Sensing a swelling in his groin, he turned the page quickly and thought of his Nan's false teeth. He was worried – he was losing control of his schlong. He tried not to think about how long it had been since he'd last had sex. He was getting desperate – and so was Steve if he was chatting up that middle-aged minger in the pool. They could get a cab back to that nightclub in Lassi tonight – sod the cost. He needed to pull, and he no longer cared who he pulled so long as it resulted in there being one less condom in his wallet.

Looking up from his newspaper he spotted Nikki the rep standing on the main road overlooking the complex. All of a sudden Nikki didn't look quite as podgy as he'd first thought. In fact she wasn't so much fat as top-heavy, which was a good thing. Nikki waved at him and he waved back. Result! He hadn't even had to try. She wasn't the best looking girl in the world, so it would probably be easy as pie – perfect. And he could overlook the ginga hair. These were hard times after all.

Nikki disappeared out of view behind the apartments and reappeared two minutes later by the pool. She walked straight over to him.

"How are you doing there, Craig?" she asked, perching on Steve's empty sunbed.

"A bit stiff – you know," he replied, laying his newspaper over his trunks and stretching his arms above his head.

"You poor thing, it's not been your lucky holiday has it?" she purred sympathetically.

"I'm not complaining," said Craig cheerfully, popping a cigarette in his mouth and lighting it stylishly with his Zippo lighter. "These things happen."

"Well that's the best way to look at it,' Nikki smiled.

"How are you anyway?" he asked, raising his Police sunglasses on top of his head and looking at her chest.

"Good," she replied merrily. "Actually I'm looking forward to going home. Another month and the season will be over. It's been fun, you know, but I'm starting to feel a bit homesick."

Homesick. Good, that meant she was in a vulnerable state and would welcome a strong pair of tattooed arms around her. "It'll fly by," he said. "You should make the most of it, go out and have fun. In fact, me and Steve are going out tonight in Lassi. Why don't you come along?" he smiled at her. Women usually couldn't resist his smile.

Nikki thought for a minute. "That's nice of you. Oh, why not?" she shrugged. "Sod it, I could do with a laugh. What time shall I meet you?"

"Come by here at eight," said Craig, fag in mouth, meagre biceps slightly flexed.

Nikki grinned excitedly. "OK, see you later then." She stood up. "Oh, I almost forgot, Maria the nurse is popping down to see you – oh look, here she is now!"

Craig sat up as Nurse Nice-Norks' shapely form appeared at the edge of the building, pausing to chat briefly to Dimitri before continuing towards him.

"I've got to dash – see you at eight," trilled Nikki and skipped off towards the drive.

Craig immediately regretted his hasty invitation as Triple N shimmied towards him, her long brunette mane shining like chocolate-coloured silk in the sun and – stone the crows – she was wearing a nurse's uniform. Craig bit his tongue. He noticed Steve trying to catch his eye in the pool, nodding excitedly towards the goddess in white.

"Yiasou Craig," she waved coquettishly as she weaved her way around the sunbeds and stooped below his parasol to sit where Nikki had just been sitting. Perhaps it was an illusion, Craig panicked – like a mirage in the desert. He'd gone without sex so long he was starting to imagine things – or perhaps he really was concussed after all. Ginga minger Nikki had mutated into sultry, sexy Nurse Nice-Norks and now he wasn't sure who he was talking to. He puffed out his chest and stubbed out his cigarette on the concrete beneath his sunbed.

Maria tutted. "Éla! There is an ashtray behind you, naughty boy!" she slapped his wrist playfully.

"So what brings you here?" he asked coolly, picking up his fag butt and leaning behind him to drop it in the ashtray.

"I come to see if you are OK, of course," she smiled, flashing her perfect straight white teeth.

"I could have been dead by now for all you knew," he pouted.

"Don't be silly! The doctors look after you, yes?"

"Yeah," he mumbled.

"And your brain is OK?" she giggled.

"I never had one in the first place," he joked.

"This I know from the way you are driving. You are lucky this time, yes?"

Craig blushed and tried to avoid looking at the gape between the buttons on her cleavage.

"Well, I must go now – I am working at the hospital in Argostoli today. I am glad you are OK." She stood up.

"Fancy coming to a club in Lassi tonight?" he blurted.

"Club?" She frowned. "No, I am working long shift so I cannot. But it's so sweet of you to ask me." She straightened out her dress and smiled mischievously. "But I want to ask you something, too."

Craig sat up straight, the world suddenly seeming a much brighter place – Kefalonia rapidly becoming the most brilliant holiday destination ever. "Go on," he grinned expectantly.

"I ask you to be careful and to stay out of trouble. You have *two* accidents already – maybe next time you are not so lucky." She arched a sceptical eyebrow.

"Yes I'll be careful," he nodded. "What else were you gonna ask me?"

"Nothing. Enjoy your holiday – I hope I don't see you again," she pointed at him as if giving a wayward child one final warning. "And keep out of the sun!" she giggled as she turned on her heel.

Craig stood up and opened his mouth to call after her but couldn't think what to say. As Maria turned the corner out of sight, Steve and Caz burst out laughing in the pool. Craig spun around, red faced. "What are you laughing at?" he barked.

"You thought all your Christmases had come at once!" Steve clutched his sides.

"Oh bless 'im," Caz crowed. "She's a lovely looking girl, ain't she?"

"Straight out of the Lynx advert," said Steve a little too loudly. "Only Craig wasn't wearing his Lynx, were you, Craig?" Steve and Caz howled with laughter, making Simon look up from his paper and Shantee open her eyes from her lotus position on her verandah.

Not knowing what to do with himself and not wanting to be a figure of fun for one second longer, Craig hurled himself into the pool in a foetal bomb, drenching Caz's fuzzy perm and filling Steve's mouth and ears with water.

The Hotel Flamingo's terrace restaurant was filling up fast with people sitting down to lunch. Frank stared at his egg and chips. It was unlike him to lose his appetite.

"Not hungry?" asked Margaret, lifting a forkful of salad to her glossy blood-red lips.

Frank shook his head. He could see Vasiliki's cottage from where he was sitting, and beyond it…his dream home.

"What's up with you?" Margaret prodded a morsel of chicken with her fork, stabbing the prongs into the cooked flesh and shovelling it towards her lips. A bracelet jangled on her wrist as she immediately swooped back down for the next bite. In front of her on the table sat her packet of Benson & Hedges and her gold handbag.

Frank took his sunglasses out of his pocket and put them on. If his eyes were concealed, perhaps she wouldn't be able to read his thoughts.

"I'm fine, love," he smiled wearily. "How's your Caesar salad?"

"So so. What do you fancy doing later?"

She had perked up since he'd promised to give the counselling a go, vowed to book the Como holiday as soon as they got home and started taking the Viagra. She was talking to him again, being pleasant – even being tactile. She had even cuddled him in bed last night, inviting him to make love. He had obliged and had been able to perform and satisfy her, although whether it was down to the Viagra or the fact that he'd been thinking about Carol Vorderman, he was uncertain. Still, Viagra and Carol Vorderman aside, she had enjoyed it much more than he had. What Margaret failed to understand was that there was only so much Viagra could do for a man who was being robbed of his manhood little by little by his controlling wife. He watched her spear another chunk of chicken onto her fork.

"Do you remember that old Greek myth about the fates men met when they died and went to the underworld?" he piped up suddenly.

Margaret looked at him and frowned. "What Greek myth?" she asked, crunching noisily on a slice of cucumber.

"Well, wasn't there some character – I dunno, Hercules or someone – who was sent to hell where two vultures sat pecking at his liver for the rest of eternity? And when they had finished every last scrap, his liver grew back and they started pecking it to pieces all over again. Do you know the one I mean?"

Margaret grimaced. "Really, Frank, not while I'm eating."

"It was a question on Millionaire just a few weeks ago, I'm sure of it." He scratched his head.

"Whatever made you think of that?" laughed Margaret, tearing a lettuce leaf in half and squishing it onto her fork.

"No matter," he sighed. "What do you fancy doing?"

Margaret was about to answer when her mobile phone rang from within her handbag.

"I didn't know you'd brought your mobile," said Frank, surprised. "What do you need it on holiday for?"

Margaret shrugged. "Just in case of emergencies," she said, ignoring it.

"Well aren't you going to answer it?" he asked. "It might be an emergency."

"No. I'll see who it is when they've left a message. If it's Gillian trying to work out some question in the Daily Mail crossword, then I shan't bother replying."

"Maybe you should – I quite fancy doing a crossword myself."

The mobile stopped ringing and Margaret fished it out of her bag, glanced at it and chucked it back in again.

"Well who was it?" asked Frank.

"Number withheld," she shrugged.

He frowned. "Did they leave a message?"

"No." She put her knife and fork neatly to one side and reached for her cigarettes.

"Well I wonder who that was?" he pondered out loud. "Perhaps it was one of the kids?"

"Oh do stop worrying, Frank. If it was one of the kids, their names would have come up. Could have been one of the plumbers I phoned for a quote the other week finally getting back to me – or it could have been a wrong number." She lit her cigarette.

"Odd," muttered Frank, waving her smoke away from his nostrils.

"It's not odd!" she sighed impatiently. "Anyway, why don't you look through this while I go to the little girls' room?" she pulled the guidebook out of her handbag and passed it to him as she got up from the table. "You might find your Greek myth in there."

Frank flicked aimlessly through the guidebook, not really paying attention to the chapter headings or the postcard-like photographs of churches and beaches. Looking over his shoulder to see if Margaret was out of sight, he reached for her handbag and took out her phone. He'd never had a mobile phone – he thought they were unnecessary intrusions in one's life – and he wasn't too sure how to use it. He pressed a few buttons and various words popped up on the little screen. Menu. Internet. Messages. He pressed the Select button and Messages gave way to a list of names. Aha – there was Gillian at the bottom he noticed, impressed. These things weren't so silly after all. At the top was DS, and again beneath it. Who was DS? And if it was at the top, wouldn't that mean it was the last person to call? DS, DS, Frank scratched his moustache. Not Deirdre Whatshername, surely? They hadn't been in touch for years. No, Deirdre's surname was Mills, anyway, he remembered. The only other DS Frank could think of was

Whathisname Shackleton, the husband of one of her 'cappuccino friends' as he liked to call them. The one who had a villa in Marbella. But what was his name? It definitely began with a D. Duncan, David or something. Damian, Dominic. Damn it, he couldn't remember. Anyway, why would he be calling her? Couldn't be him.

Without meaning to, he pressed the Select button again. A message sprang up – how about that! He'd have to get one of these things, they were right clever. He removed his shades to read the message more clearly – a lot of the words didn't make sense: "Drmt abt u last nite. Miss u. Call me. D xxx." Frank stiffened as he deciphered the words. Well one thing was for sure, it wasn't a number withheld. He got up slowly, reaching for Margaret's handbag. She'd been gone nearly ten minutes, he realised. He looked around and made his way towards the hotel reception area where the nearest toilets were. There in front of him was Margaret, talking on a pay phone, her back to him. He walked silently up behind her until he was close enough to hear what she was saying.

"Derek, I've got to go, he'll be wondering where I am! Don't call me again – you nearly landed me right in it for God's sake. I'll call you when I get back…Don't ask me to say it – I don't know how I feel right now…" Margaret threw an anxious look over her shoulder and caught sight of Frank standing behind her. Shocked, she spun around, holding the phone away from her ear. Slowly she replaced the receiver back on the hook, her speechless mouth open, her eyes fixed on the mobile phone in Frank's trembling hand.

CHAPTER 20

Jo opened her eyes to find Nath perched on the side of the bed, holding a cup of tea towards her. She blinked and propped herself up against the pillows.

"I made you a cuppa," he smiled, handing her the tea.

"Cheers," she mumbled, confused by his overnight personality transplant.

"I couldn't sleep last night," he said quietly, placing a hand on her leg beneath the cover.

"Me neither," she yawned.

"I don't want to lose you, Jo. You mean too much to me. I'm sorry I gave you a hard time last night. It took a lot of guts for you to tell me what you told me and I acted like a cock. I don't want us to split up."

Jo felt her eyes well up. "But it hasn't gone away, Nath. I can't pretend what happened with Shantee was a figment of my imagination or a mistake. I didn't want to pull away from her. I've unleashed all these feelings – not for her necessarily, but for that side of me. And as much as I don't want to split up with you, it wouldn't be fair to you if we stayed together."

"I understand that," said Nath quickly. "I understand what you said last night about exploring that side of you and…well, that's OK with me."

"What do you mean?"

He shrugged. "Look, I know I reacted badly when you told me, but I've been thinking about it and what kind of boyfriend would I be if I didn't show you some support? This must be really hard for you – you want to be with me, and yet you want to see what it's like to be with a woman – you're not sure what you want…it must be really confusing. You might experiment and then wish you hadn't–" Jo tried to interrupt but Nath continued regardless. "Or," he put his hand up to silence her, "Or you might experiment and realise you don't want to be with me anymore. Either way, I'm not prepared to give up on our relationship at half time. We need a final result."

A tear trickled down Jo's cheek. How come he was being so unbelievably sweet all of a sudden? It was as if he'd had some kind of epiphany during the night and transformed from an immature twat to the perfect boyfriend. Why couldn't he be like this more often?

"Are you sure, Nath? I mean, I can't promise you anything – I'm so confused. That's why I'm saying it would be fairer to split up, cos I don't want to hurt you."

"If you want to be fair to me, just keep me in the picture, that's all I ask. Don't sneak around behind my back. Be honest with me, involve me, trust me. Be my girlfriend – my girlfriend who I'm supporting in her experimentation with 'her other side'." Nath pierced her eyes with his. "You do still fancy me, don't you?" he asked.

"Yes, of course I do," she smiled. It was true, she did – especially when he was like this. She put the cup of tea down on the bedside table and pulled him towards her. "You're alright, you know that?" she whispered in his ear.

"I'm not bad, am I?" he grinned as she took his hand and put it on her breast.

Beneath her feet, Mia could see the wobbly shapes of pebbles on the seabed. The water was crystal clear – she had even seen a small crab scuttle beneath a rock. As she floated on her back, she thought back to last night's passionate embrace with Dimitri and felt an electric after-shock shudder through her body.

It had had a cleansing effect on her mind, sweeping all the negative emotions towards her mother and Max clean out of her head while allowing her to feel carefree again – if only for a short while. It was incredibly flattering to have the local heartthrob declare he was falling in love with her, and although he sounded like he meant it, he was obviously a passionate person who probably had a habit of giving voice to his emotions before he'd had time to think them through. He'd only known her a week after all – and you couldn't fall in love that quickly.

Besides, he was a caretaker in Kefalonia who, despite all his talk of training to become a teacher, didn't look like he was going anywhere in a hurry. She had a feeling that if she were to return to Skala next year, he'd still be here watering the flowerbeds and whitewashing the fences. Not that there was anything wrong with that – it was a perfectly respectable way to earn a living and one that actually seemed quite appealing to her, but it put their little liaison in perspective. He was a caretaker in Greece, she, a dentist in England. He was a carefree ladies' man, and she had no time for irresponsible men – especially not now. She'd enjoyed a holiday snog on the mountainside and it had been a gift from above in as far as getting closure over Max was concerned.

Mia swam back to the shore and hobbled over the shingle towards her towel. As the water evaporated on her skin beneath the warmth of the sun, her romantic romp with Dimitri won replay space in her head over yesterday's visit from Gwen, which she didn't want to think about anyway. For the first time in months she felt relaxed and almost happy. God knows she deserved it – after all, it was back to reality on Saturday.

Her father had said he'd pick her up from Gatwick and she knew he'd want to hear every detail of her encounters with Gwen. She'd told him a bit on the phone yesterday, but hadn't mentioned Gwen's claims of trying to call her on her twelfth birthday or after taking her exams. She didn't want to find herself in the middle of a 'he said, she said' dispute while standing in a payphone in a foreign country. She would question Dad when she got home. When she had asked him how it had felt talking to Gwen after all these years he had been strangely blasé about it. "Just like talking to an old acquaintance," he had said indifferently. "Strange to be talking to an old acquaintance who gave birth to my daughter and warning her not to do you any more damage than she'd done already, but other than that, nothing to write home about."

Mia wondered if more had been said between them than he was letting on, but again had decided not to press for information until she got home. In the meantime, after assuring him that they hadn't come to blows during Gwen's visit to her apartment, his advice to quit while she was ahead seemed worth following. The way Dad saw it, Gwen had faced her demons, acknowledged her daughter and wiped her conscience clean, a moment she had no doubt feared and dreaded for the last thirty years. Now that that moment had come and gone, Gwen could continue as she had done before – ignoring Mia. If Mia tried to pursue a relationship with her, she would only end up getting hurt again one day. So quit now – while apologies were fresh, explanations more or less accepted, and the cold war was at an end.

Perhaps the same should be applied to Dimitri too, she pondered. But as she pictured his face – his piercing green eyes, his olive skin, his soft lips on hers – she shivered all over with excitement. Could he really be in love with her?

"Can I have a word?" Nath asked Shantee as she heaved herself out of the pool, water dripping off her lightly-tanned limbs.

Shantee looked at him anxiously. "Is something the matter?" she asked.

"Not really," he said, trying to sound as warm and friendly as possible. "Well sort of," he cocked his head to one side and frowned. "I kind of need your advice."

"What about?" Shantee asked as she wrapped a towel around her waist.

"It's a personal matter," Nath lowered his voice so the other guests couldn't hear him. He looked up at the main road to make sure Jo was well on her way into town. Her figure was barely visible in the distance. He checked his watch – good – she'd be gone until at least four, which gave him plenty of time to put Stage Two of his masterplan into action.

"Shall we go to my apartment?" asked Shantee, looking both intrigued and slightly uncomfortable.

"Good idea," nodded Nath enthusiastically and followed her around the pool to the front of the complex.

Shantee unlocked the door to her apartment and went inside. Nath closed the door behind him and walked into the middle of her room.

"Your room's different to ours," he observed. "Your actual room is bigger, but your balcony bit is smaller."

"Right," said Shantee, uninterested. "So what was it you wanted to talk about?"

"OK, I'll get straight to the point," said Nath. "Jo told me what happened between you the other night."

Shantee froze.

"No, there's no need to worry – I'm not here to have a go at you. We've talked it through and I'm fine with it, honest. Well I wasn't at first obviously, but I've had time to think and it's cool."

Shantee eyed him suspiciously. "Well nothing really happened anyway," she said quietly. "I was wrong – I just got my wires crossed, that's all."

"No worries," he shrugged casually, "but you see, it was quite a big deal for Jo."

"How do you mean?" she asked.

"You, er, touched on some feelings she'd suppressed for a long time." He tried to recall how Jo had phrased it. "It's knocked her for six actually. She told me she's had crushes on women for a long time but she never paid them any attention – until now."

Shantee tightened her towel around her waist and sat down. She looked tense, thought Nath. It was important to get the words bang on – Shantee was no fool.

"Look I don't know what Jo's told you, but it was a simple mistake, OK?" she said defensively. "I have no desire to come between you and I haven't spoken to her since that night, so you don't need to see me as a threat, Nath."

"No, no, no, you've got it all wrong," said Nath, sitting down on the end of her bed. "I need your help – let me explain. Like I said, you touched on some feelings she'd tried to ignore, and now she can't ignore them anymore. She wants to explore her sexuality, she wants to find out how far her bisexual feelings go – how real they are."

"If that's the case, why are you telling me all this and not her?" Shantee narrowed her eyes.

"That's just it!" said Nath. "She's nervous, embarrassed…scared of hurting me. I told her she was free to do whatever she liked, and that I'd stand by her and give her all the support and understanding I could. She said she didn't want to go behind my back – that she wanted to keep me involved, but to be honest, I'm as lost as she is. How would I know where to start finding out if she's really bisexual or not?"

"And that's where I come in, is it?" frowned Shantee, relaxing her shoulders slightly.

"Well that's what I'm hoping."

"What do you want me to do exactly?"

Detecting a willingness to help in her voice, Nath went on. "Well I thought you could talk to her – talk to us both in fact."

Finally a mild smile appeared on Shantee's lips. "Of course," she said, softening.

Nath paused to search for the right words again. What had Dimitri said the other night? Flatter a woman and the ice will melt, or something along those lines. "I mean, you seem pretty good at understanding people's problems – Jo was saying not only do you teach yoga and meditation but you usually end up helping people sort their lives out too. You're clued up – you're *sorted*."

Shantee leaned back in her chair and unfolded her arms, her towel loosening slightly around her chest. "I usually light a few candles, put on some soft music, get everyone to sit in the lotus position and just open up about themselves – say whatever's on their mind. It's fascinating what comes out. Usually people solve their own problems without me having to say anything."

Nath tried to restrain himself from punching the air. His plan was coming together like a double bill of The A-Team. "That sounds brilliant," he exclaimed. "Although perhaps we could throw a few beers in with it – what with this being a slightly different situation – *and a holiday*," he chuckled nervously, hoping he hadn't pushed it too far.

Shantee closed her eyes with an ambiguous smile. Nath kicked himself silently. He shouldn't have mentioned the alcohol. She'd see through him for sure. *Stupid, stupid, stupid.*

He cleared his throat. "I mean, I think Jo and I will need to steady our nerves, know what I mean? I've never done something like this before and well, I'm a bit nervous to be honest."

Shantee looked at him. Nath swallowed. He could do with a beer right now. Was she going to go for it, or had he just blown it?

"Sure, no problem. Perhaps wine rather than beer though…"

Nath stood up and rubbed his hands together contentedly. "Wine, beer, candles – whatever – it sounds just the ticket. Thanks, Shantee – what time shall we come round?"

"Oh, not tonight, I forgot – I offered to give a one-off yoga class at the Hotel Flamingo and to have dinner afterwards with the women who want the lesson."

Nath's face fell.

"How about tomorrow night?" she asked.

He scratched his stubble. At least it gave him a little more time to work on Jo. "It's a date!" he said cheerfully as he saw himself to the door. "I really appreciate it, Shantee – I mean, *we* really appreciate it. We'll probably see you before then, but if not, see you tomorrow night – eight o'clock sound alright?"

"Eight's fine," she said as she closed the door behind him.

Nath walked merrily to his front door, pausing to kick a pebble up the driveway before letting himself into his apartment. Once inside, he leaped onto the bed and jumped up and down, biting his tongue to prevent himself from shouting at the top of his voice. He was going to have a threesome – just wait till he told the lads! He caught sight of himself bouncing up and down in the wardrobe mirror and stood stock still. "Who's the daddy?" he grinned at his reflection before flopping onto his back and reaching for the paper.

CHAPTER 21

"Steve you can't do this to me," Craig thumped on the bathroom door.

"It's not like I'm doing it on purpose," came the reply. "I reckon it was them kebabs."

"There must be something you can take to block you up," Craig leaned on the door despairingly.

"Yeah it's called Imodium. Go and get some for me, mate."

"The shop at the hotel will be closed now. We can find a chemists in Lassi."

"No way, mate. My arse ain't leaving this pan until I've taken Imodium."

"It'll take me ages to walk into Skala," whined Craig.

"Get a cab," groaned Steve.

"We can't afford all these cabs, Steve. I've gotta fork out two hundred snots for the bloody bike, haven't I?"

"Looks like you're on your own, then," said Steve. "Anyway, that's a bonus isn't it? I mean, if you wanna cop off with that Nikki, you'll be better off without me hanging around like a gooseberry."

Craig considered this for a moment. "Not really, mate, cos once I've had her, I don't want her hanging round. Know what I mean?"

Steve groaned again from within the bathroom. "Well go and ask around here, see if anyone's got anything for diarrhoea."

"No way, mate. There's no way I'm going knocking on doors asking for anus-corks. It was bad enough having everyone stare at our beetroot faces the other day, so I ain't making a tit out of myself again."

"Cheers, Craig. You're a real mate, you know that?"

A knock on the door prevented Craig from telling Steve that he was also a real mate for deserting him in his hour of need. He checked his appearance in the mirror and opened the door.

"Alright?" beamed Nikki excitedly.

Craig scanned her from head to toe. Her trousers were way too tight for her chunky thighs, her fat feet spilled out of her strappy heels, and her ginga hair was scraped back into a tight ponytail which exploded into a fountain of fluorescent fuzz. At least her melons were bigger than they'd seemed in her rep's uniform – although unfortunately, so was her stomach.

"'Scuse the smell," said Craig as he ushered Nikki inside.

"Poo!" Nikki wrinkled up her nose in disgust.

He nodded towards the bathroom. "Steve's got the splats. Don't suppose you've got anything he can take for it, have you?"

"You should have called and let me know," said Nikki disappointedly. "I've got a cabinet full of stuff back at my apartment. I could have brought it with me."

"That's bloody great that is!" yelled Steve from the bathroom. "Why didn't you think of that Craig?"

"Why didn't *you* think of it, knob-face? It's *your* arse that's leaking, not mine!" Craig retorted. "How far's your apartment, then?" he asked Nikki.

"It's half way back to Poros," she smiled apologetically.

"Oh just go without me," Steve sighed loudly. "I'd rather you left me to get on with it."

"Sorry, Steve," Nikki called towards the bathroom door. "I'll bring you some Imodium tomorrow, although I'm sure it'll have run its course by then." She giggled into her hand. "Shall we go?" she winked at Craig as he grabbed his wallet.

"Yeah, let's get a cab from Hotel Flamingo – later, Steve!" he said, slamming the door behind them.

"You poor things," laughed Nikki as they walked towards the Hotel Flamingo. "You really have had some rotten luck, haven't you?"

Craig tried to ignore the irritating clacking of her heels on the tarmac. "Well, something's gotta go right sooner or later, hasn't it?" he winked at her and lit a cigarette.

"Of course it will," she chirped. "Oh I am looking forward to a boogie – haven't been out dancing for weeks!" She clicked her fingers and shimmied her shoulders, sending her ample bosoms swinging from side to side. Craig's eyes widened at the sight of her bouncing chest. "So what do you do back at home, then?" she grinned, noticing the direction of his gaze.

"Postman."

"So I suppose you haven't sent any post cards then, cos you'd only have to deliver them yourself when you got home!" she cackled as they reached the hotel and waited outside the reception area for a cab to turn up.

Craig feigned a smile. "Something like that." His eyes flicked back to her chest again. "Nice top you've got on," he remarked.

"Oh cheers, although don't you think it's a bit tight?" she looked at him flirtatiously.

"It's just right," he smiled at her. "Very sexy."

Nikki giggled. "Maria said I should wear it. I was having a wardrobe crisis earlier and I phoned her up as I couldn't decide what to wear. She's good with clothes, you know."

Craig grunted. He tried to put the image of Maria in her nurse's uniform out of his mind.

"She said, 'Nikki, if you're going out with a sexy man, you have to wear a sexy top'," Nikki smiled at him slyly to watch for his reaction.

"She said I was sexy?" asked Craig, suddenly paying attention.

"Yeah, she said she was gutted I was off out clubbing with a cute guy tonight while she had to work. Poor girl," sighed Nikki. "Shame isn't it? If she hadn't been working and if Steve hadn't been ill we could've made a happy foursome." A cab pulled up in front of them and Nikki opened the back door. "Still, I think we'll have just as good a time on our own – don't you?" she winked at him suggestively and slid into the back seat.

As Craig reluctantly climbed in next to her, he imagined doing a runner – jumping into a separate cab and speeding off to find Maria at the hospital in Argostoli.

"Did she really say I was sexy?" he asked Nikki again as they pulled out of the Hotel Flamingo drive onto the main road.

"Yeah." Nikki slid her hand along his thigh and squeezed it. "And I totally agree with her."

Mia blotted her lipstick on some tissue paper and sprayed some perfume on her neck and shoulders. Despite the cynical running commentary in her head, her heart was fluttering as if she was a teenager going on a first date.

Having made the decision not to partake in any more canoodling with Dimitri – especially as he was claiming feelings for her which she couldn't say she shared – it had only taken a brief thirty-second appearance from him later that afternoon to change her mind. She had just returned from the beach when he had knocked on her door and told her quite simply, "Tonight, wear something nice, be ready at seven-thirty." In fact, he hadn't even hung around for an answer, so what was a girl supposed to do?

She had showered and blow-dried her hair straight and sleek, slipped into her short orange summer dress with matching strappy sandals, smoothed after-sun milk over her arms and legs, and was looking more fresh and glowing than she had seen herself in a long time. She never looked this good at home. It was the magic of a Greek island – the sun, the heat, the sea air and…a knock at the door interrupted her thoughts.

Smiling, Mia pulled the door open. "Oh," she gasped deflatedly. It was Simon. "Hello."

"Hi," he smiled nervously. "I was wondering if you fancied coming out for a drink?"

"Er…I've already got plans, I'm afraid," she tried to look disappointed. "Thanks though."

"Oh, right." Simon's lower lip twitched. "Well, perhaps tomorrow then?" He dug his hands into his trouser pockets. "That's if you still want to…I mean, you said you did, so unless you've changed your mind…if you have, then that's…well that's up to you…" He looked away awkwardly.

Mia felt a pang of guilt and pity. "No, I'm still happy to," she said as enthusiastically as she could. "Sorry about tonight." She patted his arm apologetically.

"Have a nice time, then," he smiled sadly. "See you tomorrow."

She closed the door and inhaled deeply. Then she opened it again quickly and called after him. "Hey Simon – Shantee said she was teaching a yoga class tonight over at the Hotel Flamingo – why don't you go along? The more the merrier, she said. It starts in about ten minutes."

Simon looked down at his feet. "I'm not really the sporty type."

"It's only yoga for beginners – not aerobics or boxercise or anything."

Hands still in his pockets, he kicked gently at a pebble and missed. "I'll see. Thanks for telling me," he mumbled and sloped off back towards his apartment.

Mia closed the door again and breathed a sigh of relief. The last thing she needed right now was to be saddled with some chronically depressed and needy man who wanted to make her feel guilty for not being available to listen to his problems all evening. *No guilt*, she warned herself sternly as she touched up her mascara in the mirror. Everyone's responsible for their own problems. She was responsible for hers, and Simon was responsible for his. She had come to Kefalonia to confront her birth mother, and, as bizarre a combination as it may seem to anyone else, she had also come for a holiday. She had not come to be an on-call agony aunt to a complete stranger who was completely oblivious to anyone else's needs. Tonight she was going to enjoy herself and put all thoughts of Gwen, Andonis and everyone else right out of her head. Life was too short.

There was another knock on the door. Mia threw the mascara back in her cosmetics bag, spruced up her hair and opened the door. Dimitri stood before her in a smart black dinner jacket, his green eyes sparkling in the fading sunlight. Her heart did a somersault – he looked like an illustration on the cover of a Mills & Boon novel. She suppressed a nervous giggle.

As his eyes trailed down to her feet and back up again, he wolf-whistled softly and mumbled something in Greek.

"Translation?" Mia asked coyly.

Dimitri took a deep breath. "You're the most beautiful woman I ever see."

"Wow, that's a compliment and a half," she laughed.

"And me? You like it?" he asked, twirling around in his suit.

"It's very smart – you look very handsome," she said politely, glad she'd remembered to pack her camera in her handbag. She could just picture her friends' faces when she showed them some souvenir photos of Dimitri.

"Éla," he said, proffering his arm. "Pamé sigá sigá?"

"Whatever," she smiled, clutching her bag and closing the door behind her. "Where are we going, anyway?"

"Surprise," he winked.

As they turned from the drive onto the main road, they heard a door slam loudly in the complex behind them. They stopped and looked around.

"Look," Dimitri pointed to Simon's apartment, where a flowerpot lay shattered on the doorstep. "Do you think he's trying to tell us something?" he asked.

212

Mia shrugged. "Come on," she tugged at his arm. "I want to find out what my surprise is."

Dimitri ushered her along the road to the steps that led down to the secluded cove.

"Stop," he instructed. "Close your eyes."

Mia did as she was told as Dimitri took a tie out of his pocket and tied it around her head so that she was blindfolded.

"OK, careful," he led her slowly down the steps.

Mia giggled, nervously feeling for each step with her feet. "Well this is exciting," she said. "I just hope I make it to the bottom in one piece."

"I am holding you," he said, squeezing her hand.

Mia grinned. He was so romantic, so chivalrous – why couldn't British men be more like this? At the bottom, he escorted her across the shingle to the water's edge where he stopped to untie her blindfold. As the tie fell away from her eyes, Mia blinked at the beautifully laid picnic blanket, the candle in a glass bowl, the freshly picked flowers, the bottle of wine and the silver domes covering plates of food.

"Oh how beautiful!" she gasped.

"If I am honest, it isn't my idea," said Dimitri. "I mean, it is *my* idea to do this for *you*, but I copy Frank. This is how he surprised his wife on their anniversary. He asked me to be his waiter. Tonight I'm afraid we have no waiter, but I can tell you the chef went to a lot of trouble." He gestured to her to sit down on the blanket, and flopped down beside her.

"Who is the chef?" she asked, recalling a conversation she'd overheard between Frank and Margaret about Dimitri's mother being an excellent cook.

"Me," smiled Dimitri, removing the silver domes to reveal grilled skewers of chicken, tomatoes and courgettes, freshly made tzatziki, homemade bread, a crisp Greek salad and honey and cinnamon baklavas. He poured her a glass of wine.

"To a brilliant chef," Mia clinked her glass against his.

"You haven't tasted it yet," he grinned. "But I think you will live. My mother taught me how to cook after my sisters left home. It's funny because they are terrible cooks – they are always burning things. My mother says they take after my father – and me, I take after my mother."

Mia nibbled on a chicken kebab. "It's delicious."

"Have you ever had a candle-lit meal on a beach before?" he asked.

"Never. I bet you've had a few though."

Dimitri frowned. "No, this is also my first. I don't usually go to this much trouble to impress a woman, but as I said last night, you are a very special woman."

"Thank you," Mia smiled. "I'm honoured."

"And also, it never occurred to me before to have a proper picnic on this beach with wine and candles. Can you believe it? I've lived here all my life and until Frank told me his plan the other day, I never would have thought to do this."

"And he asked you to be his waiter?"

"He paid me of course, and he paid my mother to do the cooking. She was happy to do it for nothing, but he insisted. He is a good man, Frank. My mother was nearly crying when she saw how he made a little private restaurant on the beach with the champagne and the candle. She said his wife is a very lucky woman, and she told me one day when I finally grow up and find someone special, to treat the woman I love in the same way." Dimitri stared intensely into her eyes.

Mia held his gaze before looking away. As a schoolgirl she had dreamt of moments like this – moments when some handsome man would fall at her feet on a scenic beach, declaring his undying love as the sun set on the horizon. Now here she was, and it didn't seem real. This wasn't love, this was a cliché. This was lust – or perhaps at best it was falling in love, but it wasn't real love. Real love was not falling out over mortgage repayments, bills, whose turn it was to clean the toilet or choose a video, or who had spilt tomato ketchup on the carpet and trodden it all over the living room. And yet Dimitri had something that none of her exes seemed to have had – passion. He was full of life, energy, warmth and light. He was like a raging bonfire compared to their puny two-bar heaters. She took another sip of wine and lightly dunked her kebab into the tzatziki. It was impossible not to be attracted to him. Not only was he gorgeous and romantic, but he was a good listener too. He had been an impromptu best friend, talking through her meetings with Gwen. She looked at him again. He was still staring right at her. If he carried on looking at her like that there was every chance she would crack and say something soppy she would later regret.

She swallowed a mouthful of chicken. "So where's your mother this evening?" she asked, trying to keep the conversation on a light-hearted track.

"She is helping at the Hotel Flamingo. One of their cooks is sick, so she is helping in the kitchen. She often cooks there when they need extra staff."

"Did she know you were doing this tonight?"

"I didn't tell her but she saw me taking the blanket down the steps and said something about wanting to thank Frank for being a good influence on me."

Mia laughed. "I wonder if Margaret was as impressed with her surprise dinner as I am with mine?"

Dimitri shrugged. "I don't think she is a happy woman – her smile is false."

Mia nodded. "She looked pretty miserable when I saw her this afternoon. I thought I could hear them arguing from my verandah – although I could only hear her voice, not his. Oh well, I suppose they're bound to have a few ups and downs – especially having been together for so long."

Dimitri topped up their glasses.

"So you've never wined and dined a young lady before? I find that hard to believe," teased Mia, leaning back on her elbows.

"It's the truth," insisted Dimitri dipping a hunk of bread into the tzatziki. "Why is it so hard to believe?"

"You must meet women all the time, having so many tourists invade your island every year."

"True, but they come and they go," he said casually.

"You must have had a relationship at some point," she said. "With a local girl – or a travel rep perhaps?"

"I haven't had a real relationship since I was a teenager."

Mia looked at him, shocked. "You mean you haven't had a girlfriend for over thirteen years?"

Dimitri counted on his fingers and nodded.

"So what have you been doing all this time?" she asked.

"Meaningless sex," he shrugged, pushing his hair back out of his eyes.

Mia put down her baklava, her appetite fading. Of course she'd known

215

he was a bit of a local stud, and it didn't take Colombo to work out he'd probably had a fair few tourists in his time, but to think he'd indulged in nothing but meaningless sex for nearly a decade and a half was somewhere between a sad and a worrying thought.

"Please don't look at me like that," he said, looking hurt. "I always have safe sex – I am not stupid. And I am not having sex every night with someone new. Sometimes I don't have sex for *three or four weeks!*" he said defensively.

Mia restrained herself from making a sarcastic remark. The longest she'd been without sex was eighteen months, but Dimitri didn't need to know that. Besides it was a while ago now.

"Sometimes I meet a girl and I think, 'maybe she is different, maybe I will fall in love with her', and then I get to know her better and I think, 'no way'," Dimitri shook his head knowingly.

"Give me an example," she demanded.

"A few years ago, I met this girl who was sweet and beautiful. She told me she was twenty-three, single, and worked as an actress in a big London theatre. We spent a few nights talking and dancing in the Bora Bora. After we slept together, she told me she was engaged to her boyfriend back in England but that she would break up with him to be with me. Then she told me she was actually eighteen and wasn't an actress but a receptionist. She was full of lies, so I told her it was best we didn't see each other again while she was here. She went crazy – screaming and crying. She followed me around every day until she left. When she returned to England I had a big celebration with my friends. Have you seen Fatal Attraction? We called her the rabbit killer."

Mia laughed and lay on her side, listening to him.

"It may be funny now, but I was scared! You know my friend Vasilis – the one who works in the bar in Skala – he had a worse experience. Six years ago he was seeing a travel rep from Scotland called Sandra. It was nothing serious and they were both seeing other people. Then he met his wife Yovana and started seeing her – not seriously at first – but soon he fell in love with her and finished it with Sandra. Sandra was angry and upset, so Vasilis said sorry but he wanted to marry Yovana. Then Sandra says she is pregnant. Vasilis doesn't know what to do because they didn't use condoms and he doesn't know if she's telling the truth. Also she was seeing other men so maybe he isn't the father. He didn't eat anything for weeks, he was so worried. At the end of the summer, Sandra went back to Scotland and after weeks of begging him to come to live with her, she wrote to him saying she had a miscarriage. After that, he never heard from her again."

"Wow..." said Mia. "And you're still dating British girls?"

Dimitri laughed. "Every orchard has a few bad apples. But you know, I don't think she ever was pregnant in the first place. I think she lied to trap Vasilis. But it only made him run the other way – of course if she was pregnant and it was his baby, he would want to know his child – Vasilis is a good man – but I think she was pretending to make him stay with her."

A light breeze blew Mia's hair in front of her eyes. The sun had set and the sky was turning dark. A mosquito nipped her ankle and she sat up to slap it. *How would Dimitri react if he knew*, she wondered. Suddenly the thought of him rejecting her felt quite painful. She didn't need any more rejections right now – God knows she'd had more than her fair share lately. She took a deep breath. This was a lovely moment, but it wasn't going to last. Handsome Greek men in dinner jackets on hot romantic beaches did not plod around Safeway on a rainy Saturday afternoon filling a trolley full of cornflakes and loo roll. She smiled to herself. It was sad in a way, because he was a wonderful guy. When she got back home, she'd look back on this moment and wonder why she wasted a precious second of it contemplating Egham on a rainy afternoon. No doubt the weather would be that bit colder and the days that bit shorter by the time she got back to the real world.

"Are you OK?" asked Dimitri, reaching over and pushing a lock of her hair back behind her ears.

"Fine," she said. "I was just thinking of home."

"You miss home?"

"Not really," she smiled. "I've got a lot of things to sort out when I get back which I'd rather not think about. Anyway, enough about that. Does Vasilis have children of his own now?"

"Not yet. They are trying, but every month when Yovana isn't pregnant, Vasilis is thanking God." Dimitri laughed. "We laugh because our mothers are upset we don't give them grandchildren yet."

Mia smiled. The handsome Greek man pushing a trolley was nowhere near as ludicrous as the handsome Greek man changing a nappy fantasy. "That's right," she nodded, recalling one of their first conversations. "You told her you don't intend to settle down and have kids until you're at least fifty."

"Well I'm not in a hurry to have children, but maybe fifty is leaving it a little too late," he joked nervously while offering her more wine. Mia shook her head.

"As you know I'm slightly behind with some things," he said. "I'm thirty-three and I've only just fallen in love for the second time in my life." He took her hand, stroked it and held it up to his lips. "I know you don't believe me when I say these things," he whispered. "But you'll soon see."

Mia knew she should tell him right there and then, but what was the point? She was going home on Saturday and she was unlikely to see him again anyway. He didn't seem to have even planned that far ahead. But then why would he? He was from Kefalonia, after all – the island where there was no reason to rush.

Dimitri pushed the empty plates to one side and edged himself closer to her on the blanket. "Do you feel something for me?" he asked, his eyes wide with hope.

Mia bit her tongue. She wanted to say yes, that despite her better judgment she felt something. Despite the fact that they came from opposite ends of Europe, had virtually nothing in common and almost certainly had no future beyond Saturday, all she knew was that she wanted to be with him – at least for a few more days.

Dimitri kissed her lightly on the lips. "Do you?" he repeated.

Mia thought. The answer was yes. She sighed. "Dimitri, I just can't answer—"

"It's OK," he said, a smile spreading across his face. "I know you feel something – I can see it in your eyes."

CHAPTER 22

Tuesday 11th

Frank didn't look at her as she stood aside to let him in. He had spent the night at the Hotel Flamingo in a single room overlooking a herd of goats on the hillside. He hadn't slept a wink and it showed on his face. His eyes were tired and bloodshot, his skin puffy, and he hadn't shaved. His head throbbed from the whiskies he'd knocked back in the hotel bar late last night. He hadn't even brushed his teeth because he'd left all his belongings in the apartment.

"Frank, let's sit down and talk about this," said Margaret, her voice shaking. "I need to tell you everything. I need to explain."

Ignoring her, he walked into the bathroom and swept his toothbrush, razor and shaving cream into his wash bag. He walked back past her onto the verandah where he yanked his beach towel and trunks off the back of the chair and threw them onto the bed next to his neatly folded pyjamas – untouched since yesterday. Frank turned to reach for his suitcase which was sandwiched beneath Margaret's on top of the wardrobe.

"Please, love. Don't shut me out like this," begged Margaret, tears spilling from her eyes.

Frank continued to ignore her, opened his suitcase and threw in his pyjamas, towel and trunks. She tried to touch him but he shrugged her off with a growl.

"Shut you out?" he hissed, struggling not to raise his voice. "How the bloody hell do you think *I* feel? You've done some low things in your time Margaret, but even after all you put me through in the past, I never thought you were capable of betraying me like this." He pushed past her and pulled open the wardrobe doors.

"Frank I know what I did was wrong, but you've got to listen to me – please just stop for five minutes and let me speak," she implored him as he grabbed a handful of shirts off their hangers and threw them in the suitcase. "Firstly, I ended the affair before we came away, and secondly, I only ever started it in the first place because you would never look at me. I might as well have been invisible for all the attention you paid me. It was pointless us sharing a room – let alone a bed – you just weren't interested. And I got tired of nagging you – it only had the opposite effect. I didn't know what else to do in the end. I couldn't talk to you, you just weren't listening to me. Derek and Georgina had split up and well, he and I bumped into each other once in Carlo's and–"

Frank spun around, his face like thunder. "Do you think I want to know all the sordid little details? Eh?" he raged.

"I'm not justifying what I did, Frank, but I did all I could to get your attention, and I got nowhere – I needed someone!" protested Margaret. "Our relationship was dying and you weren't doing anything to save it."

Frank slammed shut the lid on his suitcase and picked it up. "You know what, love? Our relationship died a long time ago when you were in the habit of drinking yourself into oblivion every night, shouting at me, hurling sharp objects at me, running into the back garden naked and screaming abuse at me so all the neighbours could hear. I'd say it died back then when you nearly set the house on fire after you fell asleep with a fag in your mouth, when you ran over next door's cat and then drove off leaving it there whimpering and bleeding, when you disappeared to your cousin Betty's for three days without telling me. I'd say it died then, Margaret, wouldn't you? I'd say it's never been the same since."

He tried to push past her but she blocked his way.

"Frank, I thought we'd got over all that. I made my amends to you – remember when I wrote down every terrible thing I'd done and read them all out to you and asked for your forgiveness? I was going to two meetings a day then – I was desperate to put everything right that I'd nearly destroyed. And you can't deny I didn't try to make it up to you with all my heart over these last few years – you just gave up on me. And then eight months ago I gave up on you. When Derek came along I thought, 'Well why not? I'm allowed to be happy aren't I?' I did my time with the sackcloth and ashes and there was nothing more I could do to revive your love for me. You were happy just to plod along pretending to have a relationship. Then you

220

suggested going away somewhere special for our fortieth anniversary, and I thought maybe – *just maybe* – we still stood a chance. I told Derek I was giving my marriage one last go to see if there was any love left between us – to see if we still had a future. And I was just starting to think that we did…"

Frank took a deep breath, his cheeks crimson with anger. "Well my pet, why don't you give your Derek a tinkle on that there mobile of yours and tell him it's all gone tits up and that you'll be moving in with him just as soon as you get back." He picked up his suitcase again, shoved her against the wall and opened the door.

As it slammed shut behind him Margaret sunk to the floor, mascara-stained tears streaming down her face. A few seconds later, her mobile started to ring from the bedside table. Wiping her nose on the back of her hand, she crawled towards it, switched it off and reached for her Benson & Hedges. Leaning against the bed, she lit a cigarette and inhaled deeply. After a few minutes, the cigarette helped her to calm down and stop crying. She heaved herself up and went to the fridge to get a bottle of water. There, next to it, were the last two cans of Frank's six-pack. Margaret closed her eyes and took a deep drag on her cigarette. Who was going to know?

Craig woke up with a start. His pillow was on the bedside table, his plastic bottle of water on the floor. He reached down to pick up the bottle and took a long refreshing swig of water. It was a miracle – he had no hangover. He smiled and then remembered the unfortunate ending to last night's events. He pulled the pillow back into place and lay back down. Had Maria really shown up at two o'clock in the morning or had he just dreamt it? Had she really snapped at him and called him a malaka or whatever it was that definitely didn't sound too complimentary? He rolled over and groaned.

"Craig I hope that's a cry of pain and not ecstasy," mumbled Steve from his bed.

"Eh?" grunted Craig.

"Cos if that Nikki's under your covers then can you at least wait until I'm in the shower before you start getting jiggy with it? And if you're on your own – well, you should use the bathroom for that kind of activity you dirty bastard."

"Shut up Steve," grumbled Craig.

Steve sat up and saw that Craig was in bed alone, his hands free of sin above the covers. "What's up with you then?" he asked. "Did you shag Nikki or what?"

"No I didn't!" Craig muttered into his pillow, turning to face him.

"Why not?"

"I cocked up, mate. She got upset cos I kept asking her about Nurse Nice-Norks – who apparently thinks I'm sexy. Anyway, she got well trashed and by two o'clock she was throwing up outside the club and whingeing that she wanted to go home. I thought if I don't make a move now it'll be too late, but it already was too late cos she threw up on my trainers – my brand new fucking trainers – and shouted at me to get a cab. She called me a prick so I called her a silly ginga cow. Then I look up and guess who was standing right in front of me?"

Steve's jaw dropped. "Not Nurse Nice-Norks?"

"The one and only," groaned Craig.

"Unlucky, mate," gasped Steve. "So what did she say?"

"She ordered me to call a cab for Nikki immediately, so I did. Then she put Nikki in the cab, told me I was a malaka laka maka laka maka, got in the cab with Nikki and drove off. Oy, do you think malaka is Greek for 'sexy bastard'?"

Steve roared with laughter and rolled from side to side, slapping the mattress. Craig stretched an arm towards his fags, retrieved one and stuck it in his mouth.

"Mate, let's face it, we're jinxed," said Steve as Craig lit up and blew a plume of smoke towards the ceiling. "We've had nothing but bad luck since we got here. I think we should give up and just concentrate on working out and building up our tans so that when we go home, the birds'll be queuing up at the door."

"I hate to admit it, mate," Craig stared up at the ceiling and sighed, "but I'm as randy as a monk in a knocking shop. I'm like a lion in mating season – I'm prowling in the jungle but there ain't nothing but fat hippos and geriatric gibbons around."

"I've seen a few lionesses," said Steve.

"Yeah, there's that stuck-up Mia next door who's all over Dimitri, that weirdo yoga hippy who looks like a lezzer, and that fit black bird who's got a fella."

"And Nurse Nice-Norks," added Steve.

"Who thinks I'm scum," wailed Craig. "Mate, if I don't get my leg over soon…" he trailed off. "I've got wild oats that need sowing for God's sake!"

"I know what you mean," Steve replied despondently. "My nads are like fucking space hoppers."

Mia waited at the top of the drive as Dimitri sprinted towards her.

"Kali mera beautiful woman!" he beamed, picking her up and spinning her around.

Mia laughed as he put her down. "Kali mera yourself."

"Pou pas?" he asked.

"To buy a paper – that is what you asked, isn't it?"

"Nai," he nodded, impressed, and gave her a kiss on the cheek. "Do you still like me?" he asked suddenly, frowning.

"Why do you ask?" said Mia, surprised by this rare display of self-doubt.

"I saw Frank early this morning. He was eating breakfast alone at Hotel Flamingo. I think he and Margaret are not such a happy couple."

"Ah," nodded Mia. "That would explain the kerfuffle I heard this morning as I was waking up."

"The what?"

As Mia tried to explain to him what a kerfuffle was, a car pulled up beside them and honked its horn.

"Yiasou, Dimitri!" a blonde girl in a travel rep's uniform leaned out of the window and smiled at him.

"Hi Karen," Dimitri nodded casually. "Ti kanis?"

"Kalá, and you?" she asked edgily, pushing her sunglasses on top of her head. "I haven't seen you since last week. I thought we were supposed to be getting together for a drink last night?"

"Oh shit – did I say last night? I completely forgot. Sorry," he shrugged.

Karen eyed Mia suspiciously. "Aren't you going to introduce us then?"

she asked dryly.

"Karen this is Mia, Mia, Karen," he smiled uneasily.

"Staying at Eleni?" Karen asked Mia.

Mia nodded.

"Nice apartments, aren't they?" said Karen. "When are you here till, then?"

"Saturday," Mia replied.

Karen squinted in the sun and lowered her sunglasses back onto her nose.

"Well Dimitri, that was fun the other night," she said coyly as she released the handbrake. "If you fancy doing it again – Saturday night, say – you know where to find me." She stepped on the accelerator and drove off.

Dimitri clasped Mia by the shoulders and stared into her eyes, panic-stricken. "Don't listen to her," he said firmly, gripping her tightly. "She is a mad, crazy woman. She is just jealous because she can see I am with you. I went out with her once before I met you and it was a big mistake. Say you believe me, please," he pleaded.

Mia tried to give him a reassuring smile, but inside she could feel her logic and reason stirring, trying to disentangle themselves from her heart after a long, happy, almost drug-induced sleep.

"Mia I promise you, you are the only woman I want to be with." He smiled and kissed her forehead.

She gave him a friendly squeeze on the arm. "We all have exes we'd rather forget," she shrugged. "Anyway, I'm off to get a paper. See you later alligator." She kissed him lightly on the cheek and walked off towards the Hotel Flamingo.

"In a while, crocodile!" he called after her.

As she walked along the sun-baked road, Mia considered Karen's flirtatious smirk and Nikki's comment the day she arrived about Dimitri and not trusting the local men. This was obviously the price you paid for going out with a Greek Adonis, she sighed to herself.

Frank sat down on a crumbling brick wall behind the cottage and looked out over the sea. A tiny lizard scuttled out from between his feet and darted beneath a nearby rock. This could be the patio, he found himself thinking. He would have a table and chairs right here on this spot. And perhaps a hammock hanging between those two trees for when the kids and grandchildren came to stay. Was he only hurting himself further by entertaining this dream? Could he really do it without Margaret by his side? And did he even want to be out here on his own?

Frank dabbed his forehead with his handkerchief. He hadn't meant to throw Margaret's years of alcoholism back in her face. It was in the past where it belonged – and she had, like she said, apologised to him profusely for everything and done her best to make it up to him. She had cleaned up her act, got sober and never touched a drop since. That was quite an achievement and he did sincerely admire her for it. He also respected her for apologising to everyone who had been on the receiving end of one of her vodka-induced tirades, from the kids to the nextdoor neighbours. She had nothing to apologise for anymore, it was true. And what she had said about him was also true. He had made no effort to keep their sex life alive for years. It wasn't so much that he'd lost interest in sex, but that he had lost interest in *her*. He just wasn't attracted to her anymore. Frank shrugged to himself. He couldn't help it. Perhaps it was the night she made her nude foray into the back garden that did it. She had driven home drunk from Gillian's house and he had given her an earful in the kitchen. The argument had escalated until he'd taken her bottle of vodka out of its latest hiding place, unscrewed it and poured it down the plughole. How that had led to her ripping her clothes off and running out into the garden naked and singing at the top of her lungs he couldn't quite remember, but the image of her chubby white body squatting in the middle of the lawn, peeing and belching simultaneously in the shaft of light cast by the next-door neighbours' bedroom window – at which they were standing watching aghast – had haunted him ever since.

There was no going back. And Carol Vorderman had more than paid her dues on many an occasion when he had succumbed to Margaret's unsubtle hints. Perhaps if she hadn't been so against soft pornography, he could have satisfied her more often – as well as himself. But Margaret wouldn't hear of such filth – a secret lover was obviously far more acceptable. He huffed noisily. It wasn't so much the sexual betrayal that bothered him, but the lies and deceit that went with it. She had deliberately lied to him – for eight months she had misled him, fobbed him off with fictitious accounts of shopping, cappuccinos and God knows what else with her friends. Who else knew? he suddenly wondered. No doubt, Gillian – she'd probably served as an alibi on countless occasions.

She had made him a laughing stock. She had ridiculed him. Why didn't she just tell him she was leaving him for someone else? It may have hurt but at least it was honest – unlike snooping around behind his back having a laugh at his expense. The reason she hadn't left him was because she needed him – or rather, she needed his bank account. She wasn't going to leave their four-bedroom house which she'd so lovingly decorated and furnished with their four-poster bed and whirlpool bath. She wasn't going to abandon the prospect of a holiday home in Italy. Frank stood up and angrily kicked a stone, making a cat dart out of the bushes and into the derelict ruin behind him. As he turned round to see if the cat was Vasiliki's, he found himself looking at Vasiliki herself, leaning against the open doorway of the cottage, her arms folded, her head cocked to one side.

"Yiasou," he said awkwardly, realising she must have seen him kicking the stone and mumbling to himself on the wall.

"Yiasou," she smiled.

He noticed she wasn't wearing her usual black, but a flowery shirt over a pair of jeans, and an apron wrapped around her waist. Her hair was loose, and hung over her shoulders. It was dark brown – dyed, he supposed – not the grey he had imagined it to be when it had been hidden beneath a headscarf. She looked years younger than the first time he'd seen her.

He gestured to her casual attire and smiled. "You look very nice."

"Efharistó polí," she said bashfully.

"I am crazy," he grinned, trying to explain his odd behaviour. "I am mad, bonkers, nutty, loopy, schizophrenic, crazy." He pointed to his brain and made himself go cross-eyed.

Vasiliki laughed. "Yes, you crazy!"

Frank looked at his feet. He was tempted to tell Vasiliki everything, just pour his heart out to her. She was kind, sympathetic and warm-hearted, and she wouldn't understand a word anyway.

"You're probably wondering why I'm sitting out here all alone huffing and puffing and feeling sorry for myself," he announced, putting his hands in his pockets.

Vasiliki gave a confused shrug.

"It's because I've found out my wife has been having an affair, our marriage is over, and I can't blame her for doing what she did because I stopped being in love with her a long time ago. I couldn't sleep with her anymore because I no longer found her attractive. It's not that she isn't attractive – it's a long story – she had a drink problem and peed naked in the garden and now I can't have sex with her without imagining myself with Carol Vorderman. Anyway, I'm digressing. The point is, it's forty bloody years down the pan – plus your jolly nice cooking the other day – and I'm not sure whether I feel devastated at all the wasted weeks and months of arguing and compromising, or euphoric because all I really want to do, all I *really, really* want to do, Vasiliki, is sit on this here wall and watch the sun set over the sea."

Vasiliki nodded and held her hand up to shade her eyes from the sun. Frank sighed and shook his head sorrowfully.

"One problem, Frank," she said calmly. "The sun, it not go down over the sea. It go down over the hills – behind you. Other direction."

Frank blinked at her. "You speak English," he gasped.

"I no speak so good – many years, no practice – but, I understand," she gesticulated, stepping down from the doorway.

"Oh crikey. Did you…er…did you under–"

"Frank, you want Greek omelette?" she plucked an egg out of her apron pocket, tossed it gently in the air and caught it. "I cook you omelette, you tell me everything…OK?"

Gobsmacked, Frank nodded. Vasiliki smiled and turned towards her house. Frank caught up with her and walked silently at her side, stunned by this revelation. In front of her cottage she pushed open the gate and ushered him into the front garden.

"This Carol Vorderman," she announced as she opened the front door. "She is good friend of yours?"

Frank chuckled. "Only if I eat too much cheese before bedtime."

Mia put down her book and shifted her chair back into the shade on her verandah. It was no use trying to read with those two talking at the tops of their voices. Emily Brontë was no match for Caz and Babs, so she might as well sit back and surrender to the unwanted poolside entertainment – a debate on whether TV did kids more harm than good – which by the volume of their voices suggested anyone could join in.

"Your kids are the only kids in the whole school who don't watch EastEnders," Babs scoffed, while reaching for her suntan lotion. She held the bottle upside down and squeezed it, which made a farting noise that sent the pair of them into a giggling heap.

Dimitri looked up from where he was hosing a flowerbed and laughed, glancing at Mia to see if she was listening, too. He caught her eye and smiled. She smiled awkwardly back. Caz and Babs weren't the only reason she'd read no more than three pages of Wuthering Heights in the last half hour. Karen's allusion to 'the other night' had started to bug her. Even if 'the other night' meant just three days ago, three days ago she and Dimitri had been no more than friends – acquaintances even – so it wasn't like it really mattered. And yet it was a bit too recent for comfort. And Karen would be here after she was gone…

"That's cos my kids are the only kids in the whole school who know how to amuse themselves without watching television," boasted Caz.

"They watch it when they come round our house," sneered Babs. "And they bloody love it."

"So?" shrugged Caz. "They also love their judo lessons and cooking in the kitchen with me."

"That's not what I heard."

"Oh? What have you heard?" demanded Caz.

"Your kids told me they both hate cooking and your Ricky says he doesn't like judo cos he always gets the shit kicked out of him."

"Yeah, well your Debbie told me she wants to be a glamour model after you let her stay up to watch some programme about popstars who go out with Page Three girls. And – I almost forgot – you better get saving your pennies, Babs my love, cos your daughter's been busy compiling a massive list for Father Christmas after she saw that documentary on rich kids and how they spend their pocket money."

Babs smirked. "Oh yeah? What's she got on this list then?"

"A Moschino jacket, Gucci sunglasses, Tommy Hilfiger jeans, a boob job, and she wants a massive birthday party at some trendy club in London where all the stars go."

Babs let out a loud shriek of laughter that echoed around the pool. "In her bleedin' dreams! Oy – Dimitri! D'you hear that? My daughter thinks I'm a millionaire. You don't wanna have kids, Dimitri – they'll rob you blind, believe me!"

"I know," he said gravely. "I see it happen to my cousin and his wife. All their money goes on their kids. They never spend anything on themselves. Me, I already have no money, so kids are out of the question!"

"You *have* got money," Nath piped up from his verandah. "You cleaned me out the other day. What about our re-match? I liked that version of Poker you taught me – Boo or whatever it was called."

"A re-match…" repeated Dimitri as Shantee opened her French doors and stepped out onto her terrace. "I don't know my friend – I think my blessing from Father Yorgos has been used up. I'm not winning so often anymore." He looked at Shantee who gave him a foreboding look.

"Suits me fine," grinned Nath, rubbing his hands together excitedly. "Come on, you owe me a chance to win back my money."

"OK," sighed Dimitri. "I finish doing this and I come to your terrace." He gathered up his hose and hung it over a nearby tap.

Mia watched as Nath cleared newspapers and plates from his verandah table and Jo appeared by the pool with a book and a towel. She smiled at Mia. "I know when I'm not wanted," she joked, spreading out her towel on a sunlounger and sitting down with her back to her boyfriend.

"Oy Dimitri," shouted Babs as he walked past her towards Nath's front door. "If you lose, you'll be playing me next. Remember our re-match an' all?"

Dimitri smiled. "In that case, Babs, you will definitely be next because I'm on a losing streak."

Babs grinned. "That's what I like to hear, my son! And we're playing Arsehole – none of that Poker nonsense."

Shantee settled on her verandah with a bottle of water and opened her book. As she looked up she caught Jo's eye. They smiled nervously at each other before looking away.

As Caz and Babs wittered on, Dimitri took a seat on Nath and Jo's balcony and started shuffling the cards.

Mia took out her sketchpad. She hadn't touched it all week. She focused on Dimitri and began to sketch a rough outline of his body, sitting at the table opposite Nath. She scrutinized the smooth curves of his biceps, the sturdy muscles in his thighs. Who was to say he wouldn't be visiting Karen again after she'd gone home? If not before? She scribbled over the drawing and turned her attention to a stretched-out Jo instead. But her eyes drifted back to him as he dealt out two cards each, paused, and pushed some notes across the table. She watched as he glanced over at Shantee and smiled confidently, before dealing out two more cards. Shantee did not return the smile, but seemed to have a troubled expression on her face.

"After you," Dimitri said to Nath.

"Eh?" Nath gasped as he eyed the pile of notes in the middle of the table. "Are you sure? I don't think I've even got that much on me."

"You won't need it. You will win," grinned Dimitri. "I told you, my luck has changed."

"How can you be so sure?" asked Nath.

"I don't win a single game of Poker or Boo this week," Dimitri sighed. "I don't win a single game of anything."

"So why are you gambling all that?" Nath nodded to the pile of money, frowning.

"Because I feel bad for you losing last time – when you wanted to hire the car."

Nath squinted at him, a cynical smile on his lips. "Hmm…do I trust you?" He scratched his head.

Dimitri shrugged. "Last time I warned you I was on a winning streak – did I lie to you?"

Nath unfolded his arms and picked up his cards. "Let's play," he said.

Checking to make sure Jo was looking the other way, he pulled his wallet out of his pocket and plucked out a hundred Euros to match Dimitri's.

Nath took a card from the top of the pile and flipped one back onto the table. He considered his options as Dimitri plucked one of his hand and dropped it on top. Nath studied his hand, slapped a mosquito on his arm and drew another card. Dimitri quickly played his turn and started humming to himself, his leg jogging beneath the table.

"Alright, alright, don't rush me," murmured Nath, deep in thought.

"Remember the rule about hooch cards?" asked Dimitri.

"Yes, yes. Sshh."

"And you remember what a skunk is?"

"You're putting me off," hissed Nath.

They continued in silence, Nath carefully considering each move, Dimitri seemingly considering his. Even Caz and Babs were quiet as they watched the two men play from the other side of the pool.

Suddenly a shriek pierced the air and Jo leaped up off her sunlounger, trembling. Everyone jumped.

"What's the matter?" asked Nath as he got up and leaned over the railings, followed quickly by Dimitri.

"There was a spider on me," gasped Jo, madly brushing herself down and shaking out her towel.

"Bloody hell!" snapped Nath. "You scared the living daylights out of me, woman!"

"And me!" called Babs, clutching a bottle of Evian. "I spilt water all down me boobs."

"Sorry," said Jo, spreading her towel out again and checking it anxiously before sitting back down.

Nath and Dimitri returned to their seats and picked up their respective hands.

Nath scratched his head. "I've lost my bleedin' concentration now," he moaned.

"Me too," said Dimitri, lighting a cigarette and jogging his leg under the table.

"Oy, what's that?" asked Nath, pointing to the ground by Dimitri's feet.

"What?" Dimitri looked down and saw three playing cards lying on the floor. "They must have fallen when I was shuffling," he shrugged and picked them up.

"I don't think so," said Nath snatching the cards from him. "A ten of spades, a nine of hearts and an eight of diamonds – all cards you thought you'd slip back into the deck when it was my turn to draw?"

Dimitri shrugged again and inhaled deeply on his cigarette. "I wasn't concentrating when I was shuffling," he said coolly. "I must have dropped them."

Jo turned round to see what all the fuss was about.

"They weren't there five minutes ago after you dealt out the cards," said Nath.

"How do you know?"

"Cos I bent down to tie up my shoelace," Nath's voice grew louder as he stood up, pushing his chair back abruptly. "I don't believe it!" He chucked his cards on the table.

"You are mistaken," laughed Dimitri, stubbing out his cigarette in the ashtray.

Mia leaned forward in her chair watching them anxiously.

"You bloody cheat!" shouted Nath.

"No my friend, I promise you," Dimitri stood up and in an effort to calm Nath down, took his arm. Nath shrugged him off aggressively.

"I should fucking thump you!" he boomed.

"Nath, calm down!" Jo intervened, standing up and coming towards them. "I'm sure it's just a misunderstanding, right?" she asked Dimitri.

"Yes, of course," said Dimitri. "I must have dropped them when I was dealing."

"You said you used to work as a croupier in a casino," said Nath. "Since when do croupiers drop cards while dealing?" Nath shook his head. "All that bullshit about Father Yorgos and his magical blessing. I don't believe it – I'm a right sucker. I thought it was funny the other night when you creamed every single game we played. I mean, the odds were that you had to lose at some point, but you never did."

Dimitri looked nervously to Shantee for help, but she stared coolly back at him, her arms folded, an unsympathetic look on her face. "I promise you Nath–" he began.

"You know, Nath's got a point," said Babs, standing up and strutting towards them. "We must have played eight or nine games and apart from the first, you won every single one." She eyeballed Dimitri angrily.

"How much did you lose?" Nath asked Babs.

"A hundred bleedin' Euros." She glared at Dimitri. "He thrashed Frank the other day an' all."

"You creamed a hundred and fifty off me the other night," snapped Nath. "And you were about to do it all over again you slimy bastard!" Nath prodded him in the chest and pushed him up against the French doors.

"Nath!" shouted Jo. "Just leave it. He's not worth it!"

"Actually," Dimitri faltered as Nath snarled at him, "I was trying to—"

"You know what, Dimitri, me old mate. I think that belongs to me." Nath took a step back and swiped the stash of Euros off the table. He folded the bundle in two and shoved it into his pocket.

"I want my money back an' all," said Babs. "A hundred exactly."

"And I bet Frank will too when he finds out you've had him like you've had the rest of us," Caz joined in.

Mia stood on her terrace, speechless at the scene that was taking place before her.

Dimitri raised his hands in surrender. "I will give you your money—"

"NOW!" demanded Babs, hands on hips, face pink with anger.

"Endaxi, ohi problema," nodded Dimitri. "I return to my home to get it."

"I'll go with you," said Nath, roughly taking his arm.

"It's alright, love," said Babs. "I'll make sure he pays up. Dimitri, you wait here while I put some clothes on and then we'll go for a little walk back to your place. You can give me my money and then that's that. End of story."

"End of story?" huffed Nath. "We should report him – I mean, God knows how many other people he's ripped off."

They glanced at each other thoughtfully as Dimitri eyed Mia's shocked expression, before looking dolefully down at his feet.

CHAPTER 23

"Bora Bora?" suggested Steve, pouring a can of lager into a glass.

Craig shook his head and crushed his empty fag packet beneath his fist.

"Hotel Flamingo?"

"Going there tomorrow night," said Craig, putting his feet up on the verandah railings and leaning back on his chair.

"Are we?" Steve asked, surprised. "We've already seen the Greek dancing though."

"Well there isn't anywhere else to bloody go."

"S'pose," Steve agreed. "How about we go for a big fat pizza in Skala?"

Craig shrugged. "Can't be arsed to walk back into town. We only got back an hour ago. To be honest mate, I just fancy staying in and getting twatted."

"Come on mate, I need to go out. I was ill last night – I missed out."

"You should've watched what you were eating. And thanks for forgetting to buy some more bog roll whilst we were out."

"*You* forgot as well."

"*You* used it all up."

"*I* was ill."

Craig rolled his eyes and looked at his watch. The sun was setting, the pool now in the shade. He could see Simon the Pie-man putting aftershave on inside his apartment. *Twat.*

"What time is it?" asked Steve.

"Time to slit my wrists," mumbled Craig.

"Dear oh dear," a woman's voice tutted from behind them.

They looked round. Two balconies away, Caz was towel-drying her hair and looking at them pitifully.

"Tell you what, lads. Seeing as you need cheering up and we've just got some money back that we thought we'd lost for good, why don't you come

234

over to ours for some drinks on us?"

"Thanks but–" began Craig.

"Cheers Caz, we're well up for that," interrupted Steve.

"Great! Give us half an hour to put me slap on and clean up a bit and then come on over. Toodlepips!" Caz hurried back inside their room.

"Whatcha do that for?" squeaked Craig, incredulous.

"Like we've got anything better to do," complained Steve. "Besides, the drinks are on them and all you're up for is getting twatted. Or you can slit your wrists, which was your only other suggestion."

Craig grunted. "Alright," he sighed reluctantly, heaving himself up from his chair.

"Where are you going?" asked Steve.

"For a shit," snapped Craig.

"There's no bog roll," Steve reminded him.

"Well you've got five minutes to find some before I break both your legs," he growled.

"How are you gonna do that while you're sitting on the bog?" laughed Steve as Craig slammed the bathroom door behind him.

As she sat on the terrace of the Hotel Flamingo bar, for once Mia was grateful for Simon's presence. She had no idea what to say to Dimitri after that afternoon's shocking revelation and thankfully, she hadn't seen him anyway. When Simon had knocked on her door, she had panicked thinking it was Dimitri. Adrenalin had surged around her body in a mixture of fear, anger and jealousy. Fear – because she knew she had to tell Dimitri that from now on they were no more than just friends; anger, because he was a thieving con-man who duped innocent people into parting with their hard-earned money; and jealousy because he obviously wasn't to be trusted, which meant that there was undoubtedly more than he was letting on about that bitchy travel rep. How she could have entertained the idea for one minute that he was serious about her, that it could be the start of something, was beyond her. At least she hadn't slept with him – thank God. Then she really would be kicking herself. Damn, she was stupid when it came to men. She fell for their promises and lies every single time.

Simon sat back down at the table with a pint of lager and a bottle of mineral water.

"So how come you're not drinking?" he asked.

"I don't like to drink every day," she shrugged.

"You're on holiday though," he said, taking his glasses off to polish the lenses.

"Is there a rule that says you have to drink every day on holiday?" she asked.

"No but it's a good excuse," he smiled faintly.

As Mia poured herself a glass of mineral water she caught a whiff of Simon's aftershave on the breeze. She glanced at him. He was freshly shaven, wearing a smart short-sleeved pink shirt tucked into his long, unflatteringly tight jeans. This did not bode well, she thought. Especially as he'd informed her that Shelley had finally called him to say it was officially over.

"So, er, I hear Dimitri got caught out cheating at cards," Simon said cautiously.

"It would certainly seem that way," said Mia.

"Told you, didn't I?" said Simon. "I knew there was something shifty about him. He's probably ripped off everyone who's ever stayed here."

"I don't think we should jump to too many conclusions," said Mia.

"They should definitely report him."

Mia watched as Simon took a thirsty swig of his pint, his teeth magnified in the bottom of the glass making him look like a horse.

"He could lose his job," she said softly.

"Serves him right," shrugged Simon. "How would you like it if it was your money he'd swindled?"

"Has anyone reported him?"

"Don't know. But they should, otherwise he'll only carry on doing it to the next lot that stay here."

Mia looked over his shoulder into the bar where Dimitri had entertained everyone with his dancing the week before. She tried to blot him out of her mind. She was going home on Saturday – there were more important things to worry about. Things that needed immediate attention. Dimitri could look after himself. He was obviously a resourceful enough person. And besides, if someone did report him, it was unlikely anything would come of it – her fellow holidaymakers would all be gone so they'd be none the wiser if he went unpunished, and in the meantime it was hardly worth the fuss of replacing him with only a month until the end of the season. He'd be alright...

Shantee pressed play on her portable CD player and topped up their glasses. So far, so good. There had been no awkward silences, no tension in the air, nothing. It was almost as if nothing had happened and they had simply erased and rewound back to a week ago.

She sat back down on her cushion. She had moved the chairs and table out of the way and scattered the floor with pillows and cushions – some of which she'd asked Jo and Nath to bring with them. It made the apartment feel a bit more like her bedroom at home – a nice, cosy den where you could lean back, stretch out and relax. Candles twinkled around the room and joss sticks burned in the ashtray. A breeze filtered through the open French doors from the balcony outside, the white muslin curtains giving them privacy from the other apartments.

"This is nice wine," she said, looking at the label on the bottle.

"Yeah well, after getting my money back off that slimy twat I thought I'd splash out," winked Nath, easing himself out of the lotus position and stretching out across the cushioned floor.

Jo took a large gulp of wine. "You were a real hero today, weren't you?" she grinned at him and stroked his leg.

"Well if you hadn't made us all jump when you screamed, he'd have got away with it," said Nath.

Shantee sighed. She felt sorry for Dimitri. She had thought about stepping in earlier and sticking up for him, but had decided it was best to stay out of it. Besides, this was karma taking its natural course, just as she had warned him. What on earth had he been thinking? He had sounded so keen to turn over a new leaf. Perhaps the effort involved was too much for him – some people never changed and wondered why their lives went round and round in circles, never getting to where they really wanted to be. It was so odd, though. They'd had a really in-depth conversation, and he had seemed so ashamed of himself – so eager to become a different person. She hadn't honestly expected him to go around handing everyone's money back, but to carry on cheating and stealing more money? She was well and truly baffled. Hopefully she would get a chance to talk to him tomorrow – that was if no one had reported him already.

"I'll tell Nikki tomorrow when I see her," said Nath, as if reading her thoughts.

"I'm sure he's learned his lesson," said Shantee. "I doubt he'd do it again. He's not a bad bloke really – I bet he really regrets what he's done."

"*I bet he does*," smirked Nath, "now that he's lost two hundred and fifty Euros in one day. And he still owes Frank. Anyway, enough about that tosser – what's this CD Shantee?"

"Morcheeba." Shantee passed him the CD cover.

"I love this album," said Jo. "You've heard it before, Nath. I've got it at home."

"Thought it sounded familiar. Yeah, I like it." He took a swig of wine and topped up their glasses again. "So, when did you realise you were…you know…?" he asked Shantee.

Shantee laughed. She looked at Jo who rolled her eyes.

"Nath, could you be any more subtle?" groaned Jo.

"Eh? Well I don't see the point in beating around the bush – if you'll pardon the pun!" he laughed. Jo and Shantee exchanged looks and then burst out laughing too.

"Fuzzy duck!" shouted Babs.

"No that's shit," protested Craig.

"Harry One-Spot?" suggested Caz.

They all groaned.

"Truth or Dare," said Steve.

"YES!" boomed Babs and Craig unanimously.

Babs picked up the bottle of Jack Daniels and topped up each of their glasses, glancing across at Frank and Margaret's verandah to make sure they weren't about to get told off for being noisy. Luckily there didn't seem to be anyone there.

"Blimey Babs, you ought to get yourself a job down our local," said Steve, his eyes bulging at the amount of neat whisky in his glass.

"I'll drink you under the table any day, my son," Babs boasted, taking a loud slurp from her glass.

Steve grimaced while Craig smiled in mutual awe and disgust.

"Truth or dare! Truth or dare! Who's going first?" Babs bounced excitedly in her chair, her boobs bouncing with her, mesmerising Craig whose vision was starting to blur.

"Steve first," said Caz, winking at him.

"Go on then," he groaned.

Caz bit her lip while she tried to think of a question.

"How old were you when you lost your cherry?" Babs butted in.

"Babs!" Caz scalded her.

"Well, that's what this game is all about!" said Babs defensively. "We're not asking him what he had for breakfast or what his favourite colour is, are we? What's the point of that? We want to know dirty stuff. So go on Steve – answer the question."

Steve blushed.

"And you can't lie, cos I know the answer," grinned Craig.

"I can choose a dare," argued Steve.

"Go on tell us," Caz nudged him. "I won't laugh at you, I promise."

"Fine. Seeing as I've made up for lost time it doesn't really matter," said Steve proudly. "I was twenty-one."

Craig cackled.

"See, I ain't laughing am I?" said Caz. "I think that's nice. I hope my lads hold on to their virginity that long an' all."

"What about you?" Babs pointed at Craig.

"Fifteen," he replied smugly.

"Tart!" Babs suppressed a belch.

"You can talk," Caz sneered at Babs. "You was only fourteen, you old scrubber."

"How about you, Caz?" asked Steve.

"A respectable eighteen," Caz said haughtily.

"In a not so respectable alleyway shag with the local butcher – who was married!" blurted Babs and guffawed with laughter.

Caz rolled her eyes.

"You're next Babs," said Steve. "Truth or dare?"

"Truth." Babs looked him boldly in the eye.

"How many men have you shagged?" asked Craig.

"Pass us the calculator, Caz," she quipped. "I dunno. Twenty?"

"I'm afraid we need an exact number or you'll have to do a dare," Steve grinned, revealing his wonky teeth.

"Twenty-five or twenty-six. Hmm…I haven't totted them up since before I married Trev."

"I reckon it's loads more than that," teased Caz.

"Your final answer please, Babs," demanded Steve.

"Shit. Dunno. Sorry."

Craig and Steve rubbed their hands together and grinned mischievously.

"Sorry Babs, looks like you'll have to do a dare," laughed Steve.

Babs rolled her eyes. "Come on then boys. Hit me with your best shot."

"Flash your boobs," said Craig, taking a mouthful of whisky.

"Craig!" Steve laughed. "We're not drunk enough for that yet."

Before Craig had had a chance to swallow, Babs lifted her pink vest-top up and twisted from side to side so that everyone got a good eyeful of her bra-less, large white breasts. Craig choked on his drink as she lowered her top.

Caz howled with laughter. "You'll have to do better than that if you want to make Babs blush," she said. "Although I should say that's where the two of us is different."

"You're next," Babs eyed Craig with an evil smile. "Truth or dare?"

"Dare," Craig stared at her coolly without blinking.

"Swim the length of the pool naked." She raised her eyebrows at him smugly.

Steve laughed. "Come on mate. Don't be a chicken – you can't let the side down."

"Shut up, Steve! I'm not a chicken." Craig picked up his glass of whisky and downed it in one, shook his head briskly like a dog and peeled off his football shirt.

Babs started singing the striptease song loudly.

"Sssh," said Caz. "We don't want the whole world to know or we'll get in trouble."

"Stop worrying woman – most of 'em are out anyways. And I saw Nath and his bird going into Shantee's room with an armful of booze, so we have carte blonde to do as we please."

Craig leaped over the railings in his boxer shorts and walked over to the deep end of the pool, proudly displaying the tattoo on his back.

"Get them boxers off!" hissed Babs.

"Come on mate!" cheered Steve.

Craig ripped off his boxer shorts and dived in with a whoop.

Caz and Babs cheered and clapped as they followed his pert white buttocks the length of the pool until he stopped in the shallow end gasping for breath, and smoothed his floppy wet highlights back into place.

"Chuck us a towel then," he panted.

Babs grabbed her towel from the laundry rack behind her and dangled it up in the air. "Come and get it," she sang.

Caz snatched it from her and threw it as far as she could towards him. Craig rolled his eyes as it fell into the pool. He reached towards it and wrapped it around him before climbing up the steps out of the water and punching the air victoriously.

"Steve fill my glass," he ordered. "That's sobered me up."

Standing in the flowerbed he hoisted himself over the railings, facing away from Caz and Babs so that they didn't get a close-up of his crown jewels. It wasn't until he stumbled back onto the verandah, steadying himself on the back of his chair to wails of laughter from Caz, Babs and Steve, that he realised the towel had got left behind on the railings and his jewels were fully exposed within tickling distance.

Mia looked at her watch. It was half-past eleven. Twice she'd dropped hints that she was getting tired but they had sailed over Simon's head without even grazing the tips of his hair.

When she had got up to go to the loo, she had seen an agitated Margaret hovering around in reception by the payphone. She had smiled but Margaret was so preoccupied that she hadn't even noticed her. Then, when Simon had gone inside to get himself another beer, she'd spotted Dimitri walking past on the road. In the distance she watched as he stopped to greet another figure. It looked like Frank. Frank patted him on the back and together they walked off in the direction of Dimitri's house. Mia wondered if Dimitri had paid Frank back – Frank would have probably found out what Dimitri had been up to by now, and yet they seemed to be on good terms.

"Saw Margaret back there a moment ago," said Simon, drumming the side of his glass. "She completely ignored me."

"I wouldn't take it personally – she ignored me too," said Mia.

"And Frank walked straight past me this morning without saying hello."

"I think they're having problems," said Mia.

"Even so, he could at least say hello. It was just plain rude."

"Simon, sometimes people are so overwhelmed by their own problems they act in ways they wouldn't normally act." She entwined a lock of hair around her finger and released it.

"Well I've had my fair share of problems lately and I don't ignore people."

Mia bit her tongue. If she didn't leave soon, she might not be able to keep up the level of politeness and patience she was struggling to maintain. He had done nothing but moan all evening. The only positive words that had come out of his mouth were in praise of the beer he was drinking.

"But how hard is it just to say hello?" he continued. "Takes a nanosecond of your time. It doesn't matter what your problems are, you shouldn't take them out on other people, should you? I mean, I've been jilted at the bloody altar, and I haven't given anyone a hard time, have I?"

"Simon, it's late and I'm really tired. I think I'm going to have to turn in now," said Mia, standing up abruptly.

"Oh," said Simon, startled. "Had too much to drink, have you?" he nodded sarcastically towards her empty glass of mineral water and took a large gulp of lager.

Mia breathed in deeply. Patience, patience. "Good night, Simon. See you tomorrow. Thanks for the drinks." She turned to go.

Simon snorted and muttered something under his breath. Thinking she had heard the word 'bitch', Mia froze. She turned to look at him, anger burning on the tip of her tongue, itching to be released.

As he stared at her half-brazenly, half-sheepishly, she realised his eyes were glazed. He was pissed. And he'd only had three and a half pints. She turned her back on him and walked off.

Shantee passed another bottle of wine to Nath to open. Despite feeling control of her mental faculties slipping away, she somehow knew what question was coming next.

"So you admit the best sex you ever had was with a bloke," said Nath as he clumsily filled their glasses, sloshing wine on the floor.

"The best *penetrative* sex," Shantee corrected him loudly. "And I should hope so too, seeing as men have a natural advantage in that area."

"Well most men, anyway," teased Jo, nudging Nath in the ribs and giggling.

"Watch it, you!" he grinned, tickling her. Jo squealed and pushed him off, knocking over an empty wine bottle and sending it spinning across the floor.

Shantee ignored the stray bottle as it rolled under her bed. "Behave, you two, or I'll make you do the crab posture for the next hour," she joked. "What about you Nath? Haven't you ever fancied a man?" she asked with a sly smile.

"Ugh! You must be joking! I'm as straight as a pole – I could never fancy a bloke, never, never, NEVER! The thought of shagging a bloke makes me wanna barf!" he grimaced, taking a large glug of wine.

"Hang on!" protested Jo. "You said you could happily shag Wayne Rooney the other day," she reminded him, prodding him in the chest.

"I was only joking," Nath prodded her back.

"What about David Beckham or Michael Owen? They're better looking," teased Shantee. "And supposing you were drunk?"

Nath shook his head. "Uh-uh."

"Supposing Michael Owen scored a hat-trick in the World Cup Final, leading England to victory," said Jo, draining half a glass of wine in one mouthful.

"Hmm," mused Nath. "Must admit he's getting sexier – but I still couldn't shag him."

"Suppose it was three-two to Argentina at half-time and Michael Owen came up to you and said 'Nath, if you sleep with me you'll help me get my mojo back and score two goals,'" Shantee grinned and playfully pinched his cheek. "I can see you're struggling," she laughed.

Nath downed his glass of wine and pointed to Shantee's half-full glass and gestured her to do the same. "If you want a confession out of me you're gonna have to drink a bit faster than that!" he ordered.

"Come on, Shantee!" cheered Jo. Shantee sat up straight, downed the glass in one while Nath quickly shared out the rest of the bottle before opening the next one.

"My head's swimming!" Shantee groaned and rolled onto her side. "Come on then, would you shag him if England's World Cup victory depended on it?"

Nath thought. "I still don't think..."

"I know! I know!" flapped Jo. "Not only does England's World Cup victory depend on it, but you also get a hundred thousand pounds as well."

"A million," blurted Nath.

"A million and you'd do it?" asked Shantee.

Nath nodded.

"How about a million without the World Cup win?" asked Jo.

Nath took a swig of wine out of the bottle. "Yeah, a million would do it."

Shantee and Jo pounced on him cheering and tickling him. "Let's all hear it for the million-dollar poofter!" cackled Shantee, clapping.

"You're crushing me!" he spluttered. "Ow! I've twisted my neck – be gentle!"

Jo kissed his neck. "Ah, baby...is it better if Madame Jo-Jo kisses it?

"Mmm," Nath mumbled with delight. "But I think I might need Madame Shantee to massage it as well," he slurred.

Shantee groaned and slipped her hands around his neck and gently went to work, pinching and rolling the flesh.

"Ooooh, that's gooood," he sighed. "Jo, I think she's got the edge on you when it comes to massage," he teased.

"Well I trained as a massage teacher before I got into yoga and meditation," said Shantee and hiccupped.

Jo pouted. "When it comes to massage, my area of expertise is *below the belt*," she purred into Nath's ear.

"Yes!" agreed Nath. "That is definitely true!"

Jo slid her hands along his torso and down towards his groin. Nath's eyes rolled to the backs of their sockets. "Easy now, girls," he grinned. "You really shouldn't be taking advantage of me like this…"

Jo clambered to her feet, giggling.

"Where are you going?" he asked, opening one eye.

"Need to pee," she winked. "Behave now." Jo stumbled towards the bathroom, banging the door shut behind her.

"Is that feeling better?" Shantee asked softly, rubbing his shoulders.

"I'm in heaven," groaned Nath. "Don't stop Madame Shantee – you're doing wonders for me – and for Jo." He lowered his voice. "I haven't seen her this happy in ages. I think she wants to take things further but I know what she's like – she won't suggest it cos she's too shy…"

Shantee frowned and hiccupped again. "Are you suggesting what I think you're suggesting, you naughty boy?" she slurred.

"Put it this way," whispered Nath. "I have an idea that will cure your hiccups and Jo's shyness at the same time." He leaned towards Shantee and planted his lips on hers.

Startled, Shantee froze. "What–"

"*It's what Jo wants,*" he urged gently. "She wants it to come from us so she doesn't feel bad."

At the sound of the loo flushing, Shantee relaxed in his embrace and kissed him back. Several seconds passed until she opened her eyes. She pulled away from him and looked around the apartment. The front door was open and Jo was nowhere to be seen.

CHAPTER 24

Mia swam in steady strokes towards the deep end. It was early. No one else was up yet and she had the entire pool area to herself. A small group of sparrows hopped about drinking water from the top step at the shallow end. It was wonderfully peaceful in the bright early morning light.

As she turned to swim back towards the other end, she saw Dimitri standing at the edge of the pool. He was wearing jeans and a T-shirt and stood, hands in pocket, eyes downcast.

As she waded up the steps and stooped to pick up her towel, he walked towards her.

"I'm not the bastard you think I am," he said quietly as she wrapped the towel around her and sat down on the edge of her sunlounger.

"I don't think you're a bastard," she replied softly, feeling slightly sorry for him.

"You don't?" he looked at her hopefully and sat down next to her.

She shook her head and smiled.

"Yesterday I saw you looking at me and I thought, 'That's it, finito – she doesn't want to know me anymore'. Is that how you feel?" he asked, noticing her slide subtly away from him on the sunlounger.

"Dimitri, I'm really flattered that you like me so much. You're a nice guy and I've really enjoyed your company – but we both know the score. I'm just here on holiday – I go home in a few days' time," she shrugged and looked at him, hoping he would accept what she was saying without making it any harder for either of them.

He nodded thoughtfully. "So that's it then?"

"We come from very different places in every respect. I'm going back to my life on Saturday and I've got plenty of crap to sort out. Sounds like you do too."

"I paid everyone back their money – I was going to anyway."

"So how come you were cheating?"

"To pay them back without them knowing. I was *reverse* cheating."

Mia looked at him baffled. "Which means that you cheated money out of them in the first place?"

"Yup," Dimitri sighed. "I was an arsehole. I was thinking only of myself. It was the only way I could save money – but I swear I was going to pay them back. I was turning over a new leaf. Now everyone hates me – they think I am a thief. Nath wants to tell Nikki, and if she tells my boss when he comes back from Athens, then…" He drew a line across his neck. "Nath and Jo, Caz and Babs – they will all be back in England, their money back in their pockets, and I will have to find another job which will be impossible because everyone here will know what I did."

Mia put her hand on his knee. "I'm sorry…I don't know what to say."

"It's my problem," he shrugged, standing up. "I'm just glad you don't hate me – that's all that matters."

"So he hasn't told Nikki yet then?" asked Mia.

"No, she had the day off yesterday. But tonight she will be at the Hotel Flamingo for Greek dancing night. So maybe you don't get to see my Zorba The Greek again before you go home." He forced a smile and turned to go.

"Dimitri, I'll be there tonight. I'll have a word with Nikki," she called after him.

"Thanks, but don't bother," he called as he walked away. "It's time I left this shit-hole anyway."

Craig rolled over onto his side and tried to swallow, but his mouth was bone-dry. He coughed, waking himself up. As his head started to pound and his bleary eyes opened, a slumbering round face just inches from his own gradually came into focus. Craig blinked. The smudged puffy face was snoring loudly, sending hot gusts of air – so high in alcohol content they were flammable – straight into his nostrils. He leaped out of bed with a yelp and tripped over an empty bottle of Jack Daniels. Babs opened her eyes with a start.

Craig grabbed a pillow and covered his privates. *Where the fuck were his clothes? Where the fuck was he? This wasn't his room. Where was Steve?*

Babs pulled the covers up to her nose. "Morning," she mumbled shyly with a little wave. "Any chance of a cuppa? I've got a blindin' hangover!"

Craig dropped the pillow, clapped his hand over his mouth and bolted into the bathroom, making it just in time to whip up the toilet seat and stick his head inside. As he threw up, his head spun, bringing flashes of last night's drinking games back to him. He remembered Babs flashing her tits. He remembered swimming naked. But did Steve really swallow a wet teabag? And had Babs really farted the theme tune to Jaws? And had he and Babs…had they…did they…? Craig threw up again.

"You alright?" called Babs from the bedroom.

Craig reached for the loo roll and dried his mouth. He stumbled back into the bedroom, covering his penis with his hand and searching frantically for his clothes. Babs pointed to the floor under the table. Craig seized his boxer shorts and pulled them on.

"Did we do it?" he hissed as he gathered up the rest of his clothes.

Silently, Babs cocked her head towards a used condom lying next to the bed on the floor.

Craig stared at it in horror. "Not a word to anyone – alright?" he barked menacingly.

Babs nodded, her eyes welling up as he picked up his trainers and ran out of the room, still half-naked, and slammed the door shut behind him.

"Nice one, Caz!" beamed Steve as Caz placed a plate of steaming hot bacon and eggs in front of him on the verandah.

"It don't matter where you are in the world as long as you've got a little bit of home with you," she smiled, stirring her tea. "Lucky they had all the right ingredients at that little shop in the Hotel Flamingo – I didn't even know it was there, did you?"

"No," said Steve, his mouth full. "Thanks, Caz. This is a real treat."

"You're welcome. That Nikki must have forgotten to mention that shop was in there. I'll tell her tonight at the Greek dancing. 'Ere, I wonder if Nath'll blow the whistle on Dimitri? Shame about him, ain't it? I mean, I thought he was a really nice bloke until we found out he was ripping us all off. Just goes to show, you can't trust nobody these days."

Steve nodded. "He even got me and Craig to buy him drinks all night at the Bora Bora – said he'd run out of money, remember?"

"We bought him some as well – mind you I was quite gone," Caz took a sip of tea.

"Which reminds me, how's your head this morning, Caz?"

"Not too bad, thanks for asking," she smiled. "I could never keep up with Babs. Drinks like a fish, that one. Last night was a case of if you can't beat her, join her. How's yours anyway?"

Steve was about to answer when Craig burst through the door, dumped his clothes on the floor and stormed over to them on the verandah.

"Morning!" grinned Caz. "What time d'you call this then?" she teased.

Craig scowled at her. "D'you mind?" he nodded towards the door, signalling for her to leave.

"Oy!" snapped Steve. "Where's your manners, Craig? Caz just cooked me breakfast. If you ask nicely, she might do some for you as well."

Craig turned towards Caz. "If you don't mind excusing us I'd like to get dressed," he said gruffly. "And your mate was looking well dicey."

Caz got up and rolled her eyes. "S'pose I'd better tend to the old alkie. See you later, Steve. Enjoy your breakfast."

Steve showed her to the door. "Sorry about him. He suffers from bad PMT."

Caz giggled. "So does Babs. Let's hope they're not herding, eh?"

Steve closed the door behind her and turned towards Craig who had collapsed on his bed in a heap.

"What's your problem you moody bastard?" he asked, sitting back down to his bacon and eggs.

"What happened last night?" croaked Craig, rubbing his bloodshot eyes.

"We all got twatted and played Truth or Dare," replied Steve matter-of-factly.

"So how come I woke up in *her* room?" Craig jerked a thumb in the direction of Babs' apartment.

"Cos you and her wanted to carry on drinking and trying to top each other's dares all night, while me and Caz just wanted to go to bed. But what with the racket you were making, we decided to come back here and let you get on with it. You were being well larey. That old bag in the apartment next to Caz and Babs even came out and told you to shut up – we could hear her from here."

Craig clutched his head and groaned. "Make us a coffee will you?"

Steve got up and flicked the switch on the kettle.

"So," said Craig. "What did you get up to when you came back here?"

"Nothing, you pervert."

"You just went to sleep?"

"Yes, that is correct. Why, what did you and Babs get up to?" Steve waggled his eyebrows.

"Don't be an anus all your life, Steve," snapped Craig.

"Oooh-hooo," grinned Steve. "Touched a nerve, have I?"

Craig fixed him with a threatening look. "Don't even go there, mate," he hissed.

"Well, if she's as nice as Caz, I can understand…sort of," Steve laughed. "Although I think she's a bit mad that one – got a bit of a drinking problem from what Caz tells me."

"SHUT UP, STEVE! SHE'S A FAT, UGLY SLAG AND NOTHING HAPPENED – ALRIGHT?" yelled Craig.

"Alright," said Steve, the smile fading from his face as Craig got up and marched into the bathroom, slamming the door behind him. "Reading you loud and clear, Sergeant Knob-head."

Margaret pulled out a chair and sat down opposite Frank in the Hotel Flamingo restaurant.

"Frank, we need to talk," she said calmly.

Frank stood up. Margaret watched in dismay as he turned away from her, only to turn back two seconds later with an extra cup and saucer.

"Coffee?" he asked.

"Please," she smiled, relieved. Frank poured from the pot on the table.

"Frank, I'm so sorry." Margaret searched his face as he ate his kebab and chips.

"So am I," he shrugged.

"No, Frank. I'm *really, really* sorry. There's no excuse for what I did. I hurt you and you didn't deserve it. I should have confronted you properly a long time ago and made sure we sorted our problems out maturely, but I didn't. I played games with you, dropping hints, expecting you to read my mind. I knew better than to behave that way. There's no justification for my going off and having an affair. I'm sorry."

Frank put down his knife and fork and looked at her. "You hurt me, Margaret," he said sadly. "I understand why you did it, and it wasn't entirely unjustified. I did ignore you. I didn't make an effort with you, and I'm sorry about that. I know I'm not entirely blameless. But *an affair*...you *betrayed* me – in the worst possible way. I can forgive you, but I can't forget. I don't think we can get over this one, Margaret. I think we've reached..." he paused, surprised by the lump in his throat.

"The end of the road?" Margaret finished his sentence and took his hand. "Oh Frank..."

Frank sniffed and tried to hold back the tears. "I'm sorry too, Margaret. But I want a divorce."

Margaret withdrew her hand as the tears formed in her own eyes. She fumbled around in her handbag for a hankie.

"Have we really come to that?" she warbled, dabbing her eyes.

"You know we have, love. I'll always care for you deep down in my heart, and I know you will for me, but there's nowhere left for us to go now. There's too much damage been done, and I'm too old to spend the rest of my days trying to sift through it and iron it all out. You are too, Margaret. We both deserve to be happy, and we can't make each other happy any more. We want different things – you know we do."

Margaret blew her nose and nodded tearfully.

"I don't want to buy a house in Lake Como that's going to cost the earth, set me back half my savings and give me a heart-attack before I've even set foot in it. I don't want to take pills to make my body do something that should come naturally and I don't want to go to see a counsellor to talk about our sex life. Perhaps a better husband would, but I'm not up to it." Frank took her hand and lifted her chin to look into her eyes. "Maybe you would be better off with this Derek chap..."

Margaret clasped his hand. "I don't want to leave you Frank."

"Why, Margaret? Because of the financial security? I'll see you fair in a settlement – I'm not a monster, I'm not going to leave the mother of my children penniless."

"It's not that, Frank – I don't want to leave you on your own. I'd worry about you."

Frank sighed. "I'll manage, love. I'm not completely helpless you know. I've got friends, I've got our wonderful kids and grandkids – and anyway, I like my own company."

"You could buy that cottage over there you're so in love with," Margaret laughed through her tears.

"The thought did cross my mind," he winked.

"I'm not saying I'm definitely getting back together with Derek, you know," Margaret dried her eyes again and folded up her hankie. "I think I could do with some time on my own as well...I...I nearly drank your lager the other night. And then I sat in the bar over there drinking lime and soda, hoping you'd show up, all the while resisting the temptation to buy myself a large vodka tonic. But the thought of having to start all over again and confess to everyone at meetings, well, it was just enough to stop me going ahead. But I haven't come that close in a long time."

"Well done, love. You've come such a long way. I haven't said it nearly as much as I should have, but I'm proud of you for staying off the booze," Frank smiled at her. "Look, you do whatever feels right. I won't begrudge you for setting up house with him. You know what I think, Margaret?"

"What?" she smiled sorrowfully.

"Life's too bloody short for all this nonsense," he said fervently. "We're in our sixties for God's sake – who knows how much time we've got left. Let's just shake hands and be happy. We can be apart and still be friends, can't we, pet? I mean, it's possible isn't it, Margaret? I'm not talking completely out of my derriere, am I?"

Margaret shook her head. "No, Frank. For once you're not."

As she laughed, Frank's fiery expression melted into a smile and then a grin, until he was laughing with her.

"Are you going to move back in with me for the last few days of our holiday, then?" she asked. "As my new friend?"

"If you'd like me to – it's up to you."

"Yes, I would like you to. I'd like to end this holiday on a happy, amicable note."

Frank smiled at her. "That makes two of us."

"Jo, wait!" Shantee caught up with her at the top of the steps that led down to the little beach.

"Just piss off, will you?" spat Jo, as she trounced down the steps. "I'm not interested."

"Yeah, but I am!" said Shantee, grabbing her by the arm. "I want to know what happened last night." Already the words were coming out all wrong, thought Shantee. She had rehearsed it in her head that morning, meditated, called upon the divine universe for guidance. If anything, she was more confused than Jo was – but she had to be careful not to alienate her further. Then again, whatever this misunderstanding was all about, she wasn't prepared to take the entire blame. She'd had no desire to kiss Nath whatsoever – he had manipulated her into it. It was a revolting experience and one she'd only endured because she'd been led to believe it was for Jo's benefit. And, OK, if she was honest with herself, because she had hoped it would lead to something with Jo.

Jo pulled her arm away angrily. "Don't try and play games with me you twisted bitch. If you want my boyfriend, you can have him. As of last night, he's free."

"You know I don't want him," said Shantee despairingly, following her down the steps. "I'm gay – why would I want Nath or any man?"

"Well seeing as you were happy to ram your tongue down his throat, perhaps it's you who should be answering that question?" Jo stopped and glared at her.

"It wasn't my idea," protested Shantee, noticing they were half-way down a steep climb to the beach and that if Jo were to shove her in her anger, it was a long, bumpy way down.

"So whose idea was it then?" snapped Jo.

"Well *yours*, according to Nath."

Jo laughed bitterly. "You're joking."

"Nath said you wanted to find out more about your sexuality, that you wanted to experiment, but that as he was supporting you, you didn't want to leave him out of the picture. So he suggested all three of us get together – supposedly for an open, honest chat and meditation session. But then he persuaded me that some wine might help you to not feel so nervous. It wasn't until we were all plastered and being silly that you went to the loo and Nath pounced on me saying it was what you wanted."

Jo put her hands on her hips and shook her head incredulously.

Sensing a molecule of doubt in her eyes, Shantee continued. "In my drunken state he led me to believe that by kissing him, I was paving the way for you and I to…well, whatever, without you feeling guilty that you'd gone behind his back."

Jo looked out over the sea as she took in her words slowly.

"You've got to believe me, Jo – none of it was my idea. I can't believe I went along with it! I had no idea it was going to end up such a mess. I genuinely believed we were going to have a good honest chat – I was even impressed when Nath suggested it – I thought to myself, 'Oh, so this is what she sees in him…'."

"Look, I just want to be by myself for a while," said Jo, starting back down the steps.

"I'm sorry, Jo," Shantee called after her. "I'm not the slightest bit interested in Nath, I promise you. But I'd still like us to be friends…"

Jo carried on down the steps without replying. Shantee sighed to herself. How had she allowed herself to be duped like that? When she next saw that little toe-rag she'd give him the biggest bollocking he ever had. If she hadn't been in such a rush to boot him out of her room last night she would have given him an earful then. She wondered where he had spent the night – not that she cared. He'd get what he deserved.

As she climbed back up the cliff to the main road, she saw Dimitri and waved half-heartedly. He waited for her to reach him at the top of the steps.

"I guess it was too late for me to escape my karma," he said, hauling her up the last step.

"Why did you do it?" she asked, letting go of his hand.

"It's not what you think," he said. "I was reverse cheating so that I could give them the money back without having to own up to it. I guess that wasn't good enough to avoid bad karma…"

"Well, you've paid everyone back now, so you're quits," she replied, patting him on the back. "It'll blow over."

"Maybe. Maybe not. Nath said he will tell Nikki at the Hotel Flamingo tonight. If she tells my boss when he comes back, big trouble. In fact, if she

254

tells anyone, big trouble. News spreads fast on this island. I play cards with the people of Skala too – I never cheat them, but they will think I have. They will never trust me again."

"I'll talk to her," offered Shantee.

"Mia said the same, but Nikki is weird," he smiled wryly. "We had some fun together one night and since I told her I don't want to do it again, I don't know if she likes me or hates me. But if she wants to make trouble, this is a good chance for her."

"I'm sure it won't come to that," Shantee looked at him hopefully. "I saw her going out with Craig the other night, so maybe she's over you. But what about Mia? You seem to have spent a lot of time together these last few days. What does she make of all this?"

"I told her I was in love with her, and I thought she felt the same – even though she didn't say it, I could feel it. But after what happened yesterday, I could tell by the look on her face, I fucked it up. This morning she told me we are just friends – this is her holiday, on Saturday she goes home."

"You're giving up a bit too easily, aren't you?" Shantee rubbed his shoulder comfortingly.

"What's the point, Shantee? She's right. It's always the same – they come for holiday, they enjoy my company, they go home again. A few days ago, I was dreaming of leaving and going back to England with her. Today, I have my heart broken. Everything you said come true. You are the oracle of England."

"I wouldn't go that far." Shantee blushed. "Look, it's not too late for things to change, Dimitri. It's not game over. We each make our own karma every day. Things can turn around."

"You don't understand," sighed Dimitri. "If my boss finds out – or worse, my mother, they will make me give back all the money in my savings account – the money I planned to use to go abroad with."

"But there's no point – all the other people you cheated are long gone. You wouldn't be able to track them down."

Dimitri shook his head impatiently. "The church in Skala needs a new roof. They will take the money to put it towards the cost."

"How do you know?"

"I've lived with my mother for thirty-three years. I know how she thinks."

Shantee sighed. "Don't worry," she patted him on the back. "We'll think of something."

"Yeah, I already thought of it – I could take the money and leave now." He looked at her sadly.

"No Dimitri. Don't do that. Things will be alright – trust me. You don't deserve that bad a karma."

"Yes I do – I've cheated people so many times I lose count."

She looked at him uneasily. Perhaps he was right.

Caz smiled to herself as she put the kettle on. Babs had been hogging the bathroom for ages, but that was fine by her. It gave her more time to ponder over last night and the laugh she'd had with Steve. He was such a sweet bloke, bless him. A real gent. Nothing like his moody mate when you got him on his own. They'd talked till three or four in the morning about all sorts of things – things she wouldn't have expected a lad of twenty-four to care about at all. He wanted kids, he wanted to work his way up to store manager at the branch of B&Q where he worked, and then maybe set up his own hardware company. He had his future all planned. He'd be a good catch for some lucky young thing one day when he was ready to settle down. He was quite a looker as well – no George Clooney, mind, but he could certainly give Wayne a run for his money. Funny, she could have sworn just as they were about to go to sleep he looked as if he was about to kiss her. Nah – must have been her imagination. He was only a young'un. Mind you, she wouldn't have said no. It had been a while.

Caz gave herself a light slap on the cheek. Mustn't think things like that. It was incestuous…or something like that anyway.

"What are you doing in there Babs? Hurry up will ya?" Caz glanced at her watch. It was half past one. Babs had been in there for almost an hour now, and she was being strangely quiet. She knocked on the bathroom door. No answer. "Babs? If you don't answer me I'm coming in."

Caz turned the handle and found it wasn't locked. She pushed the door open tentatively and gasped. Babs was lying on the floor, naked, curled up into a ball, wet streaks of mascara lining her cheeks and chin.

"Bloody hell gel, what are you doing?" Caz squatted down next to her.

"What's wrong?"

A high-pitched squeak came from between Babs's quivering lips and erupted into a loud guttural wail.

"Talk to me Babs," Caz pleaded softly. "What's the matter? What happened?"

Babs clenched her eyes closed and continued to wail – deep, loud, fast-paced sobs that left little time for her to catch her breath in between. Caz grabbed a towel from the shelf and wrapped it around her shoulders, while trying to steer her into a sitting position. Suddenly a terrible thought sprung into her mind.

"Oh my God, Babs. Did he hurt ya? Tell me!" She took Babs' chin in her hands and turned it urgently to face her.

Babs shook her head as mucus dripped from her nose onto her wrist.

"What happened then?" begged Caz. But Babs lowered her forehead onto her knees and ignored her. "I'm putting the kettle on and I'm making you a cup of tea." Caz got up and strode towards the kitchenette. As she waited for the kettle to boil a voice called from outside. Caz opened the French doors and poked her head out. It was Margaret, holding an empty beer can in each hand.

"I believe these belong to you," she said tersely. "I found them on our verandah."

Caz took the cans from her outstretched hands. "Sorry about that. It won't happen again."

"I sincerely hope not," said Margaret. "I barely slept last night for the noise your friend was making. I certainly won't be putting up with it again – and neither will Frank."

"I'm *really, really* sorry. We'll be as quiet as mice from now on," promised Caz.

"It would be appreciated – although I won't hold my breath. Still, she won't want another hangover like I expect she's suffering this morning."

"I hope not," mumbled Caz. "Actually I'm a bit worried about her. She's really not in a good way and I'm not sure what to do."

"Is she being sick?" asked Margaret.

"Not at the moment – but she won't stop crying. I don't know what's wrong with her."

"Has she hurt herself?"

"Not that I can see. She won't talk to me though. I think she's had enough of me – I've been lecturing her all holiday about drinking too much – not that she's an alcoholic or anything, but I think she's gone a bit mad lately," Caz lowered her voice.

"Would you like me to come and have a word?" asked Margaret.

"Er…well, you haven't really hit it off with each other, have ya?" Caz smiled nervously.

"No, but I might be able to understand what she's going through. I once had a friend with a bit of a drink problem."

"Oh yeah, Frank said…" said Caz, remembering their conversation in the chrome bar in Skala.

"Did he?" asked Margaret, looking alarmed.

"Yeah, said he didn't drink no more though."

"Yes, that's right." Margaret breathed a sigh of relief.

"Well, why don't you come on over, then?" Caz smiled at her and went inside to open the front door.

"I'd better warn her first," said Caz, as she let Margaret in. Pushing the bathroom door slowly, she slipped inside and crouched down at Babs's side. The wailing had stopped, but the vacant look in Babs's eyes troubled her. "Margaret's come to see you. Said she knows what you're going through," Caz whispered. "Shall I let her in?"

Babs stared straight ahead and shrugged.

"Fine." Caz got up and opened the door.

Margaret squeezed past her and pulled the lid down on the toilet so that she could sit down. "Don't worry, I haven't come to give you a hard time," she smiled anxiously at Babs. "I'm hoping I might be a good shoulder to cry on."

"How's that then?" sneered Babs. "I mean, what do you care? You don't know the first thing about me."

Margaret looked at Caz and lowered her eyes. "I know one thing about you, love – you're relying on a bottle to make you happy."

Babs wiped her nose unashamedly on her towel and laughed an empty, hollow laugh. "Who the fuck do you think you are?" she spat.

Margaret took a deep breath. "I'm an alcoholic – a recovering alcoholic."

Babs stared at her in silence. A nerve in her temple twitched. "Get her out of here Caz," she snarled. "Before I shove my fist in her gob."

CHAPTER 25

Looking younger than her years in a striped asymmetric top and faded jeans, Shantee shook her straight red hair over her shoulder and studied her reflection in the mirror. A rogue hair needed plucking from her eyebrow. She gripped it with her tweezers and pulled, while searching carefully for any more. Satisfied with her appearance, she reached for her wallet and keys and pulled open the front door.

"Oh you gave me a fright," said Jo, hopping back off the doorstep, startled. "I was just about to knock…"

Noticing a distinctly friendlier tone in Jo's voice, Shantee smiled. "Come in."

"Are you going to the Greek Dancing Night?" asked Jo, following her inside.

Shantee nodded.

"I was hoping you might be. I thought maybe we could go together?"

"What about Nath?" asked Shantee.

"What about him?" smirked Jo. "I thought about what you said and it all made sense. The complete turnaround in his attitude – it was like the bodysnatchers had invaded and taken him over. When Nath's got a point of view about something, there's no changing it. It's obvious now – he had an ulterior motive. He suddenly realised he could turn the situation to his advantage."

Shantee rolled her eyes. "Lesbian plus bisexual plus Nath equals threesome."

"Bingo," said Jo. "He never gave a toss about supporting me at all. It was his own sleazy needs he had in mind all the time."

Shantee shook her head in disbelief. "I can't believe I fell for it. I'm astounded by my own stupidity."

"You're not the only one," sighed Jo. "I've been going out with the little shit, for God's sake."

"Where is he now?" asked Shantee.

"Back in our apartment. I told him to keep his distance from me if he wanted to go home in one piece."

Shantee laughed. "So he won't be joining us tonight then?"

"I don't think so," Jo grinned. "He knows I'll blank him."

"What about Dimitri? Has Nath grassed on him yet?"

"Not that I'm aware of. I don't think it's worth it, personally – he got his comeuppance getting caught out like that. And he's paid everyone back now."

"Dimitri told me his intention was to cheat so that Nath would win," said Shantee.

"Why would he do that?" asked Jo, confused.

"It's a long story – I'll tell you later," said Shantee.

"Anyway, Nath's probably forgotten all about it after I locked him out last night."

"You locked him out?"

"Yup. I think he spent the night on a sunlounger at the Hotel Flamingo – another reason why he won't be so keen to show his face tonight."

Shantee burst out laughing. "Where will he stay tonight?"

"I've separated the beds in our apartment – moved them as far apart as they'll go."

"Well, there's a spare bed in here if you need it – for you, that is, not for Nath."

Jo smiled. "Thanks, Shantee. And I'm sorry about blaming you for last night. I should have known better."

"Shall we go then?" Shantee stuck her elbow out, nodding to Jo.

"Absolutely," grinned Jo, linking her arm with Shantee's. "I'm seriously up for some dancing."

Caz took a deep breath as she and Babs entered the Hotel Flamingo bar. She wished she had confronted Babs properly earlier but she didn't have the energy, let alone the nerve. Besides, Babs had barely spoken to her all day. She was in the dog house for inviting Margaret in to lecture her. But how was she supposed to have known that Margaret was an alkie? Who would have guessed?

She felt dead embarrassed after the way Babs had treated the poor woman. Margaret was only trying to help – and she was right too. Babs had a problem. It wasn't just a feeling any more, it was a fact. But as Babs couldn't see it, what could anyone do?

As they approached the smiling barman, Caz braced herself.

"Ladies!" grinned the barman. "What can I get you?"

"Coca-cola please," said Caz.

"Bottle of Sol, cheers mate," said Babs, climbing on a stool and thrusting her cavernous cleavage towards the barman. She hummed along to the music tonelessly.

Caz pulled up her smart black trousers and perched on the stool next to her. "Bit more crowded than last week, ain't it?" she said to Babs.

"Yeah," said Babs absently, taking her beer from the barman and putting it to her lips. Caz winced. How she could stomach it after the amount she'd drunk the night before, she couldn't comprehend. She was looking rough too – how she couldn't see the dark circles under her eyes was a mystery. Maybe she needed glasses.

"Look what the cat dragged in," said Babs loudly, as Margaret walked in on Frank's arm, looking preened to perfection in a frilly yellow blouse with floaty white trousers and her gold slingbacks.

"Leave it out, will you?" sighed Caz. "I think she got the message what you think of her earlier. Please don't cause a scene. This is *my* holiday too, you know."

Babs took another swig of her beer. "Alright, don't wet yourself. Just so long as she keeps her ugly mug away from me."

Caz smiled as Frank walked boldly up to them. "Evening, ladies. My wife would like to send her apologies for this morning's misunderstanding. She admits she was wrong and hopes it can be forgotten."

"Nice of her to come and say it herself," muttered Babs into the neck of her bottle.

"To be honest, she felt it was best if she gave you some space, for fear of upsetting you again. However, I hope you'll allow me to buy you both a drink – a nice bubbly holiday drink?" he said warmly.

Babs narrowed her eyes.

"Thank you Frank," said Caz. "That's very kind of you. Perhaps we can take you up on that later, as we're both alright for the minute."

"Of course," said Frank. "Don't let me forget now."

"Cheers," mumbled Babs as he turned to give the barman his order. "'Ere, look," she nudged Caz and pointed to the other side of the room. "It's Nikki the rep."

Caz rolled her eyes. "I ain't having nothing to do with this."

"You've changed your tune."

"Yes I have. I've had enough argie-bargies for one day thank you. Anyway, he paid you back and said sorry, and I think he really meant it. Poor bloke. Can't be fun doing that job in this heat, you know. I bet he don't earn much an' all."

"Give over," groaned Babs. "It's the easy life. He doesn't know how lucky he is."

"The grass is always greener, Babs."

"Caz is right, you know," said Frank, turning back to them. "He earns next to nothing. And I've seen inside his house – there's no flashy wide-screen TV or surround-sound hi-fi. There's no three-seater leather sofa or fancy furniture. A lot of these locals out here, they live simple lives, love. The lad knows he's done wrong – everyone deserves a second chance, don't they?"

"Hmm," Babs pursed her lips. "Seems I'm giving out lots of second chances today."

"Well," said Frank. "That'll set you in good stead one day when the boot's on the other foot." He winked and walked back to Margaret trying not to spill two large orange juices.

"What did he mean by that?" snapped Babs, polishing off her beer.

"Let he who is without sin cast the first stone," said Caz profoundly, prodding the ice in her Coke with a straw.

"Blimey girl. You haven't gone all religious on me, 'ave you?"

"Me mum used to say that to me whenever I was slagging someone off."

"My mum used to say 'stop bleating and go and give 'em a good hiding before I give *you* a good hiding'."

Caz smiled. Babs's mum had been a right character in her day – always speaking her mind and never suffering fools. It was a shame she'd died

263

so young. Caz took a sip of her Coke and shivered as she recalled the reason why.

"Come and join us!" Shantee waved to Mia.

Mia breathed a sigh of relief and walked quickly from the bar to their table, keeping her eyes fixed on the floor. "Thanks," she smiled.

"You look a bit flustered," said Jo. "Everything alright?"

"Yes fine," she said, pulling out a chair and sitting down. "It's just that – well, I know this sounds terrible but I just saw Simon come in, and well, I spent all of yesterday evening in his company, plus last Wednesday evening, and well-"

"Say no more!" laughed Jo, touching up her lip gloss. "We've all suffered him at some point."

"We've all lent him our ears, given him advice, tried to cheer him up," said Shantee. "The rest is up to him. There's only so much negativity any of us can handle."

"You're right," said Mia. "But he's got a knack of making you feel guilty. Last night I just reached a point where I couldn't take it anymore – I just had to leave."

"Just like his fiancée," smirked Jo. "Well, here's to her, I say. Because personally, I have had enough of pathetic, useless, self-centred blokes." She raised her glass. "I won't bore you with the details," she added, noticing the confused look on Mia's face. "But suffice to say, Nath and I are currently not on speaking terms, and it'll be fine with me if it stays that way till we go home." She giggled and took a sip of her vodka cranberry.

Shantee and Mia laughed and raised their glasses.

"Uh-oh," whispered Shantee. "Here he comes…"

"Hi girls," Simon hovered awkwardly at their table. "How are you all?"

"Good thanks," said Jo boldly, fiddling with her silver hoop earring and trying not to laugh.

"Mind if I join you?" he asked, clutching his pint of beer.

"Sorry but we're full – we're expecting two more, you see," she smiled sweetly.

"Oh," said Simon, looking around for a way to squeeze in another chair.

Mia squirmed in her seat, her cheeks burning. It felt so mean – as if they were three stuck-up schoolgirls not letting the class nerd join their clique. Under the table Shantee pressed on her foot and glared at her not to crack.

"Craig and Steve are sitting outside on the terrace," Jo pointed behind her. "And I saw plenty of spare seats at their table."

Simon blushed and muttered something as he walked off.

"God," gasped Mia, taking a large gulp of lemonade. "That felt awful."

"He looked a bit drunk," Shantee mused, watching as he plodded slowly out onto the terrace to look for Craig and Steve.

"Yeah, I could smell it on him from here," said Jo defiantly.

"You'd have felt a lot worse if you'd let him sit down next to you and bend your ear all night," said Shantee. "You'd have resented it, and resentment-"

"Gives you cancer," interrupted Mia. "Yes, I know." She thought of Gwen and her invitation for lunch. It was Wednesday, Andonis would have gone on his business trip today and she hadn't called her yet – she hadn't been sure that she wanted to. But perhaps she should go. After all, wasn't that the whole reason she had come here in the first place – to find out what happened and see if she could get to know her mother a bit better? She thought of Dad's warning that she would only get hurt again in the long run. But he had his own agenda. If she kept her expectations low, and treated it as a once-in-a-blue-moon lunch with a distant relative whom she didn't particularly care for, and banned herself from hoping for any more than that, then she couldn't get hurt, could she? And besides, as yet Gwen had done nothing whatsoever to convince her that she was someone whom she actually wanted to develop a friendship with. She couldn't see how her expectations could possibly get any lower.

Craig lifted his pint to his lips and took several gulps. Each female that passed was either with a bloke or too ugly to contemplate. Not that that had stopped him last night. He cringed and drained his pint. As long as no one knew, he told himself. Steve thought he knew, but he didn't. He couldn't prove anything, all he could do was try and wind him up and he knew better than to do that – most of the time.

"Your round," said Craig, plonking his empty glass on the table with a thud.

"Give us a chance," said Steve, whose glass was still half full. "I'm surprised you're drinking so quickly after last night."

"Why's that then?" asked Craig.

"Cos you've only just got over your hangover."

"I'm alright," grunted Craig. "I can take my drink – unlike you."

"Oy, I can take my drink. The difference between you and me is I know when I've had my fill."

Craig narrowed his eyes. "What are you trying to say, Steve?"

Steve rolled his eyes. "God you're well touchy. All I'm saying is that I can take my drink thank you very much – I just know when I've had enough."

Craig looked at him, trying to decide whether it was a dig or not. He frowned. Steve was pushing his luck – if he so much as dared come out and say it, there'd be trouble. Then again, if he got too defensive, Steve would suss. Craig pondered. The best line of defence was attack. The corner of his mouth crept into a smile.

"Did you have your fill when you went off with Caz last night?" Craig smirked.

"What's that supposed to mean?" Steve asked irritably.

"You seemed quite happy to go off with her last night."

"Oh leave it out, Craig. She's a nice bird – a *really* nice bird. Just grow up, will you?"

They both looked round as they noticed a presence hovering behind them.

Craig rolled his eyes.

"Alright?" Steve nodded, finishing off his pint.

"Got room for one more?" mumbled Simon, gesturing towards the empty seats at their table.

Steve shrugged and Simon quickly sat down before they had time to object.

"Enjoying your holiday then?" asked Simon.

Craig yawned loudly and held up his empty pint glass, as if inspecting its craftsmanship.

"Yeah," nodded Steve. "You?"

"Well, it's not quite how I planned it, but at least there are lots of nice people around to make up for how it should have been."

Craig scratched his elbow and noticed a piece of dead skin that had half peeled off.

"Look at that," he twisted his arm around to show Steve.

"Allow me," grinned Steve, gripping the skin between his finger and thumb and pulling.

"Careful!" snapped Craig, inspecting his arm as Steve held up the trophy dead skin flake.

"Gross," grimaced Steve.

"You've made me bleed now, you twat." Craig stood up. "I'm going for a slash and to clean this up." He nodded towards his empty glass. "The dancing's on in a minute, isn't it?"

Steve looked at his watch as Craig winked at him and walked off towards the toilets. He stood up and picked up their glasses.

"Pint?" Steve gestured towards Simon's barely touched beer.

"Er, no thanks," said Simon. "I'll make sure no one pinches your seats."

Steve made his way hastily to the bar as the bouzouki music started and the three Greek dancing girls skipped into the centre of the room.

Shantee squeezed Mia's arm. "Look, there's Dimitri," she said, pointing across the room to where a group of locals, both young and old, were standing chatting and watching the dancing with big grins on their faces. A hunched old lady was clapping her hands and shuffling in time to the music, while admiring the younger women dancing before her.

Mia clocked him and was annoyed to feel her heart flutter. "So I see."

"I have to say, he is a *stunning* looking man," said Jo, admiring him as he stooped to kiss the little old lady on both cheeks, making her giggle and flush.

"He certainly is," sighed Mia.

"So?" Shantee grinned suggestively. "He's definitely got the hots for you."

Mia blushed. She'd imagined people had picked up on her 'liaison' with Dimitri, but as far as divulging information went, Shantee had caught her off guard. Then again, what did it matter? She wouldn't be seeing any of these people after Saturday. She could say what she liked – what did she

267

care what any of them thought? It was just idle gossip to them that would be forgotten the minute the plane touched down at Gatwick.

"He's a sweet, lovely guy," shrugged Mia.

"But…?" asked Jo expectantly. "There was definitely a 'but' on the tip of your tongue."

Mia laughed. "Well, we've had a nice time together, but I'm off on Saturday, so that's that."

"Will you keep in touch?" asked Shantee.

"It would be nice…" said Mia, "but realistically, I'm going back to my life, and he's staying put with his. So there isn't much point."

"Forget realistically," said Shantee. "Do you not feel anything more for him other than just a holiday romance?"

"Yeah, come on," Jo grinned, nudging her. "The man's a total god – how can you be so blasé? Check out that bod – how could you not fall for him?"

Mia smiled and looked over at him as he turned and caught her eye. He nodded and smiled at her and turned quickly back to his friends. Mia took a sip of lemonade. "You don't know how close I came," she said quietly, watching him as he squatted down to ruffle a young boy's hair and tickled him under his arms.

Shantee and Jo leaned forward across the table.

"And the rest!" demanded Jo.

Mia sighed. "Look, if he lived down the road in England, had a job and could pay his own way, then maybe…"

"Well he wants to leave Greece, he said so," said Shantee encouragingly.

"I sense more 'ifs'," sighed Jo.

"'fraid so," said Mia. "If he had a good track record of commitment and honesty, then…"

"Then what?" asked Jo.

"Well if he had all those ifs, he'd be perfect," said Mia. "But he doesn't, and those are pretty important shortcomings."

"Nobody's perfect," said Shantee gently. "And look, about his card scam – I knew about it before he got caught out. He told me he was going to turn over a new leaf and that he was going to pay everyone back. I know he didn't go the right way about it, but he was scared of losing his job – he just hoped he could slip them the money back and no one would be any the wiser."

Mia shook her head. "That's just cowardly."

"I know, but his intentions were good," said Shantee. "He knew he was doing wrong and he didn't feel good about it. In fact, I believe it was meeting you that led him to want to change his ways."

Mia raised her eyebrows. "You two *have* been doing a lot of talking."

"Dimitri's nuts about you, Mia."

"And what about them?" Mia looked over to where Nikki and Karen were standing, wearing extremely revealing tops that showed a lot of cleavage, belly and bare back.

"What about them?" asked Jo.

"He's slept with both of them – and God knows how many others."

"Yes, but he loves *you*," said Shantee. "Anyone can see that."

"Too many skeletons in his closet," Mia shook her head. "Too many reasons why it would never work – geography, finances, independence, trust, commitment and…"

"And?" asked Jo.

"Well that's quite enough to be getting on with," she laughed awkwardly. There was no need to tell them about the other small matter – that was no longer as small as it once was.

"Where there's a will, there's a way," said Shantee. "But you've got to have the will – which you don't. If you don't have the will, it'll never work."

This was starting to turn into a lecture, thought Mia, examining her fingernails.

"I mean, how often does a gorgeous, vivacious man turn up in your life, who's absolutely crazy about you?" asked Shantee.

"Not very often," Mia agreed reluctantly. It was time to change the subject before they managed to convince her to change her mind. She knew she was doing the right thing. And anyway, they were not party to all the information. "Look, there's your Nath," she said, looking up and spotting him by the bar standing a few feet away from the reps.

"Oh shit," muttered Jo. "He's pissed as well."

The three of them watched as Nath propped up the bar and downed a bottle of lager. He raised his eyebrows at them and waved. Then he looked over at Dimitri and rolled his eyes towards Nikki with a sly grin.

"*Don't you even think about it,*" Shantee hissed under her breath, as Nath turned towards the barman to order another drink. He turned back to face them again and waggled his eyebrows.

"He's just winding us up," said Jo. "Ignore him. *Prat.*"

"Let's keep an eye on him," said Shantee.

Mia looked over at Dimitri. He was smoking a cigarette and talking to the little old lady again. But his eyes kept darting anxiously over her shoulder towards Nath, who winked at him, and raised his bottle of beer in a mocking salute.

Simon ran his thumb down the side of his beer glass, leaving a wet trail in the condensation. Then he picked it up, pressed it to his lower lip and downed it in one giant gulp. The alcohol hit his stomach and flowed through his bloodstream, a bitter-sweet medicine numbing his inner wounds. The Hotel Flamingo swimming pool shone up at him in the darkness, its bright underwater lighting turning the water aniseed green. Behind him the music and dancing were in full swing. Despite being outside on the terrace, all he needed to do was turn his chair around to see straight through the open archway into the crowded bar area to watch the entertainment. But what was the point? He'd seen it before.

A young couple walked out onto the terrace behind him, stumbling and knocking into his chair as they walked past down the steps to the pool area. Simon watched as they stopped and embraced, then laughed loudly before walking off into the night. A tear stung in the corner of his eye. It should have been him and Shelley.

He clenched his jaws together. What had he ever seen in her? She had used him, made him fall in love with her. And now she didn't want him anymore. She had just taken over his life, his heart, his world, and now she was gone – not going, but gone. She'd already moved all her stuff out and had spoken to a financial adviser about selling the house and splitting the profit fairly between them. And the worst bit? She hadn't even met anyone else – or so she claimed. She actually wanted to be single – *alone* – rather than be with him. He was being replaced by a preferable empty space.

Simon laughed out loud to himself. His vision was starting to blur. His empty beer glass swayed before him, multiplying before his eyes. He pulled the whisky chaser towards him. It was high time he got well and truly smashed. The barman had thought he was buying a round for a large group of people – hah! Generous ol' Simon. Such a nice bloke – so thoughtful – just like Shelley's mother always said.

He imagined Shelley out at parties, getting chatted up, flirting with other men. A tear trickled down his cheek. She said she felt suffocated, trapped, bored. *Bored*. She wanted to be free. She wasn't ready for marriage and kids. She'd felt pressured into the whole thing. But she'd enjoyed choosing the dress, hadn't she? The front room had been swamped with bridal magazines. And this was her choice of honeymoon destination. *He* would have chosen a romantic, historic city such as Prague or Vienna – he certainly wouldn't have chosen to come here to this boring sun, sea and sand cliché with all these stuck-up tossers.

The clapping behind him grew louder and a wolf-whistle pierced his ear. Obviously that slimy con artist Dimitri was showing off on the dancefloor. Some people could get away with anything, he mused bitterly. No matter what they did, some people would always be popular. That stupid cow Mia was probably gazing at him all starry-eyed right now, even though she knew he was a cheat and a womaniser. Simon nearly turned round to see if he was right, but stopped himself – there were too many tears falling down his cheeks.

Out of the corner of his tear-filled eye, he noticed a bony brown and white cat sniffing at a morsel of food under a nearby table. He leaned down and whistled to it, rubbing his fingers and patting his shins, smiling as the cat eyed him suspiciously from a safe distance.

"Here, moggie," he pleaded with a futile air-kiss. The cat looked at him, startled, and bolted down the steps at lightning speed.

Simon rolled his head back and laughed bitterly. Slumping forward again, he downed the whisky chaser, reached for another one and downed that too. One left. He couldn't possibly manage any more after this. He'd drunk an entire bottle of wine to himself back at his apartment, three pints of beer and five whiskies. Good lad, Si! He stood up and grabbed a chair to steady himself. He was too pissed to make it to the bar, anyway. He picked up his last chaser and wobbled down the steps towards the fluorescent green pool.

At the edge of the pool, he downed his last chaser and plonked himself down on a sunlounger. He fancied a swim. Shame he couldn't. But you never knew until you tried. Besides, who'd miss him if he drowned? Who'd give a shit? Not Shelley, that was for sure. None of his mates – he only had two anyway. Rob and Jim. Both married with kids. His mum would miss him, but she had a new man in her life these days, and they were always going away together on some trip or other.

He imagined Shelley's face as she heard the news. She'd be mortified, wracked with guilt. And so she should be, the selfish bitch. Rob and Jim already had it in for her and Mum wanted her head on a silver platter. And after the guilt, the devastation…as she realised how much she loved him, what she'd thrown away and how it was too late to ever get it back now that he was dead.

Hopefully Mum would invite Shelley to the funeral. He wanted her to be there, to see what she had done. To face the consequences of her actions, and the hatred everyone felt for her. Rob would make sure their favourite song was played to drive the message home. Simon leaned forward until he could see his reflection in the pool. How long did drowning take? he wondered. It always looked quite quick in the movies. He didn't want to be thrashing about – he wanted to sink fast like a-

Just two feet away sat a large concrete brick, tied by a piece of rope to a volleyball net that had been taken down and left in a heap at the side of the pool. Simon lurched forward on all fours and clumsily began to untie the rope.

Dimitri walked into the centre of the dancefloor flanked by Manos and Yannis. He breathed a sigh of relief as the crowd clapped. He looked over at Mia, Shantee and Jo. They were all smiling at him. So were Frank and Margaret, who were sitting with his mother. Even Caz had given him a pat on the back as he'd walked past. The music and clapping started, and Dimitri began to relax as his nightmares of becoming Kefalonia's Most Wanted evaporated in the cheery atmosphere. Turning to face the bar, he could see Karen and Nikki were busy chatting to some hotel guests while

Nath was looking uncomfortable and alone.

Dimitri and his companions stepped and clicked their fingers in time to the twanging bouzoukis, swaying from side to side and taking it in turns to twirl around. But swinging to face the bar again, his smile faded as he noticed Nikki was now on her own, and seizing the opportunity, Nath was inching his way towards her. Dimitri missed his cue to do his solo dance as he watched Nath tap Nikki on the shoulder and say hello.

"OPA!" shouted Dimitri as he lunged onto one knee in the centre of the dance floor. Everyone clapped and cheered. Nikki leaned in closer to Nath signalling to him to speak up. Dimitri spun around as fast as he could, petrified of taking his eyes off them, but as he re-linked arms with Manos and Yannis, he was forced to turn the other way.

"SHIT!" shouted Dimitri, breaking free of the others and bolting out onto the terrace. Behind him the clapping slowed to a confused halt as all eyes followed him belting down the steps towards the pool. Leaping over a sunlounger, Dimitri dived into the centre of the glowing green pool with an almighty splash, just as an outstretched hand submerged beneath the water. People dashed out on to the terrace and hurried down the steps after him, straining to see what was going on. A crowd quickly gathered around the edge of the pool, looking down at the two distorted figures entwined and wobbling beneath the water. Pushing people out of her way, Nikki shouted into her mobile for an ambulance.

At the bottom of the pool, Dimitri struggled to hold his breath while untying the rope from around Simon's ankles. A waiter and a man in a Liverpool shirt jumped in to help him just as he rose to the surface, gasping for air, a lifeless Simon in his arms. The other men helped lift Simon up onto the concrete, where others dragged him carefully away from the edge of the pool. The plump hotel receptionist shooed everyone back as she cleared Simon's mouth and pressed her lips against his. As she breathed into his mouth, Frank helped pull Dimitri out of the pool and patted him on the back.

"Is he breathing?" asked Dimitri anxiously, pushing his sopping wet hair out of his eyes.

Frank looked at Simon's unconscious face. "Hold on, son," he murmured, gripping Dimitri's shoulder.

All eyes were on Simon as the receptionist crouched over him, pressing her ear against his chest. Karen asked people to stand back as she and Nikki squatted awkwardly on the ground and watched helplessly as the Greek woman breathed into his mouth again. Patiently, she took another deep breath and leaned towards him, but promptly sat back and broke into a wide grin as Simon coughed and spluttered back to life. She fired off a round of incomprehensible instructions in Greek and various people quickly dispersed into the hotel and nearby out-houses.

Dimitri leaned over Simon and smiled. "Sorry, my friend. Your number didn't come up today."

The crowd laughed nervously as a waiter returned with towels and blankets. The woman put a folded towel beneath Simon's head and rubbed him gently with another one. Simon looked up at the blur of heads with glazed eyes and closed them again.

"An ambulance is coming," the receptionist informed him. "Don't worry. You will be fine."

"Oh thank God he's alright," said Mia, standing on top of a sunlounger and straining to see Simon through the crowd.

"I feel a right bitch," frowned Jo, as a few people brushed past her on their way back up to the bar.

Shantee sighed. "Look, none of us could have predicted he was about to do something like that."

"I'm going to ask him if he wants me to go with him to the hospital," said Mia, hopping off the sunlounger and squeezing through the crowd of onlookers.

As she bent down next to Simon she found herself face to face with Dimitri. He smiled at her.

"He's had a lot to drink," said Dimitri, wrapping a towel around his shoulders, as Simon's eyeballs swam backwards and forwards unable to focus on them.

"I thought I could accompany him to the hospital," said Mia.

"He is alone, yes?" the receptionist looked at her. Mia nodded. "Yes, he will feel better if someone is with him."

"Are you sure?" said Nikki. "Why don't I go instead?"

"No, honestly," Mia smiled, "I'd feel better if I went with him. I spent all yesterday evening with him. I wish I'd realised how badly in need of a friend he was."

"That's very kind of you," said Nikki. "Here, let me give you my mobile number if you need anything." She took a pen out of her handbag, scribbled it on a scrap of paper and handed it to Mia. "I'll come to the hospital in the morning and check up on him," she said standing up. "OK, everyone, let's make some room for the paramedics when they get here." She ushered people away from the pool.

"I can come too, if you like?" Dimitri suggested to Mia, clenching the towel closer to him.

The receptionist spoke to him in Greek. Dimitri smiled at her and rolled his eyes.

"Don't worry," said Mia. "I can manage. Besides, you're soaking. You should go home and get changed."

"Is what I tell him," said the receptionist. "But he don't listen to me as usual. Only listen to pretty faces, this boy," she babbled something affectionately to him in Greek and reached forward to give him a sloppy kiss on the cheek. Dimitri grinned and looked at Mia.

"The ambulance is here!" announced Nikki as a wailing siren and flashing lights screeched into the Hotel Flamingo driveway.

Mia and Dimitri stood back as the ambulance parked and a couple of paramedics jumped out with a stretcher.

"Well done, mate – you saved his life," said Steve as he walked past and patted Dimitri on the back. Several other people also came towards him, wanting to shake his hand and congratulate him.

"You're a hero," smiled Mia, as the paramedics lifted Simon into the back of the ambulance.

Dimitri shrugged. "But I'm not *your* hero?" He looked at her intently.

Mia looked away and noticed the driver climbing back into his seat.

"I'd better go," she said and raced towards the ambulance, climbing into the back as a paramedic closed the door behind her.

Jo and Shantee made their way back up the steps.

"I need a stiff drink after all that drama," said Jo.

"Me too," agreed Shantee.

"That goes for me as well," said Nikki, overtaking them.

"Oh God," Jo rolled her eyes as Nath slid out of the shadows and resumed his position at the bar.

"Perhaps you should talk to him," said Shantee.

"No way," muttered Jo.

"So sorry," said Nikki as she reached Nath. "What were you about to say to me earlier?"

Jo fixed Nath with a menacing look.

"Er, it's about Dimitri the caretaker at Eleni Apartments," smirked Nath, throwing a smug glance at Jo and Shantee.

Shantee restrained Jo as she clenched her fist.

"Oh isn't he a star?" gushed Nikki. "Did you see him just now? He's made me go all weak at the knees again, and I thought I'd finally got over him – *damn!*"

"Eh?" Nath looked at her confused.

"Didn't you just see what happened outside?" asked Nikki.

"What happened?" asked Nath.

"Didn't you see Dimitri rush out of here in the middle of his dance?" Nikki squealed in disbelief.

"Yeah, I saw that, but I thought he just ran off," said Nath impatiently.

"Why would he just run off?" Nikki looked at him oddly.

Nath shrugged awkwardly.

"So you didn't see what he did?" she asked.

"No I bloody didn't – are you going to tell me or what?" he snapped.

"Well not if you speak to me like that, I won't," she snapped back.

"Sorry," mumbled Nath.

"Dimitri dived in the pool and saved Simon from drowning," Nikki explained. "He was wonderful. He didn't hesitate – just plunged straight in, held his breath under water as he tried to free him from the rope."

"Rope?"

"Looks like the poor man was trying to kill himself," she whispered. "It's tragic. What would make a person do such a thing? If it hadn't been for Dimitri he might have succeeded. Anyway, what was it you were going to tell me about him?"

Taking advantage of Nath's hesitation, Shantee butted in. "He was going to tell you what a sterling job Dimitri's been doing at Eleni Apartments. We all think he's great."

"Yeah," Jo joined in. "He's so polite and friendly and always willing to help if anyone's got a problem – and he keeps the place spotless."

"Aah, how sweet of you," sighed Nikki. "He's a lovely guy. All us reps fancy the pants off him you know." She guffawed with laughter. "I thought I'd managed to seduce him once but he said he wasn't looking for a relationship. Boy did I cry – but rumour has it he's finally fallen for someone. And I've a good idea who – the lucky madam. Oh well, perhaps one day I'll meet my own Prince Charming."

Nath rolled his eyes and ordered himself another drink.

"Aren't you buying one for these lovely ladies?" asked Nikki, surprised.

"No," laughed Jo. "Cos these lovely ladies are about to head off to the Bora Bora without him."

Shantee grinned. "You read my mind – I could do with a bit of Abba."

"Which means poor old Nath's all on his own tonight," Jo pouted teasingly. "His first night of singledom, all alone, on a foreign island…but you'll keep an eye on him for us, won't you Nikki? Make sure he stays out of trouble." Jo winked at her.

"Of course I will," Nikki's eyes lit up as she sidled up to Nath. "Mine's a vodka tonic, darlin'."

"Dimitri!" Karen ran after him as he walked towards the drive.

He stopped and waited.

"I just wanted to say well done. You were amazing just now," she said, twisting a finger through her long blonde hair.

"Thank you," he replied. "But anyone would have done the same thing."

"Are you going home to get changed?" she asked.

He nodded, clutching the towel around his shoulders.

"Can I offer you a lift?" she smiled.

"Karen, it takes less than three minutes to walk to my house from here. But thank you." He turned to go.

"Whoa there!" She reached out to stop him. "How about we go out for that drink tomorrow night?"

"I'm sorry Karen, but I don't think so."

"Is it because of that girl I saw you with – Mia or whatever her name is?"

Dimitri ignored her question and walked off. "Kali nikta," he called over his shoulder as he turned the corner out of sight.

Caz nudged Babs. "Did you hear that?" she asked, pulling Babs away from the edge of the pool.

"Hear what?" asked Babs, tripping over a sunlounger and dropping her glass on the ground.

"Oh bloody hell, Babs. Look what you're doing!" Caz bent down to gather up the broken glass.

Babs sat down on a sunbed and tried to focus. "Hear what?" she repeated.

"Dimitri just told that girl that he weren't interested in her. And he more or less said it was cos of Mia." Caz put the shattered glass in an ashtray on a nearby table.

"So what," groaned Babs, clutching her stomach.

Caz looked at her. "Are you alright?" she asked.

Babs stood up. Caz looked quickly about her for the nearest toilets. "Are you gonna be-"

Suddenly Babs lurched towards the edge of the pool and vomited. Caz covered her eyes and groaned. "I don't believe it," she exhaled heavily.

Babs threw up again, her vomit rapidly spreading across the surface of the pool in a chunky pink cloud.

"For Christ's sake get away from the pool," Caz barked through gritted teeth, and yanked her towards a potted plant just in time to direct the next deluge into its soil.

A panicked waiter came running out of the terrace restaurant, frantically waving his arms around. "Please you take her to the toilets *now*," he ordered.

"Yes, alright," snapped Caz. "I'm doing me best."

She gripped Babs' arm tightly and pulled her towards the Ladies' as the waiter shook his head in disgust. Enough is enough, thought Caz.

Tomorrow, when the stupid bint had sobered up, she was going to give her a piece of her mind. It was long overdue.

"Where d'you think you're going?" asked Craig, catching Steve by the arm.

"I'm gonna see if I can help them out," he replied defensively, putting his drink down and starting after Caz and Babs.

"Mate, I'd keep well away if I were you – we don't want anyone thinking we're hanging around with those two for fuck's sake – I mean, look at the state of 'em." Craig grimaced as Caz guided a staggering, dribbling Babs into the Ladies' loos on the other side of the pool. "I can't believe that fat slag just puked in the pool. That's disgusting!"

"She looked like she was in a bad way," protested Steve. "They looked like they could do with some help getting her back to the apartments."

"That fat cow has looked in a bad way pretty much every day we've been here. She's a total alkie!" Craig grabbed his arm and held him back again.

"Yeah, well Caz ain't. She's alright. She was hardly drunk at all the other night."

"Blimey Steve, you're starting to sound like you fancy her. Are you sure you didn't shag her the other night?"

Steve glared at him. "Why don't you shut up for once, Craig? Just cos you shagged Babs and don't want anyone to know. In fact that's probably why she's gone and got trolleyed – cos she'd rather forget it ever happened."

Craig put his pint down on the ground and clenched his fists. "I never fucking shagged her, alright?" he hissed, sending spittle flying into Steve's face.

Steve took a step back. "It's written all over your face, mate. Don't worry, I won't tell anyone."

"You won't tell anyone cos there ain't nothing to tell," Craig lowered his voice as Nikki and Nath walked past and sat down at a table on the far side of the pool with their backs to them.

"Whatever, Craig. I'm gonna ask them if they're alright. See you later."

"God, you're sad!" spat Craig as Steve walked away from him. "Why are you fannying around after a couple of old, fat'n'ugly alcoholic Essex slags? Can't you pull a normal bird or something?"

Steve stopped in his tracks. "What did you say?" he said calmly, his back to Craig.

"I said, can't you pull a normal bird instead of a fat, old ugly slag like those two?" Craig jeered.

Steve spun around and drove his fist hard into Craig's face. Clutching his nose, Craig stumbled backwards into a tree and slunk to the ground. As he struggled to stand up, Steve marched off towards the Ladies' loos. But before he'd got half-way, Craig grabbed him, spun him around and punched him in the stomach. Steve threw himself at Craig and wrestled him to the ground as a few people looked down from the bar terrace to see what the latest commotion was.

"Hey – stop that!" shouted Nikki, leaping up from her chair as Nath sat back and chuckled.

"I've had just about enough of you!" snarled Steve, his hands clasped around Craig's neck. Craig pushed him off and kicked him, sending him stumbling over a sunlounger.

"You think you can take me on?" he spat. "Do ya? Come on then!" He launched himself at Steve again, but Steve tripped him up and leaped on top of him.

"*You're a cunt!*" Steve shouted in his face. "Always bossing me around, telling me what to do, being rude to people you don't even know. I've had enough of you, you bag of shit!"

"Break it up, you two!"

Steve felt a hand on his shoulder yank him backwards. It was Frank.

"Get out the way, granddad!" growled Craig as he stumbled to his feet, fists at the ready.

"Who are you calling granddad?" Frank growled back, rolling up his sleeves. Seeing that the muscles in Frank's arms were bigger than his own, Craig backed away.

"What's going on?" shouted Caz, rushing out of the loos, a slightly sobered-up Babs in tow. They scurried over towards Steve, Frank and Margaret, as a few other people gathered at a short distance.

"There's your old woman, Steve. She can kiss you better now!" Craig taunted him as blood poured from his nose.

Frank lost his grip as Steve burst forward and landed a punch on Craig's cheek. He hurled him to the ground and grappled him into a half-nelson. Craig cried out in pain as Frank and Caz rushed to pull Steve off.

"Stop it Steve!" shouted Caz. "He ain't worth it."

"She's right, son," said Frank, gripping him firmly and hauling him away.

Caz slid an arm around Steve's shoulders. "You alright?" she asked. He nodded without taking his eyes off Craig.

Babs swayed at Caz's side. "What's going on? Blimey, your nose is well messed up, mate." She blinked, trying to focus on Craig's blood-smudged face.

"Piss off, you drunken tramp," Craig sneered at her in disgust. "You're nothing but a sad old alcoholic."

Babs looked at him. Her lower lip trembled and tears sprung into her eyes. "Well at least one of us has an excuse for doing something they regret last night, then," her voice shook. "What's yours? Won't anyone else have you cos of this?" She held up her little finger and waggled it at him. Caz burst out laughing. "Honest to God," blurted Babs, encouraged by the giggles erupting around her. "It didn't look too bad when it was soft, but it was deceptive. Know what I mean? We're talking *mini chipolata*. The poor bloke – no wonder he's so full of himself, his ego's the only big thing about him." Babs looked around her, pleased to have a growing audience of sniggering onlookers. "You've seen the tattoo in Punjabi or whatever on his back, haven't ya?" she said. "Well, it ought to be in bloody English, cos if I'd known it said 'Warning – big head, small donger' I might have thought twice. Talk about shortcoming – if you'll pardon the pun."

Hoots of laughter rose up from the crowd. "Come on, let's go," said Caz, taking Babs' arm. "What about you Steve?" she asked, noticing he was clutching his leg and wincing.

"Tell you what," said Frank. "Margaret will go and find Nikki and see if she wouldn't mind taking these two to the hospital. I think they should get checked out – make sure they're still in one piece. That nose needs tending to for a start," he nodded at Craig.

"I'm right here," said Nikki, gloating cheerily at Craig's bleeding nose.

Steve groaned. "Not the bloody hospital again."

"Can't you take us?" Craig asked Frank.

"No, sonny Jim, I can't – I don't have any transport. Anyway, Nikki'll make sure you're alright, won't you, pet?"

Nikki grinned mischievously. "It'll be my pleasure."

CHAPTER 26

Thursday 13th

Mia yawned as she walked through the hospital's main entrance. Last night had been a late one – despite sleeping until almost midday, she was still tired and her head was still whirring with Simon's attempt to drown himself. She dreaded to think how the evening would have ended had Dimitri not seen him and rushed to save him in the nick of time. She shuddered. What a horrible way to go, tied to a large brick at the bottom of a swimming pool. What on earth had driven him to do it? She couldn't imagine wanting to kill herself, no matter how terrible things got.

She paused at a junction in the corridor as she tried to remember the way to Simon's ward. Glancing about her, she found herself looking at a familiar face sitting on a chair, a bandage on his nose and his arm in a sling. It was Craig, looking like he'd just been sent back from the trenches. She wondered what had happened to him – a moped accident, most likely, although hadn't he had one only last week? She followed the direction of Craig's eyes over the top of a Greek motoring magazine to where a svelte young nurse was making notes on a clipboard. She wondered whether or not to go up to him and ask if he was alright, but the nurse turned around and started talking sternly to him. Perhaps now wasn't a good time. Turning the corner, Mia did a double-take – there was Steve lazing in an easy chair, engrossed in a battered English translation of The Odyssey, his ankle wrapped in a thick swathe of bandage. What in God's name was going on? Either they had collided into one another or they'd been on the same bike – or, perhaps they'd got into a brawl with some other similarly unintelligent life forms.

The young nurse who had been talking to Craig tapped her on the shoulder. "You are looking for Simon Dwyer, yes?" Mia nodded. "Follow me. This building is like a – how do you call it – a labyrinth."

"Yes," said Mia. "Um, what happened to Craig and Steve? Are they alright?" she asked, pointing over her shoulder at them.

The nurse smirked. "Those two are like Laurel and Hardy – best friends and worst enemies."

Mia smiled. It was an apt comparison. She observed the name badge pinned to the nurse's chest – Maria. It was what people usually called her by mistake.

"They had fight last night," continued Maria. "Craig say something stupid and Steve lose his temper." She shrugged and drew to a halt in front of a ward. "Simon is there." She pointed to the bed furthest away from them.

"I take it they haven't made up yet?" Mia tried not to laugh.

Maria folded her arms. "I am trying to make them shake the hands but they refuse to talk to each other – like children!" She laughed.

"Men," laughed Mia. "Some of them never grow up."

"I think they change if they have a good woman in their lives," whispered Maria. She cast a glance back down the corridor towards where Craig was sitting. "Especially this one. He is naughty, but cute, no?"

Mia smiled politely. That was a matter of opinion. As Maria turned to attend to another patient, she walked over to Simon who was lying in bed, his head propped up by two large pillows so that he could see out of the window.

"Hello there," she said as he watched her make her way towards him. "Look what I found." She pulled his glasses out of her pocket and handed them to him.

"Did you find them by the pool?" he asked, putting them on.

"Under a sunlounger. So, how are you feeling?"

"Where to begin…?" He gave a weak smile.

Mia sat on a chair next to his bed. "I brought you some honey baklava from a bakery just round the corner. It's delicious, I just had some." She presented him with a paper bag. He took it and put it on the bedside table. "I'm sorry we didn't ask you to sit with us last night. It was rude and hurtful of us."

"I didn't try to top myself because of that," he said irritably.

"No, of course not." She bit her lip. "So…why…?"

284

Simon took a deep breath and looked up at the ceiling. "I was feeling very, very sorry for myself. Shelley had sent me a text message saying she had put our house on the market and it was already under offer. I couldn't believe how fast it was all happening, so I decided just to go out and get drunk," he paused and shook his head woefully. "The drunker I got, the more angry I became. It seemed like no one cared about me – no one would miss me if I was gone. So I thought I'd teach them all a good lesson. I could see them all at my funeral, wishing they'd treated me better."

Mia looked away. "Has the hospital contacted your family?"

"I asked them not to," he replied. "I don't have any family apart from my mum and I didn't want to worry her."

Mia gave him a baffled look. "Good job you didn't pull it off, then."

"Funny," Simon gave a wry smile, "I only thought about that when I was at the bottom of the pool. I pictured her face when they told her the news and I panicked. I tried to untie the knot but I couldn't see a bloody thing without my glasses. I suddenly thought, I should have gone for a less 'final' act of self-destruction, if you know what I mean."

Mia looked at him, fascinated. "*Less final?*"

"You know, like taking just enough pills to give everyone a good scare."

She cringed. This man needed help – counselling, therapy, anything, as long as it helped him to get over the bitterness.

"Anyway, that was what I was thinking as I was running out of air. It's not what I'm thinking now."

"What are you thinking now?" she asked, wondering if she wanted to know the answer.

"I'm thinking I'm an idiot," he sighed. "An idiot who's glad to be alive."

Mia smiled with relief. "Well, I'm bloody glad you're alive, too. Life always goes on, you know, Simon. I know it's a cliché, but it's true. I have days when I feel so miserable I start to wonder if I need anti-depressants. And then I have days when I feel great, and everything's wonderful, I'm a happy bunny and the world's a fantastic place. And then I think, God, we're all allowed to feel down every now and again. It's normal, it's just a part of life – it passes."

"I can't imagine you feeling so down you'd need anti-depressants." Simon looked at her with surprise.

"Why not?"

"You always look happy. You look like one of life's winners."

"Simon you've known me for less than a fortnight. Just because I walk around with a smile on my face doesn't mean I necessarily feel that way inside. I'm not saying I bottle up my problems and never share them – I do, but generally not with complete strangers…" She was going to say 'apart from Dimitri' but stopped herself. "I talk about how I'm feeling with friends or with my family. And if I think they can't help me, or if I worry that I'm boring them too much, I go find myself a counsellor."

"Really?" Simon seemed astonished. "*You? You* would see a counsellor?"

"What's wrong with that?"

"Nothing. I just can't imagine someone like you needing to see a counsellor."

"What's all this *someone like me* business?"

"Well you're clever, pretty, popular, you've got a good job – like I said, you're one of life's winners."

"I'm flattered you think so highly of me Simon, but all those things have nothing to do with the way someone feels inside. Look at Marilyn Monroe – on the surface she had it all. And anyway, why do you keep saying I'm one of life's winners? What does that mean?"

Simon shrugged. "Just a turn of phrase my father used to use."

"Who are life's winners then?"

"You know," Simon sighed impatiently. "People like Bill Gates, David Beckham, JK Rowling."

"You see, I disagree. I would say Mother Theresa was one of life's winners. Or Nelson Mandela. Or even the guy who sells the Big Issue outside my local supermarket, because he always smiles and asks people how they are, whether they buy it or not."

"Yeah, yeah, yeah," Simon rolled his eyes.

"You're talking about success, fame and popularity, Simon. Is that what your dad meant by life's winners?"

Simon frowned and looked away. "Nothing I ever did was good enough for my dad. According to him I was one of life's losers. He used to say I wasn't born of his blood and that Mum must have had it away with someone else cos I was nothing like him in looks or personality. I hated him. When he died I hadn't spoken to him for almost ten years." Simon's eyes welled up. "Imagine hating your own father so much you don't even say goodbye when he's on his deathbed."

As his lip quivered, Mia reached out and squeezed his hand. "I've felt like that about my mother on many occasions."

"I didn't realise your mum had died," he said, restraining the tears and gaining control of his emotions.

"She's not dead. She's alive and well and living in Kefalonia. I've just seen her for the first time in thirty-one years. She walked out on Dad and me when I was a baby. I came here and looked her up to find out why."

"I thought you said your Mum and Dad lived in Egham?"

"My Dad and my step-mum live in Egham. She's brilliant, my step-mum – I love her – I call her Mum. I don't really know my real mum, Gwen. I'm not sure I want to get to know her. She didn't exactly welcome me with open arms."

"So, have you found out why she left you?" Simon propped himself up against the pillows.

Mia shrugged. "She didn't love Dad and she wasn't ready to be a mum. She thought she could do it, but by the time I was born, she realised she couldn't hack it. So when you say you hated your dad, I know how that feels. I hated Gwen for leaving me, for not contacting me my entire life."

"And so how are things now that you've seen her?" he asked eagerly.

"Hard to say. Tense, unresolved. She's got teenage kids and I don't know if she's told them about me yet. She only told her husband last week and he wasn't too pleased. Anyway, he's away this week and she's invited me for lunch. I don't know whether to go or not, though. She says she wants us to be friends but it feels like lip service – it's obvious she doesn't want me to interfere with her life. She's got too much to lose now."

"Give her a chance, Mia," said Simon, listening to her intently.

"I want to, but then I think *why should I?* Why should I have to come all the way to Kefalonia to remind her of my existence? I shouldn't have to make all this effort – *she's* the parent, it should be coming from *her*."

"I know, but Mia, don't do what I did. Don't miss a chance to put the past behind you and become friends. I did and I regret it. My dad begged me to visit him when he was dying. He wrote saying he wanted to patch

287

things up so he could die with his mind at rest. I didn't reply and I never saw him. I hurt my mum deeply by not letting him make amends, but most of all I hurt myself." Simon sighed and shook his head. "I don't half mess things up sometimes – losing Shelley, trying to top myself. Perhaps the old man was right – I am one of life's losers."

"You're not a loser Simon," said Mia sternly. "Don't ever let me hear you say that again. Anyway, there's no such thing as winners and losers. It's not a bloody competition. We all have our good times and bad times. Sometimes we screw up, sometimes we score. But no one scores all the time." Simon smiled at her. Mia looked at her watch. "How long are they keeping you in for?"

He shook his head. "Dunno. I'm hoping they'll let me stay until this monster hangover disappears." He smiled. "They measured the amount of alcohol in my blood. Said if I'd drunk anymore I wouldn't have needed to go to the trouble of drowning myself. Oh, and I've damaged a tendon in my ankle that they need to look at – can't feel it though."

Mia smiled. "Are you going to try some of that honey baklava I bought you?"

"Yes," Simon reached for the paper bag and opened it.

"Why don't I go and get us some tea to go with that?"

Simon looked at her as she got up. "Thanks Mia."

"What for?"

"For coming to see me."

"That's what friends are for, aren't they?" she winked at him. "Right then, there's got to be a vending machine around here somewhere. I'll be back in a minute."

As Mia walked down the corridor she noticed a payphone. She paused. Gwen's number was in her bag. Without further ado, she swung her bag off her shoulder and rummaged around for her address book inside.

Balancing the book on top of the shelf and slipping some coins into the phone, she dialled the number. Her heart started to race as the phone rang.

"Embros?" a young boy's voice answered.

Mia hesitated.

"Embros?"

Mia put down the phone and cursed. She looked at her watch again. It was half past four – later than she'd realised. Katty and George must have come home from school. Perhaps she should have spoken to him – but then, had Gwen told them about her yet? Angrily, Mia threw her address book back into her bag. Best to wait until tomorrow. She would have to phone early – it would be her last chance.

"I was wondering if I could have a word," said Babs awkwardly.

"Of course." Margaret stood aside and let her in.

"Hello, love. How are you this fine morning?" Frank looked up from his paper and smiled.

"Paying for my sins," Babs smiled weakly.

"I'll put the kettle on," Margaret winked.

"Are you two ladies wanting to talk in private?" asked Frank, folding up his paper and scratching his moustache.

"Um…" Babs fumbled with the bow on her draw-string shorts and looked hesitantly at Margaret.

"Ohi problema, as they say." Frank stood up and slipped his sandals on over his socks. "I was just thinking I fancied a little walk, so I'll leave you two to have a good gas. Margaret, where's my hat?"

Margaret plucked his hat off the kitchen table and threw it towards him. Frank caught it and put it on. "See you later, then." He pecked Margaret on the cheek and opened the door. "Back in an hour or so."

"Take your time, love," Margaret called after him as she took the tea bags out of the cupboard.

No sooner had Frank closed the door behind him, Babs burst into tears. Margaret pulled out a chair for her and ushered her into it, rubbing her on the back as she did so.

"Let it all out, love," she said and pushed a box of Kleenex towards her. As Babs wailed into a handful of tissues, Margaret quickly made two cups of tea and sat down at the table.

"Sugar?" asked Margaret.

Babs shook her head and caught her breath. "You were right."

Margaret continued to stir her tea without looking up. It was best to let Babs do most of the talking – she had been too quick to leap in the day before, and Babs hadn't been ready. She'd been there before once or twice with newcomers to meetings. Pumped them full of teetotal wisdom, sent them off with a smile on their face, never to see them again – until a few months or years later after they had hit their *real* rockbottom.

"I'm getting worse," Babs mumbled nasally and blew her nose. "I'm getting like my mum used to be – she couldn't go a single day without a drink. Up until now, I've kept it under control – just two or three a night usually – sometimes only one – but here I haven't had to worry about the kids seeing or Trev standing over me." More tears.

"So Trev is aware of your drinking?" Margaret ventured cautiously.

Babs sighed a deep, long sigh. "He was aware of it for ages. Caz has guessed an' all. But this is the first time I've said anything to anyone."

"Does Caz know you're here with me?" Margaret took a sip of tea.

Babs shook her head. "She went to the hospital to see if the lads were alright after their punch-up last night. She left before I got up."

Margaret smiled warmly. "Admitting you've got a drink problem isn't the end of the world, you know, Babs. On the contrary, it's the beginning of a whole new chapter-" She stopped herself launching into a long lecture on the joys of not drinking.

"How much did you used to drink then?" asked Babs, slurping her tea.

"More than enough," Margaret nodded sagely.

"I remember puking in the pool last night," Babs closed her eyes and cringed as the memory came flooding back. "And then I started showing off, spouting my mouth off at that nasty little toe-rag. So I s'pose everyone knows that I, er, did something with him I don't 'alf regret."

"Babs, for every ugly drunken thing you've done, I've done something just as bad – if not worse, I'm sure."

Another tear fell from Babs' eye. "I was a complete cow to Trev. He annoyed me sometimes, you know – trying to put me off me diet, making me wear frumpy things, asking me where I was going all the time and whether or not I was gonna get drunk. One day this bloke at work says to me, 'Oy Babs, if you keep losing weight like that I'm gonna start fancying ya'. It might not sound like much of a compliment to you, but it was the first time anyone had said anything nice to me ever since I can remember. Trev kept saying he liked me the way I was but *I* didn't like me the way I was."

"Do you like yourself now?" asked Margaret.

Babs shook her head. "I hate myself. You heard what that little tosser called me last night – a drunken tramp, a sad old alcoholic. And it's true."

Margaret grabbed a wad of tissues from the box and passed them to Babs as she broke down again. She remembered the first time she had admitted having a problem. It was to their daughter Shirley one rainy afternoon. She had expected Shirley to be shocked and say, 'Don't be daft, Mum, you're not an alcoholic'. But she had slowly nodded her head, tears forming in her eyes, and said, 'Yes Mum, I know.' Everyone had known. Everyone, except her.

"Babs, once you've realised you've got a problem – once you've acknowledged it, said it out loud, you're half-way there. You've broken through the denial, pet. Good times lie ahead. Things will get better I promise you. They might get worse for a while first, but they *will* get better."

"I miss Trev!" Babs wailed. "What have I bleedin' done? I want 'im back – I've made a huge mistake. I love 'im. I really, really love 'im. You're alright, you've got Frank – I'm all on me own with the kids."

Margaret reached forward and squeezed her hand tightly. "I'm not with Frank, love. We've decided to go our separate ways." Babs looked at her, confused. "We're still friends, mind. We've broken up amicably – well as much as can be expected. But our marriage went stale a long time ago. Perhaps it's not too late for you and Trevor to work things out?"

Babs blew her nose again. "I doubt he'd have me back after the cow I've been."

"One day at a time, pet," Margaret smiled at her. "One day at a time."

"So am I back in your good books then?" Craig grinned mischievously as a smile broke out on Maria's face.

"Maybe." She folded her arms.

"Are you gonna forgive me before I go home on Saturday?" he asked, pretending to pout.

"Maybe. Maybe not."

"God I don't 'alf fancy you in that uniform. Please forgive me – let me take you out tonight."

"You should rest."

"I need someone to look after me."

"Steve can look after you."

"I'm not talking to that plonker."

"Then I don't come with you for a drink." She turned on her heel.

"OK, OK!" Craig called after her. She stopped in her tracks and turned around, smiling.

"Go, shake the hands with Steve. Apologise also to the ladies you upset, and I will pick you up in my car tonight for dinner."

Craig's eyes lit up. "Dinner?"

"Yes." She smiled. "Steve is over there." She pointed round the corner. "Go!"

Craig stood up and grinned at her.

"Go, go, go!" she ordered, marching on the spot like a sergeant major.

He tried to salute but remembered his arm was in a sling. Maria giggled and followed him as he limped around the corner to the row of seats where Steve was sitting.

Craig halted abruptly. There, sitting next to him was Caz, helping him fill in a form. Craig cleared his throat. Caz looked up and nudged Steve.

"Alright?" mumbled Craig.

Steve ignored him and turned his attention back to the form. Craig glanced at Maria and shrugged. She arched an eyebrow at him and tutted.

"Steve, I'm sorry mate." Craig bowed his head and looked down at his feet.

Steve looked up again and nodded thoughtfully. "Big deal. Now piss off," he replied.

Again Craig glanced at Maria helplessly. She shook her head disapprovingly, daring him to back out.

"Steve, I was bang out of order – I acted like a prat. I shouldn't have treated you like that, and I swear it won't happen it again." Craig could feel his cheeks on fire. He wasn't used to begging for forgiveness. "Come on Steve, you're my best mate."

"So how come you treat me like shit?" snapped Steve. "Not just last night – but all the bloody time."

"Cos I'm a knob, that's why."

Maria nodded approvingly.

Caz tried to hide a smile. Nudging Steve, she whispered, "Go on Steve, put it behind ya."

Steve thought for a moment and nodded. "If I'm your best mate, you've got one last chance to prove it. Cos if you ever talk to me like that again, you and I are history. Got it?"

"Got it," Craig sighed.

"And another thing," added Steve. "You owe Caz and Babs an apology."

"Yes," agreed Craig. "Caz, I'm very sorry for my behaviour last night. I was out of order. I'll apologise to Babs as well, when I see her."

"I can't vouch for how she'll react, but ta," smiled Caz. "I was just saying to Steve we should order a cab to take us back to Skala. You two could probably do with catching up on some sleep."

"I will call you a taxi," smiled Maria and trotted off to the reception desk.

"How's your leg?" Craig nodded to Steve's bandage.

"Could be better."

"I'll be your nurse for the day – if you're good." Caz grinned at Steve.

"And I will be your nurse this evening," smiled Maria, pinching Craig's cheek. "But only if you're *very, very* good. Your taxi is outside. I come at eight tonight. Be smart, please. No football shirt."

Craig grinned as she ushered them towards the foyer. "If you see a glowing light above Eleni Apartments as you park the car, that'll be my halo," he joked as Maria held the door open for them.

"And if you smell this strange odour that smells like disinfectant mixed with rat's piss – that'll be his aftershave," quipped Steve as he hobbled down the steps towards the waiting cab.

Shantee opened her eyes as a shadow fell over her, blocking out the sun. Dimitri smiled down at her as he lit a cigarette. Squinting up at him, Shantee pulled the headphones out of her ears and rolled them up. Jo opened her eyes as she felt the wires of the personal CD player positioned between their sunloungers vibrate on her bare stomach. Seeing Dimitri, she unplugged her ears.

"Morning ladies," he winked, exhaling a jet of smoke out towards the sea and perching on the next sunbed.

"Good morning Superman," teased Jo.

Shantee laughed. "You certainly are the talk of the town today. I heard a couple talking about you in the supermarket this morning. They must have been from the Hotel Flamingo. They were telling the shopkeeper how this handsome man dived into the pool to stop this guy from drowning himself. Even the taxi driver who gave me a lift back was talking about you."

Dimitri smiled. "I will go and see Simon after I finish work. I think maybe Mia is seeing him now because she isn't in her room. Have you seen her?"

Jo nodded. "She was off to the hospital when I saw her getting into her car earlier."

"So, has your act of bravery won her over?" asked Shantee with a sparkle in her eye.

"No." He looked out at the calm blue sea, twinkling beneath the sun.

"Have you tried talking to her?" asked Jo.

"Sort of." He shrugged.

"What does 'sort of' mean exactly?" asked Shantee.

"She knows how I feel." He took another drag of his cigarette and pushed his hair out of his eyes. "But she doesn't trust me."

"Dimitri," said Shantee in a firm tone, "you have got to sit down and talk to her properly. How serious about her are you?"

Dimitri took a deep breath and looked her in the eye. "I want to spend the rest of my life with her."

"Aah," Jo sighed wistfully. "That's so sweet."

"And how do you propose to do that?" asked Shantee.

"Move to England. Get a job."

"Easier said than done," said Shantee.

"I talked to Frank – he can get me a job. He was manager of a big furniture company before he retired. And he said he can help me find somewhere to live."

"So, you need to be telling Mia this – not us," urged Shantee. "I should think as far as she's concerned, all your talk of coming to England is just pie in the sky. For all you know, she might be thinking that if you did come over, you'd want to move straight in with her and sponge off her till you got a job. She's not some gullible nineteen-year-old, you know, she's an intelligent, grown woman."

"I know that," said Dimitri defensively. "I wouldn't ever expect her to support me. I can pay for myself."

"Without getting into trouble?" asked Jo, eyebrows raised sceptically.

"Believe me, I learned my lesson. I'll never touch a pack of cards again. Anyway, I want to train to become a teacher eventually. That is my plan."

"If Frank can help him when he first arrives, then that's brilliant," said Jo, turning to Shantee.

"Get a move on and talk to her," said Shantee impatiently. "You're running out of time."

Dimitri nodded and stood up, flicking his fag butt over the cliff. "So, what about you two?" he squinted at them in the bright sunlight, head cocked to one side. "I saw Nath earlier. He was walking into Skala to watch the football – alone."

Jo giggled. "Yes, he'll be spending a lot more time on his own from now on."

"I think he has finally forgiven me for what I did," said Dimitri. "Although he said I should have let Simon drown."

Jo rolled her eyes. "Typical Nath. So sensitive and caring."

"He even asked me a favour," said Dimitri. "He wants me to get Nikki off his back – apparently she has taken a fancy to him. But I said he has a girlfriend, so what's the problem?" He looked at Jo expectantly.

Jo and Shantee exchanged furtive looks and grinned.

"OK," Dimitri smiled. "I think I get the picture."

"Don't go jumping to conclusions now," said Jo. "We're just friends, getting to know each other. But Nath is most definitely back on the market. So you tell Nikki she can help herself with my blessing."

Dimitri flipped another cigarette into his mouth. "I better do some work," he said.

"Good luck with Mia," smiled Shantee.

"Thanks," he replied. "I'll need it."

A horn beeped outside on the driveway. Steve and Caz wolf-whistled and jeered from the terrace as Craig hurriedly sprayed his neck with aftershave and arranged his blond highlights so that they flopped across his forehead.

He cursed as he looked in the mirror at his bandaged nose and broken arm.

"Don't worry Craig – her heart will go out to you looking like that," joked Caz.

"It's not funny," said Craig. "She's probably only taking me out cos she feels sorry for me."

"Well you should be used to that by now," chuckled Steve.

Outside the car beeped again.

"Hurry up!" urged Caz. "You should never keep a lady waiting."

Craig grabbed his wallet. "Don't wait up," he winked and bolted out the door.

As he limped up the drive, Maria leaned across the passenger seat of her battered old Citroen and pushed open the door.

Craig got in and beamed at her. "You look nice," he said, breathing in her perfume and admiring the way her glossy brown hair fell over her smooth bare shoulders.

"So do you," she smiled flirtatiously. "Did you apologise to the other one – Babs?"

"She was out. Don't worry, I will just as soon as I see her – honest."

She eyed him doubtfully. "OK, I trust you."

"So, where are we going?" he asked as she pulled out of the drive.

"Poros."

"Where's that?"

"Next town after Skala."

"And where are we going for dinner in Poros?"

"Spiti tis Maria," she gave a mischievous grin.

"Sounds good," he nodded. "What is it? Greek? Italian? French?"

Maria laughed. "Greek – *very* Greek."

"Great, I love Greek food."

"I'm so glad," she giggled. "My mother will be very happy!"

"Your mother?" The smile dropped from Craig's face.

"And my father, my aunt and uncle, and my brother – who you met already – and my grandmother." She glanced at him and grinned.

"*We're going to your house?*" Craig looked at her, panic-stricken.

"Relax! I bring you back in one piece. Anyway, you have no choice – if you run away I think I can catch you." She glanced at his bandages and hooted with laughter.

Mia sat on her verandah, admiring the perfect stillness of the pool and the upside-down reflections of the parasols. Daylight had faded, the air had cooled down and her holiday was almost over. She crunched on a piece of cucumber. Tomorrow morning she would get up early and phone Gwen before nine. Hopefully her kids would be at school by then and she could jump in the car and drive straight over. Suddenly it really mattered that she saw Gwen one last time before going home. She couldn't leave with things the way they were – especially not after hearing Simon's story about his father.

Now that she looked back on it after a few days to digest everything, Gwen had seemed quite keen to spend more time with her. After all, she had driven to Skala to find her – she had even picked up the phone and called Dad, which must have been a hard bullet to bite. She thought about what Simon had said. How would she feel if she left Kefalonia without saying goodbye to Gwen, only to find out several months or years later that Gwen had died? Her nose tingled and her eyes welled up at the thought. She didn't want that. She didn't want to spend the rest of her life feeling either bitterness or regret. Whether they forged a relationship or not, she at least wanted to come away feeling that they were no longer strangers – or enemies as they had often been in her mind. Mia slid her hands down to her belly. Perhaps she should just come right out and tell Gwen what had prompted her to come now, at this particular point in time. Maybe that would bridge the gulf between them? But then again, it could have the opposite effect…

A knock at the door made her jump. She got up and went to open it.

"Can I come in?" asked Dimitri, an anxious look on his face. "I need to talk to you."

"OK," she said reluctantly, letting him in.

He followed her through to the verandah and looked around to see

Frank and Margaret reading on their terrace and Caz and Steve eating on theirs. "Perhaps we can go inside?" he asked quietly. Mia sighed and followed him back inside, closing the French doors behind her.

Dimitri sat down at the table and gestured for Mia to sit opposite him. She looked at him apprehensively. He seemed nervous – his leg was jogging under the table like a small boy needing the loo.

Dimitri noticed her frowning at him and stopped jogging his leg. "Sorry."

"What's the matter?" she asked him, concerned. "Is everything OK?"

"No," he said. "Everything is not OK. You are leaving the day after tomorrow and you don't seem to understand how I feel about you – *I love you*. There, I said it – I love you. Not just *in love* with you. *I love you*. Do you understand?"

Mia sighed. "Don't do this, Dimitri. I really like you but it'll never work."

"Why not? I can come to England in October. Frank said he can get me a job at the company where he used to work, no problem. He even said he can help me find a room to rent. He has a few friends who take in lodgers. Then I can be nearer to you and I can start looking for a training course to be a teacher. You see? I have it all planned." He grabbed her hand and clenched it, stroking her palm, entwining his fingers with hers. "I know you feel something for me – you can't hide it."

Mia looked away.

"You can trust me, Mia. I'm changing. I'm not interested in other women and I already swear never to touch a pack of cards ever again. I'm even going to give up smoking – look I haven't touched one since I came in."

Mia glanced at her watch. "That's less than five minutes, Dimitri."

"I'm serious. You can trust me. I'm not the same person I was when you first met me. I'm different, and there's no going back."

"And let's say you never see me again? You still won't smoke? You still won't shag around and you still won't con innocent people out of their money?"

Dimitri stood up and let go of her hand. "Even if I never see you again, I won't shag around, I won't cheat people, and I won't–" he turned his back towards her and paused. "Look, what is stopping you wanting to be with me?" he turned to face her again. "I don't understand it. I know you like me, I know you care about me. I promise you can trust me, I won't expect you to help me when I come to England – *and I can come to England* – so what is the problem?" He leaned over the table and looked at her intently.

"I'm pregnant," she said, looking into his eyes.

He stood up straight and stared at her. "What?"

"I'm PREGNANT," she said louder.

Frowning, Dimitri pushed his hair out of his eyes and exhaled deeply. He fingered the outline of his cigarettes in his shirt pocket and then dropped his hands to his sides.

"When – whose – who is the father?" he stammered.

"My ex-boyfriend Max."

"So you are getting back together?"

"No."

"He is supporting you?"

"No."

"You are still in love with him?"

"No."

"He is still in love with you?"

Mia shook her head. Dimitri turned away from her and stared blankly at the wall. "You are really *pregnant*?" he sighed.

Mia didn't reply.

"How many months?"

"Two."

"Why didn't you tell me before?"

"There was no need for you to know."

Dimitri took his cigarettes out of his pocket and lit one, his eyes still fixed on the wall in front of him. Mia rolled her eyes. "So now you know why I won't get involved," she said wearily. "I'm not in a position to take risks with my emotions or my future right now."

Dimitri remained silent. Eventually he turned around and looked down at her stomach with a doubtful frown.

"I'm not showing yet," she said defensively.

"Are you definitely keeping it?" he asked timidly.

"Listen Dimitri, there really isn't anything else left to say. I'm genuinely

299

touched that you feel – or rather you *think* you feel so strongly about me, but now you know the truth, I think you should go away and reconsider those feelings. I expect it will change things for you."

"Mia, I…" Unable to find the right words, Dimitri flapped his hands defeatedly against his sides.

"I think it's best you go now," she said, standing up and guiding him to the door.

"Are you sure you're pregnant?" he asked as she opened the door.

"Quite sure, thank you." She pushed him gently outside onto the doorstep. "Good night Dimitri." She closed the door behind him and sighed.

Standing sideways in front of her wardrobe she looked at her reflection in the mirror. "Yes I'm quite sure I'm pregnant – and yes," she took a big breath, "I *am* keeping it." A tear trickled out of her eye. "But even if I had chosen to have an abortion, I wouldn't want a pathetic useless man like you in my life anyway."

Mia sat down on the bed and burst into tears. For a moment – the tiniest, most wonderful moment – she had thought he was going to scoop her up and kiss her, overwhelmed with excitement. But the colour had all but drained from his face, leaving his olive skin pasty grey and the sparkle in his eyes replaced by fear.

This would be her lot for the foreseeable future. One man after another would see the bump, the cot, the pushchair, and say, 'Nice meeting you, see you around'. Not that she cared too much. Fear of not having a man at her side wasn't the reason she had contemplated having an abortion. It was fear of herself. With Gwen for a mother, who knew what little horrors of personality lay undiscovered in her genetic make-up. What if she couldn't handle motherhood either? And she had even less of an excuse than Gwen, because at least she knew there was a risk of history repeating itself. At least she knew there was a good chance she wasn't fit to be a mother. And with Max for a father – a cold-hearted, absent, totally uninterested father who had accused her of lying and then dared to question if the baby was his – there was no one else for this child to fall back on. But she had made her decision, and now she had no choice but to overcome her fears.

CHAPTER 27

Friday 14th

Frank burst through the front door as Margaret stepped out of the bathroom wrapped in a towel, surrounded by a giant cloud of steam.

"Oh you made me jump!" she squealed, patting her heart.

"Good news, Margaret – guess what?" he clasped her by the shoulders.

"What?" she smiled.

"The cottage is mine!" he hugged her and laughed joyously.

"What? When – how did that happen?" Margaret tried to smile through her confusion.

"Yesterday when I left you and Babs to have a chat, I went and put in an offer and I've just found out this morning that it's been accepted – *it's mine!*" he beamed.

"Congratulations," Margaret said awkwardly, the smile fading on her lips.

"Come on, pet," Frank rubbed her arms. "Try and be happy for me. This won't affect what you get when we sort out the divorce. I told you I'd see you right. You might have to forget a holiday home in Como, but love, we were never going to be able to afford that."

"It's not that," shrugged Margaret defensively. "I don't begrudge you the cottage – it's just brought it home to me, that's all…we really are going our separate ways."

"Oh love, we're still friends. Look how well we've been getting on these last few days. Once I've got it looking all nice and comfortable, you can come and stay whenever you want. I know you prefer France and Italy, but at least you'll always have the option of coming to visit that useless old ex-husband of yours for a free holiday!" He tried to make her laugh.

"You're not useless," Margaret put her hands to her eyes and sobbed. "You're not useless at all. You're a good man, Frank. If anything I've been a useless wife."

"Stop that now," whispered Frank, pressing her to him and stroking her wet hair. "I won't hear such nonsense. Neither one of us has been better or worse than the other."

"But Frank, just listening to that poor woman Babs regretting leaving her husband has made me realise we might be making a huge mistake. I've found myself wondering if I can bear to let you go."

"It's just fear of the unknown, Margaret. We've been over this. Our marriage is over – but what we've got left is friendship. If we were to go back home and carry on as we were, eventually even friendship would become impossible. We both know it, love. You'll be alright. We both will."

She nodded into his chest. "I'd like to come and stay at your cottage – when you've converted it from a pile of rubble to a luxury villa." She looked up at him and smiled through her tears.

"Come on, let's go and look at it now!" he squeezed her excitedly.

"Actually Babs is coming over in a minute. I said I'd go for lunch with her in town."

"OK then," shrugged Frank. "Come and look at it later. I'm going to pop up there now."

"Frank?"

"Yes, love?"

Margaret took his hand and squeezed it. "I am happy for you – I really am," she smiled.

Mia checked behind her and reversed into a space outside Gwen's house. Inspecting her reflection in the visor mirror, she felt positive. Gwen had sounded pleased to hear from her on the phone and had told her to come straight over and she would start preparing some lunch. What did she like – chicken? lamb? Or was she a vegetarian? Katty and George wouldn't be home until after five today, so they had pretty much the whole day to talk and get to know each other.

Mia closed her eyes and took a minute to calm her nerves. Hopefully things would be a bit easier, now that the initial confrontation was out of the way. The atmosphere would be less tense. Her anger had died down to a smaller flame, and Gwen had seemed willing to drop her defences. Not that they were about to become best friends by any means, but perhaps the idea of friendship was no longer as unthinkable as it once was.

Simon's regrets about his father had made her think. What had his father wanted to say to him? *Sorry, son. Sorry I wasn't a better father, sorry I was so hard on you – the truth is I'm proud of you. I only wish I'd told you sooner?* But Simon would never know. How sad, thought Mia. Fortunately Gwen was still around to work things out with – and willing. Apprehensive, but willing.

Mia opened the car door and got out. She walked up to the front door, straightened her skirt and rang the bell. She could hear voices inside. The door opened and Gwen poked her head out.

"Hi," smiled Mia.

"Mia, I'm really sorry but something's come up," whispered Gwen with an anxious glance over her shoulder.

"What?" asked Mia, puzzled.

A face appeared behind Gwen. It was an older woman with white hair and heavy eyebags. She said something in Greek, looking at Mia. Gwen shrugged and muttered something back, feigning a smile. The woman continued to stare at Mia, a curious look on her face.

"Anyway, so if you turn left at the end of this road, you'll find it." Gwen spoke loudly and pointed over Mia's shoulder. "Just pretend you're following my directions," she added cheerily through a fixed smile, turning her back on the old woman and accompanying Mia to the front gate. "My parents-in-law just turned up half an hour ago. I don't know how long they'll be here – have you got a phone number I can call you on?"

"No," said Mia, her cheeks flushing with frustration.

"As soon as they go I'll drive over to Skala and we can go out for dinner or something," she whispered under her breath.

"What about your children?"

"I'll think of something. Look I've got to go." Gwen gestured to the end of the street again. "Yes it's on your left – you'll be there in two minutes! Bye bye." She turned and went back indoors, throwing a distant smile over her shoulder and ushering her frowning mother-in-law inside. The door closed behind her with a clatter, leaving Mia standing on the pavement, alone and bewildered. Slowly she walked back towards her car, the small flame of anger within her prickling in the pit of her stomach.

Perhaps it was her own fault for not going sooner, she reasoned. It wasn't Gwen's fault her in-laws had turned up unexpectedly. But why couldn't she get rid of them? Just make up some excuse? How hard could it be? She could have pretended Mia was an old friend from England who had looked her up and whom she had invited to lunch. She could have made up anything if she'd put her mind to it. But the lies and pretense pricked and prodded at her. She was a secret – a shameful secret that Gwen couldn't bring herself to come clean about.

For a brief moment she considered turning around and going back and thumping on the door and shouting out that she was Gwen's daughter – Gwen's abandoned secret daughter. But of course she knew she wouldn't. What would it achieve? Nothing but a greater rift, more anger, more hurt and more tears. She climbed in the car, closed the door and turned on the ignition. Back to Skala it was, then. To wait as requested.

Out of the corner of her eye Shantee could see Caz and Steve walking past on the road, towels slung over their shoulders and cheerful grins on their faces. What an odd pairing, she thought to herself as she spread out her yoga mat on the grass slope next to the Hotel Flamingo pool terrace.

A group of women did the same, some of them using beach towels as substitute yoga mats.

"OK, now everybody stand in the centre of their towel facing me, feet hip-width apart, knees loose, tail-bone tucked in. Feel your feet on the ground, feel the pull of the earth beneath you."

Jo grinned at her from the front row, and pushed her shoulders back and chin up. Nikki perched on a nearby sunlounger, watching with keen interest, just a few feet away from Nath who was lying with his back to them, reading the papers.

"Why don't you join in?" Shantee smiled over at Nikki.

"I'm in my uniform," she shrugged down at her blue knee-length skirt. "Won't be able to do the moves."

"Yeah you will," urged Shantee. "Come on."

Nikki looked at her watch. "OK then," she smiled.

"How about you, Nath?" asked Shantee with a friendly smile.

"No thank you," came the distinctly uninterested reply from the back of his head.

"Go on!" said Nikki. "You look like you could do with some exercise."

Nath rustled his papers loudly and turned the page without replying.

"Come on," grinned Jo. "I won't bite you, I promise."

A few of the other women joined in. "Come on! Be a sport!"

Nath turned around and looked at them, squinting through one eye in the bright sunshine. "I'll be the only bloke," he complained.

"Lucky you!" shouted a woman on the back row.

"I thought the more women the merrier was your philosophy," teased Shantee. "Oh come on, Nath. Let's let bygones be bygones and release all our negativity with some deep breathing exercises."

As the chorus of calling women grew louder, Nath arose reluctantly from his sunlounger and walked towards them, an embarrassed smile on his face. Everyone clapped as he took his place next to Nikki.

"OK," smiled Shantee. "Chins level with the ground, eyes closed, lips closed and breathe in through the nostrils. Good – hold it – and release through the mouth. And again…"

Caz let the shallow waves wash over her and retreat as she lay on the shore at the water's edge. A short distance away in the sea, Steve took off his mask and snorkel.

"See anything?" asked Caz.

"A crab," he replied.

"Blimey, not near me I hope!" she shivered, sitting up right and wriggling her bottom up the shore out of the water.

Steve waded towards her. "You're safe," he said. "It was heading in the other direction."

Caz breathed a sigh of relief. "So what's Bromley like?" she asked. "I've never been there."

Steve shrugged. "Nothing special. Shops, bars, restaurants, a few clubs. And near enough to London if we fancy a Saturday night clubbing up the West End."

"The West End," sighed Caz. "Ain't been up there for donkeys' years."

"You're not missing much," said Steve, lying down next to her, his feet touching the water. "We don't go that often to be honest. Too expensive and too much hassle. It's easier to go out in Bromley."

"You know, I ain't been clubbing in years," said Caz, trying to wash the sand off her large white feet.

"You were clubbing only the other night at the Bora Bora," said Steve.

"Yeah, well that was the first time in bloody ages. I'd almost forgotten how to dance. When you get to my age-"

"What do you mean *your age?*" asked Steve. "You're forty – not sixty."

"Yeah, but I ain't young like you. I ain't got your energy no more – what with kids and all that."

"You seem lively enough to me," Steve smiled at her and threw a pebble into her lap.

"Oy watch it, sunshine," she laughed. "I suppose when I see young lads like you and Craig, and young girls like Mia, I become aware of how old I am – and how fat I am." She smiled a melancholy smile at Steve and gently tossed the pebble back at him.

"You're not old and you're not fat," he said, sitting up and looking directly at her. "You're beautiful." He blushed and quickly looked down at his feet, digging his toes into the shingle.

Caz's eyes widened. "Beautiful? Me?" She giggled. "You're a lovely lad, Steve. You'll make some lucky girl very happy one day."

"I mean it," he said. "I think you're beautiful."

Caz felt a lump in her throat. "No one's said that to me for as long I can remember."

Steve leaned towards her and took her face in his hands.

"Oh blimey," her voice trembled as his lips came towards hers.

After a few seconds, Steve sat back and looked at her. "How far is Southend from Bromley?" he asked.

"Well I'd better be getting back to Margaret," said Frank, looking at his watch and draining the last of his coffee.

"Don't worry, Frank," said Vasiliki. "She will understand."

"I hope so," sighed Frank, looking worriedly into her deep green eyes. "It's a bit of a surprise to spring on her."

"You are ending your marriage, so you will be apart. Maybe now is good time to start," she gave him a comforting pat on the hand and walked him to the door. "Dimitri is so grateful for your help," she said. "I will miss him so much if he leaves, but I can't stop him, and I will be happy that he is with your good friends. And," she smiled at him, "I am happy to have my new neighbour."

Frank squeezed her hand. "I couldn't have found a better place, or a nicer neighbour if I'd tried," he smiled back. "So your nephew will come tomorrow evening to talk bricks and money?"

"Seven o'clock," she nodded, twisting her long hair up into a bun and sticking a pencil through it.

Frank saluted her and opened the front door. As he turned to go, she caught his arm.

"Frank, please think to stay here – we have one more bed and Hotel Flamingo is not cheap. Here the price of your room is this – happy face." She pointed to her smiling lips.

"You're too kind," he said, patting her shoulder.

"It is the Greek way."

"Perhaps next week, if I'm still here, then I'll accept your generous offer."

She nodded and waved as he headed back towards Eleni Apartments.

Craig sat in the car and watched glumly as Frank walked past. The sun was setting over the hills and in twenty-four hours he'd be back in Bromley. Back at his Dad's cramped, grubby flat, back in his postman's uniform, back at The Boar's Head – that stinky, revolting shit-hole of a pub. Maria turned the engine off and rested her hand on his leg. It made his hairs stand on end. He didn't know what was happening to him – he had never felt like this before.

"Sorry I am working on your last night," she smiled sadly. "But I will come and wave bye bye at the airport tomorrow morning."

Craig stared straight ahead. "I'm not going," he said flatly.

"Don't be silly, Craig," she whispered. "Of course you go. I will write you. You have email, yes?"

"No. I can't type anyway – I'll never see you again," he blurted.

"Yes, you will see me again," she smiled.

307

"When? I can't afford to come out here again till next year, now."

Maria leaned over him, dunking her bosoms into his lap, and opened the glove compartment. She reached inside, pulled out a glossy colour brochure and handed it to him.

"St Mary's Hospital," he read the heading on the cover and frowned at her.

"This hospital is in England – not far from London," she pointed at the address on the back cover.

"Kent," he read, surprised. "*I* live in Kent."

"Maybe I am doing a course there next year," she beamed.

"When next year?" he asked eagerly.

"It start in September. But first I must pass my exams here."

"September's ages!" whined Craig.

"You don't wait for me?" she looked at him, eyebrow raised.

"'Course I'll wait for you," he leaned towards her and kissed her.

"My father, he likes you," she said, pressing the tip of his bandaged nose with her index finger. "My mother, she likes you, too. All my family think you are nice boy." She slid her hand down to his shorts. "I think you are *very* nice boy," she purred into his ear and pressed on his crotch.

"Come inside for five minutes," he urged, pulling her towards him. "Steve won't mind taking a quick walk."

"*Five minutes?* You think you can please me so quickly?" she teased. "No. I must be at the hospital in forty minutes. Already I am late. I will see you at the airport in the morning."

"*Please*," he begged, his lips on hers.

She tutted. "The longer you wait, the better it will be."

"Don't make me wait till *September*."

"So come back in May. You can work in a bar – or be a travel rep like Nikki. You know the island now."

A smile spread across Craig's face. He could do that – he could be a travel rep. So long as he didn't have to wear some poncey boy scout-type uniform.

"Where would I live?"

"My brother's flat in Argostoli." She kissed him on the cheek. "Go now, please. I am late. She pushed him towards the car door.

"Alright, alright, I'm going," he smiled and got out. "Tomorrow morning, yeah? My flight leaves at eleven."

"I will be there." She blew him a kiss and pressed her foot down on the accelerator, screeching off along the coast road towards Argostoli.

Craig watched the exhaust fumes billow out behind her as she went. She waved out the window as the car disappeared around a curve in the cliff. He counted on his fingers. May was still eight months away. She'd have met someone else by then, he was sure of it.

As he walked down the drive he saw Babs letting herself into her apartment. Catching sight of him, she quickly tried to get her key in the door.

"Oy, Babs! Wait!" He limped towards her.

"What do you want?" she snapped under her breath.

"I just wanted to say sorry."

"Blimey, you feelin' alright?" she glared at him sarcastically. "Didn't think you had that word in your vocubularlary."

"I'm sorry. I acted like a c– idiot. I didn't mean what I said. I was out of order."

Babs stared at him. "Actually you was right." She smiled at him fleetingly. "I've been doing a lot of thinking these last couple of days – spent a bit of time on me jack jones – and you was right."

"No I wasn't Babs."

"Yes you was."

"No I wasn't."

"Alright then, let's compromise. I ain't old, I ain't sad, but I *am* an alcoholic. However, I ain't drunk nothing today, and I never drunk nothing yesterday. So touch wood, I'll soon be able to call myself an ex-alcoholic."

Craig looked at her sheepishly. "Well I ain't perfect either."

"I know *that*," Babs huffed, opening her door.

"Look, I'm sorry, yeah?" he held his good hand out towards her.

She hesitated and looked at him. "Wouldn't it be funny if you went home with two broken arms? You wouldn't be able to carry your suitcase then."

As Craig looked at her unsure of whether she was joking or not, she took his hand and shook it. "Big of you to apologise," she mumbled. "My

309

turn now. Gotta go and tell Caz what a lousy mate I've been. Oh well, onwards and upwards." She closed the door behind her.

Craig turned back to his apartment and smiled to himself. What was going on? He felt almost euphoric and yet bloody miserable at the same time. In the last twenty-four hours his world had turned on its head. He'd met a woman like no one he'd ever met before and he'd fallen arse-over-bollock in love. She was a stunner, an angel. She was sexy, kind, mature, fun, *and* she liked football *and*, most incredible of all, she liked *him*. She had the power to make him do things he wouldn't normally do – like grovel to people he'd pissed off. And the mental thing was, it felt alright. It was no big deal. If anything, it made him feel good. Maria was a real Greek goddess, and she was all his. His heart soared. Until she met someone else. His heart plummeted. Craig leaned against his door and pressed his forehead against the warm brown wood. He wasn't sure his heart could handle all these emotions.

"Simon, I was going to come and visit you!" Dimitri walked up the drive towards him and greeted him as he climbed out of the taxi. "How are you, my friend?"

"Still alive, thanks to you," Simon smiled sheepishly and held out his hand. Dimitri shook it and slapped him on the back. "You saved my life," he said gratefully. "I'll be forever in your debt."

"No debt," smiled Dimitri, lighting up a cigarette. "You saved my life too. I am a hero now. Two days ago I was not so popular – remember? Dimitri the cheat, Dimitri the con-artist. If my mother had found out what I was doing she would have made my life hell. No, my friend, we are *both* lucky – we have both been given a second chance."

Simon smiled and took a card out of his pocket. "That's my mobile number and email address – ignore the home address, that's about to change – if you ever come to England, if there's anything I can ever do for you, just give me a call."

Dimitri took the card and examined it sadly. "Who knows, maybe one day I will give you a call. But I don't know when I'll be coming to England. I thought it might be soon, but..." he looked in the direction of Mia's apartment, "but now I'm not so sure."

"Well, even if ten years go by, I'll still be glad to hear from you," shrugged Simon. "I'll never forget you."

Dimitri smiled. "You must be the millionth person to say those words to me the night before they leave this island. And you know what? I think you are the only one I believe."

Simon chuckled. "Is…er, Mia about?"

Dimitri nodded. "She told me I can't come in because she is waiting for her mother to come."

"Oh," said Simon, disappointed.

"She doesn't want to talk to me anyway," said Dimitri. "But maybe she wants to talk to you."

"Why doesn't she want to talk to you?" asked Simon.

"Because I'm an arsehole."

"She said that?"

"No." Dimitri smoked his cigarette down to the butt, stubbed it out on top of the fence and flicked it down into the small parking bay. "It's a long story – she says she has nothing more to say to me and it is best to say goodbye now so she can leave Kefalonia with a nice memory of me – in other words, forget about me quickly."

Simon looked at him, confused.

"Like I said, it's a long story. But maybe she is right – *all* women are right. You know that. Anyway, I am going to Skala. You want to come? I go to my friend Vasilis' bar – I need a drink."

Simon shook his head. "Not sure I'm up to it, mate. Will I see you tomorrow?"

"I don't think so," Dimitri shrugged. "After everyone is gone, I will come to clean the apartments and the pool area before the next group arrive."

"Don't you want to say goodbye to everyone?"

"My friend," Dimitri smiled and slapped him affectionately on the shoulder. "They forget me already – and I forget them." He flipped another cigarette in his mouth and walked to where his moped was parked in the lay-by. "Have a safe trip home," he grinned as he revved the accelerator and sped off.

Simon walked down the drive and knocked on Mia's door.

The door opened a fraction and Mia's face appeared. "Hi. How are you?"

311

she smiled, opening the door wider.

"Feeling much better thanks. How are you? I hear you're waiting for your mum."

Mia rolled her eyes. "Yeah, I was hoping she might be here by now."

"Why don't you call her?"

"No," said Mia firmly. "She knows where I am. Anyway, I can't – her in-laws are there."

"Well, I suppose if you're waiting for her, you won't be able to join me for dinner tonight?" he asked timidly.

Mia smiled. "I'm supposed to be going for dinner with *her* – that's if she turns up. Thanks for the offer though."

"She'll turn up," said Simon. "She'll probably be here any minute."

"Well, she'll just have to wait while I take a nice, long shower."

"I'll leave you to it, then. See you on the coach in the morning."

"Yes," she said sadly. "Back to boring ol' Blighty, eh?"

"See you then. Have a nice evening with your mum." He turned and walked over to his apartment and let himself in. They could have a proper chat on the way to the airport tomorrow, he told himself. They could swap numbers then. Besides, they'd arranged to meet up – tentatively. He had told her he was anxious about attending his friend's wedding next month. Shelley would be there and he knew everyone would be feeling sorry for him – or relieved for her. Either way, he was dreading going. Mia had promised she'd be his date for the occasion – that was if he hadn't found someone else to go with him, which of course he knew he wouldn't. Besides, if Mia could be his date, why would he want to go with anyone else?

He opened the French doors and breathed in the mild evening air.

"He's back!" cried a voice.

Caz and Babs waved at him from their terrace. "Alright mate?" shouted Babs. "We thought you was a gonner. Fancy joining us for a drink? Soft drinks only I'm afraid, we're detoxing."

Hearing the noise, Frank and Margaret emerged on their verandah. "Welcome back, son," boomed Frank. "How are you feeling, pet?" called Margaret.

Cheeks aflame with embarrassment, he tried to smile at the friendly faces. "M-much better thanks," he stammered.

Shantee lifted herself up gracefully from the lotus position on her terrace and smiled at him.

"You're back!" squeaked Jo hurrying out behind her to see what was going on. "We're so glad you're alright. I think we should all go out for a drink to celebrate the fact that you're alive and well. What do you say?"

Simon twitched.

"Bloody good idea," said Frank. "Come on everyone. It's our last night, let's all go into town and have ourselves some cocktails – or non-alcoholic ones for those of us who feel they've had enough alcohol for one holiday."

Steve appeared on his terrace, covered only by a towel from the waist down. "Did someone say a last night drink?" he asked with a grin on his face and a sideways glance at Caz. "Craig, fancy one for the road?" he called over his shoulder towards the bed. "That was a yes," he reported to the listening faces.

"Simon? Are you up to it, love?" asked Margaret, concerned.

Simon looked across at Nath who was reading a magazine and listening to an iPod, oblivious to the communal spirit buzzing around him.

Steve aimed a bottle top at him. "What a shot!" he cheered as it dropped between Nath and his paper, landing on his lap. Nath looked up and scowled, pulling the headphones from his ears. "You – drink – Skala – tonight – with the rest of us?" Steve pointed at him.

Nath looked around him as his fellow holidaymakers stood on their verandahs all awaiting his reply. He looked round at Simon and sat up. "Alright mate? Heard you took a bit of a dip the other night."

Simon smiled timidly. "That's one way of putting it."

"Come on, Nath," said Jo. "Let's all end our holiday on a good note."

Nath put down his magazine and nodded. "Alright – just don't invite Nikki. The girl won't leave me alone."

Jo rolled her eyes. "OK, everyone, let's all meet at that trendy bar with the TV sets at nine o'clock. How's that?"

A ripple of agreement spread throughout the complex as people went back inside their apartments to get ready.

"Looks like you haven't got much choice." Shantee leaned on the railings of her verandah and winked at Simon.

Simon smiled. He wondered if Dimitri would still be there when they arrived. It would be nice for them all to get a chance to say goodbye. Besides, Dimitri should be the one they all raised their glasses to – not him. He was no hero, he was just lucky to be alive.

Mia sat on the small beach watching clouds pass across the moon. No tears this time, she was all cried out. Gwen hadn't shown up, and she was damned if she was going to call her. If that woman couldn't think up a reason to shake off her family – who she saw all the time – the night before her estranged daughter left for England, then she could go to hell. She knew where to find her – she could get on a plane and come and see her, if she could tear herself away from her cosy little Greek family life. Mia had done her bit now. She had done more than her bit. She had got on a plane, come to Kefalonia, looked her up and taken the courage to introduce herself, not knowing what kind of reaction she would get – *she, the child, the abandoned one*, had made the first move. Now it was Gwen's turn.

Mia sat still on the shingle, hugging her knees and listening to the silence. Despite the rawness of her feelings and the sadness in her heart, she could see the beauty all around her – the rippled sea whooshing gently against the rocks and the shore. The breeze tickling her skin and ruffling her hair. The occasional flutter of a bat above her in the moonlit sky. She could have stayed in Kefalonia forever if it wasn't for the fact that the island was tarnished with her mother's presence. And then there was Dimitri – another good reason to leave. If she had stayed any longer she wouldn't have been able to keep him at bay. He was too tempting, too beautiful, too romantic, too sweet and caring…too petrified of the word baby to be of any use to her now or ever. She couldn't afford to lean on someone like that, knowing full well they'd only let her down when the going got tough. Would he come to England anyway? He seemed so keen to leave this place, but did he have what it took to up sticks and move to another country? Who knew? He had his choices to make and she had hers. And now she knew without the shadow of a doubt, that she'd made the right one. A person was growing inside her. Initially she had tried to ignore it, detach from it, not picture its tiny, little body forming in her womb. But now she couldn't wait to know what it felt like when it started kicking. It was as if a bond had already formed and she had always known what her decision would be no matter how hard she had tried to push it away. Meeting Gwen had changed nothing. She was going to have this baby. And she was not going to desert it, no matter what. *No matter what.*

CHAPTER 28

Saturday 15th

"Welcome back on board everybody," Nikki smiled at everyone as the coach pulled away from Eleni Apartments. Mia looked out of the window at the deserted pool and empty verandahs. "I hope you've all enjoyed your stay here in Skala, and that you've each managed to see some of the other parts that make up the beautiful island of Kefalonia."

Mia watched as Nikki reeled off her well-practised return-trip speech. She noticed her eyes kept resting on Nath who was sitting on his own in the row in front of Jo and Shantee.

"We'll be making a few stops on the way to pick up more people and should be at the airport in just under an hour's time, leaving you plenty of time to check in and do your last minute shopping."

Mia tuned out as Nikki started to ask people where they had been on the island and what their favourite places were. The coach bounced over a pothole as it crawled uphill past a crumbly old café. Mia looked at the old men sitting outside playing dominoes or just staring contentedly into space fiddling with their worry beads. There was something so peaceful about this place, this life. Of course, she was looking at it with a tourist's rose-tinted glasses – a bit how Dimitri seemed to view England, exciting, busy, crazy, land of opportunities, a better standard of living, more money, more cosmopolitan. It was an outsider's perspective that usually evened out after spending a certain amount of time there.

As the coach stopped to pick up holidaymakers from the marshmallow-pink hotel on the other side of Skala, she felt a stab of guilt. She hadn't said a last goodbye to Dimitri. She was sure he would have been hanging around the apartments as they all boarded the coach, but he was nowhere to be seen. Still, it was probably best this way.

"You alright?" whispered Simon in the seat next to her.

"I'm fine – how are you doing?" she whispered back. "Looking forward to going back?"

He frowned at her. "Not exactly. I'm going back to an empty house – literally. She's taken most of the furniture."

Mia patted his arm. "New beginnings, Simon. Look to the future."

"What's Egham like?" he asked.

Mia shrugged. "It's OK. It's got its nice bits and its not so nice bits. It's not Kefalonia though."

Simon smiled. "I could live here, you know."

"I think I could too."

"I wouldn't miss a thing."

"Really?" She looked at him.

"Seriously. What's there to miss? The rain, our useless public transport service, our rubbish TV channels – all those bloody property programmes and talent contests for teenagers who want to be the next Kylie? Tesco's, Starbucks, KFC – who needs it?"

"I shouldn't get on the plane if I were you," smiled Mia. "You're in the right place right now, so you might as well stay."

"No, not Greece," Simon looked at her with a knowing smile. "Every Tom, Dick and Harry is moving to Greece, France or Spain right now. If I were going to do it, I'd go somewhere no one else would think of, like Bulgaria for example."

Mia raised her eyebrows. "Interesting choice."

"Dirt cheap, too…" He closed his eyes.

"Tired?" asked Mia.

"Last night was the best night of this holiday," Simon smiled. "You should've been there."

"Yeah, well, if I hadn't been waiting for the mother that never was, I would have come."

"There must be a good reason why she didn't turn up," he said, frowning.

"Well unless there's been a death in the family, it won't be good enough for me."

The coach jerked to a halt to let an old woman on a donkey cross the road.

"Look at that!" sighed Caz loudly from a few rows back. "Ain't that lovely?"

"Quick – pass us me camera," said Babs excitedly. "Excellent – got it!"

"So did you manage to find Tom Hanks' house?" Nikki smiled into her microphone, looking down the aisle at Caz and Babs.

Babs shook her head. "We thought we saw him when we was in Fiskardo, but it was someone else."

"And we thought we saw him somewhere else," said Caz. "Where was it? Anyway, it weren't him. From behind, he looked just like him, though."

"I doubt Tom Hanks would have a property here," said Margaret from across the aisle. "I mean, think about it – he lives in America, why come all this way? He probably has a few luxury villas somewhere nearer to home, like the Caribbean, Mexico or Bermuda."

"Well who knows?" said Nikki, "but word definitely has it he owns a villa on the coast just outside Fiskardo – and a yacht, apparently."

"Well we'll make sure we find it when we come back next year, eh, Caz?" boomed Babs.

"Yeah," came a less enthusiastic reply.

The coach pulled into a parking bay at the airport and everyone hopped off, one by one and waited patiently for the driver to unload their luggage.

"Please make sure you only have ONE item of hand luggage," Nikki repeated above the melée. "Otherwise you'll either have to leave it behind or pay a fine."

Craig limped off to find a trolley.

"You alright, babe?" Caz asked Steve, pinching his bum.

"Yeah, I'm *well* alright," he grinned, getting out his camera and taking a photo of her.

"Oy – I weren't ready for that! I need to re-do me lippy!" she protested.

"Too late," he smiled, putting his camera away. "Anyway, you look beautiful to me."

Babs rolled her eyes and turned her back on them as they embraced. "OY! LOOK!" she shouted, making everyone jump. "IT'S ONLY BLEEDIN' TOM 'ANKS!"

Caz spun round. "Where?" she said disbelievingly.

Her heart racing, Babs pointed towards a slim man with short dark hair, dressed in jeans and a short-sleeved shirt. "*It's him, it's bloody him, I tell ya!*"

"Bloody 'ell! It *is* him!" shrieked Caz.

Word spread across the crowd of holidaymakers as everyone turned to look in the direction of Babs' index finger to where Tom Hanks was helping a porter load up the back of a shiny blue Toyota 4x4.

"Come on, you lot!" Babs barked at Caz, Steve and Craig. "We're going over!"

Craig groaned.

"*Come on!*" hissed Babs, taking hold of his good arm and dragging him towards Tom Hanks. "Take me camera, and don't bloody mess it up or I'll kill you!" she instructed.

Babs pressed a hand against her heart in a futile effort to stop it beating so fast. She took a deep breath.

"Scuse me, Mr 'Anks."

Tom Hanks turned around and looked at her. "Hi there," he smiled awkwardly.

Babs gasped with delight. "Would you mind if my mate took a picture of us with you?"

"Sure, why not?" he shrugged cheerfully.

Babs grabbed Caz and shunted her to the other side of him. Grinning, Craig held the camera up to his eye and clicked.

"There you go, ladies. Nice to meet you," smiled Tom.

"Thanks ever so much. We love your films – Forrest Gump's me all-time favourite."

"Gee thanks," he smiled.

Before he could turn back to his luggage, Craig had thrust the camera at Babs.

"Er, is it alright if we have a picture as well, Mr Hanks?" he asked.

Tom looked at his sling and the bandage on his nose. "OK – er, what happened to you guys? I didn't know there was a war on here," he joked.

Craig and Steve sniggered as they stood either side of him. Craig tried to put an arm round his shoulders, but quickly discovered he was restricted by the sling.

"Cheers, mate," grinned Craig.

"Yeah, cheers," said Steve.

"Well, nice meeting you. Have a safe trip," Tom saluted them cheerily and turned around to find himself face to face with a grinning Jo and Margaret at the front of a jostling crowd all holding out cameras and pens.

Craig lit a cigarette and sat down on top of his suitcase in the check-in queue as Jo and Shantee squeezed past him and headed in the direction of the toilets. In front of him, Nath shuffled their luggage forward, a frown on his face as he watched Jo across the crowded check-in hall. Craig looked over his shoulder. Jo and Shantee were holding hands and giggling in the queue for the Ladies. Craig smirked. So it was true.

"What are you looking at?" snapped Nath, noticing his smug expression.

Craig shrugged. "Nothing, mate. They make a nice pair, that's all."

Nath's cheeks filled with blood. "You should watch that mouth of yours, pal. Seeing as everyone knows you shagged that fat heifer with the big gob."

Craig gave him a tight smile and looked away. Across the hall he saw Maria searching for him, still in her nurse's uniform looking tired and slightly dishevelled. He waved until she spotted him and came running towards him.

"I miss you already," she pouted, wrapping her arms around him.

"I miss you too," he smiled, pleased that she looked genuinely upset.

"Will you write to me, text me and call me?" she asked, gazing sadly into his eyes.

"Every day," he whispered. "And then I'm coming over in May – if not sooner. I'll get a job as a rep – and if I can't do that, I'll work in a bar. Just like you said."

She grinned and kissed him happily all over his face.

"Hey – watch the nose!" he laughed.

"You will come back for me?" she asked.

"If you'll wait for me," he smiled. "You might meet someone else and forget all about me."

"Impossible!" she protested, and fiddled to undo the shiny gold crucifix fastened around her neck. "Here, take it," she ordered, slipping it into his hand. "This once belong to my great grandmother. I give it to you to prove that I wait."

Behind her Nath rolled his eyes and yawned loudly. Craig ignored him and took his silver Zippo lighter out of his shorts pocket.

"I can't give you anything as nice as that," he said, clutching her crucifix. "But my granddad bought me this lighter for my birthday a few years ago, before he died. Look – it's got my name engraved on it. So this is my proof to you." He put it in her hand, closed her fingers around it and pulled her to him. "I'll call you the minute I get home."

"I'll be waiting," she replied.

As Margaret handed over her luggage and took her boarding card, she could restrain the tears no longer.

"Oh, pet, I'll be home in a week or two. And I'll call you tonight to make sure you've got back safely," said Frank, mopping her eyes with his hankie. "Don't cry love – you'll smudge your make-up."

Margaret took a deep breath. "What are we going to do about the house?" she asked.

"Nothing just yet," he shrugged. "There's no rush. We'll talk about it when I get back. You need some time to think about what you want to do anyway."

She nodded and looked at the seat number on her boarding card.

"I want you to go home and relax. Ring the kids, tell them you're back safe and sound and when you're ready, fix a date to get them both over for lunch and we can sit them down and tell them what we're doing. Margaret, I've only one request, which I'm sure I don't even need to say, but-"

"Frank, I would never do anything with Derek in our house. Never."

"I know you wouldn't," he sighed, squeezing her hand.

"What about your new friend Vasiliki?" she asked, trying to sound indifferent.

"What about her?" he frowned.

"I get the feeling she has a soft spot for you."

"How would you know that you silly woman?" laughed Frank, rolling his eyes.

Margaret looked at him and smiled. "Oh Frank, you really are slow sometimes, love. *Women know women.* We understand each other perfectly without having to say a word. She likes you, Frank. Take my word for it."

Frank shook his head and laughed. "Whatever you say, dear. Now then, why don't I accompany you to the shop over there and help you pick out some presents for the kids and the nippers?" He put an arm around Margaret's back and ushered her towards the airport gift shop.

Mia stood in the queue for passport control. In front of her, Shantee was trying to convince Simon to come to one of her yoga workshop weekends, while Craig was slobbering all over that pretty nurse Maria. And behind her, Margaret was drawing a map of how to get to Tunbridge Wells by car for Babs, while Frank held her hand-luggage and scanned the TV monitor for their flight number.

Mia glanced at her watch. It was ten o'clock. She was nearly at the front of the queue, but just like every other Kefalonian she had come across, the passport controllers took their time doing their job. As she rummaged in her hand-luggage to get out her book, a voice called out her name.

Turning round, she saw Gwen running towards her, a look of panic and relief on her flushed face.

"Thank God!" Gwen gasped for breath as she reached her, beads of sweat poised to slide down her forehead.

Mia stared at her as people looked at them and turned away again. She knew Simon was listening, despite pretending to read Shantee's yoga leaflet.

"Mia, I'm so sorry – it wasn't my fault, you've got to believe me," panted Gwen.

The queue shuffled forward, bags between feet, like a colony of penguins minding their eggs.

"I'd say you've got about ten to fifteen minutes before I walk through that door," said Mia quietly.

"My parents-in-law turned up without warning because they'd just come from the hospital where my husband's aunt had just been taken following a heart attack," Gwen tried to explain quickly. "They were very distraught and after you left they told me they wanted to stay the night so that they could keep going back to the hospital to check up on her – they live on the other side of the island, you see, so it made sense for them to stay. Of course, I also had to go with them to the hospital – it would have been unthinkable not to have visited my own relative after a heart attack. And then Andonis flew back early from Athens because they had called him and told him his aunt was ill. By six o'clock I had a full house and I couldn't get away. I was praying you would call me so I could explain."

Mia looked at her coldly and shrugged. "What do you want me to say?"

"That you understand?" pleaded Gwen.

Mia looked down at her feet. "What difference does it make?" she asked. "I'm going home now and I won't be coming back here again. I've done my bit now. If you want to get to know me-"

"I thought I'd come over in January," Gwen interrupted her. "I was thinking I could stay for a week – or even two. It would give us a chance to spend some time together, get to know each other properly."

The queue shuffled forward again. Mia considered Gwen's suggestion and sighed despairingly.

Suddenly Gwen dived into her shoulder bag and pulled out a large, tattered brown envelope with an elastic band tied round it. "I almost forgot," she said, pulling off the elastic band and tugging out a smaller white envelope with Mia's name on it. "I found them right at the back of the attic in a carrier bag. I'd obviously hidden them so well, even I couldn't find them. These are the letters I was telling you about Mia, the ones I wrote to you. There's seventy-four of them – I counted." She handed them to her.

Mia opened the small, musty white envelope and took out a lined piece of paper with large looped blue writing on it. As her eyes scanned the page, a tear trickled down her face.

...It doesn't matter if you don't get top marks at school, if you don't come first on sports day. What matters is that you're happy, and you've every reason to be happy because you have a wonderful daddy who loves you to pieces, two wonderful grandparents who adore you, a new mummy who loves you very much, and a far-away mummy who loves you with all her heart...

Mia looked up at her and wiped her eyes.

"Read on," urged Gwen, a tear welling in her own eye.

You're very young now and although I know you're very clever – much more clever than I am – you might not understand until you are much older, that although you never see your far-away mummy, she thinks about you often. One day, when the time is right, we'll make up for all this lost time. That's if you want to. I suppose I'll have my work cut out convincing you that I'm not the heartless individual you think I am. It'll be hard for us both, as I can't take back my mistakes, and even if I could go back in time, I can't promise you that I would have done things differently. The only thing I can promise you is that I'll always love you, even if you choose never to know me. And maybe it's naive of me, but I believe that somehow my love will reach you, even if this letter doesn't. Your far-away mummy, Gwen.

Mia stared at the words as the tears flowed down her cheeks.

"Give me another chance, Mia, *please*," whispered Gwen. "I won't let you down again."

As Mia looked up she saw Simon looking at her over Gwen's shoulder.

"Alright," she mumbled.

"I'm telling the kids tonight and the in-laws tomorrow," said Gwen. "No more secrets. I don't want to risk losing you again." She reached forward to wipe a tear from Mia's eye, and then wrapped her arms around her. Hesitantly, Mia put one arm around Gwen as she tried to halt the flow of her tears. Gwen stroked her hair and pressed Mia to her. "I'll call you. Think about January. Let me know how you feel. I'd really like to come and see you – and Mum and Dad, if the idea isn't too much for them."

Mia nodded. "I *would* like to see you in January."

Gwen smiled with relief. "That's wonderful. We could go to the sales together. I'd like to buy you a present – a pretty dress or something."

Mia smiled awkwardly. Now was as good a time as any to tell her. "It might have to be a maternity dress," she said in a lowered voice.

Gwen's eyes popped out on stalks. "Mia…" she gasped. "Oh my gosh, this is all too much to take in…I'm going to be a *grandmother*?"

Mia nodded and watched her face carefully, but Gwen reached towards her again, smiling and clasping her warmly.

"Oh Mia, that's wonderful – oh, I wish we had more time…"

Babs coughed loudly behind them to point out that the queue had moved forward.

"That's truly wonderful, Mia. Quick – give me your number. I've only got your father's." Gwen passed her a pen and a piece of paper. As Mia scribbled her number and address on it, she became aware of another pair of feet next to Gwen's. Looking up she found herself looking at Dimitri.

"Mia, you're next," said Gwen, tears forming in the corners of her eyes. Mia picked up her hand-luggage and abandoned her place at the front of the queue, waving Margaret and Babs in front of her.

Confused, Gwen looked at Dimitri.

"Sorry Gwen, could you give us a minute?" Mia smiled at her apologetically.

"Of course." Gwen walked over to a nearby row of seats and sat down.

"Dimitri, what on earth are you doing here? This is pointless, there is absolutely *nothing* left to say," she insisted in a hushed tone, casting a glance over her shoulder as the queue continued to shuffle forward without her.

"You are wrong," he said, staring at her meaningfully. "I *do* have something to say – something very important."

"What?" she looked at him expectantly.

"I want to help you bring up your baby."

Mia's jaw dropped as she shook her head, not sure whether to laugh or cry at this touching but naive attempt to win her over. "Oh Dimitri-"

"Don't Oh Dimitri me," he interrupted sharply. "I stayed awake all last night thinking it over, and these are the facts – one," he batted his thumb, "I love you. Two," he batted his index finger, "I am coming to England to be with you. Three, I have a job and an accommodation to go to. Four, I have found two colleges near London on the internet that train teachers – I already email them for information. Five, by the time your baby is born, I will be living near you, coming every day to help you feed it and wash it and change the nappies. Everything I do will be to make you see that I am the man you want to spend the rest of your life with."

"Aah," sighed Caz from the queue a few feet away. "Ain't that lovely?"

Mia pulled him further away from the others. "Dimitri, I'm really touched, but it's all just big empty words as far as I'm concerned. Call me when you get to England. Then we'll see if you mean what you say, OK? I've got to go, now – look they've all gone through to the departure lounge." Mia looked over at the passport control area where Maria the nurse was blowing her nose into a tissue and Frank was waving through the gap between the booths.

Dimitri reached into his back pocket and pulled out a small paper wallet. "Look," he said opening it and pulling out a ticket. "October 14th. One-way ticket to England. My job at Frank's company starts on October 17th – stacking and lifting in the warehouse. Go and ask him if you don't believe me." He nodded to where Frank was standing looking watery-eyed.

"I believe you," said Mia.

"Will you meet me at the airport?" he asked, gently reaching for her hand.

"England isn't like Greece, Dimitri," she frowned. "The weather's usually cold and wet, there are no beaches in Egham, the people aren't as friendly when you meet them in their native habitat, and as for bringing up a baby...I've had just over two months to get used to the idea and I've got serious doubts as to what kind of mother I'll be. So how you've decided you're going to be the perfect father overnight is beyond me."

"I won't be perfect," Dimitri pulled her closer towards him. "But I'll try my hardest. I've changed a nappy before, you know. And yes, it was disgusting. But I can do it, because I would do anything for you." He lowered his lips onto hers, but Mia pulled back.

"You could love another man's child?" she asked seriously, her hand pressed against his chest to restrain him.

"If there is one thing better than having one Mia in my life, it's having two," he grinned.

"It might be a boy."

"Even better. Then I can take him to the brothels, teach him how to play poker, help him learn how to ride a motorbike."

Mia balked and wriggled free.

"I'm joking, Mia," he laughed. "I swear I'm just joking! A little boy or a little girl – I will love them just the same and try and help them not to make the same mistakes I made." He looked at her warmly.

Slowly she smiled. Dimitri grabbed her and scooped her up in his arms. "October 14th! Will you be there? My plane lands at Gatwick at five-thirty in the evening."

Mia tried not to grin. "OK, I'll be there – but I'm not making any promises."

"I have a promise for you, though," he beamed. "I promise I'll make you the happiest woman alive." He kissed her and held her tightly. "Oops, I hope I don't crush little Mia," he smiled, putting her down.

"Mia, you should go through," said Gwen, walking towards them.

"Gwen, this is Dimitri. Dimitri, this is my mother, Gwen."

"I remember – we met outside your apartment," smiled Gwen, shaking his hand as Mia picked up her bag and stuffed the large envelope of letters into it. Gwen leaned forward and pecked her on the cheek. "Don't lose those letters. I want you to read every last one of them. I'll call you later," she smiled.

"So will I," said Dimitri hugging her and kissing her on the lips. "I love you, Mia," he whispered.

She kissed him back and held him close. "See you in a month," she said, turning to go.

"Mia!" he pulled her back. "*Say it.*"

"I love you, too," she smiled.

He grinned as she turned to present her passport at the control booth, waved at him and disappeared.